BOOK 5

OF

The River Quintet

YOUNG LIVES IN A CHANGING WORLD

Mary Walsingham

COMING OF AGE IN
TWO SILENT WORLDS

Ray E. Phillips

Quill Publications | USA

QuillPublications.com
Illustration by Arturo Aguirre

ISBN: 979-8-9899062-8-4

Typesetting by C'est Beau Designs

Preface

One condition—if not recognized in early childhood—can separate you from those all around you. Being born deaf means that you cannot, at an early age, understand how other people navigate so easily among themselves. If this condition is not acknowledged by your family, no one can understand why you do not behave like other children and do not learn how to talk. Modern technology, by diagnosing deafness in the infant, avoids this oversight. How the lack of hearing plays out in Mary Walsingham's early, unruly life and what resources she develops after its discovery is a major theme of this story.

In Book 4, Mary's inability to hear is recognized by Sky Flower, a Mohawk girl serving the Walsingham family in England. A long, transformational period ensues during which child and governess develop a language through hand-talking and cursive writing. Inevitably, they become deeply bonded. In Book 5, with the sudden departure of Sky Flower, Mary experiences unbearable loneliness, and later finds solace in the stables. As she raises a new-born foal, she finds a focus for her energy and love. A rash plan brings the two companions to an English plantation in the New World.

Fortitude describes the characteristic most required to make the transition from a comfortable life of privilege to one of hardships among the fervently religious settlers in New England. Mary leaves a family of Royalists to live with a Puritan family, underscoring the political upheaval of the time.

Along the Connecticut River at Hartford, we share the customs and events that make up Mary's new life. Harsh weather and bare subsistence living are explored, as are medical and psychological conditions and their treatments. Her experiences take on an additional dimension in new relationships with Native Americans and with one of the Dutch traders.

The STORY closes with Mary needing to make a heart-searching decision. NOTES ABOUT THE STORY invite an in-depth exploration of three major areas: historical facts and social customs of Colonial life in America; improvised development of visual communications; and the care, training, and shipboard transportation of horses, each discipline a profound and meaningful educational experience.

—R.E.P.

Special Thanks

A note of heartfelt thanks to all those people who have contributed their advice, assistance, and constructive criticism to the creation of The River Quintet:

The late Kenneth Little Hawk, Mi'kmaq-Mohawk storyteller
William "Chip" Reynolds, (formerly) Captain of the *Half Moon* Replica Ship
Janny Venema, author and (formerly) Dutch translator and Associate Director, New Netherland Research Center, Albany, NY
Walter Woodward, Connecticut State Historian
Stefan Nicolescu, Research Scientist and Collections Manager, Division of Mineralogy and Meteoritics, Yale Peabody Museum of Natural History, New Haven, CT
Barrie Kavasch, author, Institute for American Indian Studies, Washington, CT
Teachers at the American School for the Deaf, West Hartford, CT
The late Frank Kozelek, Tarrytown, NY
Research staff at various libraries, including those at Kent Lakes, Corinth, and Glens Falls, NY, Windsor, CT and Shepperton, England
Joan G. Sheeran and Wendy Phillips Kahn, editors
Sophie Seypura and Arturo Aguirre, illustrators
and Patrick Seypura, digital publisher and website manager.

—R.E.P.

This reissued and corrected version of Mary Walsingham *was prepared and published following the death of Ray Phillips in July, 2021. The editors have made minor changes and proofreading corrections and now offer this edition in loving memory of the author. Throughout the writing of The River Quintet, Ray Phillips devoted himself during his last decades to bringing history alive with accuracy and compassion.*

—Joan G. Sheeran and Wendy Phillips Kahn

Contents

PART I

The Story of Mary Walsingham

CHAPTER 1

The Letter

Leave-Taking

THE WRINKLED LETTER slipped from her trembling hands, fluttered to the floor, and there lay like a crushed dream. To Mary, who would never hear the wondrous sounds of the world around her, the words she had just read echoed throughout her heartbroken body.

First of May 1637
My dearest friend Mary,

Seven years have come and gone since I came to your Manor House in Littleton. During these years in England I found a new world and learned much. Most cherished of all is coming to know you. You are my best friend ever.

These many years have been ours to share. Remember all the wonderful times we learned and played together, times that will bind us forever. I can never forget what fun we had making names for everything with our hands. You learned so quickly. Think of those happy days under great clouds when we dallied along the River Thames and watched the barges laden with sheep and cows turning 'round the bend. Oh, how I have loved your drawings of animals! Your horses, for me, truly came alive.

This night I write to tell you that the time has come for me to seek a new path. For you, England will always be. For me, I feel a pull at my heart toward where I came from and that is an ocean away. I must now return to the forest and mountains of my early life, to the colonies, and to my Indian people who are so much a part of me.

I know that, at first, parting will be painful for both of us. During these precious years, we have become sisters out of our love of one another, not separable by time and space. You will soon become sixteen years old and have already grown into a gracious and quick-witted young woman. These are gifts that will always serve you well whatever direction you follow.

I know that times past have been difficult for you as they have been for me, but we helped each other make the best of it. We, in truth, grew up together. I was meant to be your teacher, but it was you who taught me the most valuable lessons—to overcome a hardship, to rejoice in the little things of everyday life, and to hold precious all the creatures, big and small, around us.

Though the pox has scarred my face, I want you to know that my heart is without blemish in my love for you. Some time we will meet again in another place, of that I am certain. With these humble words, I must say goodbye for now. I am proud of you in every way possible. Please think of me whenever you look at your glass-that-makes-a-rainbow.

Sky Flower

CHAPTER 2

Early Life

Birth

The story behind those soul-stifling words begins almost sixteen years earlier. The Registry Book at St. Nicholas Church in Shepperton has the following entry:

Mary Abigail Walsingham, Girl
Born to Walter and Catherine Walsingham
On the 15th day of May 1621

On that day, a sense of anticipation flowed through the hallways of a windswept mansion standing alone on the broad fields of Littleton, England.[1] That hushed spell was mercifully broken by a small cry from a large bedroom at the top of the stairway. An heir to nobility made herself known to the world. To princess-like adulation by her parents, Mary Abigail Walsingham had arrived. A life extraordinary was just beginning.

Curious and excited well-wishers snaked up the long, winding stairway to the bedroom of the Manor House. Butlers, maids, and cooks led on tiptoes and whispered voices. The gardener, the blacksmith, and stable hands—scrubbed, perfumed, and in Sunday clothes—were just behind. All were eager to see the newest member of the Walsingham clan. The subject of their rapt attention lay quietly in the arms of Lady Walsingham and showed no indication of acknowledging the soft-spoken "oohs" and "aahs" of the gathering throng. Yet all admired her performance as an early example of Walsingham breeding and reserve.

Mary was a robust infant with cheeks the redness of roses. A tiny smile appearing within her first few days slowly broadened over the weeks to follow. Her eyes, the blueness of sky, seemed to glow. The light-colored hair was silk-like in its fineness. Left by herself, she tended to squirm about excitedly. Yet mother, sisters, and governess all remarked on how calm she became when held by them, the closer, the calmer. They delighted in seeing a little smile come when snug in someone's arms. There was something else quite special; she cried softly and even that was seldom. At times, her cooing was like a dove when tiny bubbles formed at her mouth. In short, baby Mary was perfect in every way.

Growing Up

As the months went on, the baby showed that she was quick to learn. By Christmas she was able to pull herself up to a stand. By Easter that followed, she was walking without holding on. She already knew how to use a spoon (with a mishap now and then), to climb into her rocking cradle by herself, and to stroke a cat gently, all before she was a year of age. And always, she did so quietly without a babble or scream. Crying came only after a tumble and then even that was tempered. How her older sisters fussed on this doll-come-alive!

Mary's first two years passed happily, yet all wondered why she had not started to talk. Mumble, groan, and sometimes shriek she did. Surely, she was agile at play and she turned the pages of picture books with joy. She had a sharp eye for finding the tiniest movement in the grass: a worm and sometimes a beetle. "Fast to do but slow to say" was an old expression that seemed to apply to the little girl.

It is fair to say that our earliest memories probably go back to the age of four or five. While that first memory may cling for decades, it is clouded in vague perceptions of a child learning to navigate the world within its swirling vortex. Mary's first memory was no different, aside from the fact that it was not vague but was as starkly vivid as a midday shadow. She remembered standing knee high in the grass, wearing all white and holding a biscuit. She remembered a rather large bird of two colors hopping over toward her, looking up at the biscuit. It was most certainly a magpie.[2] She remembered reaching out to hand it the biscuit. Its head turned up with the beak a hair's breadth away from her hand. At that moment, a shadowy figure all in black (probably her nanny) came rushing out of the house with arms thrashing wildly. The bird flew off. The biscuit fell to the ground. Mary remembered collapsing in a fit of despair as if the world had collapsed in on itself.

The child remembered, too, in those early years, a man setting up a big box on a table. Through an opening, dolls appeared and suddenly became alive. It was, of course, a puppet show put on by a traveling puppeteer, as was common in the privileged homes of those days. The dolls—a splendid red gown on one and a jester's costume on the other—bounced up and down and struck at each other madly, as if having a great quarrel. All the time the man hid behind the box. Finally, a third doll appeared, he in a soldier's uniform with shiny medals and big black hat of fur. The soldier cuffed the jester, hauling him away. The grand lady bowed in many impossible positions.[3]

Throughout the performance Mary's sisters, Amanda and Veronica, wigwagged with amusement. They, along with their mother and their nanny, beat their flattened hands together mightily. For Mary, the dolls in the box, bumping and flinging themselves about for no reason, were simply tiresome.

Such was the beginning of an endless string of everyday events that made little sense to her. Everyone around her seemed to know what to do, but Mary did not. Her sisters left her out of their games. Unable to understand, the youngest sister felt as if she were in another world, floundering hopelessly in a sea of swimmers. And so, her life was becoming ever lonelier, while to others she was becoming increasingly mysterious.

As Mary grew, her aloofness from events surrounding her was considered good manners until finally it was not. Her attitudes and actions became more and more erratic, unseemly and rude to the point of continuing unpleasantness. She generally refused to follow rules set by family conventions. Games with her brother and sisters often became violent contests of will. During this period no one ever noticed that one of the few things that did not cause any reaction by Mary were the irritating and sometimes alarming sounds that occurred from time to time around the household.

During these first few years, learning the simple disciplines of childhood proved Mary's undoing. To give a most ordinary example, manners at the dinner table—always taught at an early age—lagged for Mary; a scolding or a rap on the knuckles had little effect. Trying to join her older sisters in play became more annoying than fun. For their part, Amanda and Veronica found their little sister less and less likeable.

In truth, Mary did not follow the rules of any game but rather created her own antics. What's more, she seemed to become ever more determined in her will, often thumping on her sisters for attention. She did her best to disrupt their skip-the-rope and bouncing a ball. Exclusion then led to anger, and anger sometimes led to her thrashing out in blinded rage. When so shut out from her sisters' games, Mary would seek comfort from her mother but found little. Her father provided a much-needed pat on the shoulder now and then, but little more. Night after night, she would cry into her pillow.

Mary, too, was beginning to sense that there was something inside that was different about her. Her sisters responded to each other as if by magic. Her parents looked at her as if expecting something, but she did not know what. There was something in the air that she could not grasp. Mother, father, servants all moved about as if guided by some otherworldly force. She began to suspect that it all had something to do about how their mouths moved. Try as she might, Mary could not grasp what was happening around her. Talking requires sound and for Mary, the world was soundless. She did not know what hearing was; she did not know that she was deaf.

A small comfort came from her brother, Charles, barely two years less her age. At first, catching his attention with moving fingers, tickling him into a smile, helping to dress him and curling his already curly hair provided her no end of pleasure. Later, steadying him during those first steps and amusing him by making funny faces were important activities of her everyday life. As he passed the toddler stages his willingness to play games with Mary began to wane. Charles was drawn more to rough and tumble ones than those favored by his sisters. He learned to spin his tee-totum with a long string and keep a stick-driven hoop rolling along the garden path. He tossed knucklebones into the air, catching them with the skill of an acrobat. Clay balls covered in leather he rolled expertly, one into the other, across the grass.[4]

Charles seemed to find even more delight in stomping on a puddle; the bigger the splash, the more the delight. The closer a sister was for splashing, the more the fun. To Mary's despair, her brother preferred solitary games where things were set in motion, not games that they could play together.

What most flustered her parents was that Mary, now in her ninth year, did not talk. Not one intelligible word! No matter how everyone tried, they could not get her to say anything. They began began to view her as a dull-witted little girl and wholly unmanageable. Easier it was to separate her from their lives as best they could.

Mary's only solace through those first years of loneliness came from an aging governess named Nora. Although thought by many as not inclined to show any feelings at all, Nora would hold her closely for hours after many of the disputes that had so angered Amanda and Veronica. Even Nora, however, had given up hope of finding a way to explain the stubborn and rebellious character of the youngest girl.

Those in the family daring to say so hinted, "Perhaps there could be a touch of insanity in the child." After all, the Walsinghams cared for two live-in aunts, sisters of the Lady. One was fine, but the other one babbled continuously and made no sense. She had been declared insane by the most famous doctors in London. "Stone in the head" was enough of a conclusion to let the matter rest there. The doctors said fools tended to run in families. This "mad auntie," as the servants referred to her in private, was tolerated but kept well-shrouded in the shadows.[5]

Nora harbored a slight suspicion that deafness could be at the root of Mary's contrary way. She knew that people lost some hearing in old age. Even she was having trouble hearing normal speaking voices and, embarrassing as it was, often had to request that words be repeated. Could it be possible, she wondered, that a beautiful little girl could not hear? Her Scottish religion had led her to believe that any misfortune at birth could happen only as an act of punishment from God. In her view there was no transgression in this household that deserved so great a blow as deafness. She needed to hold her tongue on the matter.[6]

It was the tutors—those teachers of writing and music and dance who visited the Manor House, one each day of the week except Sundays—who had the most trouble with Mary. Too restless to sit through a moment's explanation or to follow simplest instructions, she was impossible to teach. Troublesome was her learning of the letters, of forming a spoken word, and linking it with a real thing or feeling. Lessons of music and dance held even less promise. "No sense of rhythm," said the teacher, "more like a donkey in wooden shoes." During these lessons, Mary preferred to hide or to play with one of the cats. The tutors, in turn, were only too willing to accommodate her absence.

Lady Walsingham, who despaired of Mary's unruly behavior, took refuge by inventing excuses for her lack of manners. It was Mary's father, Lord of the Manor, who insisted that the girl have every chance to participate in play and attend every lesson. More than once did an exasperated tutor give notice of finding work elsewhere, staying on with the family only because of a sumptuous meal or a trifling gift.

Enigma

THE BAD-TEMPERED DISPOSITION of the Walsingham's youngest girl was strangely counterbalanced by her appearance. She was of delicate features: soft sky-blue eyes, a narrow nose that pointed a little upward at the very end, a pointed chin, and a mouth with red velvety lips. Fleeting dimples appeared when she smiled. Her blond hair fell to the shoulders. She was tall for her age, with arms that were long, even spidery. There was also a natural grace that Mary's parents had noted, even in the simple movements of walking and tossing a ball.

Solitary pursuits gave some pleasures. Of these, the household cats provided diversion. For fun, she pretended to be a cat, crawling on all fours, looking into every crevice, and scratching at the back of a chair. Her daily nap was not taken in her padded corner but on a broad window sill, lazing cat-like in the afternoon sun. On sunny days she played in the grass, slowly stalking a magpie the way a cat does and, when close, she would suddenly jump up with arms flapping; then she would cavort gaily in a circle as she watched the frightened bird fly off. With such mysterious antics, household whispers of early-onset madness came more often. A cat, she was not. It is, however, ironic that a cat would in time be part of the solution to the mystery of Mary's odd behavior.

More than once during her early years the girl would disappear from the play yard. An alarm sent a flock of servants scampering along the River Ash that flowed around the Manor House. Some ran upstream; some ran downstream. Predictably, they would find Mary happily wandering somewhere along the banks. Usually, there were some colorful wildflowers held in each hand.[7]

Most of all, Mary sought the pleasure of drawing flowers, animals, and other ordinaries within her world. Faces were more perplexing to put on paper, but she tried, starting with copying those life-like portraits on the walls of the main room of the Manor House. There was no shortage of paper or nubs of graphite; all were provided liberally by her befuddled parents. They felt blessed that drawing kept her distracted. Although no one favored her sketches with much attention, these drawings became an increasingly important part of Mary's mostly solitary childhood. And she saved them all.

The customs of Mary's father and mother were too frozen with form and rules to understand a child who floated from sweetness to aggression with no apparent cause, a child who could not follow the simplest family ritual. Thus, a great divide began. Mary started to create her own world outside the confines of the family. That world was with the animals in the barns and stables and all the creatures that lived in the fields. To Mary, trees, flowers, and waving grasses seemed to preen just for her. The beauty she saw around her led her to start making rough sketches of the world as she knew it.

A particularly fascinating image was the horse. Once with her father when she was a very little girl, she saw a horse grazing in the field and switching its tail. As if in response, she waved back. To her surprise, the horse slowly came toward them. As it stood towering over her head, her father grasped a handful of tall grass and gave it to the child. She eagerly held it out. The horse nibbled the grass from her outstretched hand and shook its head as if to show thanks. A life-long love was born.

There was something of a magical touch that Mary seemed to possess with animals. Sheep did not shy away with her slow approach, but merely looked up with amiable tolerance. When the hunting dogs came barking toward the Manor House, Mary boldly walked among them. Even the feistiest of the dogs quieted. Fearless, she drew the admiration of her father and the dismay of her mother. What drew Mary's interest most avidly was simply being around the horses. She watched spellbound as they moved with ease along the pathways that weaved around the Manor House. She spent hours in the meadows watching the horses graze in tall grass. She thrilled at the sight of a team of horses arriving with a great wagon or coach in tow, and would run toward them as if a moth to a lighted candle. Above all, Mary loved being close enough to a horse to touch it.[8]

Always, when her father took her to the stables, it was a time of great excitement. She stood as close to the horses as allowed, even standing on a box and reaching way up with a little hand to run it along the velvet-like neck that curved overhead. Mary stood small but smiling and unafraid in the presence of these towering animals. Often as she got older, she wandered alone to the stables, or sat quietly in the tall grass, well-hidden from tutors and well-placed to watch the coming and going of the horses.

And so, the first few years of Mary's life passed: becoming ever-more estranged from her family but ever closer to the animals that came into her world. And then everything changed—almost overnight—for Mary. The change happened unexpectedly. The cause of it all came from a world away. The Walsinghams' utter frustration with their perplexing daughter led to the grudging acceptance of a trader-friend's suggestion that they employ a caretaker who was especially gifted with difficult people. The well-traveled trader had in mind a young woman observed in his last visit to the Colonies. She tended a Dutch tavern in New Amsterdam.[9] Somehow, she proved miraculously able to foil the rude behavior of men who often inhabited the tavern where they drank rum to excess, be they gentlemen or rowdy sailors. She was clever at calming agitated, drunken men acting at their worst. She worked hard and knew something of the many tongues spoken there, including some of the King's English. He had reason to believe that she would rapidly master their language.

Perhaps the girl so described would have a settling influence on a contrary daughter who so vexed the entire family and her minders. It was on this point that the parents agreed to take on a servant from the New World. They were taken back a breath on hearing that she was an Indian. Skeptical they were, but arrangements for her journey were agreed upon with a letter sent on the next colony-bound ship. And so, a girl bearing the name Sky Flower arrived at the doorstep of the Walsingham Manor House several months later, she knowing little of life in England, they knowing little of the first people of America.

CHAPTER 3

Sky Flower

Gwendolyn's Duties

In the autumn of 1629—the second day of October to be exact—a servant arrived without fanfare from the Colonies of the New World. She was fully grown but still a girl. To all at the Manor House in Littleton, she was as exotic as the green parrots, silver-tipped spears, and feathery headdresses brought home as souvenirs by seagoing ship captains. Being a novelty, she caused much excitement among the children who displayed unbridled glee at the sight. They could hardly ignore the darker skin or the heavily pox-marked face of the new servant nor miss her piercing, deep brown eyes that peered through strands of tar-black hair. They stared aplenty at this visitor from faraway lands. Even her name whispered among the older sisters—Sky Flower—gave a sense of exotic worlds.

Much, of course, had already been made in England of the "Indian" woman, Pocahontas. Married to an English planter, she had come from the Colonies of America some years before. Some said that Pocahontas was a princess among the noble savages who roamed the forests of the New World. People regarded her with the curiosity given a many-colored parrot brought from Africa or China. They dressed her in splendid clothing with a tall, conical hat and ruffed collar, and exhibited her to the upper sorts, including royalty. Even the Queen extended her hand to Pocahontas. On one occasion, it is said, the princess visited the Manor House in Littleton. Her life, however, was short. Within the year, Pocahontas had died from smallpox.[10]

The new girl at the Manor House was neither a Mohawk princess nor exotic parrot. Indeed, Sky Flower began her duties as an assistant in the laundry, spending long days with endless piles of clothes and tablecloths to wash and hang for drying. She had neither feathers on her head nor paint on her face. Instead, a plain smock was enough. She ate left-overs and slept in the servants' quarters.

The children saw little of Sky Flower other than her walks to the stream that bowed around the Manor House. There, she toted the laundry's waste water and, with a great splash, dumped her buckets into the nearby River Ash, making a great cloud of gray water that was slowly swept downstream. This emptying of laundry water happened many times every day.

All this the children watched as the unworldly creature carried out the worldly chores expected of a laundry assistant. During the first few days, they marveled at the sparkle in her face as she took in the new world around her. She smiled as she passed them out at play and playfully clanked her pails together, when empty, to make a dull ring. As the days went on, they found more and more sadness in her eyes. Her steps were slower, and her pails no longer rang. What, the older girls wondered, was wrong?

Within three months after her arrival, indeed in the new year of 1630, Lady Walsingham sent word that Sky Flower was to meet her in the Great Hall. There, speaking slowly and accenting every word, she told of her own great interest in the American colonies. She spoke of hearing about Sky Flower's talent for quieting misbehaving tavern-goers in New Amsterdam and that she might try to assist Nora with the care of children. The Lady spoke slowly and seemed to emphasize every word. Perhaps, she thought, this seemingly gentle young savage could rein in the rebellious ways of their daughter. Surely, all else had failed. Giving notice that Sky Flower would not suffer the same fate as Pocahontas were the many deep pox-marks on her face.[11]

The name Sky Flower, to be sure, was colorful enough. It captured the romance of the wilderness and the spirit of the simple people of the forest. Yet, it was a name hardly suitable for a proper English household with high-born children. The older girls, at the urging of their mother, soon gave her another name, choosing Gwendolyn. Their chosen name poked fun, for it was the name of their caged canary. The Lady of the Manor announced that from now on she would be known as Gwendolyn. It was expected, she added, that the new child-helper must soon learn to speak in proper language. With this dubious distinction of a new name, Sky Flower felt for the first time since her arrival a wary sense of welcome.[12]

Escape from the laundry! The exhilaration of the newly named child-helper was matched by her impassioned effort to learn to speak as the English do and to care for children as quickly as she possibly could. Granted, she had much to learn about the ways of this new society. But learn she did: diction, manners at the table, everyday etiquette, proper dress, and all the trappings of the favored English household. Little inflections of the language were soon mastered. What the Walsingham family soon discovered was that their new hire learned quickly.

It was not many weeks before Gwendolyn could engage the children in stories at night as they huddled around a warm and glowing hearth. The halting accent and sometimes misplaced words made the storyteller even more spellbinding. Indeed, the children were deeply immersed in the stories, except for Mary who seemed content to nod off at Gwendolyn's side. There were stories of America, of a great ocean journey, of mystical beings or, their favorite, made-up stories of chairs and tables, candlesticks and fireplace tools around them that would come to life and talk to each other in voices, high pitched or deep according to the size of the object.

The new child-minder threw herself into the lessons with the children's tutors, finding that she was the one learning most. To learn faster—no matter how complex the lesson in numbers or dance or writing—she helped the children prepare for the next session. They resisted greatly but less so as the new child-minder invented little games for learning. As the tutors found week after week the astonishing improvement of their previously lackluster students, they began to think of themselves as fine teachers.

In Gwendolyn's view, Mary was most extraordinary because, now at age nine, indeed, almost ten, she never spoke. Rather, she would utter a grunt, or a squeal now and then, but never was a single word ever formed in her mouth. There was something quite mysterious about the girl. Indeed, there was a mismatch between the sparkly intensity of her eyes and the silence of her voice. The eyes missed not the slightest movement. Strong coaxing, however lively, brought not a sound.

For Mary, the new servant was sent from a happy dreamland. Mary now had someone who looked carefully at her drawings. Out of a wooden box came scores of pages, one of which was the Manor House showing the great entrance door with its lion-head knocker. Other drawings depicted trees, cats, and the Great Hall with fireplace and grand chairs. There were several more of horses in perfect proportion of head, neck, body, legs, and tail. They were running, grazing, or just standing still looking at the artist. Ants and spiders were drawn huge and looked ready to bite. Some drawings were the faces of her brother, each with a different expression. What Gwendolyn found most curious was the realization that not one drawing showed Charles's sisters.

With Gwendolyn's prompting, Mary found herself more and more welcomed into the simple play of children: jump rope, hopscotch, dominoes, and other games. She learned quickly, once shown how. With each passing day, she felt more like a whole being, able to keep up with the rest in any activity of motor skills. Word games, however simple they might be, remained impossible.

As the days merged into weeks, then months, the lives of both girls became ever more entwined. Mary brought out the older girl's awareness of and appreciation for certain sights and textures. Together they spotted a many-colored butterfly and followed the play of sun and clouds against the far hills at dusk. They felt the joy of feeling the textures of different stones and of molding mud at the stream into fanciful bowls and cups that hardened in the sunlight. The Mohawk girl found ways of bringing her "Indian" ways to Mary. Together, they made dyes from berries and painted leather patches with triangles, circles and wavy lines of purple, blue, red, and black. While teaching some simple but graceful steps once danced around a fire a world away, Gwendolyn was sure that Mary was no donkey.

As the new child-minder became more adept at language as well as in her duties of childcare, the old one became increasingly frail. Nora often retreated to her room "to rest" and let Gwendolyn manage as best she could. Barely four months after Gwendolyn's arrival at the Manor House, Nora passed on. A simple funeral was held at the churchyard of St. Mary Magdalene.

Gwendolyn was now charged with full care of the children. By then, she had caught on to the ins and outs of her responsibilities. Her ability to speak English at the time was not perfect but it was good. Only now and then did she forget something such as the proper place setting at the Sunday dinner table: an extra spoon for plum pudding went on the right side of each trencher.

Revelation

By mid-winter, Gwendolyn felt more secure in her care of the children. The trials were certainly more agreeable than those long days with her hands immersed in laundry suds. She worried nonetheless about the mystery that lay hidden behind Mary's beautiful but silent face. A household calamity was soon to solve it.

After dinner one night the children huddled around the hearth to listen to another story from Gwendolyn's Mohawk childhood. Mary, as usual during the nightly storytelling, lay cuddled in deep sleep in Gwendolyn's lap with one arm draped around her neck. Meanwhile, Sir Francis Drake, the oversized cat, had jumped from a chair onto the great mantel.[13] Here was a good place to feel the rising warmth from the fireplace, and, for a cat, to hear the story. He found a comfortable place to lie, settling behind a large vase of stunning beauty, its blue designs on snow-pure white. It was a vase from an exotic land and lovingly treasured by the family.

The tale told of a mountain monster called the Stone Giant, who the elders said, ate children when they misbehaved. When a lightning storm with thunder awoke him from his nap, the giant became enraged. The listeners braced themselves for the next part. As the storyteller made a deep-voiced and angry growl, a tiny motion on the mantel caught her eye. The vase seemed to totter, then slowly wobble toward the edge. There it tilted forward and then toppled over.

There is an instant when an impending disaster seems suspended in time, when an observer freezes down to the core. So, for a moment, to all watching, the vase appeared to hang in midair. Then, with the horror realized at its falling, came a collective gasp. The precious vase struck the stone hearth with a thunderous crash. Shattered pieces flew in all directions. The astonished children, now wide-eyed, jumped up and shrieked.

Yet through it all, Mary slept peacefully. Gwendolyn felt not even a twitch in Mary's limp body. At that instant she knew that the child in her lap had heard nothing. Sir Francis Drake had opened a new chapter in the life story of Mary Walsingham.

The Doctor

At first, Gwendolyn's opinion that Mary was deaf did not sit well with her parents. They preferred to think that no such calamity could occur in their family. After all, God had a reason for casting such an affliction on a child, and surely the Walsingham family was not deserving of such a reputation. They had accepted the possibility of imbecility or insanity, but not deafness! A child who could not learn to speak was unacceptable in the extreme.[14]

Surely, they could not agree to such a conclusion by a servant, and certainly not one brought up in the wilderness. They had always ignored the times when Mary did not react to the many audible calamities that befell any normal household. They favored idiocy for their daughter because it was more socially acceptable among the ruling class of the day.

Then, there was also the matter of the shattered vase. It had been purchased as a wedding present at a shockingly unfavorable exchange of silver from a Dutch merchant ship. Its swirling blue streaks against a pure white gloss gave eye-catching reflections from candlelight. The vase had come without a scratch all the way from Batavia on the other side of the globe.[15]

Lord and Lady Walsingham, of course, could do nothing about repairing the vase. On the matter of failing to hear, could they take the word of a servant on an issue of such immense importance? They tried shouting, but that did not help. They confronted Mary with worried looks, then agitated behavior and ever widening movements of their mouths. The angrier they looked, the more perplexed their daughter became.

Yet, Mary's parents knew that they had ignored the possibility of deafness too long. Now they must seek the best opinion in the Kingdom. Chosen for his knowledge in such conditions was Sir Gideon Albright of London, a distinguished member of the Royal College of Physicians. He was well-known for his treatment of maladies of the ears as well as the eyes and mouth. He minded the King for his every sneeze and had a reputation for keeping dignitaries within his court well supplied in spectacles, ear horns, and apothecaries for sore throats and coughs.[16]

Within days, Sir Gideon came to the Manor House. His reception was a small version of a visit by the King. The doctor and his attendant arrived in an ornately decorated carriage drawn by two high-stepping, white horses, each festooned with floral headdresses and driven by an elfin man in a tall black hat and pixie-like garb who sat high in front. The household of people, both family and servants, poured outside to greet the entourage.

The good doctor needed the help of his attendant to dismount from the carriage. In truth, he was of rather large proportions. The exchange of weight was noted by the sighing springs of the carriage as he alit onto the gravel. There he stood with a flowing wig that extended to the shoulders and a long red robe that fell to the ankles. As he adjusted his wig and pulled aside his fur collar, all could see a pudgy face with no beard, but instead multiple chins. Sir Gideon made the point well that wealth was attained by good eating and that only the very wealthy (and, he might have added, the "successful") could attain his size. He was certainly a man of importance within the learned profession of the healing arts.

Having been handed his tiny poodle by the attendant, the doctor tucked the creature into the nook of his arm as a final badge of honor. He coolly acknowledged his hosts while haughtily ignoring the servants. Following the doctor was the attendant who lugged a bulky leather trunk. Despite its bulk, none of the house servants had permission to assist.

The formal welcoming was majestic in appearance and solemn in spirit. The receiving party proceeded to the drawing room where patient and nanny waited. Lord and Lady Walsingham chose to attend the examination along with the attendant and the dog. Just as the doctor was about to begin his testing of Mary, he spotted Gwendolyn. A bit unnerved by her presence, he insisted that she be excluded. "Only a distraction," he sighed.

When all the participants were properly arranged, each one awaiting eagerly the gift of an opinion about Mary's hearing, Sir Gideon proceeded to open the trunk. He removed items that looked like children's toys and laid each, one by one, neatly aside on a table. There were bells of many sizes, whistles, squeeze horns, tuning forks, a trumpet, and strange instruments with many windings. Each one was meant to make a noise of certain pitch and quality.

So, Gwendolyn waited outside the drawing room but near enough to hear every ring, squeal, and honk. Each one started softly but grew steadily louder until it could sound no louder. She even heard a deep inhalation that was instantly followed by a blast on the trumpet. And through it all was yapping of the little dog. Then, suddenly, all was quiet except for muffled voices. Gwendolyn heard the outside door open. She supposed that the examination was to continue in the garden but could not imagine the reason. There followed a moment of perfect silence. She strained to hear more. Then, her ears were shattered by the blast of gunshot.

On a rash impulse, Gwendolyn burst out the door. A pistol was in the hands of the attendant standing behind, smoke issuing from its barrel. The Lord and Lady stood motionless and ashen in the face. Mary looked perplexed but was otherwise unfazed.

Ignoring Gwendolyn, Sir Gideon spoke his opinion. "The girl can hear. You saw her flinch at a sharp sound that exploded behind her, out of sight. I have seen many cases like this. She is stubborn and finds advantage in acting helpless. She gets anything she wants simply by pretending not to hear. I fear that she will not improve. These cases never do. No, the gunshot proves that she could not trick us into believing she is deaf. My advice is to keep her content with the bare necessities but have little expectations in her achievements in life. Should you need my services again, I shall be pleased to be consulted."[17]

Gwendolyn could not follow much of the rapid speaking but knew that the good doctor did not believe that Mary was deaf. She had not seen the reaction to the gun blast. Yet, she knew that she was right. Mary was not acting.

His conclusion stated, Sir Gideon graciously accepted an envelope, had his instruments packed, and waddled, dog under arm, toward his carriage. All, nevertheless, did not go as planned.

As was the custom, the family and servants stood together, smartly lined up by a carriage, there to send off their eminent visitor with measured pomp. The assistant had placed the trunk of instruments close by the carriage to serve as a footstool. The doctor stepped with one foot onto the trunk. Just as he raised the other leg to enter the carriage, he brought the hand with the envelope to his chin and began to sweep it downward, palm-side up, in a courtly gesture of self-satisfaction. At that moment the cover of the trunk fell in. The doctor's foot, while plunging into the trunk, stepped on a squeeze horn, thereby setting off a loud blast. His wig flew off, the dog jumped into the carriage, and the envelope fluttered slowly to ground. Soon, all was right again and with the snap of a whip the entourage was off, save for a single shoe left on the gravel.

Glancing toward Mary, Gwendolyn saw the hint of a smile. She, too, could barely hold back a snicker. But they did not laugh until inside and away from the others. There, they giggled until the power of laughing was fully spent. The doctor's visit had been difficult for both girls. But from then on, merely a hand, palm up, sweeping down from the chin by one of them was enough to provoke a fit of laughter in the other.

Treatment

AND SO, THE most experienced doctor in "these cases" offered his conclusion. Gwendolyn was devastated by the opinion of an expert on the subject of deafness. Yet, she was unable to explain her shattered belief to Mary. What cheered her a bit was the opinion of Lord Walsingham. He came to her that evening, saying that he did not believe the doctor. The doctor's whole case was based upon Mary's flinching to a gun fired unseen with its chamber held only a hand's breath from the back of her head. "In my opinion," Lord Walsingham went on, "the blast causes a shock that can be felt as well as heard. Mary felt the gunshot, and she acted by nature. I believe she is bright and well-meaning. She is not trying to fool us. Simply put, Mary cannot hear.

"Long ago, I heard that a remedy for deafness was dripping the fat taken from a boiled hedgehog and put into the ear." Lord Walsingham went on to say, "I believe it superstition but am willing to try. Do you agree?"[18]

It was most extraordinary: The Lord of the Manor asking an opinion of one of the lowest of the servants. "No," Gwendolyn found herself saying, almost as if it were beyond her control to say so. Somehow her inner voice came out, and she said what was on her mind. "The shaman used gentler means. I wish to say that I may be able to help but in another way."

"Then, I will listen," he returned.

"In my world," offered Gwendolyn, "people who travel far speak to strangers by using hands. I know a little about that." By rubbing her abdomen to mean "I am hungry" and twirling her arm skyward to say, "I am lost," she had already shown Mary how to express ideas. "May I try?"

"Yes, then, of course, you must try." He continued, "we must do what we can to make Mary happier. I will support what you think is best."

Gwendolyn could hardly believe her ears. She would try her best. She knew but a few hand signs, but was determined to invent what might be useful.

Coming to grips with a child's deafness was not easy for the parents or others in the household, including the other children. The sobering fact remained that there was a reason for the girl's rebellious nature. Knowing this and begrudgingly accepting it, the family tried to adjust in their day-to-day lives to accommodate Mary. The challenge of teaching her to speak with hands would fall upon the servant from the Colonies.[19]

Talking Hands

GWENDOLYN, ONCE SKY FLOWER, was nurtured in the forest. Talking with hands was for her a natural language. Her people traded over great distances, along rivers and through woodlands, speaking with hands to form ideas or words where the voice was useless among strangers. Even people speaking the same basic language may have had problems with the great variety in dialects spread over long distances. For example, people speaking Algonquian lived in territories as far apart as present-day Virginia and Maine. For them the visual language of hands was essential for long-distant trading.

A traveler may declare to strangers, "I am from the People of the Longhouse." He might say, "My village is two and one-half day's run from here." Or, "We will meet in nine days' time in Onondaga." In answer to a common query, a runner from far away may respond, "I have three children, two girls and one baby boy." All was understood with ease.

Within a day, she and Mary were exchanging positions of hands to represent words. Of course, they had already begun without realizing it. It took only a hand sweeping down from the chin, reminding them of the good doctor's mishap, to bring a secret smile. And so, they agreed, everyone needed to have a name. Mary's, they agreed, would be palm up, all fingers pointing up. Gwendolyn's was drawing an arch with the pointer finger. As for Mary's sisters—Amanda, the older blond sister, was referred to by a hand held high and pointing to something yellow, while Veronica, the shorter sister with darker hair, was designated by a hand held at shoulder height and pointing to something brown.

After the family came hand words for ordinary items of the house: first, door, table, chair, window, and then, parts of the body and body positions. Food, clothes, and toys soon received hand names. Each day, their vocabulary leaped ahead, taking in the world about them. "Sun, sky, cloud, grass, river, rock." The days brought a new sparkle to Mary's face. It was exciting to think of a sign for all the animals: cat, sheep, dog, pig, butterfly, horse, bird. Easiest of all were ways of saying feelings: sad, happy, scared, silly, sleepy, or surprised. Here, the face became as much of a voice as did the hands. Within a fortnight Mary and Gwendolyn had devised a simple language of their own. Even this expanded rapidly with each passing day. All the time, the quick temper flare-ups seemed to have vanished.

For Mary, her thirst for expressing thoughts shown by hands was unquenchable. Her signs were quick and specific. Others, that is, her parents and sisters, tried to learn, but only Gwendolyn had the tenacity to persist.

Late in the afternoon after a cloudburst, a rainbow appeared across the field, a vision shared by both girls. Gwendolyn remembered how hand-speaking said "rainbow." She held both arms high above her head, and then with hands closed, slowly lowered them. She opened her fingers, waving them to say "rain." Then with one arm and holding her palm down, she swept her hand in a wide arch. That meant, of course, rainbow. Pointing to herself, Gwendolyn made it known that her real name was the same.

Thrilled at the notion, Mary straight away brought out a slant-sided glass from her toy box. She placed it on a white tablecloth in just such a way that it caught the rays of a newly emerged sun. Now it was her friend who marveled. There on the cloth, a tiny rainbow appeared. She turned the glass this way and that, looking for the trick that might explain such a wonderful thing. Mary, for her part, marveled at the intense sparkle of those dark brown eyes as they looked on a mere toy that somehow seemed to bridge their lives.[20]

The language of hands now helped Mary grasp the meaning of letters. The process of learning them became a consuming passion. Mary soon assembled letters into words, beginning with

"C-A-T," the animal that turned a precious "V-A-S-E" into shards. More animal words, siding towards Mary's favorites—"D-O-G, H-O-R-S-E, B-I-R-D"—soon followed. Simply adding a letter to a word could change one thing into quite another: turning "CAT into C-A-R-T" was, for her, something magical. Then came learning the craft of writing. The hand that drew pictures so nimbly caught on quickly; her penmanship within weeks became an art form.

Months after the discovery of Mary's mysterious malady, Gwendolyn and her pupil happily exchanged words by hand. Indeed, there were times when they seemed to carry on a silent babble. Her sisters learned a few of their signs, but they did not have the patience to sustain their interest. Her brother refused to learn any. Mary's father tried his best, but he, too, gave up. Her mother did not even try.

Mary read well and found much joy in practicing the art of writing. Within the next few years, she was writing a short reminder of each day: some event or thought that had happened. These notes made a steadily growing pile. One such note read:

April 7. Today in forest, Gw and I came on baby deer. It lay still. I almost stepped on it. Two big, brown eyes look up at me. Most beautiful creature ever. I try to stroke it. Gw drew me away with a little push.

Another entry for another day read:

April 11. Rain came all day. My father loses tooth from ache. Charles angry at me but I know not why.

Gwendolyn now concentrated on Mary's total well-being. She helped the girl understand both lessons in arithmetic and geography as well as the common changes of mind and body that come with growing up. There were many days when the two would explore the River Ash, the stream that curved around the Manor House. Together, with the attention of a jeweler for tiny things, they searched the flowing water for tadpoles, snails, and minnows. Everything along the way compulsively had to have a name, and the number of hand-words grew and grew. Sometimes during the sunniest of days, they followed the river's edge, treading carefully along the moss-laden, often slippery rocks. Once passed this part of the path, they walked more easily beneath a wooden bridge until they came to the great river, the River Thames.[21]

Coming into view were tall reeds, boats, and fishermen with baskets full of catch. Teacher and pupil alike watched how barges overloaded with grain or animals made the turn at the sharp bend. On some days the two girls would lie hidden in the tall grass, watching the struggling river traffic while billowy clouds slowly drifted directly overhead.

Even with gradual acceptance of a reason for Mary's disruptive ways and her newly found inner peace, her mother remained distant in their necessary daily exchanges. The father, who had heretofore shown but lukewarm interest in her welfare, began to be more attentive. While seldom close enough to Mary (or, in fact, to any of the children) to put an arm around her or even to extend a hand, he did, on occasion, write a brief letter. It was his custom to leave it late at night pinned to her pillow. As time went on, these night-notes became more frequent. They revealed an ever-growing affection. Her father's letters over the years were treasured by Mary if not all understood. One letter read:

17 April 1635
My dearest Mary,
It pleases me to see your growth in body and soul. You show yourself to be quick in thought and more taken with the world around you. Your mother and I find good reason to be proud. The Scripture tells us that the contented mind and heart are the ornaments of a meek and quiet spirit.
Your loving Father

The Manor

On rainy days the two girls would often visit the orangery, a place where Gwendolyn had often found solitude. The quiet comfort of Harold, the garden master, always offered a harbor for a storm-tossed servant. As time went on, Mary, too, felt its appeal. There, sun filtering through the roof of oiled cloth softened everything to a dreamy glow. The smell of spices in the air was sweetly delightful. Always, the warmth by a slowly burning fireplace was welcoming. And so, Mary passed many happy days among the sprouts and blossoms.[22]

Mary loved the feel of soil, the stroking of a slightly roughened long stem, and the many textures of leaves. The soft petals of a daisy barely touching her cheek and drawn slowly across her face had the power of a cloudburst. She took delight in the endless fragrances of the spice plants and blossoms. It bears noting that her parents had different thoughts about the hands of a Walsingham child touching dirt. Plants meant little to them until they were eaten or stood in a bouquet that graced a table. Even so, they were permissive about their daughter's earthy calling.

The horses at the Manor provided another attraction. Mary's eyes beamed when she was anywhere near them. Gwendolyn, herself fretful when too close to these giant creatures, was always amazed at the fearlessness of the tiny figure standing but a hand's breadth away.[23]

Always kept in the stables at the Manor House were twelve to fifteen horses. Some worked in teams of two at the plough. These were the strongest animals, thick in body and legs, and high in stature. For pulling a cart, a single horse was needed, but only if one or two persons rode and if the load was not heavy. Although these horses were not very big, they were faster in their gait. Most of the Manor's horses, however, were for saddle. Surely, there was no more impressive image in England than of a gentleman riding a high-stepping horse with grace and command.

For Mary, no sight could be nobler than her father on his favorite horse. Bronze in color, it was the largest of the riding horses. Red velvet draped from beneath the saddle, the edges trimmed with pearls. The stirrups and bit were made of silver, as were the sparkling spurs. And the rider, with well-trimmed grizzled locks and beard, sat tall and graceful, always splendidly upright.

The upper sorts of the social class trained horses to hunt in parties of a half dozen or more. They would race through the fields with dogs leading the way, all in frenzied pursuit of a fox or boar. These were the finest of the horses, slender and good-natured, fast on gallop, and trained not to flinch at the explosion and smoke of gunfire next to their ears.

Five or six servants looked after the horses. Directing their work was Arthur, a heavily bearded man, neither young nor old.

Careless in dress but exacting in care of horses, he was stern in his overseeing their everyday needs. He gave an air that the horses at the Manor were his children. His father had spent his entire lifetime at the same work at a nearby estate.

Arthur had long noticed the lure of horses for Mary. Lord Walsingham allowed her to spend time in the stables provided that she stayed out of the workers' way. At first, Arthur tried to keep one eye on her while she wandered among the stalls. Already burdened with many tasks, he was leery of the added duty but had no choice. He soon came to know that the girl had an instinct for being close—but not too close—to animals that loomed over her. She was a careful and patient observer. The stablemaster felt he had little need to worry.

The days passed with Mary's absorption in all that went on. She watched the grooming from mane to tail, the trimming of the hooves, and the fitting of horseshoes. She came to know how the saddle maker made a saddle from huge leather sheets. One sheet at a time from a thick stack was cut and stamped and sewed into strips and shapes. The carpenters worked everywhere with their saws and files, repairing wagons, stalls, roofs, and door latches. Mary walked into the fields to watch the cutting of hay by men swinging large cutting blades, then piling the hay into stacks, loading these onto wagons, and then, with great pulleys lifting them into the lofts of a barn. In the fields she came to cherish the sweet smell of newly cut grass.

Always, when it was time to leave the stables and return to the tutorials or to meals, Mary balked. It seemed that she pulled on Gwendolyn's hand with ever greater resistance with each passing day. Her resentment at being dragged away sometimes led to sobbing outbursts. Yet Gwendolyn persisted. Mary sooner or later gave in. The next day would be the same.

Slowly, Mary blended into the everyday workings of the world of horses. After all, the men were absorbed in their never-ending chores of stablemen and having to keep an eye on the Lord's child was hardly helpful. In truth, the girl's eyes looked at them as a barn owl might on a skittering mouse, and the workers, soon accustomed to the silent witness, gave little attention.

Blacksmith

THERE WAS A place at the Manor that Gwendolyn and Mary had not yet explored. It was one that would soon exert a strange power over Mary that would draw her back many times for another look. It was the smithy, a small building of brick with a huge stone chimney that gave off great puffs of smoke. On their first visit there, Gwendolyn stepped through its heavy door with her small companion following at half a step. Upon entering the dark room, the visitors were immediately overpowered by the rush of sweltering heat and the smell of hot coals. Their eyes were drawn to a glowing flame that rose from a huge beehive-shaped, open topped furnace. They watched with fascination.

A man of gigantic proportions wearing a leather skull cap and leather apron stood before the flame. In one massive hand, he held the end of a long, metal rod. After hitting it on the anvil with his hammer several times, he slowly bent it into a graceful curve, dunked it into a barrel of water, and finally broke off the end piece. Only after he had set aside the flattened object to cool did he smile at his visitors.[24]

Surely, here was a magician, fully as clever as those strange sorcerers who appear from time to time in the village square, who make things disappear and reappear at will, who keep three or four balls in the air all at the same time, all to turn into a few coins from a passerby. Here in the dragon's den, an unyielding metal rod melted and was turned into a horseshoe.

There was something else that drew Mary back to the bending of red-hot iron. It was a feeling she had as she watched the pounding of metal. With each strike of the hammer against the anvil, she felt a tiny shake rising from the stone floor. When the hammer struck the thin end of the anvil, there was a slight tingle in her feet. When it struck down on the thicker side, the tingling went up her knees. When it gave a particularly hard blow, the feeling went all the way up to her spine. These were experiences like no others felt before. She soon learned to tell where the hammer struck the anvil (on the thick end, the thin end, or somewhere in between) by how far the shiver passed up her body. She made a game of it, closing then opening her eyes to test her newfound ability. She thought: *Does the quiver go all the way up to the head in everyone else? Is this how they make their mouths send thoughts unseen to each other? Such a mystery it is.*[25]

Iron Horse

On one of her many visits, the smithy handed Mary a fist-sized lump of metal. It was ordinary iron, black as tar. She rolled it about in both hands to feel its smooth face and craggy edges before handing it back. The blacksmith heated, pounded, and cooled it. He put the end result, a thin slab about the size of a shoe, on a pile of sand along with an assortment of hinges, wheel rims, and horseshoes.

Mary thought nothing more of the event until several days later when the smithy brought out the same hammered iron, now turned dark gray. With a nail he scratched a curved line across one side, gesturing for Mary, in the same way, to draw a picture. This she scratched out with puzzled amusement. Hers, no surprise, was the figure of a horse that stretched across the entire sheet. Once done, the smithy cut out the head, neck and body and separated out the legs and the tail.

Curiosity brought Mary to the blacksmith shop within a day, to see what had happened to her iron horse. The blacksmith at the furnace nodded to Mary but did not pause in his work. Finally, as he finished drawing out a piece until it was little more than a long wire, he brought out Mary's horse. There was a body, four separate legs, and a tail. After more work at the flame and on the anvil, the magician completed the amazing project. All legs were now attached, with the fore legs stretching far forward, and the hind legs reaching way back, not straight down the way Mary had scratched them. The horse now galloped.

Next, the blacksmith brought out a feathery long object, its edges trimmed with delicate strands. It soon appeared on the horse as a tail that stretched out straight behind, just the way it would in full gallop. Mary's eyes widened as she witnessed the horse come alive. The next day, she urged Gwendolyn to see the marvel made from a lump of iron. The toy horse now stood upright on a peg. The blacksmith pointed his bellows toward the horse causing it to face the sudden burst of air. Blown from another direction, the horse turned again toward it. A simple but beautiful object now appeared. It was a weathervane.[26]

Even more astonishing, the blacksmith bowed politely as he presented his handiwork to Mary. She, in turn, curtsied politely as she was taught to do on receiving any favor. Inside she felt a joyous bubble about to burst. Gwendolyn placed her hand in Mary's free hand, so soft and warm and extended the other to the blacksmith, feeling his calloused palms and knurled fingers. It was one of those moments that are so fleeting in a lifetime, a moment of perfect joy all around.

Deciding on a hand-word for a weathervane was easy: one flattened hand held close to the mouth and turned with a quick puff. "But what shall we do with it?" both girls thought at the same time. Hands flew as each came to the same answer: fingers spread around the closed extended fingers of the other hand. *Harold! Yes, Harold can have his own weathervane above the orangery. We can surprise him,* they agreed, and so they did. It was a secretive nighttime action with ladder and rope. Done, they could barely wait until morning to see his expression. Harold was not one to show his feelings but come morning there was a smile.

Stables

ONE MORNING, LORD Walsingham came upon Mary at the stables. In flowing skirt, pinafore and shiny black shoes with silver buckles, Mary balanced on the edge of a trough for water. He found her brushing along the back of Surrey, a mare nearing birthing. His horror was counterbalanced by a beaming happiness in the girl's face; it was a look he had seldom if ever seen before.

Of course, Lord Walsingham scolded the stable master for allowing such a dangerous transgression. Yet, there was a softening of his tone. Perhaps, he reasoned aloud, Mary might be allowed to groom a gentle horse. But first, Arthur had to teach her all about grooming. There were conditions: he had to find something more suitable for her to stand upon; a stable hand had to be there until Mary had proven herself to the task; the area around the horse had to be swept clean, and she should not wear her finest clothes!

By long tradition, the place of animals depended upon the social status of humans. Those of the upper sort were meant to drive or ride horses, not groom them. That task was for people of the laboring class. Her own children learning to care for horses was not to the liking of Lady Walsingham. Indeed, such activities, she thought, were hardly suitable for girls of any class.

At times Gwendolyn overheard some bickering between the Lord and the Lady regarding this point. The argument was countered by the admission that their wayward child was far more cheerful when occupied with care of horses. She should continue, said Lord Walsingham. The impasse between Lord and Lady, Gwendolyn sensed, was hopelessly locked in place.

Then the unthinkable happened. The Master came to her saying, "What do you think we should do about Mary and the horses?" Once again, he was asking an opinion of a servant! Gwendolyn tried as best she could to hide her sense of astonishment. She managed to answer quietly but firmly: "Mary should do what Mary is happiest doing."

"Yes," said Lord Walsingham. "You are right. I agree. The stable is a better place for her than the drawing room. She will be free to go there as she likes. Lady Walsingham will, in time, share this opinion."

Never had Mary, on seeing her father's written blessing, flashed such a big smile. Gwendolyn sensed that her charge had found a purpose among the horses. There was a communication, not like that between people but a far more understanding yet unspoken one. From now on, Mary returned from the stable each afternoon pleasingly tired and smelling powerfully of horses. A hearty scrub in an out-of-doors tub rounded out the day with the animals. Evenings found the girls together after a day separated by horses and tutorials.

As time went on, the girls were becoming separated in another way. Mary's consuming attention was on tending horses. Horses for Gwendolyn were creatures that, when too close, caused something between discomfort and sheer terror. Before dawn on her monthly one day off duty, the servant left afoot for London, returning during the wee hours in time to take up her duties once again, a reason she shared with no one.

Letter, Re-Read

On the morning of the 2nd of May in 1637, Mary awoke to find at her bedside the letter that brings our story to this point. Carefully written, the letter was meant to comfort. It clearly did not. There had been seven close-knit years of love, understanding, and growth. Now Gwendolyn, the writer, had a new life waiting for her an ocean away. Mary, the reader, clutched the letter to her breast before letting it fall. The letter told her that the one person who helped her embrace an imperfect world was now gone. That was the person who had been the building block upon which she learned to play out a role of life on an unequal stage. As she read the letter on that awful day, Mary felt her world flutter to the ground.

For Gwendolyn, the life of a servant had been endured for years, but now she heard a voice beckoning her from a distant land. Until now she had honed her inner resources to make the best of one misadventure after another. Her self-satisfying success with Mary, she thought, was complete. Each had come upon a new interest. Now, as Sky Flower, she was ready to emerge into a new life—one drawn by a matter of the heart. Absorbed now completely with these thoughts in body and mind, she was ready to promise her soul to another in a way that was as natural as growth itself. Her transformation centered on a play-actor who befriended her at a London theatre. Friendship became love. Love meant commitment. The power of attraction to join him in a northern city and then return with him to her motherland could hardly be resisted.

Could Gwendolyn have given any thought that her hasty and unexplained absence might cause Mary to plunge into a colossal abyss? Perhaps the anticipation of a fresh life with an improbable love and thoughts of her forest home blinded her to the effect that her leaving would have. Perhaps she reasoned that Mary's all-consuming interest in horses was diversion enough.

For Mary, it was different. Gwendolyn had gradually opened the stifling layers of her early dark isolated cocoon. Misunderstood for so long, Mary was now emerging like a butterfly into daylight. The awakening brought forth a new person. With the gift of language through expression of face and hands, Gwendolyn had showed her how to access the minds of those around her. But now, the giver of this gift had vanished.

Imagine a perfect bow. Once untied, it is difficult to retie the ribbon into its original beauty. Mary had not the means to understand the varying winds that tear at life nor to know that the bow may be tied once again, if not in the same way or to the same degree of perfection. This story now goes on to tell of Mary's quest to retie that bow into a perfect world.

Abandoned

As the days passed everyone knew that Mary, now almost sixteen years of age, suffered tremendously. She did not eat, and she barely took any morning ale. She kept to herself, staring through the window for long spells, or drawing topsy-turvy figures on paper. She left the grooming of horses to the stablemen. She wandered aimlessly along the River Ash and down to the River Thames, sitting statue-still, on a familiar grassy mound at the sharp bend where she and Gwendolyn often sat to take in the colors. Now, the blue of sky was not so blue, the white of clouds not so white. Rust-colored sails had lost their reds. Fields that stretched to the horizon were no longer green. The world, for Mary, had lost its color, save for a dull hue somewhere between gray and brown. The teams of men who struggled to round the bend with their overloaded barges knew naught of the colossal turmoil that went on within this girl who sat quietly up on the knoll. With her eyes she followed all their movements as if she were watching a puppet show.

Passing days of gray clouds or drizzling rain were all the gloomier for lack of sun. Lord Walsingham seemed most worried about the bottomless depth of Mary's melancholy. He came to see her, to take her on walks or to let her ride with him on his horse. Yet, try as he may, he could not find a way to reach her broken heart.

"Let her alone," advised her mother, "she will get over it. Children always do." The state of Mary's mind was not of much concern to her sisters, Amanda and Veronica. They were happier with their own playthings and dressing up in once-worn women's clothing. Charles, too, was caught up in his self-contained amusements.

As the days passed, the girl sought some comfort in the orangery. At first, she sat, hardly moving, on a wooden crate where the morning sun filtered through an oil cloth and stared ahead at Harold as he tended his plants. From time to time, he would look at her with a trace of smile. It was several days before a smile was returned. Harold knew that her smile was a narrow opening—but an opening nevertheless—for allowing a sliver of light to pass into the depth of her darkened soul.

Harold had not the ability to tell Mary that he, too, despaired of Gwendolyn's leaving. Instead, he spoke aloud to God to ease their burdens. After some days, he acted by placing a flat of dirt on a bench before Mary. He then gave her a handful of tiny seeds, pointing out how far apart each should be sowed, how deeply each should be pressed into the soil, how firmly each should be patted down, then the whole lot of them watered. Done, with a flourish of his uplifted hands, he foretold what each seed would become.

For Mary, planting seeds that break the soil with their tiny sprouts was the first step in a long path toward mending a grievous wound. There were other days and other seed flats. In small increments, Mary became livelier in the orangery. Harold saw that there were more ways for her to nurture flowers and vegetables into life. Within a week or two, she planted, she raked, she weeded, she pruned, and she watered. Surely, however slow in coming, there was a lifting of her spirit. Harold felt that God the Almighty in Heaven was behind it all.

For Harold, the presence of Mary was a godsend. (Godsend was a word not taken lightly by this pious man.) Ordinarily, his long days in the orangery meant total solitude. Since a child, he was ashamed of his stammer. He, long ago, chose the silent world of plants. In the orangery there was no one to laugh at the way he spoke. Mary brought no such fear. She was the perfect companion.

Of course, the horses were still a magnetic charm for Mary. Afternoons in springtime, they grazed in the meadows, wandering along the fences, and lolling in the tall grass. There was something about the gentle flow of the movement of these immense creatures that held a fascination for her. Sometimes the mare, Surrey, would saunter toward the fence where Mary stood. There, nose to nose, Mary found a kindred being. A handful of grass passed between the pickets pleased both of them.

Mornings in the orangery with plants, afternoons in the fields with horses; it was a cycle that seemed to suit Mary. Each day, her place close to the natural world seemed to ease her sorrow a trifle. Her mother at last agreed with her father to let her be.

Mary's father attempted to alleviate her burden with written words. He knew that his words might seem hollow but wrote them anyway.

My dearest Mary,
Your despair affects me with much worry. It is true, we cannot replace your governess. Your mother and I believe that some

force of nature has drawn her back to the uncivil world of her people. God knows that we did everything possible to bring our culture to her, but it seems for naught. Now, you must let her go in your mind.

You have a birthday coming soon. Sixteen years old! Your mother and I are planning a surprise for you. We are of a mind that a special gift will lift your spirit.

Your loving Father.

Mary read the letter over and over. But there was no surprise that could raise her spirits. She had to be content with the small joys of the orangery and the fields. How could a birthday gift take the place of the one person who, for most of the years she could remember, was a life-giving spark that kindled her inner flame?

CHAPTER 4

Outward Bound

Birthday Gift

It was at last the 15th day of May 1637, the day of Mary's birth celebration. On going to bed the night before, she tried to imagine what surprise her mother and father had in mind to fill up that great emptiness inside. She woke to find a note on her pillow. It was written on blue and yellow paper with a simple drawing of an angel at the top. The words read,

> *Mary, this day celebrates the day of your birth. Sixteen years it is. We have a gift for you marked with a yellow ribbon. You will find our gift in the stable next to the mare, Surrey.*
> *From your loving Mother and Father.*

Mary bounded from her bed, and hardly aware that she was still in her sleeping gown, stepped out of doors into a sparkling early morning sun. She dashed barefooted to Surrey's stall.

There was the gentle gray horse that she so often came to groom. Surrey seemed to welcome the visitor. Suddenly, in the darkened corner of the stall, there was a movement. Mary glimpsed in the shadow a tiny foal lifting its head. A shaft of light that streamed through the doorway brought the little creature into full view. Huge eyes sparkled. And there in the center of its autumnal leaf-brown forehead was a white patch in the shape of a winged angel. Around its neck was a yellow ribbon.

Mary took baby steps toward the foal. Rising awkwardly on sticks for legs, the foal stood against the stone wall with skittish uneasiness. Mary approached closer, slowly, and deliberately. The mare turned toward her, took a few steps forward, then paused, her head lowered. Mary hesitated but only for a moment, then reached forward far enough to touch the foal on its forehead. It drew away with a frightened jerk. Another attempt; another flinch. Mary did not give up. Again, and again the gentle hand came forward; the withdrawal seemed to lessen with each attempt.[27]

It was a long moment before Mary touched the foal's forehead. This time, there was no pulling away. She came closer still. Then, as she crooked an arm around the foal's neck, she felt a strong and rapid beat of a heart within that little chest. How long was the embrace? It could have been an hour; it could have been a few minutes. When she finally looked up she saw, standing there at the entryway, both of her parents.

Mary, who had sorely displeased them at times, now saw in them a sense of contentment. Her father gestured, using both hands, pointing to the foal, then to Mary, then with a placement of his arms meant to cuddle a baby, as if to say, "She is yours if you would like." Mary clutched the foal with both arms, secure enough to have held the universe true to its orbit. She could not hold back tears of joy.

And so it was that a deaf child with the gravest of sorrows had a reason for rejoicing. Standing in the sunlight was her just-born horse, chestnut brown except for an angelic patch of white between its eyes and four white ankles. Mary thought, "She will always be my Angel."

The following morning found another note pinned to Mary's pillow.

Dear Mary,
Your Mother and I see that you are happy with the foal and that the foal takes a liking to you. If you wish to take on its complete care, we agree that you may do so. Raising a horse is not easy. Arthur will show you all that must be done every day. Should you find that the chores are too much, he will see that his men will take care.
With wishes for your success. Father

That afternoon Arthur, the stable master, came to present his lesson. He brought along one of the stable boys. Young Warren was rather slow-moving and dull-witted but reliable to a fault. Arthur wasted no time. He stood in front of Surrey. Forgetting that he had been told of Mary's deafness, he began to talk. His lips moved but Mary knew nothing of his words, "My lady, a horse is a fine and noble creature, one of the most useful animals of all. But first you must..." With this there was a tug on his shirt tail. Arthur tapped it aside and continued, "The most important thing you must do is to show a horse that you are the master, the horse must learn to obey. So, the first..." There was another yank that was quickly brushed away. "As I was saying," the stable master continued though not a little annoyed, "you must..." This time Warren held his master's sleeve with one hand and pointed to the girl's ear with the pointer finger of other. That hand drew a circle in air. Only then, did Arthur remember that Mary was deaf. Slapping his forehead with the back of his hand, he muttered, "Oh, what a goose I am!"

The lesson in horse-caring then began again, this time in silence. First, Arthur touched Surrey's forehead gently, then with both hands stroked down the neck on each side, and across the back to the hindquarters and tail. Next, he showed how to brush the mane, first with his fingers, then with a firm-bristled brush followed by a soft-bristled one. Next, he demonstrated how to examine each hoof, leaning slightly against the horse and lifting and bending one leg to see underneath. A flattened spoon scraped off debris that clung here and there on the hoof. Surrey stood dutifully still through it all.

Angel was less obliging when it was her turn. She stomped and shook her head with nearly every touch. Finally Mary stepped forward and gently placed one hand on the side of the foal's neck. To Arthur's astonishment, Angel thereafter flinched not a twitch throughout the grooming and inspection of hooves.

Mary's training went further that day under tutelage of the stable boy. Warren showed her how to carry water to the trough. Water must be warm; cold water for horses causes mischief in the stomach, a point made with dramatic demonstration on himself. Keep the feeder filled with hay. Leftovers from the kitchen made good food for horses, as Warren demonstrated from a great serving tray. Carrots, apples and potatoes can be given as they are, as he took a big bite out of a crimson red apple. Clearing the dirt floor and piling all the waste outside, Warren mimicked with uncommon zeal. Next came a well-practiced show of replacing the straw covering the stall's floor. Mary all the while followed intently as she sensed that from now on her life was going to be different. The change excited her wildly. Bucket, broom, shovel, pitchfork: such mundane items formed the vocabulary of her new tutorials.[28]

There was more for Mary to learn but on another day. But from then on, it was she who would take care of Surrey and Angel. From sun-up to dusk, Mary was there, taking grain to them, finding left-over carrots and apples for treats, carrying water from the well, and scrubbing the stall to keep the floors clean. The sheen of their often-brushed coats became known throughout the manor and beyond.

Bonding

THE FRIENDSHIP BETWEEN girl and horse grew with each passing day. Mary found her sorrow slowly fading. The men of the stables found no need for their services and were pleased to have Mary carry on. Only once did they come to show her a better way, but more often they came to give praise, as best they could with hands and face expression, for her skillful care. In truth, the stables had become for her a home, pulling her to a place she deeply loved and that loved her in return. There was a natural resistance of her parents to see their daughter performing what servants are meant to do, but even their misgivings were slowly fading.

Mary noticed that Angel's ears pointed backwards every time she entered the stable. A strong rubbing of the neck caused the tail to swish. With a shake of the head, Mary came to know that Angel was thirsty. The quick nod that came after drinking, Mary knew, was Angel's way of thanking her. Angel often nudged her muzzle across Mary's shoulder. She tended to stand as close to

Mary as she could, touching gently, sometimes interfering with chores getting done. She liked to bite onto Mary's sleeve and hold it there, tugging this way and that.

For all her playfulness, Angel had another side, one that Mary had seen but to which she had not given much attention. Over time, this other side could not be dismissed as a quirk of no consequence. Whenever one of the stable hands entered the stall, the horse would act strangely. Her ears turned straight up, her legs seemed to lock in place, her eyes showed white all around, and her mouth was pulled in tightly. The change from playful to fearful was instantaneous. No coaxing or apple treat by anyone other than Mary seemed to make a bit of difference. Yet, all the tension melted away almost as soon as the person was out of sight.

The coming of spring brought life to the meadows. Horses needed to eat fresh grass after having little but straw and dry grain throughout the long winter. With confidence, Mary led both animals out into the fields where she watched them as they nibbled on the tall grass. Angel, however, did not only nibble. Here in the open space was a place to romp and cavort. Suddenly, she would jump, then run in frolicking bursts, and whirl in small circles; then she would nudge Mary playfully with gentle tosses of her head as if to seek approval for such talent. At times, the girl imitated the leaps and turns until she fell to the ground laughing.

And so, Mary spent the balmy days admiring the antics of her filly, walking the fields, or napping in the tall grass, while taking in the flitting butterflies, the sweet smell of clover, and, overhead, many-folded, puffy clouds and, now and then, a hawk in its effortless soar.

There in the field, Mary saw Angel growing taller, stronger and surer afoot. By summer's end, Angel's shoulders were nearly as high as Mary's. They took long strolls along woodland paths, with

Angel at first tethered by a rope. Since the horse always followed along closely without hint of tug, the rope was soon abandoned. Their meanderings extended farther along the River Ash, the way that Mary had ventured many times with Sky Flower. Sometimes, horse and girl went as far as the bend in the River Thames where, with mixed feelings of nostalgia and happiness, she rested and watched the barges.

On another late afternoon in the pasture Angel looked up from grazing and, as is the way with wild creatures, suddenly began to gallop. She ran to the far side of the field, then turned, making a profile against the border of trees, her long tail streaming straight out. Here in Mary's sight was the blacksmith's perfect weathervane come alive. She spent that evening trying to preserve the details of that wonderful moment.

Horse Training

It was now 1638. Angel had indeed become a fine yearling, admired in every way by family, servants, and stable hands alike. Her muzzle was narrow, as with all intelligent horses. Her eyes were bright, as if afire. Her ears were erect and well-pointed, the neck curved in a graceful arch. Her hair was long and finely textured and thick as velvet, her legs slender, straight, and well-braced with hooves alike in thickness. And that tail: it was nearly ground-touching long, soft and shiny, the object of countless long brushes and admiration. People said that Angel walked like a dancer, seemingly to float easily; she was never short-winded and had no wheeze or rattle. It was clear that the horse with the white angel on her forehead had become the darling of the Manor.

Few, however, noticed that Mary at the same time was growing taller, and, in fact, growing up. She was lanky but graceful in motion. She appeared happy in a world that could only comprehend silence. On many days when the sun warmed the fields and filled the tall grasses with flitting insects, she would stroll aimlessly along the fence that bordered the forest. There, always in her view, was Angel. At times, the horse would follow her along the perimeter of the fence. Sometimes, Mary would run alongside Angel and, breathless, would jump, too, in full circles.

Some wondered if Angel might have already become hopelessly spoiled. After all, a horse was a valuable possession of a family; it must provide a service, as do all others at the Manor, animals as well as persons. Yes, a change for both horse and caretaker was necessary. A chilling breeze of change was soon to come. A note found one morning on Mary's pillow read:

> *Our dearest Mary, we admire how you have made your foal into such a fine horse. The time has come that we need to train her for duties, as we do with all the other horses. Training is meant to begin during the second year of every horse. We know that you will understand and will allow Arthur to begin to teach Angel in the proper way. I believe she could become one of our best horses for hunting. Who knows but one day, your Angel may be of service to the King. In case of war with the French or even our own Parliament, she would be properly trained and ready.*
> *Your loving Mother and Father.*

Having seen something of the harsh training of horses, Mary wanted her Angel spared. She remembered when a one-year-old horse—fully grown but untrained—came to the Manor and was taught to obey its smaller Master. It had to learn to stand still for hours, carry a heavy weight, pull a loaded wagon, or run through a field, jump across ditches and wade chest-deep across rapidly flowing streams. She knew that a "working" horse, which was a naturally spirited, wild beast, must be brought to submission to serve the owner, no matter what measures were required. It was the duty of Arthur and the other stable servants to do just that. For the horse more resistant to full subjugation, it could be (and often was) brutal. Mary, with wonder and too often horror, saw the ugly side of training a beautiful and stately horse.

Teaching a horse to pull a heavily loaded cart or plough or to carry a saddle with a rider takes weeks, sometimes months. Training for the hunt takes longer. The horse must learn to run fast on rough ground with a rider and to become accustomed to the sound of shooting guns.

Mary knew that a trainer blended reward with fear of punishment to make a horse submit to driver or rider. She had seen that an apple or carrot coupled with a firm pat down could be reward enough. The horse that submitted early was best off. Otherwise, a horse might be beaten and bound into submission. The whip was meant to make a sharp, ear-snapping noise but a horse felt its sting if it did not quickly submit. Those that resisted further were considered vicious; they were trained with more severe methods. Horse trainers took pride in molding even a "weak" horse—one rebellious or too sluggish from want of spirit—into an obedient one. A horse that resisted all attempts at training was doomed. Would Angel be better suited as a draft horse, pulling a cart, a heavily laden wagon, or a plough? Or was carrying a saddle and rider more befitting her nature? Lord Walsingham wanted Arthur to spare Mary from seeing the meaner aspects of training horses. He instructed him to carry out the harshest methods, if necessary, out of her sight. They were to be exacted only in early morning and toward evening when her father could persuade Mary to attend to inside pursuits.

Both Arthur and the Master favored Angel for the hunt. For hunting, a horse needed to be both fast at the gallop and enduring at the trot. All along the chase, gopher holes, ditches, hedges, and streams needed a sharp eye and nimble legs. There was one more requirement: that a horse must remain calm when the rider fires his gun. Training for staying calm after loud noises began with faint and distant sounds getting louder and louder, closer and closer, until the horse remained unflinching at a gun blast next to its ear.

Mary realized that training Angel meant that their carefree days in the fields were over. She was ready to accept any role for herself but could not bring herself to think of what might happen to Angel. The strained look on her face made her father write more. He pointed out that Angel belonged to the Manor, not only to her. Depending on her make-up, Angel must learn to pull a cart or a heavy log or to carry a rider.

No, the page went on to explain, *a horse cannot be an idle pet. Angel must do her duty, as we all must. Every animal requires our care; every animal in turn contributes what it can. You know that the dogs stir foxes and boars out of hiding, and that cats catch mice. Even our canary has a duty, singing sweetly to us.* (The canary was beautiful but the point about its singing was lost on Mary.)

A lightning bolt of reality awoke the girl from her anguished thoughts. Having always believed that Angel was hers and hers alone, she was startled to read that she had been merely given the privilege of being its caretaker. She was stunned! Where was Sky Flower to brace her at such terrible time?

Seeing Mary at the stable on the following afternoon, Arthur bowed respectfully. Complying with the Lord's note, he had come to begin the training of Angel. It would be gentle. First, he needed to place a bridle. Mary, of course, had seen much of bridles and knew that the bit was meant for steering and control. She knew, too, that it would be fitted across the mouth and that it seemed to cause pain; indeed, that is how the horse is mastered when gentle nudging of the reins is not sufficient. Besides, Angel had long followed Mary's natural lead, with and sometimes without a loosely tied rope. What, Mary wondered, was the point of the bridle and bit?

Arthur did not have much success with his harness. Even the touch of the stable master caused the horse to spring upward, her eyes showing fear by turning full white. Trying to force the bit in her mouth caused agitated snorting and shaking of the head. At last, Arthur, in exasperation over a "bad-tempered" horse, abandoned any further effort—for now. Mary watched it all with unendurable discomfort.

At the Seashore

It was but a few days after the failed trial of a bridle that Lord Walsingham announced that the family would soon take a fine trip to the seacoast. The weather was already very warm, surely an excellent time to enjoy the sun, the surf, and a favorable breeze. Charles was expected to return from school. The house servants, of course, were to attend them. Furthermore, there would be no essentials of a good life left behind. There would be picnics and happy days sunning at the beach. All this, Mary learned from her father in writing.

But who would take care of Angel? The question burned inside of Mary for sleepless nights. Letters were exchanged. Arthur, her father reassured, had many years with horses and would know better than anyone what is best for a young horse. He will try the bridle again.

No, I will stay, wrote Mary. But that was not to be. Her father wrote that all arrangements had been made; there was no turning back. Besides, her mother insisted, they need to have the whole family together. When would be the next time? With Charles away at school, and the sisters being often courted, who knows when that would be? Besides, cousins from London planned to attend. The best news of all, her father wrote, was that they would be at the seashore for a whole fortnight.

Within a week, carriages were packed for seashore life. The family would lead the procession. Servants with the trunks and paraphernalia would follow. Charles and his sisters were overjoyed with anticipation. Mary had no choice.

Sleepless, Mary rose soon after dawn on the day of their departure. She went directly to her Angel. Mary stroked her forehead, gave her a handful of rye grass picked up along the way, threw her arms round her neck, then slowly walked toward the family carriage. She could not bring herself to look back.

The seashore, a day's ride away, meant days of relaxed comfort for the family. The procession consisted of six carriages, four of which carried servants, trunks, food, and sundry items of comfort. The Lord and Lady and the two aunts rode in the lead carriage. The children followed in their own carriage, amusing themselves with endless chatting and teasing. Mary, crouched down to avoid the commotion, felt every bump in the road, and knew that each one took her farther away from Angel.

Once there, the picnics were numerous and bountiful and just a long jump from the water's edge. Recreational activities were organized: playing in the surf, of course, collecting seashells, tennis, and long strolls. Grown-ups enjoyed just sitting on lawn chairs savoring the ocean breeze. Children jumped the rope and built miniature fortresses out of sand. The cousins of various ages were four in number. They were courteous to Mary but, finding themselves unable to converse, left her alone.

The children's cabin was not far from those of the adults. All the girls slept in one room, the boys in another. Of course, after dark, the boys could not restrain from making eerie sounds outside the girls' window. The more frightened the girls, the eerier the sounds became. Finally, one of the girls raced out screaming all the way to her parent's cabin. On close inspection with lamps alit, the fathers found no ghosts, dragons, one-eyed monsters or other causes of alarm. They peeked into the boys' cabin and found all "fast asleep." And, of all the girls, Mary was the only one who slept through it all.

During another night howling winds stirred up the waves, putting a strong taste of salt in the air. A swirling rain pelted the cabins while lightning danced across the sky. For Mary, peeking through cracks in the shutters, it was all a wonderful spectacle. Yet, there was something foreboding about the storm. Was Angel frightened? She should be by her side. The night was long for wondering.

The visit to the seashore proved longer than she could bear. Her father tried to lessen her anxiety.

I know your Angel is fine, he wrote. *Arthur sends word that he has made some progress in the training. There is no need to worry. When we return, you will see that Angel has become a fine horse in every way.* That last assurance made her worry even more.

Conflict

AT LAST THE day came when the family and their servants returned to the Manor House. It was twilight when they arrived. Mary, with her father, went directly to the stables. There she saw the mare with Angel crouched behind her. Angel was shaking. She pulled away from Mary's approach. There were streaks across her rump and along the neck. Her tail had been cut short, almost to the hilt.

Mary, stunned with horror, shrieked. Enraged, she turned to her father and began to strike him fitfully over his chest with her fisted forearms. Lord Walsingham pulled back in shock but Mary, screaming, came at him once again, thrashing wildly. This time, her father wrapped his arms around her, pulling her so close that her arms were too restricted to budge. Slowly, his clasp tightened, rendering Mary powerless. She sobbed quietly.

The scuffle of screams and futile reassurances brought others to the unimaginable sight. This action came from a child who had come to her parents every morning of her remembrance to bow and state her undying honor, as best a deaf girl could understand. Not even the oldest of the lot had ever witnessed such a spectacle. A parent switching a child—seen often! A child protesting a parent—seldom! A daughter striking her father— not imaginable!

In that flash of volcanic eruption there was another, invisible side. Mary realized suddenly that her father had never held her in his arms. Beyond her rage, she felt his sheer strength and warmth around her, at first restricting, then comforting. Her great sorrow, her anger at her father's deception, her being subdued all slowly fell away as her stiffened body slackened. They stayed in each other's arms for a very long time.

The father slowly released his hold, set her afoot, then hand-in-hand guided his daughter into the Manor House. Sitting with her on the great chair by the hearth, he attempted to wipe away the tears that had streaked across her cheeks. Mary turned her head away. He directed a servant to bring in some apricot pudding, just made and still steaming. The girl refused to eat.

Lord Walsingham sat at the desk and began to write:

Mary, know that our holiday at the beach was meant to give our stablemen time to train your horse. Angel struggled against every attempt. Arthur believes that she has been spoiled by too much attention. The Manor House cannot continue to support a horse meant only for a pet. This problem is serious. You, Mary, just help us to find a way to bring Angel to serve her duty. Please know, too, that I have never loved you more than I do today.
Your Father.

Mary read. Her head fell onto her chest. She crumpled the paper until it became a tight ball. Then, after a few moments, she pressed out the wrinkled paper and began to write, just beneath her father's words.

What can I do, Father? I not let Angel suffer. Too delicate is she. Punish me instead.

Lord Walsingham wrote on the other side of the crumpled paper.

> *No, Mary, there will be no punishment. Arthur is a good man. He does not cause any animal needless harm. His purpose is only to bring a wild animal to submission in the gentlest manner possible. Go to your room now. In the morning, I will engage a trainer from Cambridge. People say he knows new ways of taming a nervous horse. You will be there to help Angel learn to be a proper horse.*

Even this letter was not enough. The struggle between opposing cosmic forces could not be resolved easily. But a small step made a temporary compromise. That very night, Mary lay down to sleep on a stack of hay next to her beloved horse. She fell asleep consoled only by her vow to protect her Angel, no matter how strong the forces against her.

The Trainer

Within days Master Wetherspoon, the famous horse trainer, arrived. The man was pleasant enough, offering a hand to Mary that was accepted in good grace. She felt honored at such a gesture, not one meant by custom for children.

Without further ceremony he went directly to the stables and he looked at Angel's face, muzzle to muzzle, for a long minute. He then lay one hand on the animal's forehead, slowly running it along the back to the flank. The yearling did not flinch but rather stood stiff-legged. The trainer next tried to place a loose-fitted bridle on her, but had difficulty because Angel kept tossing her head from side to side. Rather annoyed, he handed it to Mary, urging her to try. By first removing the bit, the bridle slipped on easily.

Mary took the long rope of the halter and, in response to Master Wetherspoon's waving, led Angel into the open air and out into the field. They walked slowly, but the trainer hurried them on by rapping on Angel's hind legs with a long rod. Waiting for them were Arthur and Warren, eager to see the work of this most famous horse trainer.

Master Wetherspoon took the rope from Mary, brought it around Angel's neck and, to Mary's horror, tied it to the stub of Angel's tail. With a sharp pull, the rope tightened so that Angel's neck was forced toward the side. Angel was now held in the shape of a comma. The strangeness of it all caused the horse to turn rapidly round and round until she became dizzy and fell to the ground. The trainer helped pull her up. Still dazed, Angel started turning in tight spins again. Once again after a few turns, she tumbled to the ground.

Mary could endure the sight no longer. She raced to the fallen animal, falling herself and throwing her arms around Angel's neck. Arthur tried gently to pull her off, but there was no letting go. There the two, Mary and her yearling, lay as if attached to the ground. Nothing, Mary vowed to herself, would separate them now.

Lord Walsingham was soon called to the improbable scene. Arthur explained as well as he could, asking if they should draw Mary away and continue with the training. "No, we will not press on," returned the father. "My daughter is dearer to me than having a well-behaved horse." Some exchange of coins went on with the trainer from Cambridge who, presently, mounted and went his way.

By now, Mary knew that her horse was different from the others. Perhaps she had spoiled Angel, she admitted to herself. What could she do now to prevent her beloved horse from being cruelly trained again? And how would she do this without gaining the wrath of her father?

During the terrible weeks that followed, Mary's anger and Angel's fear slowly lessened. Then, by accident, she discovered something rather wonderful. On one of those dismal, drizzling mornings in the stable, Mary stood once again directly in front of Angel to admire the beautiful white marking on her forehead. And as Angel was accustomed to do, she lifted one forefoot, the left one, slightly and tapped just ahead, then withdrew her foot. The curious action amused Mary. Although she had noticed the movement before, she had given it little attention. Now, the tapping continued until she moved to the side. Then it stopped.

Mary went about her chores, but she pondered the odd behavior, even late into the night as she tried to fall sleep. On returning to the stables the next morning, she found that there was no more tapping. Of course, she went about the grooming, watering, feeding, and sweeping as usual. Then, as she stood in front of Angel to begin brushing her forehead, the tapping started once again. She moved to the side and the tapping stopped. After a few trials, Mary realized that Angel's response stayed the same. A tap of the left foot happened only when she stood directly in front. The action was most peculiar. What was Angel trying to tell her? Instead, it was a fly that told her.

As Mary tried her best to understand the mystery, a stable fly buzzed in her face. She blinked and waved it off. It was then that it appeared to her that Angel was responding to her blinking. Then, she blinked purposefully, and with each blink came a tap. Blinking outside of Angel's view brought no tapping. They now played a game. The prediction of action and reaction was true. Suddenly, for astonished Mary, a new world of possibilities opened in her mind's eye. Could this newly found connection between blink and tap be the miracle that might spare Angel from the suffering of further horse training?

Counting

WITHIN A DAY, the Lord of the Manor received a note. It bore a strange message.

Dear Father,
You will be happy to know that Angel can count. Please come to see.
From loving daughter, Mary

Lord Walsingham had heard many tales of marvelous things that horses can do, but news of a counting horse had never fallen on his ear. He suspected that his daughter had a vivid imagination and worried that the love of her horse and surely the vulnerable state of her voiceless world might have finally brought some loss of reasoning.

On the day that followed he went to the stables to see this astonishing feat. There, standing directly in front of the horse, Mary held out four fingers. There came four taps of Angel's left hoof. The man looked with wide-eyed amusement. When she held out two fingers, two taps followed. On seeing three fingers and then quickly four, Angel responded with seven taps. Five fingers shown on top, with two fingers of the other hand held just below, produced three taps. Further trials at recognizing numbers were unfailing. Mary, mischievously, chose to keep the clever feat her secret. In some way, she hoped, this hocus-pocus would improve the fate of her dearest friend. Her father knew that he had just witnessed a most remarkable event.

Not many days passed before everyone at the Manor House—family, servants, stablemen, and gardeners—had observed Angel's unnatural talent. The skill of a horse counting was certainly nothing anyone had ever dreamed possible. That horses were intelligent if well-trained, there could be no question. But what magic had Mary cast to teach Angel?

Of course, everyone wanted to try to outsmart a horse. Calling out numbers did not work with Mary, but showing fingers did. Those observers who held out nine or ten fingers were sometimes disappointed, but Angel appeared to all to be unerring at a lesser count. After each sum or subtraction, people expected to see Angel take a bow. This she did not. Meanwhile, no one noticed that Mary's blinking was behind the miracle in the stable. She always kept her place directly in front of Angel. Certainly, everyone blinks and often too; blinking, after all, is not unnatural and certainly never suspected of deception.

For the moment, Mary knew that her trick would buy some breathing space for any decision made about Angel. Yet, she did not feel comfortable in continuing the sham alone and was keen on sharing it. Harold was the only person she truly trusted, yet she hesitated to reveal her trick to this very pious man. And so, Mary decided that she had best keep the humbuggery to herself. For the first time in her sixteen years, she reveled in the exquisite pleasure of having the upper hand. Mary, in her lifetime, came to practice three deceptions; this was the first of the three.

Over time, the novelty of a horse that could count wore off. Angel's place at the Manor came up again on fatherly notes. Mary's mind raced feverishly to concoct another scheme that might delay a fateful decision. Try as she might, her head abuzz, no clever ideas came that would stave off the "proper" training of Angel.

As sometimes happens in situations where there is no answer to a burning question, a solution comes in an unexpected way. For Mary, it began when she found the letter that—one year before—had left her incapacitated in spirit and body. Sky Flower's letter was tucked away in a stack of drawings; rereading it now gave her a renewed sense of herself.

Mary unfolded the crushed and tear-stained letter. No, the words had not changed. Sky Flower's message was the same. Her friend was gone, never to return. But Mary began to realize what that friendship had meant. It had created in her strength for dealing with the sorrows of life as well as seeking out its joys. Sky Flower shined a light into her world that remained bright. From her, Mary learned that she should believe in herself and that she could make realistic choices. Such a choice was about to come, purely by accident.

Lord Walsingham had been talking with a gentleman who dealt in horses. He shared with his daughter the written agreement to bring young horses for training to the Manor. After all, Arthur had earned a fine reputation for exactly this task. It was also agreed that two older horses, good as a team at the heavy work of ploughing, would be sold. A buyer had already been found. The buyer lived in the colonies, in a place called Boston, where there was much need for powerful horses to break the soil. The gentleman was an agent for a man named Jeremy Adams. Master Adams was a childhood friend and schoolmate of Lord Walsingham. As a Puritan and an adventurous soul, Master

Adams had sought an opportunity for a new life in the abundance of the New World.

Those few words on paper—the New World—set Mary's imagination ablaze. Yes, there was the answer to her great question. Of course, she had learned a little about the Puritans and their search for a new life across the ocean. She would take Angel to the colonies! There, they would be free to roam the forests and explore the sandy beaches as they pleased. At that moment it was an idea that offered an easy solution. On impulse, Mary wrote:

My dearest Mother and Father,
Happy I am to write you of wonderful plan. I go to Colonies with horses. Angel comes, too. We return after many adventures. I tell you about the New World.
Your loving daughter, Mary

Surprising Return

For Lord and Lady Walsingham, Mary's plan was little more than comical. Yet they did not how to rid Mary of such a fanciful idea. They found her brooding day after day at the Manor House, preferring instead to be out in the field or within the closed world of stables. There, they saw a lively girl among the farm animals who shadowed the chores of every stable hand and who delighted at the skill of the blacksmith and saddle-maker. At dinner, on the other hand, no one failed to notice that Mary remained locked inside herself as if her soul had been, for the moment, extinguished.

Mary's parents came to realize that she was no longer a child and instead more of a young woman quite determined in her ways. The event that brought them to this realization came one day towards dusk with news of the disappearance of both Mary and Angel. They had gone into the forest in early morning, as they often did. Nothing was seen of them as nightfall approached.

Called forth by their master, a worried group of stablemen had gathered to begin a fitful search. As they were about to fan out into the woodland, torches in hand, Mary in her flowing skirt and blouse with the puffed-up sleeves emerged from the edge of the forest. Relief there was! Surprise, too! Mary rode Angel.

The stablemen were amazed to see Mary mounted without saddle, bridle and bit, or stirrups. Her mother was shocked to see Mary riding not with both legs flung to one side the way all women on horseback were expected to ride, but straddling her mount the way a man would ride. Her father, instead, saw a regal bearing in his daughter as she rode past the crowd, head high with a faint smile, every inch the bearing of a queen. Dead silence held until Mary had reached the stable and disappeared within. There followed collective exhalations as stunned observers slowly meandered back to their duties, each with his or her own impression of the astonishing scene just witnessed.

A trained horse without training! How was it possible? What was the special bond between girl and brute? Lord and Lady wondered mightily, as did Arthur and the stable hands.

When chores were finished near the end of the following day, the curious urged Mary to show them her gift with horses. Once more mounted astride Angel, Mary treated the gathering to how the horse could move ahead with a quick nudge of the knees. They watched as she gaited faster by a gentle poke of heels. Their astonishment was further peaked at how she turned Angel by a rubbing on one side of the neck, and how she stopped in an instant with a sharp tug on the mane. It was all so simple. Arthur and his men returned to their tasks with a sense of disbelief, each lost in his own thoughts about the long-honored traditional art of training horses.

Lord Walsingham, too, shared in smiling admiration of his daughter's horsemanship. Lady Walsingham was less enthusiastic; it was not proper. Mary's father soon let her know in writing that her mother begrudgingly allowed her attention to Angel, but only if she rode sidesaddle. The practice of a woman riding a horse like a man was certainly immodest. It might be tolerable for a woman who sold fish or collected rags. For a woman of the upper sort, it was unspeakably abhorrent.

Lord Walsingham's night letter to Mary explained all.

Dearest Mary,
Your mother and I talk often about you and Angel. We marvel at your way with her. We laugh at the idea that you and Angel seem to have become a single being, beautiful and in every way perfectly matched. Your mother now allows liberties hardly suited to any girl in our station. Yet, she asks that you always ride with both legs on the same side as do proper women of the gentles. Your mother will not yield on this point. I respectfully request that you honor her wishes.
With all my love, Father

Mary read the letter over and over. She did not know many of the words but there was no doubt about the meaning. Despite the ruckus she caused her parents while growing up, Mary had no desire to dishonor them. She had seen women riding in the manner called "sidesaddle." That meant riding a horse with one leg propped up into a sling but only at a slow walking gait while the horse was tethered by rope and led by a servant who walked ahead. Better it is to ride with one leg on each side so that rider and mount moved in harmony as one.

She mulled over these thoughts as she and Angel made their daily excursions along the Thames, each day venturing a little farther upstream. But suddenly a big smile replaced her troubled expression. The solution to her mother's restriction was simply a small but harmless deception, at least in her mind. She would ride Angel in the morning at her mother's pleasure, then change to riding astride when out of sight of the Manor, and return to sidesaddle on nearing her return home. Who would ever know? Who could care about such a tiny deceit? It was, for anyone counting, Mary's second turning of the truth.

Saddle Deception

Early morning was the best time to leave the Manor for a long ride along the River Thames, and so began one day. As the mist slowly lifted, the hubbub of men with barges came alive. Fishermen dotted the shore on both sides with baskets empty and hopes full. Girl and mount passed small villages along the way, often impeded by grazing sheep, and other times by teams of draught horses hauling barges. Now and then, a horse-drawn cart raced by, bearing some dignitary on some important mission. There was frequent stepping aside where the pathway narrowed to wait the passing of animals and men, but surely Mary was in no hurry.

A favorite place to visit was the village of Staines, a market town. It was here, at high sun, that Mary liked to walk among the throngs of people. Angel followed never more than a step behind. There were endless stalls of vegetables, pottery, pots, candles, and hanging slabs of fresh meat. Cattle and chickens, unsuspecting of their fate, waited for buyers. Tailors, knife-sharpeners and cobblers, all hawking their skills, were aplenty. Jugglers and magicians worked their way through the crowds. Beggars, blind or with missing limbs, livened every corner with their piteous opened palms.[29]

Afternoons meant a leisurely return from Staines to the Manor House. And no one noticed, Mary was certain, that she rode most of the time in a man's way of sitting on horseback. Along the way, back and forth, fishermen had come to know Mary. She had come to realize that a broad smile announced a full basket. A dour face hinted that luck had been elusive at the great contest between man and fish. A happy fisherman with a particularly large fish would sometimes hold it up for Mary to admire.

It was on one long-remembered morning that Mary and Angel left the Manor House especially early, at dawn. They meandered northwest along the River Thames, arriving at the market town even before the stalls had opened for the day. Mary made a quick decision to continue, and soon realized that they were now far beyond Staines. All the way, the morning fog cast a mysterious peekaboo over fishermen and houses and barges.

There were a few stops for water, but Angel continued at a determined gait as if she were as eager as Mary to see what lay beyond the next bend. About midday the fog lifted a bit. Ahead rose a story-book-like castle with mist-covered tower tops that seemed to reach into the clouds. Rider and horse paused for a better look at this splendid sight. After dismounting, Mary quickly found a good place to sit: a cushion of pine needles beneath a stand of evergreens. And what a sight she saw!

All at once though a black space in the wall of stone came two horses, side-by-side. Silver glistened from the helmet and breastworks of their riders, and the tips of their lances pointed straight up. Then followed another set of horses and soldiers followed by another and another, eight sets in all. And just behind them pranced four black horses, two side-by-side. They drew a huge black coach with two drivers sitting high in front. They wore identical black derbies and scarlet tunics. As suddenly as they had come, the train turned and disappeared into a bank of fog. Of all her grand memories, this memory of the Queen's Castle was surely one of the grandest.[30]

The moment had come when both girl and horse could rest from their journey. Clean river water and shoots of tall grass springing up along the shoreline were there for Angel. Basking in the earthy smell of moss, Mary opened her sack of pastry and jar of tea. Where the dappled sunlight fell, the moss glowed in a brilliant, deep green. She looked up through the trees at the sun trying to peek through the mist, musing all the while that life at that moment could not get any better. The tangible reality of her life in a privileged home was becoming ever more replaced in her fog of lofty dreams. Surely, every day would be like this in the Colonies if only she and Angel could get there.

To all observers Mary was clearly a member of the gentle class. And, of course, when she and her horse were noticed by many along the stretches of the River Thames, tongues began to wag. It was not long before gossip reached the Manor House concerning the unlady-like manner of a young woman, full-skirted and with puffy sleeves, who rode a horse astride. Her horse, rumor went, had a perfect angel on its forehead.

Lord Walsingham had mixed thoughts about his daughter's way; her mother was shamed beyond words. Yet, both knew they could not expect their youngest daughter to be like other girls of her position. Angel, too, was not like the other horses; it was now about eight months since the training fiasco. Mary's proposal weeks before was no longer comical. Her parents sensed that nothing short of her going to the Colonies with Angel would satisfy her. More notes from her father urging her to turn these thoughts around had only redoubled her resolve.

Within two months her parents had arranged for Mary to embark on the ocean voyage. They knew that she had no notion of the miseries and dangers of such a journey, and rather suspected that she imagined it as a long holiday in an enchanted land. To her the plan was like a wonderful birthday present.

Plan Unfolding

ALTHOUGH TORN APART with misgivings, Lord Walsingham arranged for Mary to travel to the Colonies with the workhorses that Master Adams, a Puritan, had agreed to buy. He had learned that the colony in Massachusetts was prospering after nine years. After all, it had been granted full rights by King Charles, and the Puritans were hard-working people. Moreover, the colony was a land rich in natural resources and at peace with the Indians. Not least was the blessing of a favorable climate.[31]

Emigrants from England now, in 1639, were not like those who settled in the New World in 1620. The purpose of the earlier group was to establish a colony, a new Plymouth, according to their ideals of worship. These emigrants were more radical religious thinkers who wanted nothing more than to sever all ties with the Crown and to reject all its Royalist religious trappings: the statues, stained glass windows and robed bishops that distracted from the simple and true worship of God as the Bible taught. They were the "Separatists," not the people who brought with them a charter from the King.

Lord Walsingham assured Mary that a letter to Master Adams had already been sent on a Boston-bound ship telling of Mary's arrival there. In it, he requested that his friend from long ago offer lodging, and that the fare would be resolved equitably. He wrote of Mary's deafness and her wonderful ability with the written word. Mary's diligence in caring for animals received great praise. He went further to describe Mary as a quiet and happy girl who would cause no trouble.

Master Adams, he went on to say, would surely welcome her. On last hearing in the gossip mill, he thought that his friend had some children, perhaps a bit younger than Mary. Certainly, Mary could help in their care and perhaps perform other household tasks. Lord Walsingham went on to explain that Master Adams was once a preacher in England. He spoke freely about his displeasure with the Anglican Church, accounting for a reason to seek shelter in the Colonies away from what he called the Crown's "tyranny." Lord Walsingham further wrote that Jeremy Adams was pious, kind, and generous. Certainly, he and his family would be there to meet the arriving ship. Mary could expect a comfortable setting since the Adams family was well established in their new home. There would be warm houses well-removed from the dangers of swamps and wilderness. With the forests filled with animals running free and the rivers well supplied with fish, food was plentiful. Ships went back and forth often to carry letters and essentials.

All was arranged. Mary would go on a ship called *The Vagabond.* The captain of the ship was skeptical of taking a deaf girl along with her "play" horse, but he was enticed with a handsome sum. The investors of the journey were swayed as well, but not so cheaply.

Lord Walsingham explained on paper to Mary that the journey would be long and dangerous and that life aboard ship from all he had heard would be, at best, dreadful. The more he wrote to explain the hard life of a sea voyage, the more eager she became to go. The stable hand, Warren, assigned to care for the other animals, would offer some company. He would return on the same ship. As the plan unraveled in writing, there was a hopeless naivety in the girl's imagination; it resisted any link to reality.

Notes exchanged with her father told Mary of arrangements already made. The ship carried many supplies and a few passengers. A ship's officer named Joseph was to look after all her needs. She, in turn, was expected to take full care of Angel. That was the only arrangement acceptable by the shipping company. There would be chickens, sheep, pigs and, of course, the draught horses to feed and groom. Warren and another boy would see to these chores. Furthermore, Mary was to stay in the lower deck where she would be sheltered from harsh weather.

Littleton to London

IN THE EARLY morning of May 15th in the year 1639, her father had everything ready for their cart ride to the docks. The route he had carefully drawn. In the evening they would lodge overnight at the London home of Lord Walsingham's sister, where three of the cousins resided. Mary's mother and her sleepy-eyed sisters gave polite hugs, not forgetting to wish her a happy birthday. Charles was nowhere in sight. Mary's excitement about beginning her journey seemed to be evenly balanced by their lack of excitement and, perhaps, skepticism about the entire endeavor. Father and wide-eyed daughter were soon on their way.

Lord Walsingham chose to take Mary in his two-wheeled, open cart, a new design that had its body suspended on springs for a smoother ride. In unabashed luxury, they rode side by side, seated on cushions just behind the driver. Thanks to the new design, the passengers enjoyed little more jostling than a gentle sway. Following them were Arthur and Warren afoot leading the pair of plough horses. The way to London, of course, was slowed by rutted roads, hordes of sheep, and travelers in carts and carriages. Many on foot struggled with bulging bundles.

This was not Mary's first visit to London, yet her eyes were transfixed at the world of urban clutter and activity. The carriage passed through dark narrow streets and then merged into busier ones crowded with shops and shoppers. She stared at all manner of things for sale, including whole animal meats hanging on hooks. Crossbeams of wood layered with stucco supported the many-windowed houses that rose high into peaks. Occasionally there was an open space where an old tree sheltered a few gravestones. Although Pudding Lane, their destination, was well-hidden within the warren of streets, the driver found it unerringly.[32]

Aunt, uncle, and cousins greeted countrified Mary and her father with hollow politeness. Inside, the rooms were tiny and cluttered, the heat of day trapped throughout the night, but the noise from the street easily let in. There, ceaseless talking among people eager for news left Mary feeling alone among many.

The city-dwellers did their best to wish her a pleasant voyage. Yet, their written well-wishes all seemed artificial, and their faces exposed their doubts about the journey. Birthday gifts presented to her were all meant for a long trip: a set of silver forks, spoons and plate, a cup of tin ware with handle and a white blouse, laced at the collar and with flowing sleeves and draw-strings at the wrists. The letters MAW were boldly embroidered on the front of the blouse. There was, too, a hairbrush with soft bristles and a carved handle. To go with it was an oval looking glass about the size of the face that gave an uncommonly true reflection. A cousin handed her a pair of white, cotton gloves that reached up to the elbows. Another presented her with a scarf, as red as any Mary had ever seen. Lastly, she received a book of many pages.

With a glance at the book's front cover, she read: *Countrey Contentments or The English Huswife containing The inward and outward Vertues which Ought to be in a compleate Woman.* It was a book of recipes and remedies. Written inside the cover in perfect scroll were the words "To Mary, our valiant cousin, may you find happiness in the Colonies." For each gift, Mary curtsied with exaggerated grace and then stuffed it into her traveling bag, already jammed with clothes for cold weather, and paper and graphite for writing and drawing.[33]

In a four-page letter her father wrote more about the proposed plan. After a difficult voyage of about eight weeks, she would arrive at an English colony on the eastern coast. It was a place where the Puritans hoped to worship as they wished and where there would be no interference by the King.

The Puritans, Mary's father assured her, were God-fearing, honest people. Within a few years they had established an idyllic "City upon a Hill" in a harbor the Indians call *Shawmut.* The new settlements (Boston on one side of the bay, and Cambridge on the other) were both named for thriving towns in England. He understood that over a hundred houses had already been erected. Although their work was hard, the people were content in their situation. They raised their own food and lived with simple comforts, all the better to gain the grace of God in the afterlife.

In another letter, he wrote that the good people of the Bay Colony were blessed by peace with the savages that roamed around them. Even their numbers had become far fewer by their weakness to resist the pox and measles. Writing that Master Adams would surely welcome her into his family was meant to relieve Mary of any anxious thoughts. It was made known to her that prayers would be conducted every day and that strict adherence to the words of the Bible would be expected.

Mary understood little of her father's long letters. She cared only about finding a safe place for Angel. She knew, too, that Sky Flower was somewhere over there. Surely, she would find her.

Departure

In the morning, father and daughter met up with Arthur, Warren, the driver, and the three horses, all of whom were lodged nearby.

The entourage arrived at dockside by midday at the place of ocean-going ships. The sights were astonishing: ships displayed like a forest of masts larger than any that plied the River Thames![34]

Inquiries led them to a wharf where the masts of a ship named *The Vagabond* reached tall above all those around it. Here, a large group of people had gathered, all milling about, and many laden with great packs. Wooden boxes, great barrels, and tightly packed bales of hay were piled high. Alongside were pigs, chickens, and some restless sheep.

There is a blend of sounds that beguile a visitor to a bustling wharf: the chatter of people, men lifting great weights, squawking sea-gulls soaring overhead, farm animals bellowing, sails flapping idly, and the water lapping against the piers. Mary was unaware of the clangs, crashes, grunts, squeals, and squeaks of machinery and animals. Yet, her view at riverside thrilled her enough.

On the edge of the wharf was yet another sight most intriguing. It was a gigantic, leaning frame of timber, a crane for lifting cargo from the wharves up and over into the waiting ship. The secret behind this impressive feat was the heavy work of the dock workers. For each haul they pushed against the spokes of a giant wheel and later pulled them back. Hours passed as the crane lifted, swiveled, and dropped bundles, boxes, and barrels into *The Vagabond.*

By late afternoon the time had come to board the animals. First, the coops filled with chickens rose up and settled down into the ship. Around the torso of each of the larger animals was tied a canvas splint, and that was bound to a rope that passed through the single hook. One-by-one, each animal was lifted high, pulled over and lowered until it was swallowed by the gigantic monster in one great gulp. The swine were the first to go in this manner. They squealed piteously with each abrupt ascent into the atmosphere.

The sheep went more quietly, some without so much as a *baa*. Next came the horses. Once the canvas was fitted snugly around each horse, the men pushing in the circle did not hesitate. As they pushed in circles on the ground, the horses, too, rose, fell, and then melted into the bowels of the ship.

Just when Angel's turn came, Mary began to have grave doubts about the journey to the colonies. But before she could ponder further, the horse was fitted with canvas. In an instant, Angel was looking down from the heights, and she could see the eyes of her beloved horse grow white from terror. She gasped in horror and felt every fretful thump of her heart. Slowly the circle-walkers reversed their course, and Angel descended and then vanished into the ship. Mary felt the strongest urge to fit a canvas sling on herself and be the next to board. For people, though, it was different. They would simply walk up an inclined plank and onto the ship.

She waited not patiently as her father spoke at length to a man wearing a broad-brimmed straw hat. They were looking closely at some papers. Then her father pointed toward her. The man looked up and the raised brim put his face in full sunlight. He was dark-complexioned, his face, weathered. A huge ring hung from one ear. He, she was certain, was Joseph.

Introduction was simple. Joseph extended his hand. Mary, who was taken aback by the gesture, touched it softly with a forefinger. Her father made it known that this was the man charged with seeing that the ship and its crew worked together as a single unit. Master Joseph would soon show her where to go. Her father added that although Joseph had many duties aboard ship, he would always find time for helping with any of her necessities.

The time came near sundown when out-bound people were meant to board the ship. Arthur and Warren stood nearby. Warren, Mary noticed, stood bent over with his face in his hands.

Arthur had a hand on Warren's shoulder. For Mary, the sight of Warren sobbing was disturbing. The newness of the place in all its frenzy did nothing to ease that troubling feeling.

Mary had never been away from family and home. In the exuberance of the moment there was no way to comprehend the absence of every familiarity that had made up her life to this point. Still, she had found it easy to take leave of her mother and sisters. Now, on the dock, it was time to give a farewell embrace to her father. She found that not so easy. Mary had come to feel a special bond with him, one that had grown immensely since the disappearance of Gwendolyn.

Lord Walsingham was certain that his daughter was in for a long journey with many discomforts along the way. Although the quarters for passengers were crude, the captain promised to see that Mary had every convenience available. Because of her concern for Angel, he agreed that she could bunk near the animals and take care of Angel as she saw fit. The arrangement was agreeable with Mary's father; it was the best he could do on a ship meant to carry animals and goods rather than people.

The firm embrace by her father was only the second time that Mary could remember him holding her. At this moment and for the first time, she saw his ever noble, stern face soften, and his eyes glisten more than ever. Slowly he freed his grasp. She turned and, with knapsack tucked beneath one arm, walked in deliberate steps, following others up the long plank, taking no notice of them and never looking back. All were led to the deck, past the tangle of ropes and stout poles, then down narrow steps into the darkened space below. Mary was then separated from the rest and led to the holding place for animals.

Below Deck

Dazzling sights—the orderly disorder at the wharf, a great crane lifting crates and animals, then her father's tear—all had left the girl feeling awed and a bit weak-kneed. Still, she needed to reach her horse quickly. Had Angel safely survived her aerial boarding?

Soon finding herself deep in the innards of the ship, Mary was unprepared for a shocking sight. As her eyes adjusted to the dim light, she could make out that the horses were each standing, aligned closely side by side but separated by thick timbers. Fitted snugly round the waist of each horse was a canvas splint. The fore legs that had been bound together were lifted by a splint a short distance above the floor. The hind legs carried the main weight. They, too, were bound. In addition, each horse wore a bridle without a bit. Each side of the bridle was tied to the stall so that head movement was barely possible. A trough made from canvas hung just within reach of the horse's mouth.[35]

Seeing Angel so tethered, Mary gave out a demonic shriek. She leaped to her side and stroked her firmly along the neck. Slowly, she could feel tension in the horse wane. With hands, Mary expressed her thoughts. *Angel, you need not fret. I will soon free you. You will be able to walk about, even in this tiny, dark space. It will be a long journey, Angel, but we will see it through together. We cannot turn back. Together, we will see the New World. You need me now, but I need you as much.* She was sure that her horse understood.

Mary, at the time, had no way to know that Angel's confinement, as with the other horses, was to last until the ship reached harbor in the colonies. Transporting large animals was a complicated process. They drink huge quantities of water. Food must always be on hand. They easily become seasick and that causes colic. Large animals do not sway naturally as the ship rolls. Any heavy objects, including horses, that have become loosened during a storm endanger the ship.

Of the other animals, there were seven pigs: five small ones and two gigantic beasts. They milled about together in a small but sturdy pen. Of sheep, there were five, crowded in another pen. Hens and roosters were held, five or six to a small cage, and there were many cages, stacked one above the other. Whinnying, oinking, baaing, cackling and crowing wailed among the animals in their rudely confined world, all lit by two small lanterns. Even in Mary's soundless world, she could see that they were at a high state of anxiety. Two figures descending the steps were a welcome sight. It was Joseph and a scruffy boy. Joseph handed Mary a note. She read: *Edmund will teach you how to care for the animals.*

She reached for paper and soon had a note for Joseph, *When will horses be set free?* He scrawled, *Soon. They will walk free when the sea is calm.*

With its delivery, Joseph returned to the upper deck. Mary for the moment was satisfied. Yet, something was odd: if Edmund were to provide instructions on caring for the animals, why was Warren not there, too?

Edmund began at one end of the high wall of barrels, bales, bags, and bundles of hay, talking about how it was to be sorted out. Mary interrupted with a tap, pointing out that she did not hear. He shrugged finally just pointed out the mops and brooms. He showed her where she was to sleep—just there on a stack of old sails. The pails were for her convenience, too. Nearby, a pewter bowl and a mug were meant for her use. He mimicked eating and pointed above.

Carrying an empty pail and long rope, Edmund then led Mary up onto the weather deck and to the aft railing. Here was the place for animal waste. It was not to be tossed, he warned with a pointed finger, but rather let down into the water with a rope. He demonstrated. There he rinsed the pail, now readied for refilling.

With this lesson that she barely comprehended, Mary returned to the hold and wondered. Certain she was that she could care for Angel if only she could find the right grains. What about the other animals? Standing there in the darkened, smelly, cramped hold with restless animals, and feeling overwhelmed by the duties ahead and the meager training just given, she felt a cruel emptiness. Naturally, an ocean traveler in 1639 should not have expected a cozy journey. This traveler would be fully tested.

Mary, on the spot, had to accept that fact that Warren was not on the ship, that Edmund would be little help, and that Joseph had other duties. There by the light of two hanging lanterns, she felt her knees wobble, her breath choke, and her skin turn a prickly cold. Her footing, now changing from steady to slowly rocking, revealed that the journey had already begun. She knew nothing of Hell but, now, she was deep within its grasp. Crushed in that miserable space, ready to collapse, alone, she had to accept her situation and do what she could. *First,* she told herself, *Do not faint. Second, Use everything learned about caring for animals at the stables and the coops of The Manor. Above all,* she told herself, *I am strong. I can do what needs to be done.*

Restless animals gave a sense of urgency. First, fill all the troughs with water, find proper food for the chickens, swine, sheep, and horses among the stores, sweep up the animal waste, and lower the slop over the ship side. She must also stop for a moment on deck for a bit of food for herself; gruel and cider had been put into an iron cauldron that hung over a cookstove. She struggled at the chores through the night, falling fitfully for a short sleep on the mound of sail, feeling more than ever dreary and spent of energy. In this manner unfolded her first day aboard *The Vagabond*. The ship had started its journey. It was the sixteenth day in the month of May.

No Help

MORNING CAME WITH a gleam of light through the open stairway. Mary could feel the slow rolling and pitching of the ship. *The Vagabond* was at sea. Her crossing to the New World was no longer a dream. In the semi-darkness, animals of all sizes surrounded her. Watering, feeding, cleaning began all over again. There was no sign of help from above. What she saw were passengers on the other side of the under-deck with stomachs that appeared to have second thoughts about an eight-week journey to the Colonies.

The first days remained warm and pleasant. Mary could stay on the main deck with each bucket load and watch the never-ending swells play with the ship. She was slowly learning to become part of the ship and to respond to its moods. On climbing the stairway with her weighty buckets, she discovered that it was easiest to take a step up while the bow of the ship was going down, and to pause when the bow rose. To keep from falling she quickly learned to hold one hand on a railing while carrying a bucket, but this was not possible when she had a bucket of animal waste in each hand!

She was left alone by the sailors and ignored by the passengers who gossiped that the husbandry girl could neither hear not speak. Let her be, they seemed to say. Mary had never felt lonelier.

No prison could be more suffocating, darker, or more confining. She was, for the time, trapped alone in a strange world. But she had her Angel, and Angel was companion enough. With each passing day she would be closer to Boston.

Crossing the Ocean

THE OCEAN VOYAGE was so extraordinary that a brief account cannot do it justice. Nevertheless, a description of shipboard life and some of her activities above and below deck will try to convey that experience.

Meals were grim: salted beef or pork, gruel, and hard stale bread often laced with tiny white, squirming things. Water after two weeks tasted too foul to drink and the barrels of weak beer were tapped to quench thirst for the rest of the journey. A splash with cold seawater had to do for a bucket bath.

Storms were what she dreaded most. The ship's sudden pitching came as a surprise because she could not hear the warning rushes of wind, the madly-flapping sails, or the straining groans of the ships' beams. During this rocking motion the already weakened horses were sickened; they were seen choking and regurgitating through the storm. Toting buckets on narrow stairs became ever more challenging.

Sometimes, waves were high enough to break over the main deck. The water poured through the boards, soaking everything and everybody huddled below. Worse still, there were the times when cargo broke loose during a storm and crashed into people and animals alike. Not until a wayward crate broke apart did it no longer pose a danger to the ship. What remained scattered throughout the lower deck was broken furniture, plates, and farm tools. Clusters of precious spices floated in puddles of bilge water.

The chores for Mary lessened somewhat over the weeks. Some sailors came into the hold and hauled away one of the giant swine. On other days a sailor would come to take away some chickens. The gruel seemed to be thicker for days after these animal heists. Meanwhile, the horses were getting thinner and more restless. Some had developed sores where the canvas hammock pressed into their skin. The sea was never calm, and the horses were never free. She, too, was wearing thin and no longer strong enough to carry two buckets at a time.

Mary soon concluded that Warren had cried his way out of making the journey. By now, she knew that Edmund would be no help. Joseph, clearly, was occupied in the business of sailing the ship. Her only consoling thought was that at the end of the voyage she and Angel would be greeted warmly by a kind family.

Mary was certain that her father knew nothing of the nightmarish ordeal. This ill-use of his daughter he would not have allowed. As a trusting person who had never been on a long voyage, Lord Walsingham took the ship owner at his word. There was something else her father did not know: the ship was not destined for Boston. It was headed for a new plantation far away. The weary and unending duties of animal care allowed Mary not a sliver of time to take up her pad for drawing. One time several weeks out and with eager anticipation—to prevent herself from going completely mad—she pried her new book, *Countrey Contentments or The English Huswife,* from her traveling bag, affixed a lantern close to her canvas bed and read about the "compleate Woman," beginning just under the title:

As her skill in Physicke, Surgerie, Extraction of Oyles, Banqueting-Stuffe, Ordering of great Feasts, Preserving of all sorts of Wines, Conceited Secrets, Distillations, Perfumes, ordering of Wooll, Hempe, Flax, Making Cloth, Dying, the Knowledge of Dayries, Office of Malting, Oats, their excellent uses in a Family, Brewing, Baking and all Other things belonging to a Household.

COVNTREY
Contentments,

OR

The English Husvvife.

CONTAINING

The inward and outward Vertues which ought to be in a compleate Woman.

As her skill in Physicke, Surgerie, Extraction of Oyles, Banqueting-stuffe, Ordering of great Feasts, Preseruing of all sorts of Wines, Conceited Secrets, *Distillations, Perfumes, ordering of Wooll, Hempe, Flax,* making Cloth, Dying, the knowledge of Dayries, office of Malting, Oats, their excellent vses in a Family, Brewing, Baking, and all other things belonging to an Houshold.

A Worke generally approued, and now much augmented, purged and made most profitable and necessarie for all men, and Dedicated to the Honour of the Noble House of Excester, and the generall good of this Kingdome.

By *G. M.*

Printed at *London* by *I. B.* for *R. Iackson*, and are to be sold at his shop neere Fleet-streete Conduit. 1623.

Her book was most disappointing. Mary knew that there were joys and griefs "belonging to a household," and that each woman had her duty. Yet, she could not picture herself restricted forever to the domestic expectations outlined on those pages. What she needed was advice about the care of animals on an ocean voyage, but there was nothing within its pages on that topic. A book of recipes and remedies was a gift ill-chosen for such a journey.

The author, "G.M," was printed inside the cover. Surely, this was a fine book for what G.M. called the "English Huswife." Here was everything that a good wife of a gentle family needed to know. Her husband and his guests would always have a comfortable home ready after a hard day of hunting, hawking or other vigorous recreation. Mary discovered deeper into the book that G.M. was Gervase Markham, a man.[36]

As she looked over her book, a new idea flashed into her thoughts. *Here I am on my way to a world far removed from what every girl in every Manor House in England can expect: devotion to manners, customs of dress, fear of callouses from work, playing the lute and making pretty conversation, and then to marry a rich property owner, organize endless festivities, tend to children, and keep a proper distance from earthly affairs. Is that the privileged life I want?*

Mary looked about in her dismal, smelly prison. Tired beyond pitiful, unwashed of weeks of animal grime, unable to look at the green slop meant for a meal, aching in arms and legs, mostly sleepless days and nights, and watching Angel become weaker with each passing day—despite all this, she knew that every dip of the ship was bringing her closer to a new life for her and her horse. Angel was the reason. She was the one who made it possible. These thoughts led to a firm resolve:

No! Whatever fate is in store for me in the New World, I will not spend my life trying to please Master Markham. She put the book aside, went over to Angel, looked directly into her eyes, and conveyed, *I am the luckiest girl in the whole world!*

Passing an Island

Down in the hold, there was an awareness that the motion of the ship was changing. It was not the slow rolling from side to side, as happened during most of the journey. Now the rolling was a little faster and a bit jerkier. Mary was soon to discover the reason.

On her next climb to the weather deck, bucket in hand, Mary found a curling fog wrapped around the rigging. The bow made its way blindly through the fog. Suddenly, as if a ghost, a patch of land appeared. At last! The long, terrible crossing was coming to an end. Spars swung around sharply as men scrambled up the ladders of rope. The ship, she saw, was turning sharply. It was soon running not far from a rock-strewn beach that she had seen during the breaks of the fog. In her joy of reaching a faraway coast, Mary assumed that this was the normal way to approach land. She did not grasp how close the ship had come to a calamitous end.

As the ship worked its way along the shore, Mary lingered to take in the sight. Spring-green hues of the landscape alternated with the rolling grayish-white fog. Suddenly a giant bird, long-legged and blue, burst from behind a giant boulder and soared into the air on long, fast-flapping wings. As it flew past the front of the ship, Mary could make out a feathery plume that adorned its head. She had never thought much about symbols, but surely this handsome bird was a sign welcoming her to the New World.

The ship soon came to a clearing over the land. There were tall, narrow and straight-up plants with drooping leaves, clearly a garden. Each stalk had a long tassel that dangled from the top, looking every bit like the King's Guard on parade. Beyond them, Mary saw a few rounded, shaggy huts. They appeared to be made from the bark of trees. Each had a small opening, likely for a door. A scattering of people stood, holding their garden tools and watching as if frozen with astonishment as her ship passed by. Their hair was long and straight, their clothing, brown and loose fitted. Beyond the gardens, huts, people, and trees, she saw another stretch of water. The ship, she realized, had come to an island.[37]

Once again, the spars swung around. Sails were trimmed. The ship began to make a turn close around a point of land. A dozen or so nearly naked children swarmed to the point, flinging arms wildly and laughing as the ship passed. Two or three were seen swimming toward the ship, making as much splash as they possible could for attention. In response to Mary's wave even more children started to fling their arms, urging her, it seemed, to come ashore to them.

The ship slipped rapidly past the jubilant scene. The girl on the rail wanted to shout *Wait! Wait, Ship! Just another moment.* But Mary could not speak, and the great ship could not hear. Soon, the island was but a sliver of partially fog-covered land. Up ahead was another vast expanse of water but this time, in the far distance, a slender rim of land could be seen beneath the lifting fog.

So, these people who greeted the ship were the "savages running wildly through the forests of the New World." They were the very people about whom the cousins in London had warned. But what she had seen were gentle people working their gardens and children excited, and perhaps thankful for the diversion, to see a strange apparition moving along their shores. Onboard ship, the crew and the passengers observing along the rail seemed too caught up in the moment of a near-miss to give much thought to the people who were already here.

How Mary so much wanted to stay above deck to take in the wonderful passing sights, but there were many mouths below deck waiting for her! The date? She had lost count altogether. Her intention to write each day about the journey as it unfolded had gone wholly neglected. It was all she could do to keep up with the creatures that needed her tending. Probably it was sometime in July, but she could only guess.

Another sweep, another set of filled buckets. Then down the steps came Edmund followed by Joseph. They chatted. They eyed each of the animals with great care. Joseph gave a sign of approval, an upward turned thumb and a tap on the back of smiling Edmund. They soon turned and went above.

That night, a troubling thought came into Mary's head. Joseph had barely nodded to Mary on his venture into the hold. Did he believe that Edmund had been tending the animals, that she was just there as part of the cargo? Hadn't he seen her countless times on a long journey emptying countless buckets overboard? No, such an idea was silly, certainly not charitable, and she dismissed it as no more than her own idle and mean-spirited jealousy.

Sailing Upriver

More ascents onto the deck proved to Mary that *The Vagabond* was now in a river. Heavily forested banks lined close on each side. The water flowed straight not unlike the River Thames (except, of course, at its sharp bend in Shepperton). Here and there, a narrow column of smoke rose from hilltops. Along the shoreline she saw no one—no fishermen, no herders with their animals, and no children running along the riverbank. It was truly a land of wilderness.[38]

Mary guessed that it was near midday, although there was no sun to judge by. A light following wind meant that the sails could stretch out fully as the ship sped along. Men on high yards were pulling some canvas in and letting some canvas out. Men on deck, tugging on ropes, shifted the direction of the sails. Calls from front to back were unheard, of course, but she could see tension in their faces. One stood in front throwing out a weight and dragging it back in again, over and over. To the silent spectator, the purpose of the hard-laboring sailor's effort was entirely lost.[39]

Mary tightened from fright as she saw the ship heading directly toward a huge boulder. This massive rock stuck out into the water at the right-hand side. Knowing nothing of navigating a great ship, she was certain that those who brought a ship across an ocean could manage to wend their way up a river. There was nothing to fear.[40]

Somehow, the great boulder resembled the fist of a giant. From the way the thumb extended toward the oncoming ship, she concluded that it had to be the right hand. Where the thumb separated from the clenched hand stood a solitarybush on a barren rock. It caught Mary's imagination. She admired how brave the bush was to stand there by itself, alone, enduring the storms of winter and scorching heat of summer. Perhaps, she thought, this simple bush facing a harsh and untouchable world alone represented herself. Yes, she had proven herself enduring and no less lonely.

The ship turned away from this rock and slipped past other rocks by a hair's width. Just at that moment, Mary saw some leaves in the center of the bush separate and a pair of eyes looking out. Within another instant, the ship had moved ahead. Had she actually seen those eyes or just imagined them? She had an eerie feeling that they would follow her wherever her journey took her.

Anticipation

IT WAS DURING this time of reverie—when the sun suddenly burst into the open and flooded the ship, river, and forest with light—that Mary began to think about her situation. The endless days and nights in the dismal hold of the ship were coming to an end. She now realized that she had already said goodbye to the world that had nurtured her, and that she would soon begin life in a new place. She would have the comforts of a well-settled family; she would see a vast and plentiful continent; and, most precious of all, she would share all her discoveries with Angel. These thoughts made her feel as if she herself had burst from behind a cloud. Along with a sudden sense of homesickness, there was joy. Her breath faulted. She wanted to laugh and cry at the same time.

Now, Mary was certain. In her mind, those mysterious eyes peering at her from behind the bush would not go away. It is true that a lively imagination feeds on itself and the prospect of a new life in a new world added to an already giddy feeling. But gray clouds soon masked the sun, forcing her to regain her senses. Her day-dreaming had come to an end. She was needed below for more feeding and more sweeping.

CHAPTER 5

The New World

Arrival

A SHIP FROM home arriving in a frontier town was always a moment of rejoicing. On board the frantically working crew rolled up sails and made preparations for landing. Excited passengers flocked to the deck to watch for signs of the fast-approaching village. Word that the ship had already entered the Great River had somehow spread to the settlement. People there began to crowd onto the wharf, some shouting and waving madly, but most just waiting quietly and observing.

The Vagabond closed in on the landing. Here were not the grand docks of London but rather some floating boards held together by standing poles. Instead of a forest of ship masts, there was a lone boat for rowing. No lifting cranes were in sight. Cargo ready for shipping was not piled high at the wharf's edge. No seagulls soared about to celebrate their arrival.

The ship slammed sideways into the dock, causing a great commotion among those standing on deck. Sailors quickly used ropes to tie *The Vagabond* to poles on a small and rickety landing place and then laid down planks for off-loading.

First, passengers, fully burdened with bundles and boxes, staggered down the planks. Some knelt to kiss the dock. Others mingled with people joyous at their arrival. All gathered together where a man—dour-face, singularly tall and slender as a tree—led them, kneeling, in prayer. Afterwards, all busily tended to the bundles and boxes that had been carried onto the landing. Most of the steerage members and their possessions were whisked off by welcoming families. Mary off-boarded with the others, but was mystified because there was no one to greet her.

The animals were the last to go ashore. First the sheep and then the two remaining pigs were coaxed up the inside steps by tugging or pushing sailors. Then, one by one, they were led down to the docks. Need the reason be mentioned why there were no chickens to unload?

Work horses were next led off ship, finally unburdened by their canvas body hammocks and bonds. They wobbled slowly, having been sapped of strength by weeks of continuous restraint. They balked at climbing the steps from the hold onto the deck but were goaded along by manpower and switches from behind. If they resisted walking down planks onto the wharf, strong-armed or even sharper persuasions were applied. With his switch Edmund applied more than a little nudging.

Mary, not seeing Angel follow the black horse, raced back to the hold. There, she found men pressing their might against her unwilling, balking charge. Edmund was ready with his switch. She pressed them all away. Angel, weakened though she was, followed her up onto the deck, then down the ramp onto the wharf.

There in the open, the animals stood, tottering and dazed in the sunlight. Rightful new owners came to claim and lead or carry them away. One of the pigs broke away and ran into the underbrush with a throng of yelling boys chasing it. Wagons, quickly loaded with barrels and crates, soon rolled away. The commotion on the dock gradually subsided as boxed cargo and walking animals vanished along a rutted road. All the time, Mary, shouldering her traveling bag, stood by with Angel, wondering why Master Adams and his family were not there with broad smiles and welcoming arms.

A man finally arrived to inspect the work horses; in fact, it was the same man who had led the prayer. He inspected them all around, front to back, from teeth to hooves. Both animals had weeping belly wounds caused by the constant rubbing of their canvas slings, and both displayed ribs affected by weeks of near starvation. Mary stood close by, hoping desperately that her father's horses were still fit, wondering if her exhausting care on the way was enough.

Finally, the man, satisfied with his inspection of the livestock, turned to the lone figure on the dock, saying "Who are you?" These were the first words addressed to Mary on stepping foot onto a new continent after a dreadful journey of more than seventy days. Of course, these words were lost on her.

The man was one of the tallest she had ever seen, a head above all the other men. His hair was closely cropped on top, but there was a thick and long reddish beard that started just beneath the ears and squared off just below the chin. And those ears: they turned straight out like those of a fox when listening for the footsteps of a field mouse. His eyes were penetrating, and they gave the whole face a look of steadfast determination.

Mary stood aghast for a moment, and then gestured that she was deaf. He seemed not to comprehend. She then fetched a graphite stick and sheet of paper from her traveling bag. He waited impatiently. Feeling breathless while trembling fretfully, she scribbled before him: *Dear Sir, My name Mary Walsingham. Forgive me, please. I do not hear. I wait for Master Jeremy Adams. Know you him?*

A response was soon written: *Yes, that person I am.*

Mary, a bit relieved, returned in shaking hand: *I, daughter Lord Walter Walsingham II of Littleton. A letter he sends you, tell my journey to your Colony—with my horse, Angel.*

Now it was Master Adams who stood aghast. He jotted down: *Yes, I knew your father. We were schoolboys. He has made a good name for himself among the King's gentry. But I have received no such letter.*

Sir, went the exchange. *He wrote. Letter on ship from England more than three months back.*

With this paper in hand, he walked to the one remaining wagon still on the dock. Oxen-pulled, it sat fully loaded with crates, barrels, and two pigs. In quick steps up, Master Adams climbed onto the seat and, in deliberate hand, wrote this note: *A letter of agreement from Lord Walsingham about selling his horses arrived in Boston. I received it three or four months ago here in Hartford. There has been no letter about a daughter and her horse.*

By now, Mary was in a heightened state of anxiety. She stood before the oxen, looking up between them at Master Adams on his high perch. Her long and terrible journey had come to this. Of course, she had been in many troubling situations before but, always, she found some way to ease what happened next. Now she felt helpless. Of this she knew, she was not in the place her father had described in his letters to her.

As Mary read the letter one more time, she felt strange things happening in her body. She started to breathe faster and felt prickles spreading over her arms, tongue, and lips. She could no longer see colors, as her world became darker and darker. Everything around her began to sway and totter. She felt herself tumbling through the emptiness of space with nothing, not even an idea, to hold on to.

Master Adams saw a ghost-like pallor come over her face. Beads of sweat then formed across her forehead. Seeing these, he leaped down from the wagon and caught Mary just as her eyes rolled up and her knees gave way. His quick move saved her from crumbling onto the ground.

Now propped up on her traveling bag, Mary opened her eyes. The tree no longer whirled, and the sky was no longer dark. Breathing was much easier now. Standing before her with one hand steadying her at the shoulder was Master Adams. A few taps on her back seemed to say that the crisis was over. The brief journey to the netherworld and back was complete.[41]

A note quickly written by Master Adams read: *Child, you have had a fit. How can I help you?*

In the intensity of the moment, all Mary could think of was to beg for a place to stay. She reached into her traveling bag and brought out another sheet of paper. On it, she scratched a simple appeal. *Will you take me in? I have no place to go. I shall be no trouble.*

Our house is already too small for my family, Master Adams wrote with measured hesitancy. He then added: *If we must, I bid you stay.*

Mary, eased mightily on reading, glanced at Angel. With a quick swipe of the hand, Master Adams took the paper and added, *Yes, your horse, too!*

He beckoned Mary to climb onto the wagon and to sit beside him. At the hint of a small switch his pair of yoked oxen began to move forward. Angel and the plough horses were tethered behind. They moved slowly because the horses were pitifully weak after their long confinement. Thus, while sitting atop a rickety wagon along with bulk cargo and some piglets, Mary started her first great adventure in the New World. She also discovered the volatile meaning of "welcome." She and Angel had arrived. It was the eleventh day of July.

Introduction

NOT A THOUGHT could be shared by voice or by graphite on the bumpy ride to the village. It was not a long ride, but once there Mary did not see the beautiful city that she had long imagined. There were no rows of sturdy houses neatly stretched along crisscrossing roads, no central park with children playing happily, and no fine church with a steeple. Instead, she saw a collection of rude cabins with slanted roofs of thatch. A dozen or so of these were scattered along a curving, rutted pathway. A few were dugouts; that is, dwellings carved into the brow of a hill, the earth heaped on each side. Only the front of each structure showed a narrow door, and above each one was a slanted flat roof. A few frames of standing lumber formed the skeleton of houses-to-be. By now, Mary was certain, *The Vagabond* had not come to the Massachusetts Bay Colony. She and Angel had arrived in a new settlement that was called Hartford.[42]

The wagon came to a stop in front of one of the cabins. Master Adams helped his passenger step down. The crates and the barrel were quickly set on the ground. He then pulled opened a rough-hewn door. They stepped inside a low-ceilinged room.

Dim lighting came from the edges of two small oil-paper-covered windows high up on either side of the room. Even before her eyes could adjust to the darkness, Mary first became aware of a pleasant aroma that wafted above the smoky air. It was the sweet smell of nutmeg. After her weeks with only the foulest smells, the fragrance brought her thoughts of the Manor House where the scent of precious nutmeg brightened Christmastime.[43]

Her eyes quickly swept through the room. In the center was a table, bare, save for a pair of candles. Benches stretched lengthwise with high back chairs at each end. Directly ahead was a great maw, a fireplace of stone. Ashes glowed beneath a giant iron kettle that dangled above. The mantel held cups and plates. Nearby a ladder led to the loft. A bed and a crib with rockers lined one wall, while clothing with shoes neatly placed beneath lined another one. A woven reed mat, not unlike the one at the servants' cottages in Littleton, covered the hard-packed earthen floor.

Hardly was there space left for the people standing there, but there were several sets of wide eyes staring at the newcomer. The light flickered on the face of a woman wearing a bonnet and a broad white collar. She held a baby propped up on one hip. A boy greeted her by pinching his nose with one hand. Two toddlers stood beside the woman, each clutching her billowing skirt. Their sense of curiosity was palpable.

Said Master Adams, "Here is Mary Walsingham. She is from Littleton, near London. She came on the ship. I knew her father. We were schoolmates. He has sold us a sturdy pair of work horses. Mary will live with us for a time."

Upon hearing this, his wife gasped. He quickly added, "She is deaf and dumb, but she can write." He went on to explain, "Mary brings with her a horse. Somehow, we will have to make do. She can look after our little ones, perhaps help with the animals, work the garden... and... and... and..." With these words, the woman began to breath once again.

Aloud, Master Adams informed Mary, "My wife. And our baby John of three months. Here are Hannah and Sarah, twins born two years ago. All are healthy, thanks be to God above. Our boy is Thomas." Still forgetting that he was talking to a person who could not understand his words, Master Adams continued, "He is a good boy, but he has some mysterious ways." Thomas stood rocking back and forth nervously. His face was delicate but his eyes were the most noticeable feature. They stared at the visitor with a fierce intensely that made her feel as if she were a creature from another planet. In a way, she was.

Before Mary could fully embrace the broad scope of her new family, a final member emerged from a darkened corner. She now stood before the fireplace so that her lanky frame was backlit. Tall, she was, and oh, so thin, in truth a stalk of wheat. Her piercing eyes squinted against the glare of the dimly lit room. Long dark hair that fell around her cheeks made them appear unnaturally pale and thin.

Had she, thought Mary fancifully, *also just completed the rigors of an ocean voyage?*

"Here, too, is Rebecca," Master Adams went on.

The two girls stared at each other intently, seemingly studying for clues as to how they would get along. Perhaps they knew that there might be a quality in each that would bind them together. For now, a slight smile from Mary brought a restrained one from Rebecca before she retreated into the shadows.

Finally realizing that he had been speaking all along to a person who could not hear, Master Adams tapped his forehead as if to apologize. He took a moment to scribble on paper all the names of his family along with their ages. He handed the sheet to Mary. It read: OUR FAMILY. Jeremy age 46, Rebecca age 49, Rebecca age 14, Thomas age 11, Hannah age 2, Sarah age 2, John age 3 months. To this list, Mary took his pencil and added: Mary age 18. This was the way Mary was introduced to her new family.

Settling the Animals

With a waning sun, there was now some urgency to see to the animals. Master Adams motioned that Mary return with him to the wagon, where she helped lift the boxes and barrels and lay them beside his door. The wagon, with the driver, passenger, and pigs, followed by the tethered horses, then bumped forward. They passed between houses and a little river before coming to a large shelter, one long side being completely open. It was a hillside dugout burrowed on three sides. Stalls inside held horses and five or six cows. Some stalls were empty.

There, two men unhitched the oxen. They lifted the heavy yoke and laid it inside the shelter, and then, by using switches, coaxed the animals into a stall. The pigs went to a muddy, uncovered sty with perhaps a half-dozen other much larger pigs. Master Adams led the two work horses to another stall where he saw that they were soon watered and treated with great mounds of fresh grass. He then accompanied Mary, Angel following, to the very end of the shelter where there was a small open air enclosure possibly meant for sheep. This, he indicated, was where her horse could stay. There, Angel could walk about freely. It would do for now, and Mary knew what to do for her thirsty, starved friend.

After settling the animals, Master Adams and Mary walked back toward his house. They stopped at a well where he, with practiced hand, drew up a bucket of water and splashed it on his face. He lathered his hands with some nearby tallow. He finally dropped the bucket into the well again and brought up clean water for Mary. Thus scrubbed, he left Mary alone.

Laughing with delight, Mary poured the entire bucket of water over her head and rejoiced in the refreshing coolness. She used the left-over tallow mixed with ashes for a brisk hand wash. Another bucket-dunk gave a chilly rinse. Dry clothes were in her sack for a quick change in a tiny privy but a few steps away. Master Adams had pointed out that she should use the privy with the crescent moon on its door, not the one with the star.

Adams Family

Supper at the Adams home came well after dark. The closed shutters allowed in only a few streaks of moonlight at the edges. Oil lanterns at each end of the table gave what little light there was. Always before anyone took a bite, the father said a solemn prayer. Everyone stood around the table holding hands. Mary held the hand of Thomas on her right and the hand of squirming Hannah on her left. That custom felt a bit strange for her because Walsingham family members seldom if ever touched one another. At the end of prayer, all looked directly at their visitor. It was a moment that she felt welcomed into the family.

Then everyone sat down. Parents were at each end of the table; others sat on benches alongside. Mary was placed on a bench next to Thomas on the right side. One of the twins sat on a raised seat on her left. Rebecca sat across the way with the other twin. The baby appeared content still in the arms of Mistress Adams.

A Bible set before Mary's place had a marker at the passage read by the head of the household. Little was said during the entire supper beyond some words from the Holy Scripture. It was a scene to be played daily with every meal.

Corn mush and turnips were served hot on pewter plates, followed by some bits of boiled meat and slices of dark bread buttered with animal tallow. Strong cider was there for the parents and older children, while milk was given to the twins. It was a humble meal by any standard. From Mary's point of view, no dinner ever served to distinguished guests at the Manor House was so elegant.[44]

Rebecca, who gave the appearance of being delicate and somehow baffling, ate little and that quickly. She soon withdrew to sit in a darkened corner of the room. Master Adams pointed to his own head and making a face as if in great pain. He then found a loose paper and on it, slowly and painstakingly, wrote in graceful hand:

> *Rebecca has a condition. Grievous aching of the head. Sometimes for days. She eats nothing. Cannot abide bright light. Or noise. Stays in house. Nights give no relief. We suffer knowing not how to help. Please do not think her unfriendly. J.A.*

After supper there was time for some childish tomfoolery. The diversion was especially enjoyed by Sarah and Hannah who delighted in the pony ride on their father's foot and riding piggy-back with him down on all fours. The twin with the lighter hair shrieked with laughter at such antics. The other twin appeared more cautious of any topsy-turvy. Thomas retreated to a darkened corner where a small heap of objects held his attention.

Mistress Adams and Rebecca readied the twins for bed while her husband sat by double candlelight with his Bible. It was a flash of time that allowed Mary finally to have a good look at baby John. Never had she seen a fuller and ruddier face on a baby. His blue eyes, glistening by the candle, locked on Mary's eyes. Her playful head shake brought the hint of a smile to his face.

The morning's work would come early. It was soon time for bed. The ashes were stirred. Rebecca beckoned Mary to follow her to the loft. There, beneath the low headroom of the slanting roof, she saw that Thomas and the twins were already asleep on their pads. Rebecca pointed out to her new sister the bed they would share. The straw-filled pad was large enough for one, and just barely enough for two. Nonetheless, despite the overcrowded bed, Mary would relish a luxury not known for many weeks. She blew out the candle. As her roommate pulled a blanket over her head, the fatigued animal caretaker was elated. Any bed would be better than heaps of rope-lined canvas sails reeking of tar and propped up on a raised plank to avoid the rats and slosh of bilge water.

Poet in the Family

SOMETIME DURING THE night Mary was awakened by the familiar smell of burning wax. Candlelight came up from below where Mary, looking down, saw Rebecca seated at the table. *Oh, have I crowded her out of her own bed?* Mary wondered. Guilt-ridden, even the pleasure of sleeping on a straw-filled mattress could not offset her qualms.

Reflecting on her present situation through the remainder of the night, Mary thought of how she was no longer at the Manor House. A mattress slung on cross-ropes to make a bed was far away. There were no servants in the Adams home. She was certain that, when morning came, there would be no sweets by her pillow. *My new family,* she thought, *is a good family. I will do what I can to deserve their care. And,* she reminded herself, *Angel is here. She is safe at last. My dream has come true after all.*

When dawn broke, Mary found that Rebecca had returned to bed and was seemingly asleep. She also found a scrap of paper by her pillow. It was, in fact, sweeter than any sweet could ever be. The paper read:

Across a storm cursed sea
Came Mary to a land of mossy green
In ragged dress and weary face
To sleep on fronds of ferns, a queen. R.A.

Mary learned later that it was the headache that kept Rebecca awake. Too miserable to sleep, she always tried to endure her malady during the quiet hours of nighttime. These nights were passed at the table where she found writing a distraction from the suffering in her head.

These were thoughts from a frail wisp of a girl, suffering through a long night. A note from Mary at breakfast told of her love of poetry: *You write a fine welcome from a terrible journey. I am thankful for your perfect words. Do you have more poems?*

Rebecca brought out another paper:

A sky without a cloud in sight
Paints a field of purple sage
That floods the eye with happiness
The nose it does engage. R.A.

Such verse! What treasure had Mary already discovered in the Colonies! No, it was not the shining "City Upon a Hill." No, she had not arrived at a storied land of gold and silver; instead, she found a sparkling gem in the guise of a delicate poet hardly past her first full decade of life.

Daily Life

At her place on the table on that first morning, Mary found a long message from Master Adams. Welcoming her, he vowed that his family would share their sparse life as best they could. He let her know that the two work horses and her own horse appeared to be fit, even, as expected, scrawny and weakened from the long confinement. Gaping sores from chaffing on their rumps had to heal. No, the horses would not be ready to work for weeks.

A second page Mary read with mixed feelings:

You know that all the animals of the New World are wild. The Indians know not about taming them. It is necessary to bring all useful animals to the colonies. I am truly grateful to the captain who saw to it that the animals aboard your ship were well cared for. On my voyage some years ago, I saw how the crew struggled to tend the horses, oxen, and smaller animals. Even with their effort, one horse and four of the sheep died.

The reading brought a faint nod of thanks. Neither writer nor reader could have known that horses were in America many thousands of years before but had become extinct for about two thousand years.[45]

There was a third page. Perhaps, he hinted in language that was more like instructions, Mary could walk the horses in morning and afternoon each day as they regained their strength. There were stables and chicken coops to help clean and the never-ending chore of feeding all. To be safe, he added, she should never go beyond the border of the settlement. There were savages running around out there, he warned, and, besides, you never knew what the Dutch would do. The Dutch? What did that mean? Mary's curiosity was piqued.

Daily life in this Puritan household reflected a rigorous adherence to an everyday practice. It was as constant as the movement of stars across the sky. Everyone in the family and everyone in the plantation had a part in that constellation. Furthermore, as Mary had suspected earlier, no household had servants to carry out this all-important work.

The family broke fast at dawn, with the morning meal consisting of porridge with honey. At high sun there was bread and soup. At dusk came the largest meal, generally of boiled meat and bread. The small children drank milk and the others, cider. Conversation was sparse other than the fussing of the twins. There were no strict table manners. Over time Mary noticed something odd during the daily hand-holding at prayer time before and after meals. Thomas tended to hold his grip on her hand well after the prayer was over.

The work day started soon after breakfast when the men in the plantation left to tend animals, work in the gardens, or shape planks from felled trees. The older boys, including Thomas, worked with them or with others on various community projects. Some trekked with woodsmen to hunt. The moment of supreme success for a boy was to emerge from the forest with a rack of venison flung over his shoulders!

The Puritan woman's day included the constant care of babies and small children as well as the household chores of cooking, sewing, and spinning. Older girls were expected to help bake, cook, churn butter, spool yarn, make candles. and, of course, keep the house tidy.

Children roamed freely outside, not under any watchful adult eye. Mary was quick to notice that the children did not have to kneel before their parents every morning to pledge their loyalty.

Evenings passed with reading or telling of stories with morals about the continuous struggle between good and evil. For children, time for bed came as the night sky descended. Parents retired as light from the hearth faded but not before a reading a Biblical passage or two.

Although Mary could not hear the mealtime prayers and scripture passages read aloud, her quick eyes observed these daily rituals. With helpful notes occasionally from Master Adams, she grasped the significance of the Good Book for defining the lifestyle of a Puritan family. Gratitude must be expressed for good health, a good day's work, and the blessings of the harvest and the hunt. She came to understand that Puritan families endured cold, hunger, illness without complaining because misfortune was part of God's plan; He knew of their good works and would reward each of the faithful in the hereafter.

Although now with a better understanding of this Puritan family, Anglican Mary still felt a bit strange and even useless, once even comparing herself to another piece of furniture and one, at that, not at all needed. Yet, mother and father were kind and sharing. She found herself trying to deal with each child in separate ways. She took a special liking to baby John and was soon entrusted to hold him. With him, she could sit for long periods, slowly rocking, feeling the baby's warmth and gentle twinges as she looked into those searching blue eyes and watched tiny bubbles form and burst around his mouth.

Expectations

Mary soon learned what was expected of her: care for the horses, cows, sheep, swine, and chickens; amuse the small children; and help with the household chores of sweeping, emptying the hearth, scrubbing pans, and washing clothes. This last chore brought back the memory of Sky Flower's first task as laundry assistant at the manor house in Littleton. Mary smiled at this odd twist of circumstances. The Adams family did not attempt to teach her the more complicated workings of a loom. Thinking of her previous weeks aboard the ship, Mary considered these expectations a blessing. As the weeks passed, she realized that she was accepted in the family. Although she was one more body in a tiny home, no one seemed ill-humored over the addition.

Mistress Adams was eager to introduce the new daughter in the family to the arts of cooking, baking bread and even making cheese. All these new lessons were to be given after Mary's early morning chores with the big animals. Yet, Mary knew herself not suited to the teachings of *Countrey Contentments.* A shortnote to Master Adams changed everything. She had pleaded in writing: *I not good with housework. I more like animals and gardens. Please allow me.*

Her request was granted, although the duties expected were more suited to men than to women. The fields, stables, and coop, like the household, were never ending in demanding care. Some eyebrows were raised at the prospect, but Mary performed her chores well and mostly alone. New chores came on feeding and watering the chickens, then gathering the eggs. Within a week or two she found herself in tall grass swinging a hay-making sickle. In a note soon afterwards she requested instructions for milking a cow.

The art of milking a cow takes practice but it it was soon learned. One morning as Mary sat on a milking stool, her head snug against the cow's warm flank, and her pail slowly filling with each squeeze, an amusing thought came to her: what would her mother think of her wayward daughter now? With a smile on her face, she expertly directed a squirt into the gaping mouth of an intrepid cat.

Mary found small relief to know that she was always near Angel. She greeted her horse every day with loving pats on her muzzle and groomed her with the same attention that a lady's hairdresser would give.

There was one more chore that pleased her. It was one of pure exercise: running, flapping arms, and pushing, pulling, and even lifting. Well before the ending of the day's light, all the farm animals that roamed within the village had to be rounded up and put back into their protected pens. The task sometimes meant herding the grazing cows and sheep after a wild chase and then pushing and pulling them into place. The pigs, rooting here and there, were the most stubborn; once the sow was coaxed into her sty, the little ones followed without persuasion. Sometimes an animal strayed too far and passed through a break in the fence that surrounded the plantation. A missing animal prompted a lively search before sundown.

There were vast differences between life in this New World plantation and life as Mary knew it in Littleton. She thought back to the carefree days of walking around the Manor House, to the gardens and stable, always anticipating a new adventure. Everywhere there was a continuous bustle of people busy in the role expected of them. After all, the welfare of the estate depended on the tasks meant for each of the players. Some were meant to serve as gardeners or to take care of the animals. Then there were the carpenters, the leather workers, and the blacksmith. Many others worked at preparing and serving food.

She realized that her parents were meant to see that all elements of the system ran as smoothly as possible; they were not meant to work in the manner destined for their servants. Their children were being prepared to assume the leadership of their parents, as gentles; that is, as that small segment of society that does not need to work. Everyone was engaged in carrying out the duties that defined a station in life. All men, women, and children knew their places and did what was expected of them in some limited way. Like the workings on the clock that stood in the dining room, all carried on with the purpose of making the Manor run smoothly with nary a skip.

All was different in Hartford. There seemed to be no directors, no privileged, and no idlers. There were no stations. All shared the labor from sun-up to dusk. Children were called to do what they could contribute in helpful handiwork. All was directed at carving out a new town in the wilderness where their devotion to God could be practiced as they saw fit.

CHAPTER 6

The Puritan Plantation

Hartford

As she performed her own chores and at times had a chance to walk throughout the settlement, Mary could witness the frantic activity of houses being built, especially now that cold weather was approaching. All settlers remembered spending their first winters in the crude and cold dugout shelters along the hills; now they were most eager to finish building their houses before the first snowfall. Long-time settlers helped with both new construction and with the renovation of the old dugouts now destined for the next group of new arrivals. House building went on daily with the exception of Sunday.

Mary was fascinated to see the work involved, since in England she had never seen or, she admitted to herself, never been seriously interested in such an activity. She saw the important work of horses and oxen as they dragged in logs from the forest. After that, men with axes would begin removing branches and limbs, and finally, with giant saws, cut the logs into planks. Each plank made one small but sturdy portion of a new house but more than a hundred were needed for each house.

The completed houses in Hartford, about twenty or so, were strung out along the south shore of the Little River. The fast-running river emptied into the Great River near the dock. Except for the dugout shelters, all the houses, including the Adams house, looked alike: wood-framed of two stories, a door on the broad side and windows covered with oiled cloth on each narrow side. The back side of the roof was extended to look like what Mary remembered as a saltbox. Each house rested on a base of rocks or bricks that brought the first floor about knee high. Wooden stairs of two of three steps sat before the door. Some roofs were thatched; others were planked and shingled.[46]

How Hartford cared for its animals also interested Mary, for she was now, in fact, the family's new animal caretaker. Master Adams had already conveyed to her that each settler owned his animals, but kept them in communal stables, pens, and coops. During her walks she quickly learned where these shelters were located.

Making sure that all the animals, especially the large ones, had enough food and water was a priority of every farmer, and Mary did her utmost to tend to them. Jeremy Adams was most appreciative of her efforts. Over the weeks since arriving, the new horses were slowly regaining their strength. A few weeks passed before they were ready for heavy loads and Angel was ready for riding.

The heart of the Hartford plantation was the garden. Now this was a subject to which Harold, the gardener at the manor house, had introduced her, and one that helped her overcome the painful loss of Sky Flower. Hours spent in the fragrant orangery not only taught her much about plants but also helped heal her broken heart. Yes, the gardens at Hartford drew Mary's interest tremendously.

The community at large purchased seeds which they distributed evenly among the households. Each family vigilantly maintained its own garden, hoping to ensure a successful harvest in late summer or autumn. An especially good crop often meant that a farmer could barter or purchase needed items from a neighbor. Garden crops such as vegetables, plus eggs and tools were frequently exchanged for the temporary use of horses and oxen. All transactions, however, including donations, were made according to individual agreements of the neighbors.

Knowing this was a Puritan custom, Mary could only speculate on what she often saw happening near the grazing fields or near the chicken coops. Master Adams would be conferring with his closest neighbors, Masters Easton and Ensign. They would be pointing to some animals or showing each other some vegetables. She wondered on those occasions if a trade or purchase was being discussed.

As she worked in the Adamses' large garden, picking out weeds, Mary did not see any wheat, oats or barley. She was later to learn about the reasons why. The first harsh winter taught the settlers a vital lesson: English crops did not grow well in the New World soil. Rooted plants (turnips, potatoes, onions, carrots) fared much better. The crop that flourished most in the Hartford soil was corn. At first, the settlers fed this crop only to the animals, but that practice soon changed. Planting, harvesting, and preparing corn soon became the settlers' life-sustaining concern. The story behind corn is largely one of cultural attitudes.

The situation was explained in a letter by Master Adams:

Mary, you asked why we plant corn instead of English grains. Here is a short answer. Corn grows much better in this soil. We learned that corn was the main food of Indians. From corn they knew how to make porridges and bread. Corn, when charred, stores well over the winter. Oxen and horses will eat corn. We were slow to depend on corn instead of wheat and oats. After all, corn was the food of cattle and chickens as well as the Indians; it was not for people of different standards of culture.

I know that the Indians plant corn in clumps along with other plants. They even bury a smelly fish below each clump of seeds. Yet, the Indians do not want to learn our English way. It should be planted in neat rows and be well cared for by frequent watering and weeding.

I hope this answers your query. J. A.

Fences wove throughout the plantation but they were not the stone walls that Mary knew on the farmlands of Littleton and Shepperton. Because there were few stones along the riverbanks, the Hartford settlers looked to the forests: from the smallest wood planks they made split-rail, zig-zagging fences.

Broken fences had to be quickly repaired. Wooden fences not only marked ownership of land, but also protected the animals. After all, a cow wandering into a garden can soon eat a large portion of a future crop. Without a good fence small creatures such as calves, lambs, and chickens were not safe from marauding skunks, foxes, and raccoons. Any animal that strayed beyond the fence was doomed unless found by nightfall. And so, within a short time after arriving in Hartford, a girl from a privileged upper-class family had happily joined in a race to find a lost animal.

Diaspora

FROM SHORT NOTES written by Jeremy Adams almost every night and left for Mary to read in the morning, she slowly pieced together the story of the household. What good fortune for her that Master Adams found pleasure in writing his story! One such writing was as follows:

> *Mary, should you have an interest in how this family came together, I write a few words. I was raised as a child in Stoke-by-Nayland in the county of Suffolk. It was the village where your father and I grew up. We both enjoyed the privileges of well-to-do families. I went to the Bay Colony seven years ago, having decided that some privations were a trivial matter compared to the benefit of freedom from interference by bishops with their many trappings. I shared a deep-felt belief that the only truly acceptable life in the eyes of God was through hard work and simple worship.*
>
> *Two years ago, I married the widow Rebecca Greenhill. She is the mother of Rebecca and Thomas. Sarah and Hannah were born the following year. Baby John came but three months ago. So, there you have the whole story. J. A.*

Mary was curious about why the family had left the Boston area to come to a place so harsh for everyday life. It was the soil, she learned from another day's writing. Three years before, in 1636, they left Boston and Cambridge to begin a plantation along the Great River. Others had gone before them all because of crowding and the need for larger gardens. The soil, they said, was more fertile than the gravel-rich gardens at the Bay Colony.[47]

Master Adams wrote:

We heard that English people from Plymouth came here to start plantations. Those at Wethersfield and Windsor were already thriving despite some setbacks with Indians. Words of reassurance had come back that the People of the Forest were friendly and that they mostly kept out of sight. There was some trading with the Indians, exchanging tools and blankets for corn and pelts. The new land promised all that settlers could hope for: good crops on spacious land, peace, and a place to worship God in the most direct way that their consciences told them. J.A.

There was more written on another day. Mary learned that their leader was a pastor named Thomas Hooker.[48] He voyaged from England to the Bay Colony in Boston in 1632, the same time as Jeremy Adams. In 1636, following old Indian paths as best they could, they started their journey on foot to Hartford. There were sixty people of all ages who came with horses overloaded and many cows, oxen, and some pigs in tow. They had a compass and some axes. Men carried guns. One worry was the disappointing supply of milk from their hard-driven cows. Food gathered along the way consisted of mostly acorns, grains, and roots. All slept in the rough. The grueling journey lasted one hundred days.

If Mary learned the bare-bone story of Hartford that Master Adams jotted down from time to time, she learned its heart from the writings of Rebecca. The girl kept a diary of sorts, written in small, scattered entries among her poems. These she shared freely with Mary and, truthfully, she seemed to delight in the attention.

Snippets from Rebecca's diary about the footslog from Cambridge read:

Cold, so cold. Every day, rain. I cannot keep my doll dry. Feet hurt. My big toe comes through my shoe. Father has let me ride on a cow. At the end of the day, we eat boiled seeds and acorns found along the way. All night, every night I shivered. The children try not to cry, but they do and often. Today, we forded a fast-flowing river. I feared drowning, had I not a rope tied round my waist. All crossed except for two panic-stricken sheep that wiggled out of their rope ties.

Additional notes from Master Adams told of the arrival of Hooker's group in Hartford. By the grace of God, they found an agreeable space of fertile land along the banks of a small river near the place where it merged into the western shore of the Great River. Indeed, it was called the "Little River." Life in the new colony, however, proved harsh. People suffered in the unforgiving cold of winter. Living in a makeshift hillside dugout meant never being free from cold, dampness, and smoke. There was barely enough food. Illnesses and injuries were common and sometimes deadly. But, Master Adams reassured Mary, the Puritans of Hartford and in the sister settlements knew that they were proving their heartiness to God, and that their perseverance would be favored with the first blush of the spring planting.

Oxen and Horses

FINDING GOOD PLACES for each spring planting was a priority. To extend their gardens to the other side of the little river, the villagers knew that one of their first tasks would be to make a sturdy bridge of logs. It was now completed. Logs floating side by side were held against the current by stout ropes. Atop were planks that stretched lengthwise. The whole was wide enough for a horse-drawn wagon to cross, cautiously. The bridge meant that the gardens could spread out to the north.

Something bothered Mary one day as she walked across that bridge to the stables. She wondered why Master Adams wanted to purchase horses from her father. Why, when he already had two oxen to plough, pull wagons, and haul tree trunks? The answer came in a lengthy reply:

> *Mary, you ask about the horses purchased from your father. They are horses that are well-trained and strong. They arrived in good health. Our oxen are very old now and will probably not be useful for another spring of ploughing. This past spring, they showed they had nearly passed their usefulness. They can still pull a wagon, but you may have seen them breathless and lame at that. Still, we managed. These are oxen that brought us through the forest to Hartford three years ago.*
>
> *Oxen are best used for turning up newly cleared fields that have tangled roots. They pull with a steady force, not in the jerky way that horses pull. Oxen can move a heavier load. Now that the first clearing of our field has been done, the horses will do. They more easily make the turns at the end of ploughed rows. Also, horses are better for hauling logs through wooded trails.*

Never had Mary thought about comparing oxen to horses.[49] The animals were just there. She read on.

There is one more point. Horses are fussier at fodder. They cannot live on hay alone as oxen do, but must have some grain. Oxen can digest kernels of corn that are whole. Horses will get colic if we give them kernels that are not cracked. Did you ever wonder why we pound corn with a stone hammer? That is food for the horses. I might add that pigs have no such problems. They consume the plant with all its parts intact: cobs, husks and tassels.

Last spring, I expected to receive a pair of draught horses purchased from a trusted man in Cambridge. Both died aboard ship. Poor care, I believe. These old oxen had to do the spring ploughing for all the fields. Arrangements were soon made for another purchase, this time from your father. This time, the ship's crew took good care of them.

At this point in the reading, Mary gulped.

But now that the horses have arrived and have recovered their strength, they will haul logs from the forest. The snow cover of winter is a friend of log-haulers. Horses can work their way through the forest better than oxen can. Does that answer your query? J.A.

Yes. Quite well. Thank you, Sir, was scribbled at the end of Master Adams's letter, not mentioning the "good care" they received shipboard. *What will happen to your oxen?* wrote Mary back.

The reply was terse:

We will keep them well-fed until winter when the ground has frozen solid. After that time they will be our beef. We butcher them and keep the meat underground. Two oxen will keep our larder filled for much of the winter.

The answer left Mary with an unsettling thought. The oxen knew only heavy drudgery throughout their years. They had strained tremendously in labor for the good of the planters. Now that they were old and less useful, they would be reduced to meat. Unfair it was, and she tried to think of another way but no solution to rescue the oxen from their fate came to mind.

The Podunks

UPON RETURNING FROM the stable one day, Mary saw a throng rushing toward the river. Curious, she merged into the excited crowd and soon found herself at the landing dock. There at the river's edge she saw Indians dragging their narrow boats onto the shore.[50]

There were six Indians not counting the small boy among them. All, including the boy, wore animal skin clothes and all except the boy were bedecked with head feathers. From their boats they hefted stacks of furs, carried them on their shoulders, and laid them in neat piles up on the high ground. It was Mary's first close-up look at the native people. They seemed not at all fearsome as she had often heard they were; indeed, if anything, they looked kind by nature. Rebecca was there, too, and together they watched the proceedings as they unfolded.

The settlers soon crowded around the new arrivals. The Indians had come to trade and lost no time in getting to business. But first, they acted out a ceremony, standing tree-trunk straight with feet together, head thrown back, arms outstretched with palms toward the sky, and giving out a long wail. There was intensity in their eyes that told of confidence in their purpose. All wore one or two feathers propped in hair of shoulder length. Most noticeable, each had a design painted on his face. The one who spoke for all had three slanted stripes across each cheek.

While the Indians and settlers bickered with hand gestures over furs for metal things—pots and axes mostly—and woolen blankets, the boy scanned the onlookers. His piercing eyes looked out through black hair that was held in place with a red headband. When his eyes fell on Rebecca, a bright smile appeared. He stepped forward, handing her an object. She responded by holding out for him a favorite pastime of her early childhood: a ball attached by a string to a handle with a cup at the top. The gift-giving ended with an exchange of nods. The boy soon found his way back among the throng of traders.

The object? It was a figure about wrist-to-elbow in size and made from husks of corn. It was cleverly tied to make all the body features look real. Its hair was corn tassel. Two black dots made the eyes.

Later that evening Mary learned that the boy was a regular visitor to the Puritan village, and that from time to time Rebecca had given him one of her childhood toys. One such gift was a boat about as big as a man's foot. It had a seated figure with a paddle. Both were carved of wood and painted in gaudy colors by her father.

The Indians around them, Mary learned from Master Adams, were called Podunks. He wrote: *They are peaceful people who live by planting, hunting, and fishing. Tribes from the south and from the west have harassed the Podunks from time to time. It was perhaps mostly for this reason that they sought a closer tie with the foreign settlers, expecting that we would protect them from warring tribes.*

Mary had not seen "wild savages," as they were called by people back in England. Sky Flower was surely no "wild savage," nor were the Indians who had just come to trade. This brief encounter gave her no reason to fear but reason enough to wonder with admiration how they learned to live in a harsh world with remarkable natural ability. Somehow, they harvested corn, made tools out of stone and pots from clay. Hunting with arrows and spears brought animals for food and hides for clothing and shoes. From the full cheeks of all the Indians, Mary was certain that they did not go hungry. If there was anything to say about the good nature of the Indians coming to trade, it was told in the smile of the boy with the red headband.

Headache

Rebecca's headache afflictions were as numerous as they were dreadful. Her mother and father did what they could to help. Her mother was often at her side coddling her, braiding her long hair, or singing softly the familiar ditties of childhood. They had tried every remedy at their disposal: feverfew, salica, cider, fish oils, butterbur, lavender, peppermint oil, basil oil, flax seed, and buckwheat. Once, Rebecca drank a tea made from costly ginger. Nothing helped.[51]

Villagers added their own recommendations but no improvements were noticed: binding the head at the temples with cold and hot water cloths; crushing beetles on her scalp to make the skin blister, promising to draw out the headache-causing poisons; and swallowing ipecac to cause vomiting. Her father would not permit what others had strongly recommended: letting out of a cup or two of her blood.

Mary felt bold enough to ask Master Adams what the doctors said about the girl's terrible headaches. The response came in a long letter:

> *When in Boston, I took her to a specialist in disease of the nerves. He had studied at the Scottish University of Edinburgh and his high fee was based accordingly. That was a few years ago when Rebecca's headaches were getting quite severe. The doctor, a huge man, silent and frightening in a long, black robe, looked carefully at her tongue, commenting on its color and texture. Then he felt the pulse in her wrist for a moment, urging her to breathe faster and faster until she felt giddy. He then stood straight before her and placed both of his massive hands so that they covered her entire head. This position, he held motionless for a long time, then proceeded to rub each part of the skull. The conclusion was that he could feel no activity through the skull and therefore the headache was a matter of "no consequence."*
>
> *I have worse to tell. One doctor, well-respected in Cambridge, found defects in a few of Rebecca's teeth, although she never complained of toothache. A headache, he said, when unrelenting, was a result of bad teeth. He was certain that removing them would lessen the severity of headaches. To cure the headaches completely, he insisted that all her teeth need be removed, appearing normal or not. Mistress Adams and I refused such treatment. We were determined to find another way and wonder if our decision has caused needless suffering.*

During the worst of her long nights, Rebecca's candlelit poems revealed the torment she had to endure.

TO MARY
Why is sleep so pleasing
And nights for dreaming?
I sit, my head in hands.
Waiting, waiting, waiting.

The sounds of slumber
Our little house
Tranquil as moonlight.
Dreaming, dreaming, dreaming.

For me, the night is long
Harsh and lonely
'Til the dawn relieves
Throbbing, throbbing, throbbing.

How I yearn to be
Blessed by nature's gift
To sleep as others do
Peaceful, peaceful, peaceful.

From R.A.

On one good day when no head pain grieved her, the young poet showed Mary some of her random scribblings. One was about a bird's nest found in a nearby maple tree. Another described the pewter pitcher that now sat on the mantel. (It had been acquired from a Dutch trader in a nearby fort). On an entry dated 11 July she wrote about the arrival of an English ship that brought a curious older girl who, strangely, did not speak a word. The writer described her as unwashed and weary, but at the same time, as graceful as a deer and as having huge, inquisitive sky-blue eyes. The girl, she wrote, "would live for a time in our house and in my bed. I wonder how we will get along."

Spells

SOMETHING ABOUT REBECCA perplexed Mary. One remarkable feature about her manners was odd. There were times when she became excited to a fault. At such times, she tended to the chores of the house with bubbling-over liveliness: sweeping, scrubbing, and polishing whatever there was to sweep, scrub, or polish. All the while she spoke incessantly, rambling from thought to thought. She never sat for more than a moment. Sometimes she would go outside where she wandered throughout the village. Reports came back that Rebecca was seen at times thrashing her arms wildly, walking erratically, or ranting continually. Neighbors knew not what to make of such behavior. During the night times of frenzied activity sleeping was difficult as well for Mary who tried to sleep alongside her.

Mary's attention was caught by a glimpse of Rebecca's diary:

> *Yes, someday, I will compose sonnets like the great poets of England. I will teach the Indians how to write out their beautiful sounding words. Someday I will see the whole world on a voyage to Cathay to fetch silks and pearls.*

Such surges of excitability lasted but a day or two. Afterwards she would crumble into a state of complete collapse. She distorted herself into strange positions, sometimes curled up into a ball and staring ahead. She spoke to no one. And then would come the terrible head pain.

Mary could only comfort Rebecca during these times. She carried on but with a heavy heart, feeling helpless when most needed. Yet she kept thinking that there might be something that started it all. She appealed to Rebecca, pleading for her to write about the odd spells that came *before* her headaches. The response was polite but curt.

> *Your concern, dear Mary, about my 'odd spells' is taken to heart. I cannot speak of these for fear that you will all think me raving mad. I much prefer to endure the headache that follows than have you think me foolish. R.A.*

The Dutch

Early one morning, Mary saw four strangers walk solemnly past the stable. They wore metal helmets and metal breastplates. Below were knee-high boots and pantaloons. Each man shouldered a gun. Anger was evident in their faces. A great number of settlers quickly gathered to confront them. There was much shouting and fist-waving among the strangers, but the villagers remained calm. It was but a long breath-holding before the strangers made their point, then turned and marched off.

Of course, she was more than curious about who these men were and why they were so furious. She wrote how they frightened her. *Would there be trouble?* she wrote to Master Adams. There was much discussion at the table that evening. Afterwards Master Adams wrote a short explanatory note to Mary.

> *Do not be afraid. The men are Dutch. They come from a fort called the "House of Good Hope." They speak English well enough to say that this morning they awoke to find one of our pigs rooting in their patch of potatoes. They say that the pig ate many, and it partially chewed many more before they chased it away. Truthfully, I do not think that one pig could cause so much damage. Even so, if it happens again, the soldiers say that they will have roast pork that night. I believe them. We must be more careful in counting the animals as we shoo them into the pens at nightfall. That is all, Mary. There is no need to worry. J.A.*

The Dutch fort had been there for many years, serving mostly as a trading post administered by the soldiers. They traded with the Indians: mostly metal tools, blankets, and trinkets of diverse kinds for furs of beaver, fox, mountain lion, and otter. Most of the furs were brought in canoes by tribes farther south, near the river's end.

Small ships came from the Dutch soldiers' mother colony: New Amsterdam. They brought much needed supplies to the fort and took away ever-dwindling stores of furs. Although some scuffles had broken out between Dutch and English, the two groups mainly had little to do with each other. The Dutch, however, found that their supply ship could be a bit more profitable by bringing a few goods wanted by the English. These items were mostly lumber and tile for houses produced in the great windmills and kilns in their up-river post in Beverwyck.

Mistress Adams

MISTRESS ADAMS EXEMPLIFIED the typical Puritan colonial woman, called the "goodwife."[52] She was lean and nearly as tall as her husband, (who, similarly, was addressed as "goodman.") Beneath the ever-present bonnet her face was always calm. Her eyes, always aware, flitted to everything that moved. She wore the same blouse for weeks, one with loose sleeves that were tied around the wrists. Her skirt was long so that her ankles were never exposed to the light of day. She added an over-skirt or apron of wool when attending the fire.

The goodwife of Jeremy Adams was always tending to her housekeeping by the time Mary arose in the morning. She planned and prepared meals and kept her house clean and tidy. Though it is true that she said little, she murmured continually to her infant. She kept the twins occupied with simple toys and clapping games. She was always still up when all others had retired for the night. Her fingers flew at stitching and mending worn out clothes. In between, there was never a moment in which she seemed idle or took a moment to rest. Even so, she never rushed but took life's many trials with a steady, slow pace in mind and body. She was all that was expected of a "colonial woman."

Rebecca's mother truly cared but could not understand the troubling burden of her eldest daughter. Nevertheless, she sat with her daughter during the worst of the headaches or during the few moments she could spare. Many a night she would sit next to the suffering girl, a hand resting gently on a shoulder and humming softly.

On a whim, Mary wrote a short night note to Mistress Adams to praise her for the breakfast of hot corn cakes with maple syrup. It was Rebecca who wrote a response.

Mary, my mother wishes me to tell you that she holds your 'thank you' dearly. She regrets that she cannot write it herself.

There followed a quickly written succession of brief notes, all on the same paper.

Can it be true that your mother does not know how to write?

Yes. Mother says that she was always too busy to learn.

But I see her read the Bible every night.

True. Girls are taught to read. They visit the Bible as often as they can, whenever free of expectations. So it is the custom that there is no need for a woman to learn to write.

But, Rebecca, you write like a teacher at Oxford College. What do you say to that?

Papa taught me to write, expecting what, I do not know. Perhaps to be a great scholar of the scriptures. Sometimes I help him write a speech that he will give at the meeting house. He does not always follow the rules of our great leaders. He tells his thoughts freely and sometimes I help make them easier to understand. I think he does not like my writing poems, but he abides by it.

That put an end to the subject.

The Adams Children

There were many children in a typical colonial household. Certainly, the problems of moving caused by emigration presented a challenge for a busy mother. Older children were enlisted to help as much as they could. There is no reason to doubt that the exuberance and the diversity of children's personalities played out in the Puritan home just as they did in other kinds of households the world over. Although the Adams children had individual temperaments and character traits, they shared common traits of all children everywhere.[53]

The boy Thomas was tall and spindly. He moved about with uncommon grace. His face appeared serious, one might even say intense. Parted in the middle, his long dark hair looked like curtains around his eyes ready to open in a dramatic scene.

In the mornings he and Mary would often leave the house together on the way to their chores. There was something about the way that Thomas walked that intrigued Mary. Every step, whether around a stone, over a fallen log, or between tall weeds, was performed with the easy flow of a dancer. His whole body seemed to have a natural movement, each foot advancing as if on water, and with the rest of his body floating airily. Mary never tired of following him into the fields simply to see his wavelike walk.

The boy seldom engaged with anyone in the family but rather tended to sit by himself, poring through a wooden box of the kind that wagon drivers sit upon. Kept in the loft by the shuttered window, his oddities were picked up on his long, solitary strolls. These were his treasures and he doted over them, caring not to share them with anyone else. At the age of eleven, he did not appear unhappy. Yet he did not like conversation or even simple play, tending to shy away from other children in favor of more self-contained interests.

Mary inquired about his curious ways. In her writing to Rebecca, she said that even she—who does not know what it is like to speak to another person—had seen that he keeps much to himself. It was not the way of other children she has known.

In response, Rebecca wrote:

> *Dear Mary, your thoughts about Thomas and his wont for being left alone is not unnoticed. He is a good boy. He works hard, sometimes in the field or in the forest without complaining. He does not cause mischief like some of the other boys. Father does worry about his not liking to talk.*
>
> *Curious it is, there are odd times when Thomas talks to me about a singular thing, as if the entire world depended on that thing. It might be about his most recent discovery, perhaps a rock of strange shape or color. Once he told me excitedly about a flock of crows driving off an eagle, as if he had seen two nations at war from beginning to end. One time, not long ago, he spoke for a long time about a hole in one of his stockings. You would be surprised at how he jabbers on about such concerns with nary a word from me. Such prattle was common, but only for*

me, not my parents. Since you came to us, he has kept mostly silent.

Papa thinks that Thomas fusses too much about little things: his appearance, tidiness of his clothes and washing his hands many times in the day. Father is also concerned about his long disappearances, sometimes for a whole day. My brother says that he is "just looking for things." He has a prized collection of what may be pretty stones, turtle shells, bones and other curious objects—I am guessing—stowed away in his all-too-secretive chest. Papa thinks it is all rubbish, but collecting things seems to make Thomas happy. Pleasing God in the manner that the Puritans expect of all is not easy, and small pleasures in life may be his earthly blessing.

Rebecca

The twins, Sarah and Hannah, played well together. Both climbed up and down the ladder to the loft with the ease of mountaineers, and both ate with little help. They delighted in running outside and going to the stables to see the baby animals. Yet, the girls were as unlike as a housecat and a bobcat. Mary remembered that Sky Flower had much older sisters who were twins. But those two were so alike that they were impossible to tell apart.

The Adams twins were different. Sarah and Hannah looked not at all alike. Everyone noticed how often quiet Sarah, the curly redhead, smiled. She appeared to enjoy watching the actions happening about her. An unusual event never missed her chuckle: a dropped plate, a fallen-over candle, someone making a funny face. Hannah, in contrast, was continuously in motion: bouncing, chatting, scurrying about within the house. Her hands were always busy with simple things: twisting her long dark strands of hair into partial braids, balancing cups, playing with the cat, and treading the loom to make it turn fast.

Together, there was never a squabble. Despite their pleasure with baby animals, they gave only a wink of attention to their little brother. Perhaps it was their mother's attention to Baby John that brought out their indifference.

One sunny afternoon, Mistress Adams was outside taking in washed sheets and clothing that had been drying throughout the day. Inside the house were Baby John, lying in his own basket, and the little girls. Mary happened by in time to carry the linen to the house for Mistress Adams. As the door swung open, they saw Sarah, sitting on the floor, smiling. Hannah at the same time was standing by the basket crib, her arms thrashing in excitement. A piglet had gotten inside the house and was at that moment licking the baby's face.

Mistress Adams shrieked. Mary dropped the laundry and lunged to the rescue. But her effort was badly executed, and the piglet scampered off into a dark corner of the room. Mistress Adams and Mary then set off in frantic pursuit, but the attempt proved the piglet a clever fugitive. It ran into another dark corner. The contest was repeated, finally coming to an end when the piglet ran directly into Mary's hands.

For a moment the breathless girl sat on the floor with the piglet held securely under her arm. Mistress Adams, also panting, sat and reached over to put an arm around Mary. After all, they had accomplished a brilliant capture. They shared a well-earned grin.

Hannah closed in to pat the piglet. Sarah was content to just look on. The cause of it all stared back. Its tiny black eyes shifted from one to another as if to say, "How sorry I am to cause you so much trouble. But it was fun." Mary could feel a little heart thumping a dozen or more times within every blink of her eye.

All the other hearts in the room melted at the sight of a tiny pig's pudgy, pink face and its twitching nose.

John was only three months old when Mary arrived at the plantation, but he soon showed his personality. His blue eyes flashed at every movement. He chuckled at the slightest funny face and shaking head. With a firm grip he held onto everything that passed close by. An occasional cry was soon hushed simply by a snug hold. John was the perfect baby. But his parents worried about one thing—his left foot turned in. Perhaps the doctors in Boston would have a solution.

Dutch Fort and Trading Post

NEAR THE END of the day there was often time for strolls along the riverbanks by a girl and her horse. Mary found their outings through little used woodland trails peaceful. Oftentimes, she let the horse choose the way. It meant following a stream, climbing a boulder-strewn hill, or staying by the well-marked pathway that coursed along the riverside. The rider never worried about returning: Angel was unfailing in finding the way home.

One afternoon, Mary led Angel across the bridge of planks that spanned the Little River. She then let Angel follow along a slightly trodden pathway through forest and across marshland. It was a path that Master Adams had advised her not to take. But she was curious, and she saw no harm in the venture. She had not gone very far before coming to a rise of ground that jutted out a bit into the river. Upon this neck of land there stood a great wall of upright and sharp-pointed stakes. The wall spread out along a long earthen mound that formed a square.[54]

Behind the wall and towering over it was a large blockhouse, and, pointing out from it, were two long and thin barrel-shaped black objects. She had seen such objects before at the Manor. She could never forget the time one was brought on a wagon pulled by four horses. There was much made of it. She stood close by with her father as men rolled the object down onto the ground. She well remembered that the men put hands over their ears. Her father did the same but only after positioning Mary's hands over hers. A moment later, one of the men put a torch to one end. At almost the same instance she saw a burst of white smoke pour out of the other end. Then Mary felt a strange sensation as if a sudden wind had struck her body. But there was no wind and the sensation as quickly vanished. To her, it was all so mysterious. Here at the fort, Mary saw no blast or smoke come from the great black tube.

Caution overruling curiosity, Mary nudged Angel into a full turn. They traced their way back to the settlement. Mary could not wait to get some explanation of the awesome sight. In a letter written sometime during the night, Master Adams favored her with some details. He left the pages for her to find in morning on the table at her place.

> *Mary, what you saw was a fort. It is where the men live, the men with guns who came to complain about the pig. Here is the story as best I can tell it. A Dutch explorer ventured this far upriver more than twenty-five years ago. It was here where the Great River receives the Little River. The Dutch claimed all this land for themselves. More than twenty years ago, they built a block house on the high ground where the rivers join. It served as a trading post. There, they could safely stack furs while awaiting a ship*

from New Amsterdam. It became a small fort, one that they call 'House of Good Hope.' The Indians bring animal pelts in exchange for metal tools, blankets, sundry trinkets.

The Dutch claim all the land that the English cultivate as theirs. They say we are trespassers while we sit here beneath their noses. But the Dutch keep only a small garden and most of the fertile land near them lies idle. It is truly shameful. The Indians call this area Suckiaug, meaning black earth.

Yes, we have an uneasy truce with the Dutch and so far, thanks to God in Heaven, there has been no gunfire. It is true that we trade with the Dutch for they see some profit in the exchange. What do we have for exchange? Only gold coins will do. The time will come soon when we English can cut enough of our own lumber and fire our own tile and bricks.

We are not good neighbors. My warning for you, dear Mary, is to keep some distance from the House of Good Hope. We do not need to provoke an ill-fated incident. You know what they say in England, 'Let sleeping dogs lie.' In good faith, J.A.[55]

A Special Headache Cure

A FEW MORNINGS after Mary discovered the Dutch fort, a strong whiff of a burnt candle jolted her from sleep. Realizing that her roommate's side of the bed was empty, she looked down from the loft to see a candle flickering on the big table. There sat Rebecca, her head resting on flattened hands. She climbed down and gently laid an arm across her shoulders. The younger girl startled, bolted up, smiled weakly, and pushed a page of writing toward Mary. The words:

SATAN IN MY HEAD
On a sun-filled day of summer
Distant thunder rumbles cross the plain
And then, sudden-like, I feel a chill
That brings a drenching rain.

I know too well the cloudburst due
When fast the world about me warns
By leaves that shake and animals scatter
Oh, how I dread the coming of the storms.

The purple clouds gather close
Then, there is a blinding flash of light
It strikes my temple like an ax
The way a woodsman applies his might.

The tempest in my head may last for days
With throbs unstopped through the night
I wait until the storm passes on
When sweet serenity says all is right.

A fresh idea popped into Mary's head: what better place to find an answer for this long-suffering girl than in the book, *Countrey Contentments*! What a goose I am, she thought, not to look there before! At once she stepped up the ladder and returned with the book tucked beneath one arm.

Something in this book will help, wrote Mary. *Famous in England. Some pages on remedies for every ailment.*

Together, they found the right place for "Pain in the Head" where there were instructions on how to make a poultice: *Page 10. For the Head-ach, you shall take of Rosewater, of the juice of Cammomil, of worme milke, of strong wine vinegar, of each two spoonfuls, mixe them together well upon a chafing dish of coals: then take a peece of drie rose cake and steepe it..., and as soon as it hath drunke up the liquor and is thoroughly hot, take a couple of sound Nutmegs grated to powder. Page 11. and strew it... upon the Rose cake, then breaking into two parts, bind it on each side upon the temples of the head, to let the party lye downe to rest, and the paine will in a short space be taken from him.*

These instructions led to a flurry of activity at the break of dawn. Master and Mistress Adams felt very fortunate. After all, it was in the most distinguished book of practical matters for women known throughout the world and Mary came with her own copy!

The poultice, prepared with nearly all the assembled ingredients, they applied to the patient's head. Then they waited for the results. Hours passed. Rebecca's headache lessened by not one throb.

Sunday Prayer Meetings

Sundays were days of rest and reflection. No work was allowed. Of course, the animals needed minding but, otherwise, the day was meant for worship—and only worship. Other mundane tasks could not distract the devotion of the good Puritan from His Holy Spirit. Because there was no suitable building for them yet in Hartford, the families made their way to Windsor. Settlers in that village had already built a proper meeting house a few years earlier. The trip to and from Windsor, therefore, when combined with a long sermon, required a whole day.

The meetinghouse was not an immense building of sparkling studded stones. It had neither steeple nor deep-throated bell. What the plain wood-planked building had was a shining weathercock in the form of a crowing rooster that perched at its peak. The two windows on each long side were covered with oiled parchment. Benches faced toward the central pulpit, not like the churches of Mary Magdalene in Littleton or Saint Nicholas in Shepperton where the benches faced forward toward a slightly raised pulpit. An aisle separated benches into two rows. Men sat on one side, women on the other. Children could choose any side. All were accustomed to a sermon of three or more hours when the monumental struggle between the Almighty God and Satan was put into perspective by a fiery preacher.[56]

For the Sunday prayer meeting men changed the mud-splattered, tattered clothes of the working day to long black overshirts topped with broad, white collars, breeches and conical hats. Women wore their "good" dresses and bonnets. On the coldest days, parishioners draped themselves in blankets, finding the hearth on the far side not sufficient to stop them from shivering.

Sitting alongside the other women, Mary had no choice but to sit quietly and observe the preacher and all the villagers seemingly spellbound by the message. As is the way with people who cannot hear, she observed the minutia of all around her: the flowing long sleeves of the preacher where the stitching was unraveling near one shoulder; the nodding and sudden head jolting of a few bench sitters; a wasp crawling across the center of a window pane; the shadow of a hanging cross moving slowly until it was in direct line on an upright beam. Distinctive odors of bodies changed continually as a draft came from different directions.

People listened through a long sermon, barely shifting their bodies. Mary learned that the message from the pulpit was always in accord with the teaching of the Puritans in Boston and Cambridge. The message on this day taught that God has already decided every soul's destiny. Those so chosen could reach the Firmament in the afterlife but only if they followed a devoted religious life. Master Adams explained in writing to Mary that every person had to reach inside himself to find God and to behave according to the message that He provides, whether or not that person was among the chosen. Of course, no one knew during his time on Earth who had been chosen.

It was on one special Sunday that the preaching was given by the Reverend Thomas Hooker. He spoke with passion rising from deep within his soul. In his black, flowing jerkin and neatly pressed broad collar, his presence struck awe in the crowd. To Mary, there was something unusual in this day's sermon. People did not sit like statues. Rather, the congregation appeared surprised with the words coming from the pulpit. Many of them squirmed in their seats, looked around at each other, some with confusion, others with wonder. At the end, all slapped their hands together excitedly, over and over. It was truly an uncommon reaction during a Sunday sermon. The meaning of it all, a written explanation came without asking. Once at home Master Adams wrote of the odd behavior of the people at church:

> *Mary, our worship service today did not follow the usual quiet manner. We were all expecting the sermon to present a special message, and it did! Indeed, Rev. Hooker spoke of a new way of thinking, more in keeping with the feelings of the people in*

our river plantations rather with the beliefs of those in England. Beginning with the philosophy of the Greeks in ancient times, he spoke of the worthiness of each person. Within each worshipper there was a guiding light to be recognized. He went on to describe a new charter, written to assure that the government would represent the free consent of people. He called his proposal the "Fundamental Orders of Connecticut." It said, in effect, that people must govern themselves, not be governed by a higher power of the Church or Crown or by any other authority. We are not, the Reverend reminded everyone, obligated to the authority of the Bay Colony and its restrictions.

Rev. Hooker spoke in a language that all could understand. Our people were stunned. There came whisperings of approval and then clapping. His words on "self-rule" shatter the traditions of government since the beginning of time. I think you will see that our Connecticut Constitution, in its own quiet way, will someday ring bells that can be heard around the world.

The determination in his face as he handed Mary his letter with its remarkable message made her realize that something important was in the air.[57]

Talking Hands

As the weeks wore on, the two new sisters drew closer together in spirit and learned to cherish their differences. They realized that one was a thinker. That is, she was wont to pursue activities of the head. The other was more bent on motion. They knew that their growing friendship needed better communication. On this idea was born the possibility that Mary would teach the younger girl the magic of using hands and face to form a language.

Mary had invented many hand-words with Sky Flower for whom speaking with hands was a natural part of being a Mohawk. In time, they “spoke” to each other and laughed when they first realized that some of their gestures had been understood by the other. Others watched and wondered at the magic of it all.

At first, Rebecca was pleased to learn gestures that easily identified the objects around them, and the things that they did and the different feelings they had: kitchen utensils, sleeping, reading, happy, sad, etc. The two went out of the house to learn words for trees, sun, chickens, wagon. Neighborhood children watching them giggled, hiding their broad smiles behind flattened palms at the odd sight of the girls in their exaggerated whirling of arms and strange configurations of hands.

Yet, Rebecca was not a good student when it came to learning the language of signs. For one thing, she felt awkward. For another, her life-long love of words, both spoken or written, was well-embedded in her thinking. In addition, Master Adams felt it unnatural and did nothing to encourage her. From this coming together of two mindsets, a serious attempt to acquire a visual language did not progress much further.

Dutch Sloop

A DAY IN early August proved to be the perfect balance of sunshine, breeze, and clarity. Mary, with Angel trailing behind, visited a familiar bluff from which she had often admired the splendid view of the river below. The water in late afternoon sparkled in the way a million stars can light a moonless night. Letting Angel loose and wishing the glorious day would never end, she stretched out in the tall grass to enjoy both the warmth of the soil and the coolness of a caressing breeze. She closed her eyes and tried to embrace the perfect moment for her memory.

When she opened her eyes again, a tiny fleck in the far distance of mid-river caught her attention. It looked like a huge bird with large red wings gliding just above the river's surface. When the bird got closer, it turned into a ship, but not a great and sleek ship like *The Vagabond*. Instead, it had but a single huge red sail and appeared to float low in the water. Stubby for its short length, the vessel gave the appearance of excessive bulk. Its gigantic sail stretched out to one side and billowed into a smooth curve. Stout poles held the sail out. The pole on the bottom was longer than the one at the top so that the slanted, trailing edge of the sail gave it a graceful shape, not like the square sails of the English ship.

Unlike *The Vagabond*, there were triangles of reds and yellows all along the side of the boat, and white in front and blue behind. A bold orange, white, and blue streak in front led the way. Mary followed the boat with fascination as it moved slowly in light wind with little splash in front and little wake behind. The whole reminded her of a toy boat once received by Charles as a birthday gift, a boat that he floated and soon lost downstream in the River Ash.[58]

Closer still, Mary could clearly see two figures on the boat. A man with a long red beard and a puffy black hat stood at the rear where he was engaged in the long pole meant for steering. The other man, wearing an orange hat with a wide and floppy brim, stood at the front, a bit like the figurehead on an ocean-going ship. Thrusting an arm one way, then another, he appeared to be pointing the way ahead. At that moment, Mary could not have imagined that the figurehead would also come to point a direction in her life.

In all, the sighting was a wonderful diversion to behold. Mary could not have known, is that the boat had come from the Dutch colony of New Amsterdam, a day or two away by sail. Filled with provisions for soldiers, it was bound for the fort at the head of the river. Nor could she know that it would first stop at the dock in Hartford to unload the English tiles and bricks as well as some lumber cut by a sawing windmill in New Amsterdam. These would be paid for in gold coin, or corn, or in exchange for furs that the English, in turn, had acquired in trade with the Indians for some pots and axes.

When Mary and Angel returned to the settlement, the little ship was already tied at dockside and a crowd had gathered. Some of the cargo had already been offloaded. Tiles, bricks, and lumber sat stacked neatly on one side of the dock. Bundles of beaver and otter skins along with sacks of corn were hefted from sheds and carried directly onto the ship.

In the crowd she spotted the two men seen on the boat. In their many-colored clothes, they could not have looked more different from the English. Her own people, Mary believed, favored a drab appearance; somehow the modest outside meant a more colorful appearance before God on the inside. The logic of this idea she never questioned.

The man with the red beard was short and the contours of his face and belly had every appearance of eating well. He was now hatless. His vivid blue waistcoat was topped by a white, loosely fitted collar. Baggy pantaloons pulled in at the knees were met by tight stockings nearly as red as his beard. His shoes were ankle high.

It was he who saw that each item brought onto the ship was first inspected and duly recorded. He protested if a fur was too moldy or badly trimmed; these were turned away. He made certain that no sack of corn was underweight. Not an item did his keen eye miss.

Then, Mary's eyes fell on the glorious orange hat. It crowned a young man, tall and slender as a tree and standing above the forest of milling townspeople. He was muscular in the shoulders and, with heels together, reminded Mary of a soldier in the King's palace guard. Below the floppy brim was a broad face and square chin, not the usual narrow face and tapered chin of an English man, nor did he have the hollowed-out cheeks of the Hartford settlers.

Accustomed now to the somber clothing of the Puritans, Mary could only stare at his stunning appearance. On his chin was a small, well-trimmed flaxen beard. Long ringlets of straw-colored hair bordered his face. He wore a purple vest. At the neck, there was a loosely hanging medallion that sparkled as he turned toward the sun. His flowing white sleeves came down to the wrists. Boots were trim and folded over at the top, just below the knees. Tassels swung from the outside top of each boot.

Unlike the first man from the little ship, the second one seemed less attentive to the dealings of trade then taking place; he appeared to be more interested in keeping an eye on the crowd. After he passed a small item to a child, a horde of others instantly gathered around him. With this attention, the man knelt on one knee and delighted the children with a gyrating puppet made from a stocking. Mary, riding astride, led Angel in for a close view.

Unexpectedly, the man in the floppy orange hat turned toward Mary and smiled. It was a warm and inviting smile. At that moment, Mary felt a tingle flow down her body that she had never felt before. She could see he was speaking in a way to her. In the confusion all around, she was afraid that she might act foolishly. She turned to Angel, and they ambled toward home. On her way, the excitement of that smile lingered. She did not understand the feeling that it brought but Mary knew she needed to see his face again. The orange hat had become a flame, and a fluttering moth was drawn toward it.

In the excitement of the moment an idea suddenly came to her. She wrote of this in a note handed to Master Adams. He returned, writing that the ship would continue to the fort at the House of Good Hope where the sailors would stay to rest and await a favoring wind. A few days may elapse. Thought Mary, there may be time to put my idea on paper.

The next hours saw Mary feverishly working on her drawing. It was meant to be the wondrous sight as she remembered it from her view high above the river. In the center would be the ship with its billowing red sail. Red and yellow triangles would decorate the side, a white triangle would show in the front, and a blue one, behind. A flag out in front of the boat would be colored orange, white and blue. Of course, the red-bearded one and the orange-hatted one, tiny as they were, would stand in their places aboard. The basic sketch was completed by nightfall.

At daybreak Mary began her chores of watering, feeding, cleaning, milking, and egg collecting, completing them all by mid-morning. Her plan was taking shape. A quick walk now through the bushes behind the house would take her to the closest briar patch. And so, by high sun she had already collected some ripe berries and crushed them into dyes of blue and red. Some goldenrod provided a hint of yellow. At last, having made her drawing as colorful as she possibly could, the artist looked it over with a critical eye. With a modest sense of contentment, she allowed herself a little smile. Her impulsive idea was now a reality. At the bottom she printed her name using blackberry juice for ink: MARY WALSINGHAM.

The Reply

WITH THE COLORED stains drying quickly in the noonday sun, Mary prepared for her outing to the House of Good Hope. As she usually did, she unfolded her riding blanket to use as a saddle over Angel. The two made their way across the bridge over the Little River in the direction of the Dutch fort. She soon saw the trading boat at dock, its red sail neatly rolled around a pole. Not far stood the imposing, timbered wall of the fort, and behind that rose the towering block house.

Spotted by a lone guard, Mary was ordered to stop. It mattered not that he shouted in Dutch, *Halte. Kom niet dichter.* His musket pointed directly toward her. Of course, Mary had seen guns before; she always gazed in awe as smoke burst from their tips, but wondered what the fuss was afterwards. She, however, had never seen the results of the powder blast. Nor had Mary ever had a gun pointed at her.

Oh, Angel, she thought. *We have frightened the guard.*

Reassuring herself that they should proceed, Mary—hopelessly naïve—guided Angel parallel to the wall, and then had her walk a wide circle. In that way, the guard could see that she carried nothing that would threaten the fort. She waved her painted drawing. The sentry looked on but kept the powder in his musket unlit. Perhaps the reason why was obvious. Mary herself made an unusual picture that seemed harmless enough: a girl with flowing golden hair and with bare ankles on long legs that dangled astride a chestnut brown and unsaddled horse.

By the time she reached the gate, more faces were peering down from the wall. She held out her drawing for all to see. With that, the gate opened a trifle and a hand reached out. It took the paper. The gate closed. If she only could see the puzzled faces inside the wall soon turn to grins! By the time they returned for another look at the horse and rider, both had gone.

Within a few days, Master Adams handed Mary a letter. It was brief and written in elegant hand.

To Mary Walsingham.

My name is Pieter van Stroomer. I am the man in the orange hat. My fellow sailor, Frans Mulder, has the red beard and the black hat. We like your drawing of our little ship. We call it the Visarend. *In my language, it means Osprey or Sea Eagle. Do you know the bird that dives from high up straight down into the river to catch fish? Our boat is tub-like and slow, but two people can sail it easily. It carries much below deck.*

A fine artist you are. Were you that handsome girl on a horse at the plantation? Please draw a picture of yourself and

your beautiful horse. Our ship will return in one month's time. I will bring you a surprise when we return from our home in New Amsterdam, a two-day sail away.
Pieter

Misadventure

ON ONE LAZY afternoon while following a narrow trail toward the south, Mary and Angel came to a turn when some men sprang out from the underbrush with bent bows holding arrows pointed at her. Faces were painted in frightening designs. Headdresses were feathered. Pelts hung from shoulders. Threatening voices went unheard. These were not like the trading Indians that Mary had come to know.

Mary tried her best to gesture that she was unable to hear. They continued to yell but with fading intensity as they warily looked over the defenseless passerby, talking together. "It is only a girl," they seemed to say in a laughing smirk. "No danger is she."

Emboldened, one of the Indians grasped Mary's sack, finding only some bread and cheese. Clearly disappointed and repelled by the smell, he showed it around. Another reached out to touch her blanket, feeling with glee its fine texture. Still another began to stroke Angel's flank. That caused Mary to feel a creeping discomfort. As a fourth one tried to touch Angel's forehead, the rider had had enough. She gave the hand a sharp thwack. The hand withdrew. At this action, the surprised men spoke to each other, stepped aside, and gestured with nods and extended arms to bid

Mary pass on. A quick hand retrieved her sack, and she was on her way.

Glancing back from an easy walking pace, Mary saw them standing together. They were shaking their heads as if astonished by her audacity. Only then did she remember the Indian signs that Sky Flower had taught her years before. She brought Angel to a stop and turned to face those who had rudely tested her. Boldly, she let them know with a glance and with strong words by hands, *Do not frighten an enraged woman.* She then turned and nudged Angel on her way. The warriors, if that is what they were, were left staring after her.

Dutch Treat

THE DUTCH SHIP returned in September. Its arrival was announced by the excitement of people rushing to greet it. Again, the same two men attended the ship and, again, the trading was brisk and watchfully measured. Wooden boards stacked high along the dock were sorely needed for some new partly-built houses. There appeared some haggling because of the less than expected number of pelts for exchange.

As the quibbling went on, Pieter, still wearing the shiny medallion at his neck, amused the children as he had done before. This time he pulled a stocking out of one pocket. A hand went into the stocking. The children saw the face of a cat painted in the stocking with whiskers coming out of both cheeks. A thumb and pinky finger sticking out through holes in the stocking made ears.

The story without words was simply about a cat trying to sleep on the man's other arm. The bravest of the children stepped forward and scratched the cat beneath its chin. The cat awakened, jumped up, wiggled its ears and soon fell asleep again. Up came another hand, another scratch, another awakening, another jumping, another wiggling. Every time, laughter rippled through the crowd. It happened over and over until every child had a chance to give a good scratch and awaken the sleepy cat. When the last of the children was ready for a try, the cat suddenly sprang up and gave a good scratch beneath the child's chin. By that time, the trading was over, and the stocking went back into the man's pocket.

When the transactions were completed, the sails were readied for casting off. Mary handed Pieter a drawing that she had fussed over for days. It was a sketch of the most handsome horse in the world. Sitting on it was a girl as amusingly ugly as the artist could possibly make her. She had a warped face, a nose like a dried-up crab apple, and hair that stood out at crazy angles. The eyes were unearthly big, one bigger than the other, and far apart. Ears were like dinner plates. Her silly grin showed crooked teeth, a front one missing. She was not, in few words, a great beauty.

Pieter stepped into his boat and soon returned with a long, narrow box covered in a rich textile of many colors. With it was an envelope addressed "To Mary Walsingham." He handed both box and envelope to Mary. But a moment later, the two Dutchmen pulled their red sail to full height, cast off ropes to the dock, and were on their way toward the House of Good Hope.

Mary felt a tingling all over for the joy of receiving a gift from the stranger. She waited until evening and candlelight. Yet, eager anticipation quickly turned to grave disappointment for the paper drawn out of the envelope made no sense.

,yraM raeD
.gniward ruoy rof uoy knahT
lufituaeb erom si ohW
?esroh ruoy ro uoY
reteiP

Perhaps this writing was the way of the Dutch people. But there was a clue that suggested otherwise. A large letter came at the end of each line. Aha! Mary remembered her looking glass, a gift from a London cousin. Soon fetched, the note was as clear as daylight.

With such a whimsical treat, Mary could hardly imagine what she would find in the wooden box. She turned the clasp and lifted the lid. Inside were many brushes of different sizes for painting and four small glass bottles with colored oils: red, yellow, green, blue. Most precious of all was a roll of paper as white as snow. Her joy she shared with the Adams family. Rebecca wrote that she could now become a great artist. The others were more reserved in their opinions.

Something, minor as it was, happened that night that could not be explained. Mary had left the backward-lettered letter on the table to amuse all in the morning. But in the morning, it was not there. She looked high and low, but the note was never found.

On the following morning, a cry of fire rang through the village. Smoke always poured out of the smokehouse, but now it billowed out in great puffs, carrying sparks up with it. Flames broke out on one side. Men, women, and children scrambled with pails of water to splash on the blaze, but it was not enough. In minutes, the entire building was engulfed. For the children, it was a time of rare excitement as they watched orange-red flames lick the walls and plumes of gray smoke rise skyward. For the others, it was a disaster. The smokehouse was critical to cook large chunks of meat properly. Fortunately, the building was small and many hands could quickly build another one. At least, no one needed to sleep outdoors on this night. The fire, nevertheless, was a stark reminder: every house is but an errant spark away from the same fate.

On the next day, ashes and a brick oven were all that was left of the smoke house, in addition to a well-roasted pig. Some said it was the work of witches. Fear of witchcraft always lurked at the back of people's minds when bad things happened. For the next days, dinner in the households of Hartford included a generous slice of pork, whether they all believed in witches or not.

Late Delivery

It was on the same day as the smokehouse fire that something most extraordinary happened. A messenger on horseback arrived bearing letters from the mother colony in Boston and Cambridge. That evening after prayers, Master Adams handed Mary an envelope, so addressed:

To Master Jeremy Adams
The Massachusetts Bay Colony

Master Adams bid her look inside. To her astonishment, she read:

2 April 1639

Dear Jeremy,

I write that all is readied to transport two of my finest draught horses to you. Your agent, Master Dorset, appears satisfied with the health and strength of the horses. I think you will find them quite serviceable on your gardens and well worth the price. Please be reassured that they will cross the ocean under the best care possible.

We have received the good news that the Bay Colony is doing well in the bounty of the New World. On reading of your venture there with Rev. Thomas Hooker and his devoted followers, I trust that life has been profitable over these six years. I believe, too, that you have found a favorable place to continue the Puritan ideals to which you are so faithfully committed.

Now I write to you with a request. My daughter, Mary, will be eighteen years of age in a month. She has become determined to "see the world," first visiting the colonies in America. With arrangements made for her to journey there in one month's time, I anticipate that she will arrive in Boston about the middle of July. Should all proceed as planned, she will be on a ship called The Vagabond. *I trust that you will be gracious enough to see to her lodging and needs until she is ready to return home, and that she will not be a burden to you or your family. Mary writes well, is quiet and does not complain. She is a good worker and is exceptionally devoted to the care of animals.*

Writing this letter makes me think of the good times we had growing up in the fields and rivers of Stoke-by-Nayland. Do you remember the gay time we poured juice from boiled onions across the fields the morning before a fox chase? The sniffing dogs scattered in every direction leaving the hunters totally baffled. To this day, I do not know how your father found out that we were responsible for that farce. Oh, were we punished! Still, I break into a chuckle every time I think of the uproar we caused on that day.

If in any way I may return the favor for your looking after Mary, be certain that I shall gladly honor it. By the way, I think you should know that Mary will be bringing along her horse. Also, Mary is deaf.

By the grace of God for your continued prosperity in the colony,
I remain your obedient and trustworthy friend,
Walter Walsingham, Littleton.

The letter solved a mystery. It explained Mary's frosty reception on arriving at the dock in Hartford. The letter had gone first to the Bay Colony. Her father, of course, had not known about the farmers who left Boston and Cambridge in 1636 to begin plantations along the fertile valleys of the Connecticut River. Master Adams was simply not prepared to meet Mary and Angel on the dock that fateful day in July.

CHAPTER 7

Autumn

The Refuge of Words

THE EXCITEMENT CREATED by the new furnishings brought by *The Vagabond,* and then by the smokehouse fire and the wayward letter from Lord Walsingham gradually subsided as summer drew to a close. People went back to the noisy activities of preparing the food stores for another winter season. It would be another month before the *Visarend* would appear again.

As the villagers worked hard outside, Rebecca retreated more and more often into her quiet corner inside. The only refuge that the girl found to counter the assaults on her head was some delight in capturing beautiful words—to let night writing replace her night suffering. It mattered not whether well-chosen words rhymed, or whether they fell into a poetic rhythm. One such play on words, finished by daybreak, found its way onto Mary's pillow:

Autumn comes quiet like a cat
With welcomed beams of sunshine on my brow
And twilight falling in planned succession.

Then comes night, moonlight's long shadows
The changes as true as the evening star.
As the crunching sound of leaves pressed under foot
And above a leafy shroud of crimson reds and gilded yellows.
I hold this season close to my breast,
Not thinking of that season past or that ahead
But bathe in the present golden glory of autumn.
R.A.

One of the poems left on Mary's pillow on another night was short and did rhyme:

A drop of dew
On a willow leaf
Reflects the world
In bold relief.

Rebecca's description of autumn touched Mary deeply. She marveled at the brilliant colors of the changing leaves around her. In contrast, autumn leaves in Littleton had never been so vivid. She picked up a leaf that seemed especially colorful and left it for the young poet.

Her message said: *This bright red leaf with its many points brings to mind everything you write in your treasury of poems.*

It was not a surprise that Mary soon found another poem at her bedside:

Dancing green in summer's breath
A leaf is Nature's power
Then comes autumn's chill

In scarlet it is a flower.

It should be said that Rebecca's father did not support her passion for poetry. "Idle," he said. He wished instead that she would take more interest in the words of the Scripture. Still, he pitied her long suffering and vowed to allow what might ease her deep misery.

Gifts

A RUNNER CAME from the House of Good Hope. In addition to a message for Reverend Hooker he carried a letter addressed to Mary Walsingham:

> *Dear Mary,*
> *Thank you for your wonderful painting. Indeed, I think that is truly a handsome horse. I have never seen a more beautiful girl than the one who sits so queen-like on the horse. As we Dutch like to say about anything too good, "It is like a spoonful of Jamaican sugar dropped into a bowl of maple syrup." Frans and I will return in a month's time. Your house builders are in need of more Dutch lumber to build another smokehouse.*
> *Pieter*

His promise held true. Toward the end of September excitement spread quickly across the fields when the Dutch trading ship appeared at dockside. It was quickly secured. Men of the village dropped their hoes and axes, women picked up their babies, and children shouted in glee. All flocked to the river. It was the same ship with the same men aboard.

Cut boards were soon unloaded and stacked alongside the dock. Soon after unloading the cargo, Red Beard stood facing the crowd of eager bargainers. The tasks of inspecting, counting, and recording all that the ship brought and all the corn and furs that the settlers provided were quickly completed.

All the time, Orange Hat entertained the children. He pulled from his pockets three clay balls, each the size of a fist. He threw one into the air, then another. As he caught the first ball with the other hand, he tossed up the third. Soon he had three balls in the air all at one time. Truly, it was magic. Since children in Puritan families were not brought up amid such frivolities of the world, this amazing feat was new. But of course, each child had to try. All soon learned that keeping three balls constantly and effortlessly in the air was not easy. Mary had already seen such skills on the streets of London and found them here no less spectacular.

Using her new colors, the artist had painted another gift for Pieter. It was of her home in England. There was the Manor House with all its windows and turrets. On the grass field, a single magpie hopped about. In the foreground a few sheep grazed and some girls "jumped the rope."

Pieter had something for Mary. It was a bumble bee frozen in a bead of amber sap. Preserved were the tiny hairs around its head and the soft fuzz that covered its black and yellow striped body. The spread-out wings showed the finest lacework imaginable. A thin string of leather piercing one end made it into a necklace. Attached to the necklace was some writing on brown paper.

O
WE
ARE
BEES.
STING
OR ELSE
PRODUCE
COMBS OF
FINE HONEY.
11

Mary was so delighted with the honey tree that she left it on her pillow. When she returned to sleep that evening, it was gone. A search into everything she owned—which did not take long—came up empty. Disappointed, she began to question her memory. Perhaps it was just a fleeting fantasy. The missing honey tree was soon forgotten. She still had her frozen-in-time bee.

By now, Mary cherished the occasional visitations of this well-mannered and fun-loving stranger. The periods of absences seemed to her intolerably longer. Should he return, what, she wondered, might she do to attract his attention? Weeks passed without an answer. Then, suddenly, an idea came to her during one fitful night. Counting! Yes! She would show Pieter her number-counting horse. But first, she must see if Angel remembered to respond to her blinking.

At first sign of dawn, Mary was up and at Angel's stall. And yes, Angel did remember. Her additions and subtractions were flawless.

Counting Horse, Again

WHEN THE DUTCH ship docked again in October, Mary handed Pieter a note rolled into a scroll. Tied around it was a red string. Colorfully painted were the words:

> *Dear Master van Stroomer,*
> *The horse in my drawing is not only handsome, she knows numbers. Her name Angel. She can count. I like you come and see.*
> *Respectfully yours, Mary Walsingham*

By this time, word had spread. After the trading was completed, disbelievers and the curious alike followed the Dutch sailors to the stables to witness this remarkable horse. Mary led Angel out to stand beneath a lone elm tree where all could see. Mary faced her but two steps away.

Angel performed as promised. Each answer brought out a brisk tapping of one forefoot. All were amazed at the sight of a horse adding and taking away numbers, answering correctly without fail. Needless to say, the children were delighted and completely entranced. Others, the elders, mostly, were surprised but not altogether pleased to see an animal with human qualities. Only, they supposed, a demonic spirit could allow such a variance of nature. Perhaps the horse was an agent of the devil, and Mary was in some mysterious way part of Satan's plan.

Pieter and Frans were, like the others, astonished by the performance. "You have a gifted horse," said one. "And you have trained her well," said the other. Mary smiled at their moving mouths but did not answer. They walked away thoroughly numbed by the display. Satisfied, Mary led Angel back into the stall.

Just before the ship's parting, Mary passed Pieter a hastily written note. He placed it in a pocket for reading later. It read:

Please know, Sir, that my beloved horse Angel be not so clever with numbers as appears. I tell her by blinking, something that no one seems to notice. I deeply sorry if trick you. Kindly overlook my silence at your words. My ears useless. I do not learn to speak. I am truly sorry.
Mary Walsingham

Days later, a response by messenger arrived. It read:

To Mary Walsingham.
Your horse, I believe, is very clever, still. I was truly taken in by the flimflam and truly amused to see Angel so good with numbers. What I find even more admirable is the magician's honesty in the telling how her amazing trick is performed.

About your silence. It is not so heavy a burden. I believe people talk too much anyway. Your words in pictures for me are far more important.

Our little ship will return to House of Good Hope by November's end. After that, the river will freeze over. I will bring some items to help you through a long Hartford winter.
Yours, Pieter v S.

Riddles and Stories

IT WAS ON a mild day in November when the Dutch boat next arrived in Hartford. The people rushed to the wharf on word that the *Visarend* had docked. There was Frans with his red beard even longer. There was another man, a person barely beyond boyhood. Pieter was not among them. Mary was crestfallen.

A good supply of wide boards and some tiles came onshore from the ship. Terms for the transaction were soon settled. Frans spotted Mary. He brought something out from the boat and handed it to her. Accepting it with a polite curtsy, she discovered two sheets of leather and between them, a stack of papers. Inside, the top letter read:

> *To Mary. My absence this winter is my misfortune. During the long night you may find some amusement in these random scribbles. Pieter*

Over those endless days of winter, Mary slowly savored each piece within the stack. Each was cherished as if it were the original Magna Carta itself. Indeed, for Mary, it was. There were pages of riddles, like these:

> *What do you remove the outside of and throw away, then eat the inside, and throw away what is inside that?*
>
> *What moves on four legs in the first stage of life, then on two legs, and then finally on three legs?*
>
> *What do you find in each of the following? The beginning of eternity: What is it? The end of time and space: What is it? The beginning of every end: What is it? And the end of every place: What is it?*

There were pages of jokes, many about horses:

A gentleman always rode his horse on a handsome saddle, but he had only one spur. When asked about this curiosity, he responded, "What profits me to have two spurs? If one side of my horse speeds up, is it likely that the other side will stay behind?"

Mary's life up to that point had been devoid of anything resembling a joke. After all, each day was a serious effort to follow the social and religious expectations pressed upon each person. It is fair to say, the world that the Puritans put themselves into was mostly humorless. Their world was one of self-discipline. Her parents, too, could hardly imagine any frivolity in those who were expected to be grown up even when they are children. And so, the ridiculous story of a horse speeding up on both sides was a delightful distraction that, on its recall long after, brought a chuckle. But seventeenth-century England did have a sense of humor, although it surely differed from our modern way.

Perhaps, thought Mary, telling a far-fetched story was a Dutch way of thinking. Here is one of the dozens that entertained Mary through the long winter:

One day in spring, a man on horseback was crossing a stream when his horse stopped and bent forward to take a drink. It happened that a man walking in the opposite direction said, "My, but you have a thirsty horse there." Months went by. It was summer during a long drought. By chance the two met again at the stream, now dried up but for a trickle of slow running water. "Well," said the man, "your horse was thirstier than I thought."

And another:

He that buys a horse and does not look upon it before with a pair of spectacles makes his horse and himself a pair of sorrowful spectacles for others to look at.

There were also charming tales, each written in beautiful hand. One read:

A weary traveler carrying a heavy bundle stopped to rest where the riverside pathway made a steep rise. Suddenly, a frog appeared atop a moss-covered boulder. Asked the frog, "Where goes you?"

The traveler, though startled by a talking frog, responded, "To the village that lies at the peak of these hills."

"Why go you there?" inquired the frog.

"To speak to a wise man," came the answer.

The frog, ever more curious, questioned further. "What wisdom seek you?"

Replied the man, "To know how to free my life of its many burdens."

The frog did not answer right away, but after a long period of deep thought said, "You need go no farther."

"I beg you to tell me more," said the traveler, even more astonished.

Returned the frog, "The object of your search can be found in the little settlement of huts just beyond the next rise."

"Do go on," added the man.

Said the frog, "Look for the most beautiful maiden you have ever seen."

"Can she tell a tired wanderer where to find the meaning of life"? the man asked.

"The truth is," said the frog with all deliberate slowness, "she speaks not a word. But with a single glance she can lift your spirits."

Said the man, "Please tell me more, my good frog. How do. . . ." But before he could say another word, the frog made one long leap from the rock and jumped into the river, never looking back.

On and on went the pages of puzzles, riddles, jokes, stories, and thoroughly delightful twists of words. All were written in a beautiful hand with flourishes as if each line were a masterpiece of art.

Often after the day's chores were over, Mary would ponder the puzzles and giggle at the stories. She was grateful for the gift-giver, a special person who knew what could make the days and the long dark nights of winter pass much easier. Treasured, too, was the extra paper. Mary counted. There were twenty-seven sheets, pure white and squared to perfection.

CHAPTER 8

Winter

Red Bird

THE BITTER COLD of a New England winter soon made its presence known along the Great River. Mary, of course, had known cold in Littleton, but she generally had stayed close to a blazing hearth during this season. It was only on the ride to church in Shepperton that she and her family needed to bundle up against winter's chill. Even then, a blanket or two was enough to keep warm as the wagon bumped along.

She soon realized, even before Christmas, that winter in Hartford brought a different sense of cold. Overnight, the air changed from chilly to frigid. The first touch of morning outdoors stung the face. Puffs of smoke came with every breath. Air that felt like ice breathed in and steam breathed out. The cold bit through her long woolen coat and the layers of cotton underneath, cutting directly into the bones. The long white-dyed leather gloves (the gift from her London cousins) were hardly enough to keep her fingers from turning numb.

Despite the cold temperatures, Mary knew that she needed to get water to her charges waiting in the stables and pens. She feared that the well would freeze. Ice did form around it, but the water down below, fortunately, did not.

What happened next, however, was unfortunate and painful. While trying to pour the bucket water into the carrying pail, she felt her numbed fingers turn into icicles. But the worst part came later when trying to warm them at the hearth. No one had told her that nearly frozen hands and feet should warm up slowly. She learned that lesson only after feeling a painful throbbing that seemed never to go away. It was some comfort to count ten fingers and ten toes, reddened and puffy but still there.

The cold weather brought a small change to Angel's accommodations. Master Adams allowed the horse to stay in the enclosed part of the sheep pen, not in the open air part where she had been during the warm season. The sheep, in their thick wool coats, would continue to spend the winter in an outside pen. Inside, for reasons that Mary did not understand, the entire animal shelter was warm. Could it be the heat coming from the breath and bodies of the cows and horses?

Off and on snow flurries throughout December turned into the first full ground cover by the twenty-third day. Early that morning, Mary stepped out into a landscape turned magically white. She blinked in full sun against the dazzling vista. Boulders and roofs appeared to have vanished. White was interrupted here and there by the vertical browns and grays of trees that led to horizontal limbs trimmed white. Feathery arching of snow-laden boughs made the green of fir trees ever greener. And above, the sky had never been bluer. Only God, she believed, could create such a beautiful setting. But just when Mary thought that the scene was perfect, she saw a red bird alighting on the crown of a nearby fir tree. Having never seen a cardinal, she knew that the Magician in Heaven—like a good street performer delivering a final flourish—had completed his landscape with a bird of brilliant and dazzling color.

Christmas

Mary wanted to long remember that perfect image and to share it with her new family. What better way than to paint the whole scene as a Christmas gift to all! And so out came Mary's brushes and paints for two long evenings. On Christmas morning she left her painting on the table for all to see, a blanket of white with scattered details of gray, browns, blue and green. Looking down at it all from the top center was a beautiful red bird. She wrote at the bottom: *A Christmas Present for All.*

All through her animal chores that morning, Mary thought of the excitement of Christmas morning at the Manor House. There was always a delicious pillow-side treat for each child to awaken to: marzipan, an orange, or a tart. Each child also received a present that was wrapped in a colorful bow. The Manor House was decorated with holly boughs and sweet-smelling rosemary and sage. It was a time that her parents spent the entire day with the children, bundled up against the cold for a long walk along the river or greeting seldom-seen friends arriving with gifts.

Mary's return from the stables to the Adams house was different. Faces did not radiate in the spirit of the day. Indeed, each person seemed the same as on all the days before. Her painting was nowhere in sight. Instead, Master Adams had written a note:

Dear Mary,

Your good intentions aside, you should know that Puritans do not celebrate Christmas. Yes, it is the time of year that our Savior on Earth was born, and so it is a sacred day. But the day has become profane, and, more or less a pagan holiday. We say a quiet prayer to Jehovah but do not partake of the mischief of the Anglicans. On this day, they revel in drunkenness, gambling with dice and cards, and other mischiefs too wicked to mention.

We do not labor today only because Christmas this year happens on Sunday. A true Puritan celebrates the birthday of Jesus in quiet contemplation. Your lovely painting gift on any other day would bring heartfelt pleasure but the day celebrating our Savior's birth is too holy for anything but devout worship. J.A.

Mary could see once again that her life in "The Colonies" was far different from her life in England.

Snowfall

THE ARDUOUS WORK of preparing food for winter proved adequate. Pork or beef that had been smoked, dried, or frozen went into the daily stew. Ground corn served in porridges with herbs was plentiful. Apples stored in the cold shed provided much sustenance. There was even a generous supply of collected honey for each household in the colony - enough to last, if used sparingly, throughout the winter.

Another snowfall occurred on the second day of the new year, 1640. This time every trace of big boulders vanished from sight. Roofs appeared ready to collapse from snow weight. This was not like any winter in England that she could remember.

Pathways to the animals had to be dug free of snow. The task was done with a shoveling tool fashioned out of a long-handled wooden scoop. Each household had to clear a footpath to the main way and that, in turn, led toward the stables. Shoveling snow was a man's chore but Mary insisted on being in on the task. As did the others, she wholeheartedly gathered a scoopful of snow, lifted it high, and tossed it alongside the lengthening path. It was a blessing that the day was not too cold; the heavy work of scooping soon warmed the body.

Making pathways and trudging through the snow were not unwelcoming chores. What she found distressing was the need to keep Angel inside. A long walk every day is healthy for a horse, but she knew that deep snow made it not possible.

Rebecca, needing to try her hand at shoveling snow, proved a bit too delicate for the task. After a half dozen or so scoopfuls, she went back to her poetry, but not before demonstrating what a well-made snowball can do when tossed with accuracy. At her doorstep she took aim. Mary spotted the missile, but not in time to duck under it. She quickly patted some snow together and tossed the result at Rebecca just as she slipped past the door. It missed by a wide mark.

Finding a poem by her pillow the next morning, Mary read:

THE GIFT
God is an artist
of that I am sure

Giving us the beauty of new-fallen snow
but the cold we must endure.

He paints his canvas
with generous gobs of white
And lets us marvel
at his work of the night.

A thousand lilies
we see on trees
As if a gardener
Planted with a set of magic keys.

The graceful bend of boughs
Sparkling white from snow
Touch a horizon, purest blue of cloudless sky
Speak of creation's brightest glow.

So, God, the painter-sculptor
Sprinkles his frozen dust
That molds a new horizon
And do we tread its crust?

Mary thought it lovely. She replied that the poet must show it to her father. Rebecca was reluctant because she feared his disapproval but after another appeal from Mary, she agreed and left a copy on the table. In the morning she found a written reply:

My dear daughter, we have separate ways of reaching to our Lord in Heaven. For me, the unquestioned faith of the heart leaps across that glorious pathway. For you, the gap between Earth and Heaven is bridged with words that tell of God's mighty benevolence. Which, I ask, is the grander view? Father.

Days later another snowstorm fell on the village. Snow piled on snow. This time, a drift had built against the door. Master Adams rocked the door back and forth with no success. Then, with a strong shoulder, he pushed the door ajar, just enough to slide one hand in the little crack between door and sill. He slowly pushed aside the snow until the opening was large enough for him to pass through. Once outside, he began the task of scooping out a waist-high drift against the house and tossing the snow aside. Paths to the privy, well, and stables would be next.

Squeezing through the crack in the doorway, Mary gestured that she could relieve him as he tired. Thomas and Rebecca, too, did what they could with a snow shovel improvised from a board. Men and women from other houses applied themselves to the task. By high sun, a pathway to the stables had been cleared.

There is something about aching muscles that gives a good feeling at the end of a day of hard work. It was in just such a time that Mary sat hunched over before the fireplace, as she was often wont to do, warming her front, with a blanket around her shoulders. It was a good time to think of home. She wondered if Charles had gotten over his fear of horses and mused about her sisters becoming ever more beautiful as they preened for the expectations of courtship and marriage. There were fleeting thoughts of many peaceful times in the orangery with Harold and the endless surprises of watching the blacksmith at his fiery artistry. Her mind shifted to Sir Francis Drake, bringing a smile about the cat's troublesome way. *Has he knocked over any more priceless vases?* Thoughts about Sky Flower, as always now it seemed, were fleeting; she had long before exhausted the stream of memories and questions about whatever path her friend and teacher had taken. There was no longer room in her head to imagine any more.

There was one reality that Mary could not avoid. She was, in fact, growing up. She was feeling less and less like a child and more and more like a young woman. The puzzles and stories that Pieter had given her for the winter's diversion were well-worn. His absence over so many months and the failure of the *Visarend* to appear on the horizon were becoming more and more on her mind. There was a deeper passion brewing, clearly melting the foolish, childlike shell that she had built to protect her from common indifference by those around her. Yes, Mary found herself thinking often of the man in the Orange Hat.

Suddenly, her reverie shifted when a large ember burst from the fire. It arched up and across the hearth—much as a comet does in a startled mid-summer night sky—and then landed on Mary's skirt. With several frantic strokes with the back of her hand, she brushed it off onto the stone. There she smelled the burned wool and stared vacantly at the ember in its death throes. But it did not relinquish life easily. First glowing yellow, then turning scarlet red and—for the briefest moment—there was a flash of blue. Then, all faded and soon the light was gone. The ember became just another black fleck among the many at her feet.

Mary thought about the ember, leaping away from its original flame as it did, having a brilliant moment before its spark faded away. She waited until it had cooled, and then picked up the ashen sliver. It crumpled between her thumb and forefinger. She marveled about what had just happened and pondered the short gift of life that began with a flash and ended in dust. She could not have known that her own life was about to burst from the fading blaze of childhood and cross the sky in a brilliant glow as a woman.

CHAPTER 9

Spring

Earth's Awakening

THE COMING OF March brought an end to the snow cover except for patches here and there that lay hidden from the sun. Early signs of spring crept into awareness. Rivers swelled and their currents became rapid. Huge chunks of ice floated downstream. Every day, the footpaths to the outer buildings became muddier. Slowly, the underbrush was turning green. The first flowers of spring were popping up: snow drops and wild geraniums. Great flocks of ducks and pigeons soared high above, always headed northward. Orange butterflies with black markings appeared in the thousands, along with the cat-o-nine tails that grew tall in the wetlands. Yes, spring had come at last to the plantation along the Great River. Mother Nature, with a long and powerful yawn, was finally waking up.

A chorus of peepers continued to peep throughout the night. A pileated woodpecker pecked noisily high in a tree. A yellowthroat songbird, closer to the ground, chirped happily in the thicket. Squirrels "clicked-clicked" high in the branches. The sounds announced the full flush of unfolding spring to all but Mary.[59]

The warming days brought something refreshing to the more daring: a bath. It had been a long winter when washing meant dipping hands in a common bowl and splashing around the mouth before every meal. Soap was a mixture of mutton fat, wood ash mixture and, when lucky, salt. Washing hands and mouth was a custom respected by all in the Adams household. They believed that this habit accounted for their good health.[60]

To get wet all over, that is, to take a bath, was quite another thing. The privy was large enough for one person to take a splash bath in privacy, as Mary remembered at her arrival at the Adams home. One had to bring in two buckets filled with freshly drawn well water. First, one pail for the wash and scrub with tallow, followed by a second pail for a shivering rinse. A thick cotton cloth for wiping dry and redressing ended the ritual. For those who cared to endure such a pleasure, there was no longer a need to mask their body smells with natural oils and spices. Mary relished the refreshing opportunity and promised herself a splash bath once every week or two.

Flood

SPRING EVOLVED AS it always did in the fields and forests along the Great River. In the spring of 1640, snowmelt and rain were more than usual. Early April rain fell in sheets for a week. Each day the river and its tributaries swelled a bit more and the current ran faster. In places the water spilled over the banks, flooding the fields. Paths around the plantation turned into carpets of oozing mud. Mary had seen such overflow in her own river, the Thames at Shepperton. But life there was little affected, and the flooding caused little harm. Here, walking between house and stables now meant sloshing through almost knee-deep water and spending much of the day with wet feet.[61]

By the third or fourth day of steady downpour, the increasing level of water over the land was worrisome. The water crept across the fields and rose around the houses. By the seventh day, worry had turned to despair. About noon on that day the sun mercifully broke through clouds to the joyous relief to all. All the time, the small footbridge of logs across the Little River was under tension. Floating high in a powerful current, the holding ropes pulled taut, but did not snap. The bridge so far was holding.

Master Adams's next note to Mary reassured her that the flood was expected, although perhaps this year it was a bit more generous than in earlier springs.

> *You have noticed,* he continued, *that some of the houses are built knee-high above ground on flat stones. These houses need to use precious planks for a floor. Our house is on higher ground and needs no wooden floor.*
>
> *The fields are much more fertile than those of Boston and Cambridge, and they have few stones. God has given us rich soil. Satan counters it by the flood. It is the way of the world. On earth we are bound to let one triumph over the other. Our reward will come in life after death. This spring, God tests our will more than usual. J.A.*

It was soon after the return of favorable weather that a hunter spotted a cow happily eating grass; it was miles upstream on the far side of the Little River. One of the cows had been missing for a week, clearly having strayed from pasture, and somehow waded across the river, perhaps where the rapids were shallow. Master Adams and his next-door neighbor, Master Samuel Easton, did not delay in going to fetch the errant cow.

Mary had just left the stables when she saw the men returning with cow in tow and approaching from the far side of Little River. She watched as they came to the footbridge where they spent a moment discussing the best way to cross. As any modern engineer or old-time farmer could attest, a bridge made of logs bound together with hemp, tethered to opposing shores, floating above the level of the banks in a flood does not make secure footing. Meanwhile, from upstream, floating branches crashed against the bridge and piled up dangerously against it.

The cow seemed not eager to trust that bridge. But the persuasion of Master Adams pulling on her horns in front and Master Easton pushing from behind succeeded in coaxing their balking subject onto the bridge. There, exactly mid-bridge, the cow had other ideas. It was at this point that the cow—eyes white around—seemed to ponder the precariousness of its situation and, in defiance, planted all four legs stiffly on the bouncy crossing. This was not a time for indecision for those determined to succeed. On the count of three Master Adams gave a good yank on the horns, while his neighbor provided a mighty heave on the rump. Their labors, alas, were undone when Master Adams slipped and landed backside onto the muddy bank. The cow skidded into the torrent stream with Master Easton following not far behind.

Mary, helpless in the calamity, could only cringe in horror as the current carried cow and man rapidly downstream. The cow was the first to find a low bank and, after a frantic struggle, gained firm ground and promptly ran across the field. Master Easton, too, was soon on terra firma. Once there, quivering from the cold water, he jumped up and down on one foot. At the same time, he tilted his head to that side and banged it with the palm of his hand to rid his ear of water. All the while, he forgot for the moment God's message of forgiveness, and raising the other arm in a decidedly un-Puritan gesture, he shook his fist mightily at the cow that had already attained a good distance between them. There is something universally and inexplicably comical about someone falling harmlessly into the water.

Supper that evening went on as usual, starting with a prayer by everyone all holding hands. A meal beginning with a thick soup, followed by boiled meat and potato, was followed by a treat of baked apples with cinnamon. As usual, there was barely any conversation through most of the meal.

What made this supper different from other suppers was Rebecca speaking breathlessly even before all had finished their apples. Whatever she was saying, Mary knew that it had captured the rapt attention of Master and Mistress Adams. They strained not to miss a word. As the story went on, there came a hint of a smile on both. Only when Rebecca hopped on one leg, banged her bent head with one hand and held the other arm high with a shaking fist, did Mary realize that they were hearing the story of the bridge calamity. With the telling, it was the first and only time that Mary saw Master Adams laugh.

An exchange of notes was passed before bedtime. Wrote Mary: *How did you know what happened today at the bridge?*

Rebecca's answer:

I had just stepped out of the privy when a cow came splashing by. Looking across the field, I saw you holding your head. Your elbows touched in front as if the sky were about to tumble down on you. Farther downstream, there was Father and our poor neighbor completing the drama in a play of one act.

Leaves

BUDS ON TREES were everywhere. One of the largest trees to burst into leaves had a single very wide trunk that separated into two parts. On a warm and pleasant day when Rebecca was using the end of a low-hanging branch to dry some washed clothes, she reached up and picked a leaf. It was just an ordinary one, but she admired its details. She left it at bedside along with a note for Mary.

To search the world for perfect form
And find it here in common Land
A simple leaf from yonder tree
It seems to me the Dragon's Hand.

Indeed, at the end of a long stem there were five long fingers that had sharp points and jagged edges. The middle finger was long and the two on each side exactly alike. The leaf was bright green on one side and silvery gray underneath. Surely, only a dragon could have such a hand. It would probably be no surprise to the reader that, on the following morning, Rebecca awoke to find a drawing nearby. It showed the Dragon's Hand in all its details of edges and inside network. It was a leaf from a silver maple tree.

And in this manner began a collection of poems and drawings, each girl trying to outdo the other by finding leaves of different shapes. The very next day, Mary left a leaf for Rebecca with a drawing. Although it was quite like the Dragon's Hand with jagged points, it differed in being broader and having short fingers. It was taken from a tree with tiny reddened buds that gave a bright blush to the early spring landscape. It was from a red maple. In the morning, there was a poem with another leaf sitting on the table.

Not always beauty takes a slender form
But oft is found in lesser view
The hand of one who's short and round
A Gnome, I think, it must be true.

The search for different leaves led to a contest of discovery and an ever-increasing stack of poems and drawings. The girls did not forget to look at the lesser trees, including yellow birch and apple. Trees brought from England only a few years before had grown higher than the treasure-seekers themselves. In their hunt, there was something that they both noticed: in the endless variety of shapes of leaves, all the leaves on one tree were exactly the same without exception, save for some differences in size.

Thomas looked at the collection in silence. Whatever his thoughts, he kept them to himself. But the following day, he handed Rebecca three leaves. There was a touch of self-satisfaction in his face with the hand-over. He insisted they came from the same tree! One leaf was a simple, single blade and, another, a smaller lobe in the center with narrower lobes on each side, as if a three-fingered creature. The third leaf was most curious of all; it was a perfect mitten! There were two lobes, a small one for the thumb and a large lobe for the rest of the fingers. The leaves, all from one tree, the sassafras, changed their thinking. So, not all trees had leaves with only one leaf-shape! Thomas had made his point.

Rebecca was eager to show the collection of poems and drawings to her parents. Her mother took a few moments to savor them all and returned a look of prideful approval. She appeared to recognize Thomas's three leaves. With a slight smile she brought from the kitchen some small branches that had such leaves. It was from the bark of this tree that she made a delicious tea.

Of course, the discovery of three kinds of leaves on the same tree was destined for poetry.

A leaf that has a pretty shape
Delights me like a furry kitten
But there are trees with many forms
A spoon, a glove, or just a mitten.

Her father took another view. He knew all the trees from which the leaves came. This tree made good firewood, burning easily without sparks, that tree made the best axe handles because the wood was more flexible. One tree made the strongest beams for houses. Another tree would, in another year or two, produce much-awaited fruit. He made special mention of the straight-growing tulip tree, praising its use for ships' masts, dug-out canoes, and house shingles. In addition, it had a beautiful, yellow tulip-like flower!

Surprises from the Forest

MARY DREAMED OFTEN. As most dreams are wispy and soon forgotten, hers were mostly visions of walking, dancing, or sometimes soaring through strange lands with strange faces. But always upon awakening she found herself safe on her bed. But one night in spring, her dream brought her to the stand of pine trees where she saw teams of horses and a royal carriage emerge from the fog-laden castle. All too real was the scent of pine and—faint but true—the musty scent of moss.

In the coming daylight she opened her eyes. Lying next to her was a patch of moss sprinkled with pine needles. Around the rim was a tight circle of tiny blue flowers. In the center of it all was a white rounded stone. She wondered if she were still dreaming.

She somehow knew that it was Rebecca's way of showing thanks for caring about her terrible condition. After all, Mary reasoned, it could not have been a birthday gift because none of the Adamses even knew that she had a birthday in this month of May. The scene of flowery moss was even more surprising because Rebecca, who seldom wandered past the confines of her home, must have gone into the forest to fetch everything.

But then she sensed a curious pattern developing. A week or two later, she awoke to find next to her an arrangement of ferns in a standing bouquet, and then a few days later, she found a sweet smelling garland of boughs and tiny white blossoms with black dots in the centers but no leaves! She remembered seeing such flowering bushes, called the shadbush, along the river. But to her knowledge, Rebecca was not known to visit riverbanks.

By now, Mary knew that she had to repay Rebecca in some meaningful way. A gift of a much-treasured piece would do. The birthday of the young poet was coming up. Mary wrote:

Dearest Rebecca,
Please accept this small string of beads brought from Littleton. It was gift to me on my fifteenth birthday. Now you soon be fifteen, I want you to have them. I know your family no believe in jewelry, but this simple string is meant to celebrate us, good friends. I also must thank you for lovely plant scenes left for me. The colors and smell I remember in England. Each one cheered me many days.
With much love, your friend always, Mary.

That evening Mary found a note on her pillow. It read:

Dear Mary,
Your string of beads is the most beautiful object I have ever seen. I hold the beads in every which way to watch how the sun plays off them in different colors and sparkles. I caress each one beneath my fingertips so that I have come to know all twelve by their feel. At night, I rest the string across my forehead and find that the cool feeling quickly summons the Sleep Magician. It is truly such a precious gift that I cannot think of words to thank you enough. I am also pleased that you enjoy the gifts of nature that somehow appear overnight, yet I must write that it was not I who left them.
Yours, always, Rebecca.

Mary was mystified by the last sentence.

Growing Village

IN THE BUSTLE of the settlement, Hartford was becoming a village. The warming days saw houses replacing crude huts. The cutting of trees into boards provided lumber. The rapid building of houses created an insatiable hunger for logs, firewood, and clay. Fortunately, the river bed contained an ample amount of clay, and soon newly-made kilns were turning out a continual supply of bricks and tiles. Foundations of houses and fireplaces were being built every day. Meanwhile, more people were arriving from the Bay Colony to work in the woodlands and tend to the kilns. The more people there were, naturally, the greater the need for additional houses. The plantation had become a village.

How joyful it is, Master Adams wrote on a reflective note to Mary, *to know that God hath looked with favor on our work. We now no longer need supplies from New Amsterdam. I feel that our little settlement is on the way to becoming a great city.*

Reading the note, Mary smiled. Surely, rough-hewn Hartford will become a fine city. She had been there almost at the start.[62]

At the same time, she had a sinking feeling. She had not foreseen the shock of knowing that Pieter would not return. Her longing to see him again after a long winter was futile. She had to move on with her life as a farmer. The days passed as she did her best to tend to her chores, forgetting—or trying to forget—the Dutch sailor.

Why, she mused, should she care so much about a person from another world, a person with barely a connection to her own life? She knew that as time went on, her mind would be less and less on him and that anticipating his return would no longer linger in her thoughts. But that way of thinking did not happen. Instead, his absence became more unbearable with each day. She did her best to keep these thoughts from the others, including Rebecca, but suspected that she could not hide what was troubling her.

Illness Next Door

THE BOUNTIES OF nature are the food of life. Yet, since the beginning of time, farmers who work the soil for food have feared the ravages of nature. Drought, flood, hail, swirling wind, or a swarm of insects can quickly destroy a season of labored harvest. A blizzard can pile up drifts of snow so high that milkers cannot get to their cows for days. A heavy-beamed house can be dashed in an instant by a falling tree, or by a flash in the sky or by an aberrant spark from the hearth. But of all the whims of nature, the one feared most was sickness.

Sickness can strike the healthiest with rude suddenness. It can affect one or all in a family. No one knows the cause. Remedies for any given illness—be they gentle or heroic—were plentiful, but there was little trust that they mattered at all. The Puritans believed that good health was a gift of God. Illness was His disapproval or warning for some errant thought or behavior. Haunting the sickbed, all too often, was the gloomy specter of death. Such a visitation was to come to Hartford late in the spring of 1640.

As evening fell, James Ensign, the neighbor to the east, returned from a trading journey to the mouth of the Great River. His nose was stuffed. By morning his sniffles had turned into soreness of the throat with aches, fever, and chills. He struggled to take a deep breath. As worrisome as it was, the crisis broke within three days. He regained his strength, and within another day joined others in the planting. Whatever was God's message in this affliction, all rejoiced at his recovery.

That was, however, not the end of the story. Within a week his four children developed fever and sore throats. Sarah, Rebecca's age and the oldest, was at first the most severely stricken. John, aged thirteen, and Anne, at eight years, had like symptoms but these were less severe.

William, a boy of ten years, posed the greatest worry. Burdened with wheezes since a small child, he now had great difficulty breathing. What is more, he felt his throat burning. Swallowing was painful.

In past years, it had fallen on Sarah to care for her younger siblings in all the ordinary household chores. Her mother, also named Sarah, did the best she could despite the crippling rheumatism that left her mostly chair-bound. In this desperate situation, their father, an outdoorsman, tried his best but proved quite inept at cooking, tending the sick, and tilling the garden.

Of course, an illness of the feverish kind could spread throughout the village like a brush fire. Expected of the first stricken family was to keep within the house until every member was free of illness. Neighbors helped by preparing food. Bread, dumplings, mutton, and milk, they left at the doorstep.

It was during the outbreak of sickness in the Ensign home that Mary became aware from the tense faces and the over-worked movement of mouths that some troubling words were spoken between Rebecca and her parents. Never had Mary seen such tension between Master and Mistress Adams and their sweet daughter.

Later that night she learned the cause of such bother. Rebecca wrote of the sickness at the neighbor's home. Sarah Ensign and she had been companions since early childhood and had shared the rigors of their trek from Cambridge. Sometimes during that terrible ordeal, they rode together on the same cow. Rebecca wrote of her plan to help Sarah and her family, more than just leaving something to eat. Her father thought it too dangerous to go into a stricken home. Her mother agreed but not so strongly. A night of reflection, the parents assumed, would give her time to think again about such a reckless plan.

By morning, Rebecca was more determined than ever to be with her friend. Mary was aware from appearances alone that the protests of her parents mattered not. Eventually, the Adamses realized that it was futile to hold Rebecca back; they accepted her stubbornness as "God's will." Mary, once understanding this titanic clash of opinions, insisted that she join Rebecca. On this matter, there was less resistance.

At midday, both girls boldly pushed open the neighbors' door and recoiled at what they saw. James Ensign, surprised yet grateful for their appearance, looked fatigued beyond words. Bent unnaturally on an improvised chair-bed, his wife raised a gnarled hand of greeting, clearly unable to satisfy the needs of her sick children. They lay sprawled about the room, rolled up in blankets and battling with their own choking and aching. Their ashen faces showed varying stages of the malignant fever. The remains of meals were scattered everywhere in the dimly lighted space.

In a frenzy of activity, Mary brought in firewood while Rebecca stoked the hearth until the room was brighter and warmer. They made porridge from cornmeal and stew with the meat and carrots that they had brought from their home. They applied heated, wet cloths to painful necks. They made the air easier to breath by the sweet aroma of sassafras bark steaming at the fireside. Bedclothes were scrubbed clean and quickly dried in a bountiful sun. All the while, the mother told of her regret for not being able to help. Only at night did the girls return home for a fitful sleep. They returned to the Ensign home early the next morning.

Happily, some ravages of illness began to abate within a few days. Sarah, John and Anne had reached a turning point, and now seemed to be recovering. On the other hand, William's condition worsened. He once even coughed up blood. He was grievously ill. He had quinsy.[63]

Reverend Hooker stopped by almost every day, staying for just a short time and keeping well-distanced between himself and the sick. He recited a short prayer for each patient's recovery. All knew that a shepherd must tend to his flock and that the shepherd must stay free of contagion.

As the days went on, John and Sarah gained strength while William weakened. His voice was lost, and his senses seemed to be in a state of torpor. Taking turns with almost constant coaxing, Rebecca and Mary were able to make the boy take a few sips of broth or a stew of rhubarb. Precious honey, reserved for just such an occasion, was tried with some success. They placed cool rags on his forehead and soothed his aching by rubbing his neck and arms. It was the best they could do.

What perplexed Mary was the absence of strong remedies. Surely back at her Manor House in Littleton, someone so very sick would already have been forced to take medicines that caused vomiting or otherwise rid the body of corrupt fluids. Bleeding, sometimes to faintness, was accepted as ordinary treatment for most illnesses. Leeches were commonly applied to remove blood painlessly. These customs, however, were not carried out in this Puritan settlement. The reason given by Rebecca was simple. Her people believed that some mild herbs and pleasing aromas were enough; they should not interfere with God's way of healing.

The coming and going of illness has its own velocity and through it all is the element of crippling boredom. That was something that Rebecca could remedy. She knew that recovery is faster if the mind is kept active and free of excitement and fear. Reading could help to pass the day. She had few books and, of course, there was the Bible from which she read random passages. With each reading of "The Lord is my Shepherd and I shalt not want...," the sense of hope was renewed. Then, there were her own poems, accumulated over the past years. These she read repeatedly as all gathered close. Poems of flowers just blossoming, a rising sun, a new baby, and cavorting squirrels—all of these brought a welcome cheer.

Mary, although left out of the readings, offered her own treasure of writings. These were the well-worn pages left by Pieter, with the puzzles, jokes, and stories that had amused her through many a winter's night. Now, with them in hand, Rebecca continued to brighten the Ensign household with hours of cheerful distraction.

William continued to struggle. On the fourth or fifth night of his illness, his body radiated with burning heat and glistening sweat. He began shivering enough to make his cot tremble. Leaving for home well into the night, Mary and Rebecca felt his cold hands and saw his blue nails. His pulse was weak and quick. Those brown eyes looked up soulfully at the two as if to apologize for all the trouble he had caused them. He managed to whisper, "I have two angels."

That night Rebecca, bone weary, kept a late candle as she worked on writing a cheer-up poem. By morning, however, she thought that nothing about the poem was good enough to read to William. She handed it to Mary with a gesture of tearing it to pieces. Mary read:

TO WILLIAM
Do you remember
the day we found the wild strawberries
or the times we jumped in stacks of hay
or the night we caught fireflies in a jar
and jumped in the river one hot day?

Do you remember
the first time you milked a cow
or when the pigs escaped their sty,
the family of skunks beneath the Easton's house
and Mary's face when a raccoon passed by?

Do you remember
when we said we'd build a raft
and float downstream to places new
and learn to shoot an arrow
like the Podunk boys knew?

Do you remember
all the things we did
all the things we said we want to do
and together we will see the world
and write a book about it, too?
Get better (despite my foolish poetry),
Your friend forever, Rebecca

Flying hands and a grand smile told Rebecca that her poem was heart-warming.

No, do not tear up the poem. Read to William, went Mary's lively gestures. *It will make him happy.*

On returning in the morning, the girls saw only crestfallen faces. During the night, the Lord had taken William. Mary and Rebecca saw the boy, still lying by the hearth on his makeshift bed, his face softer and his brown eyes looking straight up. His chest no longer heaved mightily against his throat. Rebecca laid her poem between William's folded hands.

The burial service was simple. It was meant to soothe the aching hearts of those left behind with thoughts of a happy past and the promise of an afterlife in Heaven. A wooden cross stood next to the grave with the name "William S. Ensign" and underneath was his time on earth: "1630-1640." Reverend Hooker spoke. He had no need to read from the Bible, for he had conducted enough services for a dead child to remember all the words. The deep faith in God of all who stood around the grave held them strong against painful reality.

On the following Sunday, the sermon ended with, "We pray to the grieving family for strength at this tragic time. We give thanks to God for his blessings and are glad that the pestilence has not spread throughout the colony. All but one lived through that terrible trial. We had known William for such a short time when he was taken away. The reason is known only to God, but He did favor us by sending two angels to help the stricken household."

The Reverend continued, "Yes, these angels sometime act in ways that we do not understand. Each one bears a burden of great weight yet bears it with grace and humbleness. In every way they could, these two girls brought solace and nurture to the Ensign household during this terrible affliction. For this, we must be eternally grateful."

Thoughts of life and death lingered in every mind. There had to be a message in William's fate, but it remained one of the great ancient mysteries. Rebecca could hardly wait to write to Mary that they had been elevated to angels.

The Return of Pieter

AFTER HER MORNING care of animals, Mary stepped out of the stable into the bright sunshine. Squinting against the glare, she saw before her a sight more improbable than in any flight of her wildest fantasy. Standing there was a big black horse and astride it sat Pieter! She looked up into a smiling face. It was the same face imagined so often during that long winter. Mary, awed, managed a timid smile. With that, Pieter leaned forward and reached down with an open hand. Mary took it and felt the warmth of her hand in his. At the same time, the medallion worn as a necklace swung forward. It was close enough to Mary's eyes for her to get a fleeting glimpse. Letters on a heart-shaped silver disc read KATRINA.

Suddenly, Mary froze. A cold rush came to her head and numbness to her feet. She ran to the house, rushed inside and up the ladder to the loft where she curled up beneath her blanket.

Thomas came to Mary bearing a letter from Pieter. She would not open it. Instead, fearing what it said, she tucked the letter beneath her pile of accumulated possessions. Her crushing disappointment was a chasm in which she was falling deeper and deeper like in a horrid dream. She refused to come for dinner. Rebecca's playful tugging caused not a stir. The blanket in which Mary rolled herself became a cocoon that did not know how to release its pupa.

On a night's reflections, Mary had come to the reality that Pieter for her was a dream. He had no obligation to her. All stories and riddles that had helped so immensely through the winter were a gift of friendship. They were meant for amusement. She should have no expectations beyond that. Anything more, she knew, was but an illusion. Pieter had another.

By morning, Mary accepted that her duties were important, and her life was useful. She had chosen this way, and she was resolved to do the best she could. There was no reason any more to think of Pieter. And so, at dawn, Mary was back in the stables with renewed determination. With buckets, hay fork, shovel, and brushes, her work was as meticulous as always. Perhaps the horse and cows, however, sensed some loss of vigor in her touch. Pieter's letter lay unopened and was soon forgotten.

CHAPTER 10

Summer

Under the Hot Sun

THE LONG DAYS of summer meant longer days for working. The household awoke early. Breakfast was soon dispatched. For Mary, tending the animals was no different but now there were chores in the fields. Planting and harvesting went on until dusk.

For reasons that suited Mary, she was not looked on in the usual way that girls and women were considered, but rather as a much-needed stable and field hand. The distinction was fine because she liked the touch and, as much, the smell of animals and newly upturned soil. Callouses on her hands were a measure of pride.

With hoe in hand, Mary followed the plough, placing seeds of corn just so far apart, just so deep and covered with just so much dirt. She had become quite expert with the sickle and after a while with the scythe. Her stack of straw was as high as any of the men's. She hefted an axe to trim new-fallen trees of branches with the expert knack of a barber. Where she drew the line was anything to do with the process of turning animals (sheep, pigs, chickens) into meat. She was thankful that dressing turkeys and deer was a man-only task. Cooking them, that was another matter.

In the cool of late day she enjoyed the solitude of sitting by the river until the sun had long set and the landscape had slowly donned its darkened mask. The first star appeared as expected, as if set by a clock, and just as mysteriously, fireflies began to flit about her head.

On the hottest nights of summer the children stayed outside their house until the loft was cool enough for sleeping. Sarah and Hannah coiled up on a blanket and soon fell asleep. If there was enough moonlight, Rebecca and Mary took turns braiding each other's hair, creating and undoing fanciful styles. Thomas hunkered down between the girls claiming that he was there to protect them from a wolf or mountain lion.

One day in late summer, Mary realized that something had happened to her. Quite simply, she had tanned. The darkened skin began just beyond the elbows and knees where her dress extended. A mirror told her of a similar change in her face and neck. What was so extraordinary to her (but evidently not to anyone else in the plantation) was that she no longer had the porcelain white complexion that so embodied her hereditary position.

Mary had always assumed that being of very light skin separated all those who belonged to manor houses from the servants. The shade of skin color, in her mind, separated the social classes. People with the darkest skin of all came from lands far away. She gave no thought to the fact that members of the nobility had little exposure to the sun, whereas workers were continually exposed. Even domestics indoors, although less dark in complexion, had chores enough with washing and hanging clothes, scrubbing and sweeping that the sun saw much of them. Now, there was a new realization: darker skin was earned.

Eyes of the Devil

THOMAS PERFORMED HIS work as a woodsman or stable hand as best he could, even though he was half the men's size. The men spoke well of his labor, although they hardly got to know him. "Not talkative," they said. At home, he seldom spoke a word. Even so, he was not idle. The boy kept occupied looking over his boxed collection of small objects, mostly rocks of odd shapes and color. With a scrap of leather, he polished his treasures as if readying them for a royal festival. Of course, all were curious to know what was so interesting, but Thomas zealously guarded his collection from roving eyes.

One time when the family was inside, Mary noticed something quite unusual about him. When her eyes turned to him, he suddenly looked away. At first, she did not pay much attention, but as time went on, she realized that his eyes had often been fixed on her, only to flick somewhere else the instant she looked in his direction. At first, she felt flattered, but soon found his attention annoying. What was he thinking? Did others see this? Over time, the problem resolved itself; Mary simply ignored his glances.

One late afternoon turned out to be most unusual. It was one of those rare occasions when Mary and Thomas found themselves without others in the house. Mother, baby and the twins were away visiting a neighbor who had just recently given birth. Rebecca and friends were off to find blueberries along the edge of the woodland. While dozing in the loft, Mary felt a sudden chill; Thomas had removed the oiled cloth from the window. Now, a beam of the lowered sun streamed into the loft and fell directly onto his mystery box. Thomas beckoned Mary toward it. Wearily, she approached. Once she was there, he flung open the cover. Inside under the unflinching sunlight was an astounding sight.

Mary looked down at a collection of rocks, perhaps a hundred or more, some round, others flat, many oval and all of various shapes, textures, and colors. Some were gray rocks with countless glittering points like the stones that graced the front of St. Mary Magdalene Church in Littleton. Among the rocks were other assorted items: skulls of small animals, a turtle shell, an antler, and a bundle of colorful, long feathers, perhaps from the tail of a pheasant. In one corner, there was a folded page of brown paper.

The collector reached into the box and, with both hands, gingerly lifted out something that was flat and very black. With a wide sweep of his long arms he raised the object toward the open window. Mary could see that it was only a cake of dried mud about the size and shape of a herring: pointed on one end, tapered on the other end, and thin as a plate.

Thomas offered the object for Mary to hold. This she did. *Anything more ordinary,* she thought, *could not be.* If there were something special about it, she was completely baffled. Try as best she could, Mary was unable to comprehend the strangeness of it all. Was this a kind of joke? But Mary could see in the tenderness of his expression and the innocence of his manner that the boy had no mischief in mind. Clearly, this object in its ordinariness held some power that had deep meaning for him.

Mary held the object in both hands and noticed, on closer inspection, that there were two tiny rounded bumps at one end of the slab. These were of the same dull gray-black hue as the rest of the slab, and surely of no special interest.

Mysteriously, Thomas went to the smoldering hearth where he set a small candle afire and then held it close behind the slab of dried mud. Almost unbelievable was the action that followed.

Those two dull bumps instantly sprang into life, becoming a brilliant red and glowing as if each had burst into flame. Mary gasped. Her arms stiffened as if they were frozen solid.[64]

Not believing her own eyesight, Mary moved the slab away from the flame, and the bumps were once again no more than dark bumps on a dark plate. Again, she held it to the light. And again, both nubs radiated crimson red. A most common thing—a drab piece of river mud—had suddenly turned into stars in a midnight sky. She was certain that no gemstone in the jewelry box of her mother ever shined so brightly! No roaming magician seen at the Church Square in England ever performed such an amazing trick!

Were these the eyes of the devil peering from a stone fish? Mary knew enough of Puritan beliefs; the devil had eyes everywhere. She began to feel a penetrating, unavoidable power that those eyes were peering deep into her soul. Could it be that the flattened piece of dried mud held the power in which Satan could see what evil lurked inside her being? She felt at once both fascinated and vulnerable at the prospect. Misdeeds of the past suddenly flashed to mind. Now, even the devil knew about the counting horse and riding sidesaddle. Her whole body, from feet to crown, began to shake. All the while, the smile of Thomas, looking on intently, turned even broader. The moment was even more bewildering because of the simple fact that Mary had never seen Thomas smile before.

If the experience had not been enough to test Mary's capacity for astonishment, Thomas motioned as if to say, "This is my gift to you." Stunned, Mary held onto the slab with one hand and placed the other still trembling hand on his shoulder. The boy responded by putting his hand on hers. The touch lasted no more than a heartbeat, but there was no mistaking that there was some inexplicable attachment between the two.

Mary could not bring herself to accept such a precious item. *No,* she willed, *Thomas, you must keep it.* But Mary was to find out how persistent Thomas could be. She felt compelled at last to accept the eyes of the devil in a fish-shaped stone. That night she laid it gingerly beside her pillow, then covered it with her paper so that it would not stare at her through the night.

But the story of the awesome slab could not end there. On the following morning before leaving the house to feed the animals, Mary left her gift next to sleeping Thomas's mat. A note alongside read,

> *My Dear Boy Thomas,*
> *The gift you give me too precious. I feel not worthy. I return your stars in a piece of mud to you. It truly beautiful. Please know I will always treasure the close view of your night sky. That is enough for me.*
> *Your friend forever, Mary*

Shaking Tree

One afternoon Mary stopped on a level ridge where the grassy edge sparkled green under a bright sun. There, atop Angel, Mary looked down on a broad river in one direction and at a broad stand of fir trees in another direction. She dismounted and found the ground dry and invitingly warm for a short nap and where Angel could nibble on the thick growth. It was a peaceful scene on a clear day without a breath of wind.

Before she could close her eyes, she spotted something quite extraordinary: the top of a fir tree in the valley was quivering. Then it stopped, becoming as still as the other tree tops around it. The shaking, curiously, started again, and then stopped again. Start. Stop. Other treetops did not shake. Thought Mary, could there be a strong wind in one small place? But wind, she knew, does not act in such a way. There must be an explanation. Of course, she was bound to find that answer.

Afoot, Mary shuffled her way down the side of the ridge. Angel, not far behind, had more trouble finding space for hooves among the jumble of boulders. Once on level ground, they made their way into the forest toward the mysterious tree. Suddenly they came face-to-face with a huge black bear standing up on hind legs, its back rubbing against a tree. With legs now like frozen sticks, Angel stopped. Mary, too, was frightened. She had never seen a bear before. All three remained motionless and stared at each other for an instant as if they were posing for a famous sculptor.

The bear dropped to all fours. Mary was struck by the beauty of the animal, its thick coat of black fur glistening in the dappled sunlight. The bear, with mouth gaping and eyes opened wide, seemed surprised, too, by the intrusion. Wasn't Mary admired for her special gift of stepping into a pack of agitated hunting dogs and calming them with gentle motions of hands?

When she was but a few steps away, the bear rose on its hind legs and came to full standing. It looked down at the girl, sniffed, and cocked its head to one side. It finally came back down, turned, and ambled away into the underbrush. For an instant, Mary thought her heart had stopped altogether. Soon, she felt a heavy, rapid beating. With the near crisis averted, she quickly mounted Angel to continue their outing, this time with an awareness of what can cause a solitary fir tree to shake; nevertheless, she felt a trifle guilty for interrupting a bear that just wanted to enjoy a good back scratch.

The Tyranny of Noise

Rebecca was experiencing another cycle of excessive activity, then withdrawal, then headache. She was now in her fifth day of an incapacitating headache. Mary once again appealed to her to share her changing moods.

> *Dear Rebecca,*
> *You suffer much. We who love you suffer, too. I not help you but most eager to. Write me about your feelings in awful times before the headache comes. We may find answer to what starts them. I think you not foolish, nor ever will. My parents thought me foolish for not speaking before they found my ears not hearing. Do tell me all. What I ask is from bottom of my soul. Remember that I have a burden that will never go away, that leaves me lonely and misunderstood. I often try to think of what it is like to hear anything at all, but know in my heart that will never happen. We have what nature has given us, the good and the afflictions. I only ask you to share your condition with me.*
> *From Mary*

On awakening the following morning, Mary found two sheets of paper alongside her bed. Her friend had responded with a poem. As she read with still sleepy eyes, she found the title amazing and the simple words astonishing.

ODE TO SILENCE
To see a budding laurel plant
And watch a hawk soar high above
A distant clouded mountain top
Of colors, motion, beauty the eye dost love.

To smell the scent of fresh-cut sassafras
And know the scent of rambling rose
Or fragrance of a meadowed breeze
Pure delight it brings the nose.

To taste the sap of maple tree.
And sip a tea of peppermints
A porridge steeped with berries blue
Will paint the tongue with joyful tints.

To stroke a blade of pasture grass
Or baby's flushed cheek to feel
The sense of fine linen across the face
Brings to touch a blessing real.

Such a mastery of words! The second page left Mary stunned to the core.

To wake by rooster caw in early morn
A child's cry of endless needs annoys
The wheels of wagons squeal on rutted roads
My ears but bring me only noise.

To hear the words of preacher stern
Or distant sounds a cruel musket's voice
And pigs at slaughter's hopeless squeal
Allow no moment to rejoice.

When thunder tells of lightning strikes
And crows of stolen seeds of corn sing grace
How blessed are they who do not hear
And so, escape into a kinder, silent place.

Mary read the poem in disbelief. Then, having read it several times more, she struggled to grasp its true spirit. The words were simple. The thought behind them was not. Rebecca did not write about her awful times but rather hinted that Mary's "burden" was in truth a blessing. Was her poem saying that the very sense that Mary lacked and could never know was the very one that troubled her?

For Mary, this gift of hearing—or rather its absence—separated herself from the rest of the world of people. For everyone else, it was more than some quivering in the legs that is felt when the blacksmith's hammer strikes an iron rod. It somehow helped to connect people through talking. Yet, for Rebecca, this same wonderful ability that Mary could not imagine was a dreadful affliction. Did her friend find that hearing certain things led to pain? Did loud sounds have something to do with the start of the headaches? Mary believed that there could be no other meaning. She begged Rebecca to tell her more.

There came another recurrence a few weeks later. Perhaps it was the ferocity of the attack that prompted her to write of it. Mary found in the morning alongside her pillow a long letter:

To my dearest friend, Mary
You asked about these terrible feelings. Here is what they are like as best as I can tell. I beg that my telling will go no farther than between you and me. Remember your promise not to think me mad or worse?

Most times I feel as free and content as a puffy cloud passing by. Then, on another day, I want to do everything. I cannot sit still and I cannot sleep. Then I can feel my body slowing down. I want only to be left alone in a dark and quiet corner. Then I begin to have strange sensations, like floating through the air, seeing whirling colors and smelling scents, like apricot, remembered from long ago. At times, I hear screeching as if someone were falling off a cliff. I try to tighten up my body into a little ball, and that helps a little to block out everything.

My headaches feel like the steady cracking of a woodcutter's axe. Should you have any thoughts on how to soften these blows, I will not fully give up hope. Please do not give up on me.
Rebecca.

The reply:

Rebecca, you favor me with description. I honored by share with me. Now I try to understand. I promise we find a way to soften woodsman's blows. Know from my heart I think you not mad and not beyond reason.
With all my love, Mary

Finding no immediate way to fulfill her promise to help, Mary could do little more than dwell gloomily on her letter. On a long, aimless exploration with Angel, however, a new idea came to her. Words formulated in her mind: Rebecca has taken every remedy imaginable that might have relieved her headache. Instead, we should look for something that comes before them and may cause them. Could these offenses be avoided? Where to start? Her poem! She hurried back to the house, finding it where she had left it, tucked beneath her sleeping mat.

In her poem Rebecca wrote of the joys of sight, of smell, of taste, of feeling. But for hearing, it was all noise, and noise was unpleasant. Sounds that spared Mary by deafness clearly bothered Rebecca, enough to write of them so vividly.

Suppose, thought Mary, *noises were taken away?* Would that make a difference? The thought of removing the noises that bothered Rebecca was, indeed, an amazing idea! A note to Master Adams was necessary. Here was the paradox of a girl who had never experienced the sensation of sound advising that sound be avoided to cure a terrible affliction in another. After some discussion with Mistress Adams and some looks of doubt, Master Adams jotted at the end of Mary's note,

> *Mary, Yes, certainly, we should do that! God knows that we have tried all other means. Some things here that make noise we can change. I must get all to agree at our village meeting. I have faith that your ideas may help. We have failed to find anything better. Also, you should know that the rumors about Rebecca are becoming ever uglier, to our growing worry. J.A.*

Aura

A NOTE FROM Rebecca appeared next.

> *Dear Mary,*
> *Since you want to know all about my condition, I will add just one more thing. It is about the odd things I see before the head pain begins. Noise is but a part of what I feel at the beginning.*
>
> *Light is painful to my eyes. Colors change from one moment to another. A candlelight will have a halo around it. A solid object such as a milk pitcher appears zigzagged. Most frightening of all, and here you will think me totally insane, is that parts of things disappear. Last night, half of Father's face was gone. The kettle hung at the hearth was only half there. All this before the head pain begins!*
>
> *So, there you have the entire story, dear Mary. Think of me with a stone in the head. I can accept that, but the loss of your friendship would grieve me more than my miserable soul could bear.*
> *Rebecca.*

Suspicion

AFTER RETURNING LATE one afternoon from a visit to the stable, Mary found a letter from Master Adams. Written on many pages, the letter had a foreboding feel to it. What she read left her trembling in disbelief:

> *To Mary,*
> *Mistress Adams agrees that I share with you a state that brings us grave vexations of the mind. People in the village have noticed the changes in the behavior of Rebecca. You have seen her at times wandering, talking wildly, gesticulating as if mad. At other times, they find her drawn into herself so that she speaks to no one, sitting for long periods in silence. We know that these moods are somehow connected to her headaches.*
>
> *But people are thinking that Rebecca's actions bode no good, that somehow Satan has penetrated her soul and will force her to take evil actions. What fueled the fire was a report by some children; they saw you and Rebecca using hands for talking, being ignorant of the real reason. Rumor now has it that you may be the devil's agent who has possessed Rebecca with powerful magic. Some say you are hatching up a hex on the plantation or against their household. I grieve to tell you this.*
>
> *People keep their children away from Rebecca. They fear that she may turn their cows into large and dangerous dogs and other such nonsense. These strange notions are why we try to keep Rebecca in the house all we can, most especially during those difficult times that come before her aching of the head.*
>
> *And so, the truth is that word has spread that Rebecca is a witch and that you, dear Mary, may be the devil's agent. Deaf and dumb ('dumb'—a word that people call those who do not talk) have always raised this suspicion. We know not how deeply this is believed among our neighbors. Our good friend, the Reverend Hooker, has done what he can to protect us from this vicious idea,*

but he cannot convince all. You know that Puritans hold their beliefs strongly. If enough of our neighbors, who are good people, come to think of you and Rebecca as witches, I fear for the outcome.

Mary, we now seek your most gracious help against this terrible wrong. Mistress Adams and I look on you as goodness. You are the one person who knows that our daughter is neither evil nor spiteful, nor are you in any way responsible for her odd behavior. It is true that we do not understand the reason, but we turn to you for wise council in this matter. It is also true that her writing poetry rather than reading the Bible is a form of idleness. Idleness, we know, tempts the action of the devil. Perhaps you can find a way to unlock the mystery of our precious daughter. We feel with our deepest passion that Satan has no place in her soul. Still, rumors of suspicion leave Mistress Adams and me shaken. Should you advise us in any helpful way to resolve this unkindest notion, we would be forever grateful.

In the protection of our Lord and Savior, J.A.

"Witch" was not a word that Mary knew. It did not come up in the hand language of Sky Flower nor in the exercises of the tutors at the Manor House. An answer to her inquiry about its meaning came in a new letter from Master Adams.

Dear Mary,

I will try to explain the meaning of a witch. Since the beginning of Time, Satan has done his best to upend the magnificent works of God by various wiles and devices. One of his treacheries has been to enter the soul of living people who will then act as agents of evil. The most vulnerable to fall victim to this power are women, aged and in poverty with no living husband to defend them and who in some way have offended God. The other most likely victims are girls who in all innocence are taken over by the wicked power of the devil. In Boston, even a man in his most productive years was found to be possessed. The devil then disguises the afflicted agents and, at night, transforms them into roving beasts: a wolf, toad, or some other animal that has power to accomplish strange things against ordinary nature. These people possessed with powerful but hidden mischief are witches. It is sometimes said that even the witch is unaware of being possessed.

There is ample evidence here in Hartford that Satan's frightful work is being carried out by witches. Remember the gust of wind that blew off a roof but ten days ago, the sudden swelling of the river over its banks, the terrible illness in a healthy child, and the poisoning of food that plays havoc in a whole family. Our neighbor, Mistress Easton awoke one morning finding bruises around her neck. These were witch marks from a large, black cat that came through a window during the night and lunged at her throat, so claims her husband. The sudden paralysis of an arm or leg, and sometimes both, in a strong man of great piety is also well known. Such stories are too plentiful to dismiss as merely fancy.

Mary, you come from a place that offers great safety against unseen evil. Here along the Great River, we sit at the edge of wilderness, with savages running loose in the nearby forest, wild and hungry animals howling at night, under the noses of the unpredictable Dutch, no army to protect us and agents of the devil in disguise flitting within our midst. The only remedy that we have against those so possessed with mischievous powers is through prayer and knowledge of the Scriptures. Hard work is our bastion against evil and the Bible, our perfect Salvation. Idleness, on the other hand, creates a perfect opportunity for the entrance of Satan into the soul. You must now understand our worry about

Rebecca and her passion for poetry, words for the sake of words.
J.A.

For Mary, the news came as if the sky had fallen. The writer of such delicate poetry! She, who finds joy in the faintest aroma of a leaf or the soft fur of a rabbit, who shares her thoughts in beautiful words, as a great artist would paint a waterfall. Rebecca, a witch? No, it was not possible.[65]

Prevention

Mary's plan, presented to the village council, was met with much skepticism. Yet, Rev. Hooker spoke strongly in its favor of limiting noise that might affect Rebecca. After a stormy discussion and much persuasion by the Reverend and a particularly zealous Master Adams, the council agreed to try to soften the sounds of a village, at least for a time.

How to be rid of noise? Here was the strange irony that the idea came from someone who had no perception of noise. The task was left to others to carry on. Once the idea was spread around, keeping quiet was pursued with uncommon zeal. Crying children were soon attended to. Rebecca's family learned to speak softly, not a difficult demand for her mother, but surely difficult for her father, famous for his strong expressions of opinion expressed in his powerful voice. Pots and dishes were scrubbed with delicate handling. Churning to make butter was slowed to prevent any squeals of the paddle.

The chicken coop was moved to another side of the village. Roosters were no longer allowed to run free. The awful squeals that attended the transition of animals to meat were heard now only on the far side of the shed. Practice with firearms would no longer take place within earshot of the Adams house. Wheels were greased more often; wagons took the long way around the Adams house. No axes would ring out within hearing distance. Alas, the booming voice of a visiting preacher could not be changed. On days that an itinerant minister came to preach, Rebecca could be excused from the service on promise that she would read certain passages from the Bible. Of course, there was no way to avoid hearing the thunder. One of the council members advised that Rebecca stuff her ears with beeswax whenever a storm threatened.

Although Mary did not notice all these changes, she did notice that Rebecca was free of headache pain for another month, and then, not again for another three months. The anguish that the Adams family had experienced for so long was replaced by the joy coming from Mary's advice. The miracle did not go unmentioned by the Sunday worshipers.

Joyful Things

JULY CAME AND with it, a ship, but not the Dutch ship. *The Vagabond* had returned. Such excitement it brought to the people of Hartford! First to leave the ship were a dozen or so passengers. All were adults, each intoxicated with the joy of arrival that did not mask the grunge and scarcities from weeks of ocean travel. The gathering to meet them remained orderly and quiet until thankful prayers for a safe journey were offered. Hugs and news from home came soon after.

This time, there were no animals. Cargo piled up at dockside. There were crates and boxes, large and small. Last to come off the ship were sacks of mail containing long awaited news from home. Names were called out and an outreached hand readily grasped each letter. A large envelope was handed to Mary. She felt her heart jumping out of her chest on seeing her name on it. Hardly could she wait until there was a secluded time to open it. But first came the discovery of things brought by the ship.

The opening of goods addressed to the Adamses was exhilarating for everyone. Even Mistress Adams broke into a half smile on seeing her husband unpack a rocking chair from a crate. In a box was a huge iron pot along with some cups and plates of pewter. There were knives and a much-needed pair of scissors. Blankets and woven clothes were tightly packed in another box. On top were some sheets of cured cowhide for making shoes. There was a pair of already made shoes, these for the delighted Thomas. They were made of thick leather that came well over the ankles and had thick soles. They were tied with long laces of hide. A smaller box held a spinning toy and a cloth doll with a delicately painted porcelain face. At the bottom of the crate, they found a small book for Rebecca. It was the biggest surprise of all, a book of poems by famous English writers. All were items paid for by Master Adams, whose instructions and requests had been taken to England a few months earlier. All had gone as planned with the return of *The Vagabond.*

News from Home

THE TIME FOR reading her letters from home had to wait until after the evening meal, after the scrubbing of dishes and not before the final prayer for the day. The first letter Mary read was the one on top. It was from her father.

31 May 1640
Dearest Mary
Can it be almost a year since the return of your ship, The Vagabond*? Not long after it sailed from view, the owner of the ship, Master John Throckmorton, met me by chance with the distressing news that the destination was not the Bay Colony. It was a new plantation a long distance up a river. Master Throckmorton reassured me that the colony was thriving and there was no need to worry about my daughter. His apology in the humblest manner for forgetting to tell me before the ship's departure was hardly enough to overcome my deep anger at the oversight. Until word came by way of the ship's return of your safe passage, my life was in a state of great turmoil. During this time, I fretted about your having properly cooked food, shelter from the harsh elements, and safety from People of the Forest. I still am most concerned about your welfare.*
Your mother and I are forever grateful for the generosity of Master and Mistress Adams to take you in. Please convey my promise to do the same for him should any of his children have reason to come to Littleton.

You will find in a separate little parcel some of your favorite sweets. You will also see some dried fruit that Harold knows you like. Harold asks about Angel. The King has sent a troop of cavalry to Scotland where a rebellion has arisen. What a fine and noble addition Angel would be to our loyal, mounted men-at-arms! I think you would be very proud if she were part of this fine cavalry.

It was here in the reading of her father's letter that Mary felt a sudden chill. She felt her heart come to a stop, and it took a deep breath to bring it back to life. *Angel going to war!* she spoke in silence. *No, never!*

There was more.

Arthur had two new colts to break in. He told me that he tried your gentle way of teaching a young horse, but he has much to learn about your touch in this matter. He hopes you will return soon to help him with all the horse training.

Through misty eyes, Mary read on.

Please see that The Vagabond *returns to England with a letter from you. With my fondness for you and my deep concern over your situation, I remain, Your loving father.*

Another letter came from Mary's sister, Veronica.

31 May 1640
To my dearest ever sister Mary,
I have the most wonderful news to tell you! Oh, you will be thrilled to know that Amanda will marry next month! We can barely wait. They say her intended is quite rich. She is nearly agog with the preparation. I have already had made a proper dress for me, having pleated collar and cuffs. There is also a pretty sash at the waist. You would love the colors, light green with yellow accents.

As for life in Littleton, you may remember the Stevenson boy, Robert, who lives in Shepperton. He has grown up to be a rather handsome lad, standing quite straight in his military uniform despite his low rank. He comes here to the Manor House once a week, picking wildflowers for me all along the way. I think he is jealous of Archibald. "Archi," we call him, is here often enough that I quite ignore him, much to his displeasure and to my wicked pleasure.

We visit our cousins in London nearly every month. Meanwhile, I have a new dog, a little one I have named "Sniffy" (for no particular reason). Of course, I take full care of him. As you can tell, I have been busy with all. The only sad news to send is that Gwendolyn has died. Father, however, has promised to bring us a new bird. He waits for the next ship coming from the West Indies. If you could only have known how Mandy and I loved the "chirp, chirp" from the cage over our playroom! This time, I hope the ship returns with one not the color of yellow.

Do you remember the servant from the colonies we named Gwendolyn? Oh, we laughed so much over that joke, giving her the name of our canary. Of course, I miss you immensely and hope that you have suitable service and are not endangered by the wild people there who run about in the forest. Please write to me as soon as you can. I cannot wait to hear from you.
Your loving sister, Veronica

The third letter was the most surprising of all, from Mary's mother.

31 May 1640
Dearest Mary,
We hope our letters will reach you soon. You should know that your father has been in good health since your absence, aside

from his losing more teeth. I, myself, have been plagued with the persistent itching disease from those scaly patches. It has traveled from my arms to my knees. There are even patches on the back of my neck. The doctor has given me a black tar ointment. It is ugly, but it seems to help. No matter, we do hope that you remain in good health.

I am pleased with your sisters. Amanda will be wed in July, only a few weeks away. When you receive this letter, she will probably have already gone to her new home in Newcastle, a town to the far north where much coal is found. Her husband-to-be is the eldest son of a well-to-do owner of mines. They live in a grand mansion overlooking the River-upon-Tyne. At the same time, Veronica has several courtiers and seems content with their fawning attention. You know how she likes to flirt. It is only a matter of time before she brings us news of a wedding.

Charles, now in his 16th year, has become skillful with the arrow. His marksmanship at archery won him an award at the county fair in Surrey. Much to our concern, he still refuses to go near a horse or fire a gun. He seems to care not about becoming a proper gentleman but only on game playing. Your father is distressed about this manner, but has slowly become resigned to the disappointment. Charles plans to enlist in the King's Footguard. That way he proudly wears a bright red tunic with a tall bearskin hat and carries a large gun with spear at the end. In the guard, he knows that he will look the part but will never have to point and fire his weapon.

So, as you can see, there are no unexpected changes at the Manor except for one: ME. That is, how much I miss you. Your sisters have done what was expected of them, and, I fancy, little more. Your brother has not lived up the expectations of a Walsingham man.

I have slowly come to realize that if anything interesting happened around the Manor House, somehow you had something to do with it. That we did not even think of your affliction during those early years of your mischief-making continues to haunt me. Alas, I never expressed my gratitude to that Indian girl for discovering the reason. And little did I appreciate how smart you were. I now think that my failure to recognize something different and wonderful in you was pure snobbery. All else at the Manor House, now to me, seems boring. Yes, I must tell you in all honesty that if anyone has changed, it is I.

I long to receive a letter from you. Please know that I am proud of you and await with most heart-felt anxiety your early return to a home much in wanting for your presence.

With all my love, Mother

Of the three letters, this was the one that forced Mary think about a decision of some importance. Should she return to her life as she had always known it? Her mother's change of heart reached deep into her own. After all, a family, no matter how imperfect, is still a family. Her one misgiving would be forcing Angel to undertake such a terrible voyage. Leaving the horse behind, of course, was unthinkable. Yet, how could she expose Angel to that agony again? How could she leave Rebecca? Mary was becoming ever more aware that Thomas, too, was hiding a special fondness for her. And what of Pieter? Such thoughts would begin to haunt Mary.

The Podunks, Again

On a cool late afternoon day, and unmindful of the waning daylight, Mary found herself riding north along the Great River. There the hills stood boldly against the sky. What better place to look over the river and the plantations that straddled its shores! With no trail to follow, she simply kept Angel on an upward path. Near the peak of the highest hill, she stopped for an unbroken, breathtaking, view of the entire valley below. The sun just past setting and red clouds lay across the entire horizon. It was a painting, she promised herself, for another day. And there she dallied too long.

Daylight quickly turned to dusk and dusk into twilight. There was no path on which to return. The contours of the hills confused any sense of direction. With increasing darkness and the coming of a drizzling rain, Mary felt a shivering chill. Even Angel, who had an uncanny nose for finding a way back, snorted with indecision. Mary, increasingly fretful, chose to walk, leading Angel downward. She did not know that they were heading away from her village.

As they felt their way downhill, Mary smelled smoke, and thought it was coming from the many chimneys of Hartford. Now groping her way through the darkened forest, she expected to find familiar ground. Instead, she came upon a head-high fence made with stakes driven into the ground. Between a row of stakes were tightly threaded branches. Reddish light came from cookfires just behind the thicket fence.

Mary had come to an Indian village. Sharp barking had aroused the Indians. They soon swarmed around the shivering girl and her horse and led her through a narrow opening of the fence to the inside. A wolf with bared teeth greeted her but held its ground. Scattered around were small fires in open pits, illuminating domed huts beyond.

The stranger was shown a place to sit by one of the fires. She felt a blanket being wrapped around her. A cup of warm broth was placed in her shaking hand. Angel stood within arm's reach.

Safe for the time, Mary thought about her good fortune on stumbling upon the Indian village. She was also aware of her folly in getting lost. She thought, too, about the worry her absence may be having on those who cared for her.

In the flickering light, Mary recognized one of the traders by the three black stripes on each cheek. She now knew then she had come to the village of the Podunks. In a flash she remembered what Sky Flower had taught her about talking-hands. These men may understand. She would try. Her hands tried to say,

I give thanks for your kindness. Foolish me. Lost.

Against the firelight, another of the Indian traders returned with hand-speak, *We know you. We know horse, too. You rest here.*

The small fires gave enough light to see high racks of drying fish. Posts with hanging furs were scattered here and there. Now, Mary was able to gather her first close-up view of Indian houses. They were made with the bark of trees and held together with vines. How, she wondered, could people get through a winter in such flimsy houses?

While many gathered around Mary to take a close look, it was Angel who attracted more attention. The children, who had never seen such a large animal so close before, flocked around the horse. Some even dared reach up and touch her flank or neck. Angel seemed to bear it all with patience.

Once her cup of broth was empty and seeing that Angel had water, Mary was led by a woman to one of the wigwams.

There she was handed a smock of soft leather and bid to shed her soaked clothes. She would pass the night, sleeping in a warm and dry wigwam. Mary was aware of other people lying nearby but did not know how many. Noticeable was the absence of the smell of people. For her, there was one bear skin to lie on and one for cover. Her riding blanket she rolled up for a pillow. Mary's last thought before sleep was about the favor of being in an Indian village. No one else from the settlement, as far as she knew, had ever been in one. So here she was, a pampered girl from an English manor, clothed in an Indian gown and sleeping among the savages. Her smile was counterbalanced by a gnawing anxiety about her absence in Hartford. The struggle in her mind soon lapsed into a wandering dream.

Come morning, Mary emerged from the now empty wigwam, blinked into the daylight where the grass all around glistened with early dew. Fires were aglow beneath large English kettles. Her clothes hung nearby. Curiously, there was no one in sight. A quick look to the far side of the village, however, found people crowded together. Soon back in her own dried clothes, Mary made her way toward the crowd.

Everyone had gathered around a stream where water spilled over split rocks to form a cascade. The water then flowed into a widened pool of slow-moving water. Mary had seen some bewildering sights since she left her Manor House in Littleton but was little prepared for the one now before her eyes. Caring not for lack of clothing, men, women, and children plunged into the pool. They stood shoulder deep in the water, laughing, splashing and scrubbing their bodies with some sort of tallow. For all in the chilling water, it was a quick, happy dip.

After someone spotted Mary, all beckoned her to join them. The more she hesitated, the more insistent was the urging. Casting life-learned propriety to the wind, she put her clothes aside and plunged into the frigid water. She felt the shock as her whole body seemed to tighten, then shrink to half its normal size. In another moment, there was a calmness in a way that she had never felt before. A quick scrub with tallow. A rinse. She bounded out of the pool.

With teeth chattering and goose-bumped arms gripping around herself, she saw the Indians clapping, cheering for her pluck. For Mary, it was the proudest moment she had ever known. She had done something and was admired for it! If only her mother could see her now! No, on second thought, that was a terrible idea.

Soon air-dried and clothed, Mary joined in on a cornmeal mush topped with honey. Happy and fretful at the same time, she could delay her return to Hartford no longer. Mary gave thanks and said goodbye. But not before a familiar small boy showed her how clever he was with a ball on a string. He popped the ball into the cup repeatedly with unfailing skill. Yes, he was the boy who came with the traders.

Despite her splendid welcome, Mary knew that she had to be making her way home. Two of the Indians would accompany Mary and Angel part way. As they left, excited children lined the pathway to take one last, admiring look at a horse. What Mary noticed was the field of still standing stalks of corn. Even in the planting, there was a cultural difference with the English way. Indian planted corn not in neat rows but in bunches. Mary saw mixed shoots of beans that climbed to the tops of the corn stalks. Broad leafed plants covered the ground and between them lay some orange pumpkins.

Their escorts took Mary and Angel as far as the crest of the hill from where they could see the river and the clearing where the

English village lay. Finding home from there would be easy, what the English call "like falling off a log." Musing on her cold bath, she thought she had learned the secret of why the Podunks carried no odor, not as her countrymen do.

Upon returning, Mary was eager to tell all about being in an Indian village, but her return was not embraced cheerfully. Rather, it was met with concern and relieved sighs from all.

Though a bit ruffled in the face, Master Adams quickly scribbled a note.

Mary, We worried through the night of your absence, not knowing where to begin to look. You are free in the village to do as you like. All we ask is that you tell us before you wander off. J.A.

His note was terse, but it made the point.

Her written reply:

Master Adams. I sorry cause you worry. Silly me. Angel and I went too far. Lose our way. Indians at the village cared for me most kindly. I promise as you ask. Mary

That same night, she found that he had added some words to the bottom of the page:

Again, I urge you to keep some distance between you and the Podunks and the rest of the Indians. We are at peace now, but you never know when they will fall on us. I fear their true intents. J.A.

On a fresh piece of paper, Mary left a note on the table.

Dear Master Adams, The Podunks kind to Angel and me. They are peaceful. Have they harmed our village in any way?

She was eager to find an answer. On climbing down from the loft on the following morning, she found her note still there. Added to the bottom were the words, *No. We have had no trouble with them, but we cannot be too careful.*

Mary had no response. She knew only that she had been given the privilege of spending a night in the Podunk village.

With August soon coming to an end, the settlers took stock again of their foodstuffs and supplies for the upcoming winter. Master Adams hoped the Dutch boat would arrive soon. They needed boards to close the stable for the winter. Mary, too, longed for return of the *Visarend.*

Gift from Rebecca

WITH THE LESSENING of her headaches, Rebecca felt wholly indebted to her friend. She could think of no way to show her gratitude. Perhaps a token would be to give her a much better-written poem, one by Master John Donne in Cambridge. Rebecca wrote to Mary:

I have little to offer you for your help in improving my life. Perhaps this poem will suit you and I want you to have it. The writer is John Donne. He gave a copy of this poem to Father. They studied together at Cambridge College in England. Master Donne and Father were students together. Father read it to me one night on the foot-slog from Cambridge in the Bay Colony. How it cheered me up. Oh, I wish to write poetry like Master Donne.

THE BLOSSOM
Little think'st thou, poor flower,
Whom I have watched six or seven days,
And seen thy birth, and seen what every hour
Gave to thy growth, thee to this height to raise,
And now dost laugh and triumph on this bough,
Little think's thou
That it will freeze anon, and that I shall
Tomorrow find thee fal'n, or not at all.
By John Donne[66]

I hope you like it, Rebecca added at the end.
The reply was speedy.

It is a lovely poem. The flower is much like a lighted ember. It comes to life, glows in triumph and too soon dies. Have no fear, dear Rebecca. Your poems are a golden treasure of words. If only Master Donne could learn from you. These humble words, dear Rebecca, I write from heart.
Forever, Mary

Returned Rebecca:
You write to make me blush. I am happy that you find beauty in words.

Special Place

The letters from her family ignited a spark of homesickness. A sense of her deep-rooted world at the manor began to smolder with increasing intensity. She knew that she must return to Littleton and let the happenings of the past year, both good and not so good, slowly fade into memory. Was she ready to do that? Yes, she thought so. But returning to her house after her morning's work, she found a large envelope on the table. On it, her name MARY WALSINGHAM was written in flourishing scroll.

Stunned, she opened the envelope to find a single, ragged-edged paper. Written were tiny words arranged in a circle. At the very center of the jumble of words, she made out her name. By turning the page around and around she read:

Dear Mary,
I have come to our fort on the Fresh River (what you English call the Great River). Your settlement at Hartford thrives and no longer needs goods from Holland and New Amsterdam. That is good. But I would be pleased to see your bright smile once again. In two days my ship will return to New Amsterdam. Tomorrow at midday I will arrive at your village on horse. There is a place not far away that is my SPECIAL PLACE. Please, do me the favor of riding Angel there with me.
Pieter

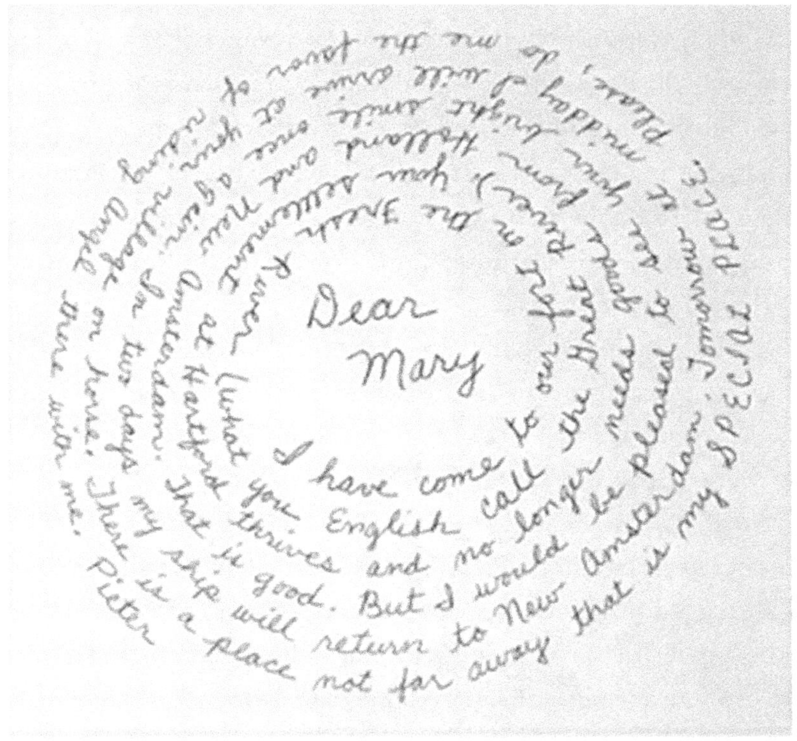

Dear Mary

I have come to our fort on the Fresh River (what you English call the Great River), your settlement at Hartford thrives and no longer needs goods from Holland and New Amsterdam. That is good. But I would be pleased to see your bright smile once again. In two days my ship will return to New Amsterdam. Tomorrow at midday I will arrive at your village on horse. There is a place not far away that is my SPECIAL PLACE. Please, do me the favor of riding along there with me. Pieter

Now it was Mary's head that spun around. She was not prepared to let Pieter enter her life once again. Her mixed-up thoughts throughout the night, however, would not allow her to refuse. She knew that whatever Pieter had in mind—if she did not learn it—would haunt her forever.

Arising at daybreak, Mary tended her chores. Feeding, watering, grooming, milking, and collecting eggs were all done well before noon. Pieter, orange hat and all, arrived as promised and looking quite striking on a totally black horse. His decorated saddle could have belonged to a prince. Knee-high black boots and a flowing blue scarf completed a majestic picture. Greeting Mary with a nod, he beckoned her to follow.

Mary went directly to the stable and Angel. They were soon on the way, Pieter on his splendid saddle, Mary wrapped in a long shawl. She rode astride, as always, and bareback except for a folded blanket. He led the way past the villagers who, to the man and woman, were flabbergasted by the sight of an unmarried woman accompanied by a man riding along a riverside trail, then turning into the woodland.

The trail took them along the banks of the Little River where their horses broke into a canter for a time, then slowed to an unhurried pace as Pieter led into the hills. Mary worried that they were going too far and that they might not return before sundown. At last, where the river had turned into high falling water between boulders, Pieter's horse turned away from the river and zigzagged into a forest of evergreens. Angel followed, stirring up the powerful scent of pine needles that layered the ground. Within a few deep breaths, they came to the foot of a sharply rising ledge of rock.

Pieter dismounted, loosened the saddle and removed his horse's bit. He tethered the horse loosely to a tree. For Angel, with no halter, he made a loop in another rope and fit it loosely around her neck. The other end, he tied to a low-hanging tree branch. Both tethers were long enough for the horses to reach some tall grass. Next, Mary saw Pieter take off his leather jacket and lay it neatly across another low-hanging branch. He signaled that she should do the same with her shawl.

She watched as Pieter first cleared needles from a patch of ground and then in the center made a pile of dry grass and twigs. Taking a piece of flint from his pocket, he struck it against a stone over and over until sparks flew out. The tinder soon caught fire. From a sack tied behind his saddle, he brought out a handful of dried and well-oiled cat-o-nine tails. He plunged the thick ends into the fire, soon holding high a blazing, red-yellow torch. The fire was quickly dampened. All the time, Mary looked on with questioning fascination. What was this "Special Place"?

Now ready, Pieter led Mary afoot toward a narrow slit between massive slabs of rock. First, he squeezed through, keeping the torch held ahead at arm's length. Mary, more curious than fretful, followed. Not many steps later they found themselves on all fours, with Pieter ahead and Mary, following. Both being slender in build, they easily crawled through a rock-bound gap with only a few turns here and there. Though they inched slowly along, in time their knees and shoulders began to hurt. The burning cat-o-nine tails broke the ominous blackness that was ahead. Space became more constricting as they crept along, keeping the chest from taking a deep breath.

As she squeezed herself through the low passageway, it seemed to Mary that the walls were pressing against her. She soon found it easier to lie on her back and to squeeze onward by pushing herself hand-over-hand against the rock above and pushing below with her feet. Inch-by-inch she wriggled along. If Pieter, who is so much bigger, can do it, she thought, so can I.

As it often happened to her from time to time at anxious moments, Mary began to feel tingles around her mouth and at her fingertips as they tugged along the rocks. Her head began to swirl. Was the cause a sudden cooling in the air or was she beginning to sense the awful terror of being buried alive? If ever there was a living nightmare, this was it. She thought of turning back, but there was no room to turn.

Fearless and trusting as she was, Mary began to think more carefully about her situation. She barely knew this man, Pieter. She found him kind and thoughtful. There was surely a trace of playful devilishness in him. But what deviltry had he led her to now? Whatever his game may be, she tried convincing herself, I must go on to the end. She braced herself in mind and in body for whatever was ahead.

As the passageway narrowed, the stone faces on opposite sides came closer together. At one point, Mary was forced to turn her head sideways to snake through the opening and even then, her ears, never useful and now in the way, scraped against the stone.

A few pushes-and-pulls later, she twisted her neck just enough to look forward. In the flickering light she saw two upright black boots. Pieter was standing. A few wiggles more, she found her head poking into an open space. One more squirm, and she could thrust out an arm. Suddenly the curious but hesitant cave-crawler felt a firm hand on hers. It was a cool hand with a gentle touch. Pieter held it for an instant. She felt a shiver race through her whole body much like the time when the blacksmith pounded his hammer. There she was, on her back with half her body still wedged between stones and yet wishing the moment would not end. A second hand came to her elbow. Slowly, the hands drew her forward until she could turn over and then bring herself to her feet.

Pieter held his torch high. Mary gazed into a black space before her. She saw a vast cavern, far greater in breadth and surely higher than any great room in any manor house. At her feet lay an ink-black pool, its water as still as glass. The reflection of the torchlight cast a brilliant streak across it, reaching to a stream of falling water on the other side. Surrounding the pool were huge and grotesque columns and crooked monster-like formations hanging from the ceiling.

Mary gasped. Was it the sudden cooling and dampness that brought a powerful chill? So overwhelming was the sight that she closed her eyes to gain composure. She looked again, aghast.

The high dome, the hanging and rising creatures of stone and the black pool with a waterfall in the distance were still there. A dream, it was not. She was surely looking into the center of the earth. She knew not any comparison in the whole world.[67]

With an extended arm sweeping across the cavern from end to end, Pieter appeared to scoop it all up, and with a grand bow offer it to Mary. The message could not be mistaken, This, my Special Place, I give it to you. In the dancing light that reflected off his blue eyes, Mary understood. Relieved of fear, she could not help but break into a smile of acceptance.

Pieter had one more surprise. He bent to pick up a loose pebble, raised it to shoulder height and threw it into the middle of the glass-smooth pool. Mary could not hear the *plunk*, but she did see a tiny wave grow out from the center, making a small circle that spread outward, getting ever larger as it moved away from the center. There followed a succession of spreading waves. Before long, the pool was a series of perfect rings. Was this like the letter written by Pieter, his quill, a pebble from which perfect words spread out?

The two tarried not long before crawling back through the tight rock-bound passageway. After much twisting and squeezing, Mary saw the glimmer of the sunlit forest. She soon emerged into the open air, stood, took a deep breath, and brushed the dust away.

There was one more heart-stopping anxiety for Mary as they emerged into the dazzling daylight. The black horse had hardly moved a step, but Angel was not there. The rope with its loop lay on the ground. Another moment of panic began but it was brief. At the edge of the forest, Mary saw a white mass flanked by two straight up ears. Angel, seeking a cool place, had found shade under some pine trees.

Mounting the horse was another challenge. There in the forest, there was no step or fence for Mary to stand on. She looked for a fallen tree, but not one was in sight. Turning, she saw Pieter next to Angel clasping his hands together to form a makeshift stirrup. Placing one foot into the hand stirrup, Mary once again felt a sudden chill beginning at the nape of her neck, shooting down her spine as far as the toes. It lasted but an instant before she bounded up on Angel. But during that fleeting moment and from under his broad-brimmed hat, Mary caught a glimpse of Pieter's smile as it widened into a big grin.

With saddle and stirrups tightened and harness fitted, Pieter was soon mounted. By not tarrying, they expected to arrive home before sundown, stopping only for the horses to drink as they crossed a stream here and there.

Mary had seen Pieter's secret place. But, as they rode, she only had a dim awareness of what had just happened beyond the black pool and the monster-like columns and hangings. Knowing romance by first touch can be blurry. Love takes time and practice. When there is doubt, as Mary had in Pieter, the pathway can be narrow, convoluted, and perilous.

Disapproval

Evening had fallen by the time that the two returned to the village. Candles in some houses were already lit. The Dutchman departed with a bow as they reached the Adams house, and Mary met with stern faces upon entering. Dinner proceeded as usual: hand-holding prayers, bread and stew, and then all the usual evening activities of reading, sewing, or the foot-horse play of the little girls.

There was something else, a feeling that Mary had as the day ended. It had something to do with an inside emptiness. She had not known such a feeling before. She needed to open her soul to someone but knew it could not be to Rebecca or Thomas or to her own mother or father. Instead she found herself thumbing aimlessly through the book of poems that came to her from England. By candlelight, she turned page after page, finding beautiful words and fleeting ideas here and there but hardly a thought to comfort. But just before closing its cover, her eyes seized upon some pleasing words:

Shall I compare thee to a summer's day?
Thou art more lovely and more temperate.
Rough winds do shake the darling buds of May,
And summer's lease hath all too short a date.

Mary did not understand it all. Yet these were words to help fill a space that came so suddenly with Pieter's departure.[68]

Master Adams wrote not his nightly message of encouragement but instead rather unsettling words that waited until morning to be read.

Mary, we have done all we can in our humble home to please you. You have been faithful in your work in the stables and countless other tasks. Your friendship with our dreamy daughter is cherished. Yesterday, you chose a path that is opposed to the ideals that we hold sacred. Both Mistress Adams and I are deeply disappointed, but we take hope in the belief that there will be no further such occasions. J.A.

Mary expected disapproval. It was perhaps not as severe as expected. Rebecca, too, left a gentle chiding, this as a poem.

SENSE OF PLACE
All creatures know their place.
The world is too complex
To forget this lesson
History teaches over time.

Trees reach for the sun
To bask where bright
Mushrooms hide in shade.
Ferns like shadows and light.

Frogs stay near streams
And trout never leave.
The robin hugs the ground,
Hawks prefer the sky.

People, too, live by natural rules,
Their feelings are held in place.
Whether on earth, water, sky
We are measured only by grace.

You are free as only I can dream.
My whole life-reward
To live within the boundaries
We know that please God.

Yet, 'tis not for hawks to swim
Nor fish to take to air

A place there is for you and me.
I think we both know where. R.A.

Mary thought this a lovely poem, however a bit strange. Only on reading it again that night did she realize that Rebecca had written it about her. The poem said politely that her action on the day before was ill-advised. Mary felt properly chastised. She had been wrong by the standards of the times and place. Did she wish that her journey to the Special Place had never happened? No, never.

A letter received on the following day was more about Rebecca's own oversight in poetry.

Mary, today, I realized something about my poems to you. You may know that I try hard to make rhymes in my lines. It is one of the wonderful things about poetry. After all this time and all these poems, I only now realized that rhyming to you does not matter. Since you do not hear the words you do not know what a rhyme sounds like. You enjoy words in a different way. And so, the joke is on me. Ha!

From the letter, Mary knew that the friendship with Rebecca was not a thing of the past.

Answers

ON THE MORNING two days later, another envelope addressed to Mary was left on the table.

Mary, I was happy that you shared with me my secret place. I was shown it by an old Indian named Guasanaca. He said his name means Runs-Like-The-Wind. He befriended me on many occasions. He told me that he discovered the cave when he was a small boy. His people do not like closed spaces and so no one else would dare enter. Guasanaca has long since taken his starry path to the sky-world, and now only you and I know about it. Now it is our special place. Have you solved those silly riddles written long ago? Here are the answers:

An ear of corn.

A human. He crawls on all fours early in life, then on two for walking, and in old age, add a cane.

The letter "e."

I hope you can match the answers with the riddles. Today we sail down river and turn on reaching open water toward New Amsterdam. I leave the fort with a fond memory of our visit to that magical underground world. I am hoping that the beauty you saw there will make up for all your bruises and scrapes. I shared this adventure with someone who is very special to me.

Your friend, Pieter

Her decision was not easy, but she chose not to respond in writing.

CHAPTER 11

Autumn, Again

Angel

Never was a morning in autumn so bracing. The days of steady rain had passed, and the brilliant reds, yellows, and oranges on trees now radiated through the sun-dappled woodlands. A faint musty scent was in the air, a blend of mosses, ferns, pond weeds, and sassafras. Here and there a puddle reflected a passing cloud. Mary did not remember being more content with life in general. In such a mood, she rode without a care along the river bank. Angel led the way.

A long ramble had brought them to a high bank that edged close to the river. It was along a well-worn path but not one they had traveled before. Rains had made the bank slippery. Here, the river was wide, and the eye traveled far downstream. Often along the Great River, Mary held Angel back to admire the sights. Sometimes there was an osprey tracing great circles above the river. Sometimes it was a lone fisherman in a canoe who had found a promising cove. Sometimes on the far side of the river, Indian women washed clothes with splashing children nearby.

But on this day, the river sparkled along its entire length. It was void of such distractions until Mary spotted a figure on the other side.

That figure, she guessed, was a boy perhaps older than Thomas. He stood at the edge of a great rocky ledge. His hair fell to the waist. He wore a dark headband, no upper clothing, and long, loose-hanging leg coverings. The boy's attention was on a fishing line cast far out into the river. But on spotting a horse and rider across the river, he instantly squatted down behind some low-lying bushes.

The ledge to Mary somehow looked familiar. It took a moment for her to realize that she was looking at the great fist-like rock that *The Vagabond* had edged by on her sail upriver. The boy stood on what she imagined was the thumb. Now she remembered that it was the spot where two haunting eyes, looking through some leaves, seemed to follow her and the ship along the way. Was he the same boy?

For a closer look, Mary nudged Angel closer to edge of the embankment, although the horse's hooves sank into the soggy ground. Angel might have sensed a tremor, a sign of weakened earth underneath. Mary sitting above could not have felt the slightest quiver. What she did not know was that Angel was now stepping on terrain that had been undermined by the heavy rains of recent days. She urged Angel even closer with gentle heel prodding. The undermined earth was ready to give way. And it did, with the added burden of horse and rider.

Tumbling down the mudslide in a headlong fall, Mary felt the crushing weight of Angel roll over her body. Once? Twice? They slid down to the water's edge. There, stunned, the girl struggled to take a painful breath. Tormenting moments passed before she regained her thoughts. Then she saw Angel foundering as she tried to rise. Despite her attempts to push and help Angel regain her footing, the horse could not stand. She soon saw the awful reality. One of Angel's front legs flailed unnaturally to one side. Angel had broken her leg.

For Mary, a dark cloud seemed to emerge from behind a sky full of softly curled, white clouds. For both, she knew, the world had just as suddenly changed. They lay together in the mud for what Mary knew would be the last time. The sun slowly drifted to the far horizon. Near its setting, she, even with tear-filled closed eyes, became aware of a long shadow.

Swollen eyes snapped open. Mary saw an Indian standing over her. He was the boy who had been fishing across the river. A canoe was beached nearby.

The boy beckoned Mary to come away, then tried to lift her toward his canoe. His fishing nets were already placed on the beach to make a place for her. This help offered, Mary shook her head, meaning *No.* He held her firmly at the shoulders, attempting to lead her away. She shrugged him off, wrapping her arms around Angel's neck even tighter. No, she could not leave Angel. After her stubborn refusal to leave, the boy paddled off.

Well into nightfall Master Adams appeared at the woeful scene along with Thomas and others, each carrying a lantern. The flickering light gave Mary a glimpse of the face of the boy who first came to her. Everyone looked over the injured ones with careful attention. Master Adams helped Mary lift her tear-stained cheek from Angel's forehead and led her, stumbling, up the hill toward the tree line.

Mary knew what happened to crippled horses. There are times when deafness is truly a blessing. Once Mary and Master Adams were beyond the next curve of the river, a gunshot echoed across the way. Mary could not hear the blast, but she felt a sudden chill in the night air. At the same time, she became aware of the gentle weight of a large hand on her shoulder as they trudged through the lantern-lit pathway.[69]

Sorrow and Healing

THIS NARRATIVE NEED not belabor the days and weeks that followed. Sufficient it is to write that grief-stricken, guilt-ridden Mary lay in her bed, chores neglected other than feeding and watering the large animals, refusing nearly all food and unwilling to engage with others. Her days were spent buried beneath a blanket, head and all.

During the period of unrelenting grief, Rebecca came to sit next to her, but Mary turned aside. Mistress Adams saw that hot tea of sassafras or nutmeg was always nearby. Also, put before her by Master Adams were underlined passages from the Bible telling of overcoming great sorrow.

Death was common in the colonies, not only among people beyond the age of forty. Sometimes it was the grippe or the fever that struck a young person who was dead by morning, the tragic death of little William Ensign being a most recent example. The burial grounds marked with flat stones of slate tell of insufferable sorrows in silence with the words "the pox" and "ague." What was different now with Mary was that no one could remember such deep sorrow at the death of an animal.

Master Adams, dour as he might be, wrote with measured sensitivity of the God-given power to accept terrible happenings.

Dear Mary,
You must know by now that you have truly become part of this family. Mistress Adams and I pray for your speedy recovery from the great misfortune that has befallen you. We can only offer you our love during these dark days. Our Book of Common Prayers tells us that "The Lord healeth those that are broken in heart." Join us in our prayers. Let Him speak directly to you as only He can in your silent world. The Scripture tells us, "May our Lord Jesus Christ who gave us everlasting comfort and good hope, comfort your heart and give you strength to every good thing you do and say."
Jeremy Adams

Rising from grief in the deepest hollow of the soul is a slow and painful journey. Others had to carry on with Mary's feeding and watering of the animals. As the days went on, she felt weaker, even light-in-the-head as, from time to time, she made her way unsteadily to the privy. She knew that she must find in some way the will to mend her broken spirit. The beginning of this inside mending came in an unexpected way.

Late one afternoon, she became aware of someone sitting by her bed. At first, there was no stirring. Mary turned away and pulled herself deeper into her blanket. A long time passed before she felt a hand reach across her shoulders and take her hand. The grasp was light, but there was a firmness to it. The hand was warm and comforting.

Mary became aware that the hand that held hers was slowly drawing her up. First, it was an arm that yielded to the slight but steady pressure. Unable to resist the upward force, Mary sat. She covered her eyes with the free hand as if to protect herself against an empty future. But a voice deep down in her being spoke of the need to get on with life. A spark of life had returned, but it was only a spark.

At last, Mary, the hands still clasped, turned to face Rebecca, a slight smile to tell of comfort given. But, to her astonishment, it was not Rebecca, it was Mistress Adams. The smile broadened. There was another kind of love not expressed by words spoken, in letters and in poetry. It was the love of someone simply being there. As dusk settled in, Mary at last fell asleep.

Within another few days, Mary was back at the well, the stable and the coop doing what was expected of her. Her movement was slow and prodding, but she saw that the chores were done and done properly. She was also more aware of the strength of a willowy soul in a bonnet.

Walk in the Woods

On one of those perfect days of early autumn when the sky was pure blue without a cloud in sight and the air was crisp, Mary set out on a walk to nowhere in particular. Taking steps slowly and walking aimlessly, she came to the edge of a clearing. Sunlight quickly gave way to gloom. She found herself in deep forest where the woodcutters had yet to come. A great dark space filled with giant ferns and smelling of decaying leaves now became a whole new world. She sniffed the heavy moist air and felt the boggy soil under her feet. The forest seemed to be calling her into its ancient depths.

The sudden change from light to dark triggered a series of thoughts and questions in her mind. *These leaves rotting under my feet were once a shimmering green. In time they turned to oranges, yellows, and reds before falling to the ground. Can a leaf, as it flutters downward slowly, feel a moment of freedom, of satisfaction, before striking the ground? The leaf will die but the tree in spring will live on with a new headdress. I see the balance of life and death. Was Angel my green who nurtured me? Did she do her duty and, at last, found freedom in dying? Perhaps I am the tree. I will live on another season.* And with this vow, Mary continued to walk deeper into the woods.

Hardly aware at first, she had stumbled upon a well-worn, inviting but strange footpath that was barely wide enough for a person to squeeze through. Rather than leading along in a single direction, it wove crookedly here and there, skirting around clearings, and climbing to the peaks of hills only to drop down to a glen. It passed almost in a full circle around a pond where the walker found a moment to pause, catch her breath and revel at an amusing sight.

From some distance Mary could see that the pond was as still as glass, and black as coal. As she approached, a frog jumped in, causing tiny ripples to expand outward in perfect circles and bringing back the memory of a magical underground pool. Now she watched the frog's throat bulge in rapid repetition. It was much like the quiver that she had felt on Sky Flower's throat when the Mohawk girl tried to explain about sending messages with the mouth. She knew that the frog was sending a message, perhaps telling all who had the gift of receiving it, that he was the bravest of them all.

Throughout her life, Mary wondered what the magic of sound was like. If the Almighty would allow her the joy of experiencing sound just one time, she would choose to hear the song of that frog as he boasted of his courage.

Now she wondered who had trampled this soil. The woodsmen of the plantation did not frequent this part of the forest. Indians, as far as Mary knew, lived not anywhere nearby. Farther along, she came upon a thicket of brambles. Why should the winding footpath lead directly through it and not around it? The walker was not deterred. She picked her way gingerly through the briars, receiving only a few scratches before reaching the other side.

Farther along, she caught sight of two enormous brown eyes looking up at her. The rest of the fawn blended perfectly with the bed of leaves. It lay motionless alongside the footpath. As much as Mary wanted to pick up the little creature for a good cuddle, Sky Flower had taught her to leave a baby deer alone. The fawn moved not a muscle aside from turning its neck to follow the girl as she slowly tiptoed away.

Not far beyond, Mary came upon a most remarkable sight. It was a boulder thrice her height, long like a loaf of bread and standing upright as if some giant baker had set it on end. The boulder was split down the middle the way a mad cook might have cut the loaf. The halves angled out slightly from one another. It was truly an impressive sight, but Mary was hardly prepared for the sight that lay on the small space between the split rocks.

There on the ground were some stones that lay in a perfect circle, perhaps an arm's length across, each stone lying at exactly the same distant apart. The rocks were rounded, each about the size of a fist. There were many shades of gray with tinges of red and yellow. Exactly in circle center was a flattened cake of dried, black soil. Like the mud-like stone that Thomas had shown her, it had small bumps in some places.

The temptation to hold the central stone was a mighty force. Fearing that a bolt of lightning would strike if she disturbed the site, she mustered the courage to reach down and gently pick up the mud cake. She held it up into a narrow streak of the sunlight coming through the leaves. Viewed in this way, the bumps glowed a brilliant red. Lightning did not strike.

Clearly, the people who found and gathered the beautiful rocks made the circle with great care. They knew about the magic that Mary thought of as "the eyes of the devil." This place was surely a sacred altar where Indians worshiped their god in their way. Remembering Sky Flower's stories of Mohawk dancing and incantations, Mary yearned to be there when the Indians celebrated such a ritual. How wonderful that would be!

Partly visible through the dark forest curtain, the setting sun warned that she must start for home. Mary dreaded threading through the briar patch again, but had little choice. *Why,* she wondered, *did the path-makers go through it? Did they want to dissuade the curious from following it?*

Dilemma

As Mary wrestled with sleep that night, new thoughts swirled in her head. *Thomas! Could the circle of stones be his work? Does it explain his frequent disappearances for almost a whole day? Did the footsteps that made a well-worn pathway to the split rock belong to him? Does it explain the scratches often seen on his face and hands? Eerily, the rocks did look familiar. The mud cake with the bumps looked very much like the one that Thomas had shown her. Was it the same? What in God's good name could he be thinking? Was this a kind of young man's fantasy or something more sinister? Could the woodland altar at the split rock be Thomas's Special Place? Perhaps, after all, it was Thomas who was a witch. Yes, Thomas was odd, but was making a circle of stones enough to mark him as a witch?*[70]

What consumed Mary's thoughts through a restless night was the "stone-with-eyes-of-the-devil." Had she seen the same mud cake before? She knew where the answer could be found. If the "Devil's Eyes" stone was in its place in the secret box, then the forest circle of rocks was the work of others. She could then put to rest any suspicion of Thomas being a witch. She could take a quick look in midday after her chores; it would be just a harmless look in secrecy.

On returning from the care of the animals, when the house was quiet, when the baby and twins were napping, and when Mistress Adams was at the privy, Mary had a rare moment to answer her burning question. She told herself, *Lifting the lid will take but an instant.* She would then know if Thomas was or was not living out a strange ritual at the Split Rock. Yet, to pry into another's well-guarded privacy was wrong. Her entire life (except for two occasions that she could remember) stayed within the bounds of honesty.

As she stood before the boy's wagon chest contemplating whether or not she should lift the cover, an inner turmoil was stirred up. Flashing through her mind were the memories of other deceptions: the many journeys on Angel sitting astride and returning sidesaddle. Then there was the falsehood of her counting horse. Should she commit one more deceit? If the strange mud cake object were there, then the devil will have already seen her. Would she then become an agent of the very devil that so addled the Puritans? If the object were not there, well, that was another matter.

Another thought popped into Mary's head. *If I opened this box, would I find the missing things? Did Thomas take the wonderful honey-tree poem from my pillow? Will the mirror letter that I left on the table be there? If I find them, then the mystery is solved.*

But a greater mystery now emerged from the shadows. She questioned herself: *Does Thomas have feelings for me that he could not find a way to express? Is he jealous of Pieter's attention to me?*

And so, the great struggle between evil and a simple curiosity-driven, quick and harmless look into the old wagon seat hung in the balance. The reaching hand hesitated.

Jumping Frog

EARLY ONE MORNING during the family breakfast there was a knock. The door opened. Pieter! In one hand he held the reins of a horse. In the other was a parcel wrapped in paper of diverse and dazzling colors. A broad smile was soon followed by an explanation. "I have come from Fort Hope with a gift for Mary."

Master Adams received the parcel, nodded and, turning, shut the door. All but Mary, of course, heard hoof beats rapidly fading.

The tightly bound parcel did not wait long to show its content to many curious eyes. Inside unwrapped was an earthenware pitcher with a flowing handle and gently curved spout. It was mostly white with swirls of deep blue, surprising for its delicacy. On one side of the vase was a windmill, as if at full tilt. The other side depicted a one-masted sailing ship. Mary held the vase against her cheek, eyes closed, partly to feel the cool and smooth surface and partly to bring Pieter closer. And as remarkable as the color and texture were, she felt a sudden, small shaking that seemed to come from inside. She quickly turned the pitcher for a look down into its mouth when a frog—fully as startled as she was—jumped out and bumped her in the forehead before skittering away into a darkened corner. It had been a long time since Mary laughed aloud, but nevertheless, she retrieved the creature and found it a new home near the Little River.[71]

First Steps

THE LETTERS FROM home prompted a growing need to be once again with her family. Mary began to ponder the notion of returning to her true home. Such a plan would surely cause a mixture of sorrow and happiness. What could she say to Master Adams and his wife who had done their best to ease her most troubling times? How could she end her precious friendship with Rebecca? Would Thomas grow more withdrawn? And what of Pieter? Whatever truth he was keeping from her and whatever caused his mysterious ways, Mary could not imagine a forever goodbye.

There was, too, a special joy for the family. Baby John was now past one year old. He had learned to crawl and to sit. Then on the matted floor, he beamed as if he had mastered a great skill. He laughed aloud whenever Mary would swing her head from side to side; sometimes he mimicked the action. He often flapped his arms as if flying in response to the flapping of his sisters' arms. Was he ready now to stand?

Holding his gripping hands, Mistress Adams drew him upright. A huge grin arising from the excitement of it all spread over the baby's face. But since one foot turned in, he stood quite lopsided, and could hold the position for only a moment. She felt John's hands grip tighter around her extended fingers as he took his first step forward. On planting his twisted foot on the floor, he lurched sideways. At that moment, his mother felt a foreboding tightness run through her whole insides.

The errant foot had been addling Jeremy Adams's thoughts ever since John's birth. On the momentous occasion of this first standing, he lamented to Mary in writing, *A plantation, I fear, is no place for a cripple.* He went on to write that a friend in Cambridge knew a bonesetter in Boston who had a good reputation for correcting this problem. It was expensive and took a long time. Treating a club foot, he was told, should have started soon after birth. The prospect of leaving John with the doctor for a year or two was too heart-wrenching for his wife. Still, it had to be considered.

With the unhappy prospects looming so heavily, Mary offered an idea. She wrote, *Need John become a farmer? Perhaps Reverend Hooker could help him find another life's work. Training in the classics? A man of letters? A preacher serving the Lord at the highest level? We already know that John has a quick mind.*

Mr. Adams adjusted the candle to read Mary's note most carefully. He read it slowly to his wife. She smiled. He sat back in his chair, as he held the letter against his forehead. Mary's misgivings about her reckless audacity melted as Jeremy nodded in approval. Mary, too, smiled.

Problem Solved

What brought the notion of returning to England to sharp attention was the arrival of a ship from Boston. It was not an ocean-going ship but rather a sloop. Its arrival at the plantation dock was the spark that set aflame Mary's thoughts of going home. An inner voice seemed to be speaking to her soul, beckoning her to return to familiar places and those who loved her.

Ships in Boston, Mary's inquiries led her to believe, return to England almost every fortnight. Surely, there would be a way for her to earn her passage. Knowing this, thoughts of the Manor House in Littleton came streaming into her consciousness. She had a vision of sleeping in her own bed with her familiar pillow, perhaps finding a sweet nearby in the morning; of sitting at the window and watching the magpies flit about the grass among the sheep; sitting at table on Sunday with her true family for plum pudding. How she longed to see Harold again and to take in the wonderful blend of smells in his orangery. And then to watch and feel the blacksmith shape blocks of iron into tools! She thought about the past joys of dawdling along the River Ash to the bend in the Thames where barges make the sharp turn. All these thoughts along with some painful memories awaited her. Mary knew, or at least thought she knew, that she was ready.

Life is a progression of unpredictable wounds and pleasures. Mary knew that she had tried her best. She felt that she had lived up to her many life-trials and proven worthy. Having decided to return to her real home, she was certain that she no longer needed the erratic support that had thus far preserved and fostered her well-being. Despite living in a world of total silence, she was now ready to meet the hearing world straight on.

Indeed, there was a new life purpose waiting for her in England. The thrill of training young horses at the Manor House with a soft touch was almost too exciting to dwell in her imagination. The end of the story in Hartford would be the beginning of a new life in Littleton as a complete person, a person who no longer needed a constant emotional crutch to shape her future. She was ready to return to her roots in England.

Yes, Mary told herself, she had seen some difficult times, but she was no longer the rebellious, misunderstood, lonely person of her early life. Sky Flower, in Littleton, brought her into the rest of the world but, innocently, abandoned her, leaving her grief-stricken. It was Harold who slowly nurtured her out of a downcast shell. Her full emergence into the real world blossomed not from another person but from a horse, Angel. It was in the Colonies, where she had taken Angel to save her from abusive training, and where their bond came to a sudden, accidental end. Fate had once again forsaken her. She was taken in by a family that barely had enough for themselves, a family that helped comfort her in her unbearable sorrow. Another person, Pieter, though not often seen, intruded now more frequently in her thoughts. Despite her efforts to dispel the notion, she realized that he was the cause of a new kind of feelings, both disturbing yet stirring. These seemed to be as powerful as life itself.

How to soften the blow to Master and Mistress Adams, who had accepted her from the beginning, even as they struggled to eke out a living in a desperately challenging world? All this for a person thrust suddenly on them, a person who could not hear or speak and who was not ready to accept fully their Holy Cause.

Perhaps they will find some relief in having one mouth fewer to fill and a bit more elbow room in a small house.

What to write to needy Thomas? Surely a letter will encourage his continued growth and his impressive collection. But is that enough? Mary did not think it would help to suggest that he reach out to others, and tell more of his feelings and share his treasured items. It would be for others to reach out to Thomas.

Most troubling was how to say goodbye to Rebecca who had grown to be a true sister. Her whirling thoughts brought to mind another sister from her past: Sky Flower who came from across the sea, who saved her from a wounded future and who, suddenly and painfully, left her forsaken. Mary knew that she must struggle to write a parting letter, perhaps about shared love and shared sorrows in a world that was not always kind, but a world that always went on. And so, the painful note to her best friend had to be written. She knew the news would not be easy for Rebecca. Mary fretted about telling her and, with much inner turmoil, wrote,

> *My Dear Rebecca,*
> *A year come and gone since I arrived on the steps of your little house. During this time, I learn much about another world and how God-fearing people choose a harsh life to honor their true beliefs. Most wonderful of all, I know you. We share our thoughts. I happy for the magic you make with words.*
>
> *Yes, we have both suffered in one way or another. We try help each other through terrible times as best we could. Always, you truly best friend I ever imagine. We remember all the good times together collecting leaves of different trees, playing in the snow, and fun to make words with hands.*
>
> *I write now my heavy heart. I decide return to my home in England. Something powerful draws me there where my family*

awaits me most eager. I fear that I never be a good Puritan. And so, I board the next ship to Boston.

I know you have heart and soul to be a wonderful poet. Your verses match that of famous poets of our mother country. Such images you write of little things in this vast world. I come to learn of them and to be a better person because of them. How proud I am of you. At some time, we will meet again in this world or in the world across the ocean.

From your friend and admirer, Mary

Mary read her much scratched-on letter many times. Yet, there was something about it that vexed her deeply. She could not tell what. In the early light of the next morning, as she re-read the words, she understood what was wrong. An old letter kept ringing in her mind. She had just written the same kind of letter to Rebecca that Sky Flower had written to her two years before. It was the letter that suddenly left her for so long in a state of unimaginable emptiness. No, no, she could not give Rebecca such a letter. And so, each page was torn in shreds and put to flame. The writing started again,

Dear Rebecca,

Living with your wonderful family and coming to know and to love you for almost a year, I choose now to return to my home in England. I have strong need to be close to my family. They need me. Mother writes. She misses me greatly. Also, I fear I not good Puritan or ever expect to be. I leave the Colony sad and joyous, sad mostly for leaving you and joyous in the thought of how you have so fully enriched my soul.

When we first met, we were two tiny, slightly damaged plants looking for sunlight. As our lives together grew, we begin

blossom and become more beautiful each sunlit day. The things we did and learned together will remain beautiful flowers forever in our minds.

How kind your family to take me in, a poor, helpless, and silent creature arrive at doorstep with a horse. I learn much from your good father who cared to write often to poor, oxen-headed me. I found strength in your mother. I leave knowing they, your little sisters, Baby John and Thomas in good health. Also, the headache demon dares pester you less often now.

Please let me take your poems to England. I promise to see them published. All England to find beauty in your verses. Perhaps you will visit me! Until then I look for more magic words on every ship from the colonies.

What pleases me is care of your brother. Thomas has mysterious ways, true, but I know him sensitive and clever. But he feels alone even in our crowded house. He reached out to me when I had nothing to offer. I believe him to be like our slow running river, but inside there is a restless tossing of the sea. Your attention to him, I believe, pleases him wonderful. Talk to him often. Attend his collection. What may seem useless for us is for him a pirate's treasure.

Goodbye for now. This does not end for us but new chance to see more blossoms to our lives. I believe with all my heart that we will meet again. Should you ever be in a sad state, think of the badly-behaved cow and poor Master E. crossing bridge. Somehow, I will feel your laughing and will laugh along with you.

Forever your best friend, Mary

The letter Mary left atop Rebecca's pillow. It was read by candlelight sometime during the night. Mary wondered about what her poet-sister would think on first reading it. She did find some writing by her morning pillow. Not surprisingly, it was a poem.

To Mary

BEAUTY INSIDE AND OUT
A bud becomes a flower
Not with a mighty cheer
But does in sublime silence
For beauty, it has no peer

Fearless, the flower shows itself
To hummingbirds and bees
And faces the world in all its glory
Then fades to those it please.

When a girl becomes a woman
And appears in our barren world
Blessed, she is, in supreme silence
Inside her shell, I find a pearl.

Fearless to walk among the small and great
A princess with natural grace
I follow in those footsteps
And find her joy left in place.

Added at the end was something not in verse. It was a surprise.

Mary, I knew all along that you would flit away. Something deep inside told me that you must go. There was no holding you in this stark world, where a fine-looking snow scene with a red cardinal perched on a perfect tree is not allowed on Christmas Day. Yes, I think that the life of a Puritan is not for you. God will find a place for all of us.

Now, you see that life here under the watchful eyes of God is harsh and unforgiving. We know that life is fragile and mysterious, as William has taught us. Yet, I feel comfort in the Puritan ways of thinking. It is solid ground, a place to stand when the mightiest of floods swirls around me. Yes, Mary, I will dream of sailing with you so far away. But still I choose to stay here in a known world. My poems are my transport to other worlds. For me, that is enough.

I will continue as best I can and pray to see you again. I keep your beautiful necklace close to me at all times. Know that you left me another gift even more precious, the belief in myself. So enriched, I will forever be grateful to you.

Love, Rebecca

Mouse

On one long walk, while Mary mulled over the prospect of returning home, she spotted a dot low in the distant sky. The dot slowly became larger until it was nearly overhead. There, it began to make diminishing circles then, suddenly it plummeted straight down. At the same time, there was a tiny movement that sped across the field. Mary was witnessing the life-and-death drama of a hawk and mouse. By the time the hawk reached the ground, the mouse had scooted into the tall grass. For a moment, the hawk, too, disappeared in the grass but soon, with strong flapping of wings, was air-borne, its talons empty. This time good fortune fell on the mouse.

Somehow, the cosmic contest among creatures caused Mary to think of her own life and wonder. Was she the hawk who was unlucky? Yet, the bird had mastered the mystery of flight, had the eyesight to see a tiny object from far way, and could scurry through tall grass to scramble for supper. Whatever wonderful abilities the hawk had, in this instant they were not enough. The hawk for now would be hungry. Another time, it would succeed. *Am I a hawk?* she mused. *Or am I the mouse?*

Yes, it is true that she was missing something that made her different from everyone else in her world. In that difference, the strength of bonding was even more intense. At her home in England it was Sky Flower who taught her how to communicate, and that was the true meaning of interaction among all creatures. Harold, in a different way, had brought her from the depths of depression into a meaningful world. Angel responded to her with the blink of an eye. Certainly, her father, Lord Walsingham, had tried his best to understand and support her. Her mother, clearly, was having a change of heart.

Here in Hartford she also felt a bonding with her new family. Rebecca, burdened with her own devil, had shown Mary a world in words that often touched her soul. Thomas, in his own strange way, was a thread to a mystery that spoke of the intensity of life itself. Master and Mistress Adams demonstrated a way of life rigidly devoted to the afterlife. Pieter had come into her life bringing ideas and discoveries. Mary knew that she was blessed with those around her. And when any terrible threat darkened her space, there was the tall grass where safety favored small creatures.

Yes, she was more like the mouse. And so far in life, like the mouse, she had been lucky.

Mouse or not, Mary knew that her life was changing. She could no longer depend on luck alone to see her through the years ahead. It was not only her body that had changed, but it was also her throbbing needs. Those needs seemed to be focusing on the new person in her life, Pieter. Each of the Adams family in his or her own way may have been the bridge. What lay on the other side of that bridge was an unknown land. Many an explorer has been lost after crossing a bridge that led to into uncharted territory.

Reassurance

WITH NEWS OF Mary's impending departure, Thomas became more withdrawn than ever. Rebecca now tried to reach out to him. Her first effort was a poem, well-chosen in words but with no thought of meter or rhyme:

Dear Thomas,

The tree that stands beside our house
began as a sprout.
Over the years it became a sapling
Then came branches and leaves.
In the heat of summer
It gives us cooling shade.

You are much like that tree.
Once a small child
Growing fast and handsome
To become the strong, long-limbed man
Who reaches out to work the fields
And make this home a better place.

You live in a world
Of which we know little
Yet, I admire and support
Those interests to which you so devote yourself.
For whatever reason you keep them secret
The more I yearn to discover them.

I hope that there will be a day
When you can share with me
The great mystery that you lock inside yourself
And may someday glow for the world to see.
I think you right-minded and kind
Know that I could not love you more.
From Your Sister, Rebecca

The poet also left a note at Mary's bedside.

My dearest Mary. It is said that a Bay Colony sloop will leave in the morning. I do not understand the meaning of "Goodbye" but will come to know it in your absence. I am happy for you and sad, too. Do not weep for me. I no longer feel helpless and alone, as I did before you came to the plantation. I now am stronger inside myself. Our way of life may seem void of necessities, but it is not joyless. You have helped me find beauty in every way possible.

You can leave knowing that Thomas speaks to me. He handed me one of his favorite rocks. It is most uncommon. I must show it to you. He has promised to take me for a long walk to show me where he has made a splendid altar to the Spirits of the Forest. I am eager to see.
Your friend forever and a day, Rebecca

Mary read the note with joyous relief. With the thought that she had already seen the secret "Altar to the Spirits," she dozed off.

Difficult Decision

THERE WAS ONE more letter to write, perhaps the most difficult of all. It was meant for Pieter. The song of starry-eyed desire is a difficult one to sing because the beginning notes have pauses and repetitions before blending into a tender and beautiful melody. Mary, having never felt the lure of romance, was ill-prepared to play the tune with purpose or finesse. She knew only that she wanted to be near Pieter, whatever his untold story, one more time even as a ship was readied to carry her away. Mary felt the forces of two opposing themes that were heard more in her heart than in her head.

My Dear Pieter,
I write this note with a giant stone lying on my chest, squeezing out my breath, for I have something giant tell you. Word came to

> *our village that your ship has returned to House of Good Hope. I hold not back my feelings of joy that I may see you..*
>
> *Well I remember your first smile to me shaded beneath that orange brim. You never know how your stories and puzzles made me laugh and wonder. Yes, they kept me from going mad during those long winter nights. The most wonderful moment of all my life stand with you at your secret place and look out at the torch-lit black pool of another world. Do you remember first and only time we touched? You put your hands together to make a stirrup for me to rise onto Angel.*
>
> *Now I like share with you my decision that comes not easy. I await you in the meadow. Please allow me the graciousness of attending.*
>
> *—From the ugly girl on the beautiful horse, Mary Walsingham.*

Throughout the evening she continued to think about her letter, but, come morning after her chores, she chose not to change a single word. Instead she reveled in a good scrub, brushed her hair with the zeal of grooming once expended on Angel, and at the last moment wrapped her very un-Puritan red scarf round her neck. So readied, Mary walked toward the House of Good Hope.

Reflections

On that brisk, sun-filled day in early October Mary took her letter and walked with determined purpose across the floating bridge and along the river toward the House of Good Hope. Joyful she was upon seeing a boat with the red and yellow triangles on the sides. Just beyond was the Dutch fort and, hopefully, there inside the wall of stakes, was Pieter.

The gate opened a trifle at her approach. The letter addressed to Pieter passed to the hand of the guard. Afterwards, Mary wandered along the outer edge of the clearing wondering what to do. Seldom had she felt a more fretful time, not knowing if she should proceed home or simply wait. She finally decided to go into the nearby field where tall knee-high grass stood on a long-neglected garden.

Walking aimlessly through the grass, she relived in her mind's eye the events of her life. Her thoughts brought back memories of endless days in the welcoming pastures that she knew so well in her childhood. It was here, in her unendurable loneliness, that she sought refuge, and where she would spend time happily watching the horses graze amid the world of butterflies and red-winged blackbirds. She recalled days during her childhood when a field of beautiful things lifted her out of her own sorrow. The field of gently waving grasses seemed to speak to her, calling her home.

Mary knelt for a moment where her view across the grassland was shoulder high. Here, she found a universe all her own. Although she knew nothing of music, the waving of the grass in puffs of wind gave her a sense of rhythm. The clear autumnal colors of sky, fields, river, and maples all came together in blue, green, yellow, gray, red, and brown. Her fingertips slid along a stalk of grass that was smooth and strong yet able to bend easily. The stalk led to a seed-filled, feathery tip much like a fine brush for painting. She relished in Nature's delicate tickle as the tip crossed her brow. Now, crouching close to the ground, she smelled the soil that was the mother of all life.[72]

These senses, altogether, gave Mary some measure of rhythm, tone, harmony and texture that—in a world of silence—was music enough. The things seen, touched, and smelled became the sounds of her imagination, and these, in turn, became the music that filled her life. Basking in the sun-touched field, she joyfully embraced her blessings.

Life at this time had taken her far away. For too long she had been far from home. Now it was time to return. As promised long ago, she would return to the Manor House with wonderful stories to relate. She imagined the supreme blessing of feeling herself once again in the sturdy arms of her father. A new understanding with her mother, so longed for and never realized, was finally to come true. Perhaps her sisters and her brother, however caught up in following their own pursuits, would have a deeper respect for their adventurous sister; after all, she had now seen a good part of the world and had proven herself hardy and resilient.

What of her new family that she would never see again? Master and Mistress Adams and their children? Each one was special and unique and would remain a treasured memory. And what would Pieter think? Would he even miss her? There was a new feeling in her soul that could not easily fit into the thought of departure. Now as she awaited Pieter for a final goodbye, a solitary, puffy white cloud slowly drifted toward her. She did not know that it was a rain cloud in her overloaded mind that was soon to burst.

Cloudburst

Mary was not long in such deep thought. She saw in the distance an orange hat bobbing across the waving grass. Pieter! Mary greeted him with constrained exuberance, extending a hand. It was taken with a deep bow and a delicate kiss on the back of her hand. Walking together slowly, they found a small rise along the riverbank where it was comfortable to sit. The bluff offered a view of the river that extended far in both directions. Pieter had brought paper, already written on. There were several pages. Mary read the first one, shading the paper from the sun with one cupped hand.

Dear Mary,
I am happy to see you again. You must first tell me of the giant stone that weighs you down. Can I be of help?
Yours, Pieter

Mary had come with some pages already written for Pieter. The message had been heavy on her mind. It was not easy to write but she knew it was the proper thing to do.

Pieter. You must know a sloop is at our plantation now. Bound for Boston it is. I decide return to England from Boston. I sad not see my family long time. My father care much about me. Now, Mother writes she needs me. I feel I need her. One sister soon marry. Without Angel I walk every day and feel empty. Puritan life not much my liking. Rebecca, my dearest friend. I take some of her poems to England. Father knows a man print books. She will become famous poet. Yet, I will look every day for Visarend to appear at bend in River Thames where is my home. And so, I have come to bid farewell. I think I will miss you beyond reason. Mary.

Pieter read the paper as Mary tried to read his face. It was as frozen as a statue. She snatched the paper from him and, emboldened beyond civil modesty, continued scribbling on the last page.

A strong voice calls me to my home. Given favorable wind, the sloop will leave in the morning. I never forget you. Know I leave my heart for you in the Colonies.

On reading these words, Pieter quickly scrawled at the bottom, *No, Mary. When you go to England, all of you must go. You must not leave your heart here. So, I will go with you, too.*

A rain cloud had burst and overflowed. It was not the cloud that was now overhead but rather the words of Pieter that flooded Mary's mind. As she read, he touched the back of her hand with his fingertips, then withdrew to write on a fresh paper. He wrote a long time, and his words led on to two more pages. He wrote quickly and distinctly.

Breathing fitfully, Mary read the first page as he continued to write the others.

You know little of me other than my arriving on a small ship and entertaining children. You and only you know of my Special Place. Here is a little more of my life.

My home is far up what the Dutch call the "North River." It was discovered by an English captain in a Dutch ship. That was thirty years ago when the Wilden lived along its banks. Since then, people from Holland have made a village. It now has many farms, some kilns and two windmills. Thirty families are there in small separate houses. I grew up there. I had one sister.

At first our people traded with the Wilden who brought great numbers of beaver pelts to trade. Ships carried the pelts to Holland where they fetched a good price. The fort on this river is another place to collect peltry in exchange with the Indians for tools and blankets. Now, the beavers are becoming scarce. Our people turn to making lumber and bricks. These are what we bring to your plantation to exchange for whatever furs...

Second page...

your men are willing to trade.

Mary stopped him at this point. She had read enough of trading. She took the paper and wrote in bold letters,

WHO IS KATRINA?

Pieter flinched and drew back. He had heard a rush in the thick grass. Movement caught the corner of Mary's eye. Just then a chicken burst from the underbrush with a dog in hot pursuit. Both were gone as suddenly as they had come.

Taking back the paper, Pieter wrote, *My sister. She had consumption. It was a condition of much coughing and sad wasting. Katrina died almost ten years ago from the pox. She was only fifteen years old.*

Mary felt a warm flush cross her face that quickly spread down her neck. She had to know more. Pieter obliged.

I was Katrina's little brother. I found great fun in playing tricks on her. But I loved her dearly. I know that she loved me.

With this, he brought out the medallion that had slipped beneath his shirt. Mary saw the highly polished ornament and its small but bold letters: You are in my heart forever. He wrote next: *My father made this for me.*

Pieter cradled the medallion with reverential care. He held it forward for Mary to touch. This she did. With the tip of her pointer finger, she felt its smooth surface across the face and the raised dots that ran along the entire edge.

He kept scribbling: *Father suffered much at her death. He asked me to keep this reminder always close by.*

The words began to blur from tears, but Mary continued the reading.

Near the end, a Wilde girl came to care for her. Katrina was getting well again. Then came the pox. They both suffered but the Wilde lived. Many years later I learned that she had gone to England. I grew up fond of traveling and that led to my work on a small ship. I am now twenty-one years old. Someday, I want to be captain of an ocean-going ship. I will make you proud of me.

Mary was astonished at the reading. There was more.

Mary, before we go to England, I will take you to Holland and to the city called Leyden where I grew up. You will meet Moeder and Vader. My Vader is a trader in furs and woolens. Our huys is always lively with visitors who have traveled around the world. In Leyden there are many fine artists. They will show you their ways and you will have all colors to paint with. I believe deep in my heart that you will become a famous painter.

Stunned again by the words, here in the full sunshine, Mary was awash in the sudden chilling drench of an imaginary rain cloud. She held back any sign of approving. Pieter took back the page and wrote on the bottom,

Before that, we must go to New Amsterdam on the North River, a day's sail west in good wind. It is the biggest city in the Colonies. There you see a harbor where masts of ships from around the world rise as if trees in a forest. There is a great battery fort, some windmills, many houses in neat rows, and a real inn. There is room for one more on the Visarend. It also sails in the morning. Will you come?

Mary smile changed into a look of disbelief.

On another clean page he continued:

Afterwards, we must go to my home, a day's sail farther up on the North River to a village called Beverwijck. There you will see large gardens and the making of tiles and lumber. With you at my side the journeys will be my greatest joy.

Thought Mary, *Can this be true? Am I dreaming?*

She was aware of a skipping in her heartbeat as if it had a mind of its own and, at this very moment, it was in a playful mood.

Then—most astonishing of all—Pieter put down pen and paper. With hands, he pointed to himself, then to Mary. His hands then came together so that the fingers meshed.

Does Pieter want to marry me? Mary knew at that moment that her inability to hear did not matter, that love did not need to speak aloud; it was there always, all ways. There are times when a simple choice determines life's destiny. For Mary, such a time had come. Two boats, pointed in different directions, each awaiting for her to step aboard.

For want of air, her breath quickened, and she read the words of Pieter one more time. Once again pins and needles came to the tips of her fingers and around her mouth. A thousand thoughts burst in her head at one time. One found its way to paper. Mary wrote, *What happened to the Indian girl who went to England?*

She waited a long time for him to write a reply.

> *She found a position caretaking children in a family of the noble kind somewhere near London. There she became good at languages and the use of numbers. She learned the manners of the gentles' class. She returned after many years, but chose not to go back to the forest with her own people. Instead, she started a little school where she taught Dutch tykes, both boys and girls. A few Wilden children also came to her school. Over the years she became a good friend. I helped her build a tiny schoolhouse on an island near my village. I could often tell that my Indian friend was very sad. Still, no one knows why. Even so, she has become a wonderful teacher of English, French, and her own Iroquois as well as numbers and other learned things. From her the children learned, too, about insects, birds, trees, and stars. She taught them much about Indian ways. They become good at speaking with hands. For fun, she taught me some hand-talking. I think you will like her.*

Suddenly feeling light-headed and hungry for a deep breath, Mary leaned against Pieter for support. With trembling hands, now both needed to hold the paper, she scribbled: *Does your Wilde teacher have marks on her face from the pox?*

Returned Pieter, writing on his bended knee: *Yes, many.*

Taking his quill, the paper still resting on his knee, she jotted quickly: *What is her name?*

By way of answer, Pieter pointed with an extended finger to a blade of grass. He stood and pointed to Mary's scarf and then to his hat. Mary could hardly believe what came next: his outstretched arm—fingers fully extended—swept across the sky in a great arch.

The next moments for Mary were a magnificent blur. She tried to clear her head, but the ideas that so completely affected her old life and that were bound to affect her new life were overpowering. Because her hands trembled so much, she could not write an answer. Her head swirled. Her feet were unsteady. Pieter's firm hands reached out to steady her. She let her weight fall against him and, for an instant standing in tall, wind-blown grass, their lips might have touched.

Thunderstruck in the extreme, Mary soon broke away and turned, knowing that she still needed to respond to his plea. She began a slow, numbing walk toward her home. She needed time to think.

Bridge

When she reached the footbridge, she hesitated. A few more steps brought her to the midstream of Little River. She turned to face Pieter but could no longer see him. She held up her handful of letters and read them all again. The last words seemed to float away from the paper and find a place somewhere in some depth of her soul. A happy tear slid slowly down one cheek, then fell onto the paper as if it were a gentle kiss. Somehow the pages took on a life of their own. They began to quiver mightily, and fluttered into the water. In an instant, the current carried the pages downstream beyond reach.

Mary knew that they would flow from the Little River into the Great River. From there, they would go into the bay and then across the ocean. She believed that somehow, they would reach the Channel, surge into the River Thames and manage to float against the current of the River Ash. Like the pages, she, too, would arrive at the Manor House in Littleton. There, amid familiar comforts and unfamiliar love, she would see again these soggy but much-cherished writings.

There was, however, another possibility, one that was impossible to ignore. Pulsating and growing more insistent by the moment, it demanded her attention. It would take a circuitous direction into the unknown world of Pieter. What joys and mishaps would such a future bring?

Yes, there was his letter, still tucked beneath her pillow. She would open it. So, one life ends as another begins. Mary Walsingham had known many trials in her short life. Yes, Nature had forgotten her in one sense, but made her stronger in others. She was ready, if hesitant, to face the future on her own. She stood on a shaky bridge and asked herself, *What direction should I take?* Mary listened once again for an answer from that inner voice.

PART II

Notes About the Story

List of Notes in Book 5, *Mary Walsingham*

Chapter	Note	Title
2	1	Littleton
	2	Magpie
	3	Puppet Show
	4	Toys & Games of 17th Century England
	5	Insanity: Changing Attitudes
	6	Hard-of-Hearing With Aging
	7	The River Ash
	8	Horse: Attraction
	9	New Amsterdam
3	10	Pocahontas
	11	Smallpox: Immunity
	12	Gwendolyn: Origin of Name
	13	Sir Francis Drake
	14	Deafness: Children
	15	Chinese Vase
	16	The Royal College of Physicians
	17	Deafness: Early Attitudes
	18	Deafness: Traditional Treatment
	19	Deaf: Education
	20	Prism
	21	The River Thames
	22	Orangery
	23	Horse: Domestication
	24	Blacksmith
	25	Vibrations
	26	Iron Horse
4	27	Foal
	28	Horse
	29	Staines

Chapter	Note	Title
	30	Windsor Castle
	31	Puritans: Plymouth and the Massachusetts Bay Colony
	32	Pudding Lane
	33	*Countrey Contentments or The English Huswife*
	34	Quayside: London
	35	Animals: Ship Transport
	36	Gervase Markham (B. 1568 – D. 1637)
	37	Fishers Island
	38	Connecticut River
	39	Leadsman or Plumb Lead Line
	40	Bodkin Rock
5	41	Fainting
	42	Hartford: The Beginning
	43	Nutmeg
	44	Food
	45	Horses: North America
6	46	Colonial House
	47	Diaspora
	48	Reverend Thomas Hooker
	49	Oxen and Horses
	50	First People
	51	Migraine
	52	Colonial Women
	53	Historical Data
	54	Dutch Fort and Trading Post: House of Good Hope
	55	Neighbors: The Dutch and the English
	56	Meetinghouse
	57	Connecticut Constitution
	58	Dutch Sloop
9	59	Spring Peepers
	60	Bathing
	61	Hartford: The City
	62	Flood
	63	Quinsy
10	64	Almandine
	65	Witch
	66	John Donne

The Notes

CHAPTER 2: EARLY LIFE

2-1 Littleton

The tiny village of Littleton sits just a couple of miles north of the Thames where the river makes a sharp bend at its southernmost reach. Fragments of spears, swords, wooden posts with lead coatings, and human bones provide evidence that Roman legions were here long ago. Vikings coming upriver and marauding villages along the way left their relics. Mention is made of Littleton in records back as far as 1165, the time of the Crusades. Today, it is a quiet, laid-back cluster of mostly brick cottages surrounded by some impressive features.

A. The Old Manor House

The manor house, where this story begins, dates to the 1500s. It currently serves as a B&B. The street view from Squires Bridge Road is that of a long, plain whitened brick wall with many windows. The rear of the building consists of two reddish-toned peaked wings (one on each side) and a smaller one in the middle. The house overlooks an expansive, tree-lined courtyard bounded by the River Ash. Modern amenities for houseguests do not mask the ambience of old nobility of early Stuart England.

The builder of the Manor House and information about its first family has thus far eluded a search for information. The name Walsingham comes up, but this has not been substantiated by the time of this writing. We do know that a much larger and far grander estate, called "Barn Elms," was built in an area now identified as the London borough of Richmond. It was the home of Sir Francis Walsingham, long the chief adviser to Queen

Elizabeth I and a strong promotor of the Jamestown colony in the New World. The estate, alas, has not survived the centuries.

B. Queen Mary's Reservoir

Across the road from the Old Manor House is an earthen mound that rises seventy-five feet above ground. The mound lies on the perimeter of a huge reservoir, London's main supply of water. The reservoir forms a lake that is one mile across. Here, members of the public have an opportunity to windsurf or sail a dinghy at forty-five feet above the surrounding terrain.

Construction of the reservoir took many years. Its enclosing embankment consists of clay, covered with gravel and over that, a depth of grassy soil. After the interruption of the First World War, the reservoir was completed in 1927 when the demand for water in the city had reached a critical point. It was dedicated in 1925 by King George V and named in honor of his deceased spouse, Queen Mary.

Water pumped from the Thames fills the reservoir. There it is rendered potable before flowing to London and its suburbs. The structure ensures that the city always has a sufficient supply of fresh water that can be delivered by the natural pressure of gravity.

In the construction of the reservoir, much of the village of Astleham (or Astlam and other variations) and some parts of the old village of Littleton were drowned, including a few houses and the church. Dislocated residents found accommodations along the "New Road." The original Astleham Manor House was relocated to the Chiltern Open Air Museum. It is said by long-time residents that on a quiet night when the temperature and the wind are just right, you can still faintly hear the church bell ringing down under.

C. St. Mary Magdalene Anglican Church

This Anglican Church goes back a long way. It was named to honor Mary Magdalene, who devoted her life to extolling the message of

Christianity after she believed Jesus had cast out her demons. She was canonized as a legendary example of mercy and grace.

Records show that monks of the Benedictine Abbey lived at St Mary Magdalene church in 1135. Its naves, font, altar, choir stalls, and pews have been preserved since medieval times. The tower was laid in the 16th century with additional height and bells added in the 19th century. Brickwork was overlaid with granite. Chips of mica within the granite provide its sparkling surface. Fifty-four gravestones surround the church. The earliest one bears the name of Edward Dyer who died in 1816 at the age of 44.

D. Shepperton Studios

Here in Littleton is the sprawling film production company, Shepperton Studios. The studios have produced and hosted the sets for many well-known motion pictures. Among them on a long list are: *The African Queen* (1951), *Dr. Strangelove* (1968), *Oliver* (1968), *The Elephant Man* (1980), *A Passage to India* (1984), *The Madness of King George* (1994), *Harry Potter and the Prisoner of Azkaban* (2004), *The Da Vinci Code* (2006), *Anna Karenina* (2012), and *Beauty and the Beast* (2017).

E. Heathrow Airport

Only five miles from Littleton is Heathrow Airport, one of the busiest airports in the world. From time to time its activities break the tranquility of the village. At the time of this story, the noise most likely to disturb the peace was the bleating of flocks of sheep on the way to a barge on the River Thames bound for a London market.

2-2 Magpie

The European magpie is identified by the striking black and white pattern of its plumage, its black beak, and a tail that is as long as its body. Rough-voiced chattering and a swaggering hop give away its identity.

The magpie is a member of the same family as crows and jays. It is renowned for its intelligence. It is the only known non-mammal that can recognize itself in a mirror. The cheeky bird has a reputation, deserved or not, of stealing little shiny things and incorporating them into its nest.

In 1817, Gioachino Rossini's opera, *The Thieving Magpie* (*La gazza ladra*), was first performed in Milan, Italy. In Act One, a silver spoon in the home of a well-to-do family goes missing. Accused of stealing it is a servant girl, Ninetta. The penalty at that time for stealing was death. As she is standing on the gallows in Act Two, Ninetta is saved when word comes at the last minute that the missing spoon had been found in the nest of a magpie.

2-3 Puppet Shows

Puppet shows go back a long time. At the time of our story, traveling puppeteers (or "motion men") went from town market to county fair to engage an audience. The characters—figures made around the gloved hand—were for entertainment, but they could also send a powerful message. Stories from the Bible (such as "Jonah and the Whale") were standard repertoire. Certainly, life's struggles were dramatized to the fullest in this miniaturized world. Using dramatic contrasts such as beautiful and ugly, conflict and peace, comedy and tragedy, heroes and villains, puppeteers commanded a rapt audience, perhaps enchanted and fearful at the same time. The puppets Punch and Judy, originally from Italy, depicted in sharp relief the eternal struggle between good and evil, all performed with a twist of humor.

Private performances of puppet shows came to the homes of the wealthy and, no doubt, portrayed what is expected of the ideal child. The familiar puppets animated by strings did not appear until much later in the century of this story.

2-4 Toys & Games of 17th Century England

Children throughout history have found amusement in simple things. The most important toy of the time (and perhaps of all times) was the doll. There were two kinds of dolls. One was meant to be cuddled and dressed up, the other more ferocious in the form of a soldier or hunter. One was made from cloth in various colors, the other from wood or metal. Toys deemed appropriate for each gender emphasized expectations as adults.

A hoop from a broken wagon wheel could be propelled across the lawn with a well-directed smack of a stick; it could be tossed into the air and caught with two sticks. A top, whipped by pulling on a wound-up string, could spin. Knucklebones were tossed in the air and caught with various positions of the hands, an early version of jacks. Knocking over nine-pins by rolling a ball was the forerunner of bowling. Balls of leather, wood or clay provided a never-ending assortment of games. The hobby horse, for most children, was probably little more than a wooden head attached to a pole that a child stood astride and pretended to gallop.

2-5 Insanity: Changing Attitudes

The mentally ill, historically, comprised a sad lot. An age-old description of the insane was the "inability to reason." In the early modern period, beginning in the seventeenth century, madness was largely a family burden. The family had to deal with a mentally deranged member as best it could, while keeping him or her secluded behind the curtains at home and out of their neighbors' eyes.

An insane person without family protection but deemed harmless might roam the streets of Stuart England, begging at passing coaches, churches, and private homes, and displaying bizarre behavior that an unsympathetic public often found amusing. In London, the privilege of begging required a license, and the license had to be displayed on the left arm. Where there was question of an addled mind that might lead to harming oneself or others, the old Bethlem Royal Hospital (aka Bethlehem or Bedlam)would suffice. Here, patients were often chained to the wall and abused in diverse and appalling ways.

At the time, there was an underlying belief that insanity meant the separation of the mind from its natural state, somehow involving God's will; it could only be remedied by disciplinary actions. One of the prevalent concepts of insanity in the sixteenth and seventeenth centuries was that the insane carried "a stone in the head." Of course, the possibility of cure by removing the stone was not left unnoticed by a plethora of unscrupulous surgical practitioners who made a well-padded livelihood in the procedure. Gowned in the exotic clothing and headdress of a surgeon, with scalpel in hand, the quack made an incision in the scalp. From within the bloodied hair came the "Ah Ha!" moment that the family had waited for anxiously. The operator pulled out a pebble, much like a modern magician pulls a live dove from behind a scarf, seemingly out of thin air. The promised results: dubious. The surgeon: long gone.

While attempts to classify forms of mental illness had to wait another couple of centuries, there are many literary examples portraying neuroses and psychoses in fictional characters in the early seventeenth century. Among them are:

Don Quixote: A dirt farmer turned knight-errant acted on delusions of serving God by removing evil from the face of the earth. In doing so, he would, incidentally, become rich. A modern diagnosis of "schizophrenia" would cover this condition.

Lear: As the king ages, his speeches become more rambling, not inconsistent with the natural deterioration of mental function common with advancing age. In a word: "senile." In addition, King Lear suffered from hallucinations with periods of morbid melancholy that were interrupted by eruptions of manic behavior. Adding to the diagnosis of senility, we can make a good case for a "bi-polar disorder."

Ophelia: a titanic conflict between loyalty to her slain father and love of Hamlet unhinges the brittle framework of a grief-stricken girl, still in her teens. She acts almost oblivious to the act of drowning herself. It is her clothes that pull her down into the water, and she does not resist. Today's diagnosis of "Post Traumatic Stress Disorder" with depression would seem quite appropriate.

2-6 Hard-of-Hearing with Aging

Of course, reduced hearing acuity is an age-old problem related, in fact, to old age. Practically everyone is familiar with an elderly person who asks family and friends to "speak up." In most cases, the cause is a developing rigidity of the three tiny bones of the middle ear that conduct sound waves.

These three bones (the ossicles) connect the tympanic membrane (ear drum) with the oval membrane that covers the inner ear. They transmit vibrations of ambient sound from the tympanic membrane and amplify the volume of sound by about twenty-two times before it stimulates the oval membrane. From there, the vibrations are converted from mechanical to fluid energy in the cochlea of the inner ear. Microscopic nerve endings along the snail-like, curved cochlear in turn stimulate the auditory nerve. The brain receives these impulses and interprets the entire experience as language, music, warnings, or plain noise.

With aging, the articulated auditory ossicular chain becomes less flexible in a condition known as otosclerosis. High pitched vibrations are usually most affected. Consequently, in everyday speech, elderly persons are more likely to ask a woman to repeat herself than to ask a man. Various designs of "ear trumpets" were used historically to help focus sound before electronics changed everything.

2-7 The River Ash

The River Ash in Littleton is a tributary of the Thames. It makes a loop near the Old Manor House at a crossing that became known as

"Watersplash." At the end of the lawn there is now a bypass canal dug out across the loop. It is this stream that separates lawn from woodland.

The Shepperton Studios filmed part of the movie blockbuster *African Queen* farther upstream. While most of the filming was shot in the jungles of the Belgian Congo and Uganda in 1951, those scenes in which actors Hepburn and Bogart had to get in the water were taken in the River Ash or in an aquatic tank on site. Tropical vegetation, leeches and other exotica used in these sets were imported.

2-8 Horse Attraction

There is something about a horse that commands attention. While it is huge compared with humans, the horse is nevertheless graceful and gentle. The noble and loyal horse has served humankind for four or five thousand years, providing transportation, power, sports, a show of wealth and, lastly, leather and food.

The only defense a wild horse has against predators is being fleet afoot. Escape from a stalking cougar is possible by a burst of speed well over thirty miles an hour for short distances and by a canter for much longer distances at a slower pace. Long legs and hooves are well suited to running on the hard surfaces of the plains. Its eyes can detect movement in an almost complete circle, looking forward and back simultaneously. Sitting near the back of the head, the eyes can see above grass when the horse is grazing. Horses sleep standing with their legs locked in place and so are ready to run at the instant an alarm startles them.

Domesticated around the world, the horse has been bred over thousands of years to run fast or pull or carry a heavy load. The race horse is slender, nervous, and delicate. On the other hand, horses bred for hauling and pulling a plough are large, thickly built, and patient. The saddle horse, with its small head and long neck, carries the rider with graceful elegance.

Horses in the British Isles, Europe, and the Near East were a major part of everyday life from the Middle Ages on. Breeding horses that were envied for good looks, stamina and speed became an all-consuming passion of the well-to-do. It led to an extensive world-wide trading industry. Of course, a horse was expensive, as it is now, for it required dedicated and complex upkeep.

But there were practical advantages, too, for having a horse. Centuries ago, the successful, common farmer may well have owned a horse. It allowed him to till a much larger garden and to transport his produce by wagon longer distances to market. In balance, the advantage was partially offset by the many details involved in caring for a horse.

The elite of English society may have had dozens of horses, some to plough and harrow and some to pull a coach. Horseback riding, requiring another kind of horse, was a major avocation for the gentry. There was no greater symbol of wealth and power than a well-proportioned and spirited horse ridden by a properly dressed gentleman who could literally look down on an ordinary passerby. Having a well-trained horse for riding, hunting and racing became an obsession of the seventeenth and eighteenth centuries in the English manor house. Of course, the nobles and upper-class gentry had a staff of caretakers who fed, groomed, harnessed, shoed, doctored, and swept up after the horses.

The king and the royalty of the ruling classes were wealthy enough to maintain hundreds of horses. Many were trained for battle and kept on a war-like footing. Certainly, a fleet of horses provided a formidable reminder of the king's power. King Charles I, ruling at the time of this story, was particularly fond of race horses. He is portrayed by Sir Anthony van Dyck on horseback in armor with sword. He appears to be surveying his kingdom. Painted around 1637, the portrait can be seen at the National Gallery in London.

A comprehensive look at the horse throughout the ages can be found in a book by Peter Edwards, Professor of Early Modern British Social

History at the University of Roehampton. His book is entitled *Horse and Man in Early Modern England.*

2-9 New Amsterdam

Dutch traders first settled on Governors Island in New York Bay in 1624. In a notorious deal with the native Lenapes in 1626, Peter Minuit of the Dutch West India Company purchased the island and established a village on the southernmost tip of Manhattan Island. They called it "New Amsterdam."

While the Dutch considered New Amsterdam but one of the many colonies for trade around the world, they did make small attempts to attract settlers. The first groups were dispersed up the Hudson River to Fort Orange (the area of Albany today), while others were sent up the Connecticut River (to the area of Hartford today). The rest were to stay in New Amsterdam. The fate of each of these first settlers has its own story. Actually, most of them were not Dutch but rather Huguenots. These were Protestants of French origin who went to Holland to evade persecution by the pursuing Catholic Spanish. Obviously, their tenuous life in the Dutch cities led them to choose the uncertainty of a new life in the New World. The story of what happened during and after these events is well-told in Russell Shorto's book *The Island at the Center of the World.*

CHAPTER 3: SKY FLOWER

3-10 Pocahontas

Pocahontas was the daughter of an Powhatan chieftain who ruled over a large territory in the Virginia area at the time of the first permanent colony at Jamestown. She is most famous for saving Captain John Smith from execution (a legend not historically validated). Years later, she was captured by the English in a conflict with the Indians. Eventually she married a planter, John Rolfe. They went to England where she was greeted as royalty or "Princess" (as if a regal system existed in the Americas) or as a mere curiosity, such as a colorful bird of paradise.

Pocahontas and John Rolfe had one son, named Thomas. It is worth noting that many distinguished Americans trace their heritage through Thomas.

Within a year, Mr. and Mrs. Rolfe boarded a ship to return to America. The ship had barely made it to the mouth of the Thames when Pocahontas fell sick and died not long after. The cause may have been smallpox. She was twenty-one years old. A statue of her stands in the Pocahontas Princess Gardens at St. George Church in Gravesend, England. A pair of earrings believed to have belonged to her were handed down through the Rolfe family. They are made of white shells from mussels that are mounted in silver. The earrings, belonging to the Association for Preservation of Virginia Antiquities, can be seen at the colonial museum in Jamestown.

The story of Pocahontas is awash in myths. A version by the local Powhatans, the tribe in Virginia, has been told in *The True Story of Pocahontas: The Other Side of History*. The book is by Dr. Linwood "Little Bear" Custalow and Angela L. Daniel.

3-11 Smallpox: Immunity

People in the seventeenth century had good reason to fear smallpox. Spread from person to person, it often came in waves to communities and persisted as an ever-present threat. It could wipe out a family overnight. Certainly, the scars on smallpox survivors were common within the general population.

Smallpox is a viral illness that most prominently affects whole body skin, causing acute blisters that eventually slough and leave scars, known as pox-marks or pocks. The illness also affects other organs, most particularly, the lung. Pneumonia is the most common cause of death, coming to about 20 to 40 percent of Europeans affected. For indigenous people in the colonies, a fatal outcome was probably closer to 80 percent.

With no known remedy for it, physicians of the seventeenth and eighteenth centuries injected people with pus-matter taken from a blister of someone with the illness. This "natural" vaccine caused smallpox, but usually it was a much milder form of the illness than in the naturally acquired disease. The vaccine provided permanent immunity. The death rate from the vaccine, however, was 3 to 5 percent. The risk was taken by some of our Founding Fathers, for example Jefferson and Franklin, for their families. President Washington ordered that all the recruits in the Continental Army be vaccinated against smallpox. This illness, common among recruits, was far more fearful and deadly than the Red Coats.

Once a vaccine derived from cow pox (a related infection) was adapted, immunity was guaranteed with an induced death rate of zero percent. It is the vaccine used today. The last case of community-acquired smallpox recorded in the world occurred in Somalia in 1977. The vaccine against it is safe and effective. Its incorporation into public health policies has provided an example of a triumph of immunization; the vaccine remains one of the world's greatest medical advancements.

3-12 Gwendolyn: Origin of Name

The name Gwendolyn goes back to the Middle Ages. Geoffrey, a clergyman in Wales and author of the King Arthur legends, wrote about a Celtic queen of that name. She was abandoned by an unfaithful husband who was beguiled by a German princess. Gwendolyn gathered together an army and, in a pitched battle with her husband's troops, was victorious. The remaining years of her realm were left in peace.

The Welsh word gwen means fair or pure. Dolyn refers to ring or brow. How the name came to be used for the canary in our story is purely whimsical, perhaps because it just seems to roll off the tongue. It is a given name that has been sustained to the present time.

3-13 Sir Francis Drake

Cats in a bygone age were not kept as pets. After all, one cannot train a cat to do anything useful, such as other domesticated animals do. Rather, they were left on their own, unfed, to do what comes naturally: catch mice. A fat cat was assumed to be a good mouser. Sir Francis Drake, an ocean-wandering and skilled predator of ships, seems a fitting namesake for a cat also with a strong reputation as a predator.

The sea captain (ca. 1540-1596) was given a knighthood by Queen Elizabeth I for his naval exploits on behalf of the Crown and for being the first one to to circumnavigate the globe (1577- 1580). He helped defeat the Spanish Armada in 1588.

3-14 Deafness: Children

The situation of the child born deaf or acquiring deafness before learning a language is different from that of an elderly person who is hard-of-hearing. Before the age of electronics, parents could only detect complete deafness of their child by inference. There was no direct way for the child to comprehend that a critical sense for communication was missing; the development of coherent speech was therefore impossible. Because the great majority of babies born with deafness have hearing parents, the suspicion of why a deaf child does not speak or play nicely with other children is often delayed for years.

In a previous era, the child who was non-verbal because of deafness was considered by family and society in general as peculiar, mindless (quite literally, without a mind), or, worse, possessed by the Devil. The deaf were forced into a life of loneliness. Menial labor and begging were the usual occupational prospects. Public ridicule and commitment to an asylum, when available, of these lost souls was commonplace.

We know that beginning to learn a language very early in life has a crucial effect on the thinking processes. This experience has a bearing on complex social interactions. The typical child has a "spurt" of developing vocabulary at about eighteen months of age and is capable of learning several new words a day. In the child with a serious hearing defect, this spurt is significantly delayed. In the profoundly deaf, there is no spurt without digital hearing devices. Children who do not learn a language by the time they enter the first grade will be severely disadvantaged in eventually learning one. To give some idea of the impact of non-assisted hearing: in the 1980s half the deaf children in the United States and in Canada did not speak with intelligible language.

In addition to the problem of language development, children who are deaf miss out on important experiences of nature: the purring of a cat, a running brook, a robin's call, and the clatter of hoof beats. Enjoyment of music for the unaided deaf is at best restricted to the beat. Even more important is the inability to hear an approaching thunder storm, a scream, a fire alarm, or an on-coming vehicle.

The predominant reason that deafness occurs in the very young is damage to the microscopic hair cells that line up along the cochlear bone of the inner ear. Normally, these hair cells respond to movement of fluid within the cochlear chamber; they convey impulses to the auditory nerve. Damage from disease or injury can also affect the auditory nerve directly. Before routine immunization, rubella (German measles) was the leading cause of deafness in children in the United States. It was probably the cause of Helen Keller's loss of hearing and vision at the age of three. Other diseases of viruses incurred during pregnancy may also be an indirect cause of children being born deaf.

Early detection of deafness is now a standard of care in the modern newborn nursery. The often shocking discovery spares the family the exasperation of trying to find out over the next few years why their child is not learning to communicate.

Testing of hearing in the infant is done by making clicking sounds at the ear and sensing its "echo" when it reflects off the inner ear (cochlea). If the results are questionable, a backup test detects the neurological response of auditory clicks by sensors of movement placed on the forehead.

3-15 Chinese Vase

Such a treasure as a fine, blue-on-white flowered vase in a seventeenth century English home could tell a world-wide story. It may have been made in China where the art of white porcelainware with cobalt blue underglaze was highly accomplished by the fourteenth century. The white clay used in the making of pottery was much envied by Europeans.

Imported to Jakarta (Indonesia), the vase may have been taken in trade by the Dutch who had established a long-distance trading venture by 1602. Renaming the city Batavia (the old Latin name for the Netherlands), the Dutch East India Company loaded its ships with silks, spices (cinnamon, cloves, pepper), and fine-crafted ceramics.

Because this part of Asia was highly self-sufficient in human creature comforts, the Dutch had little to swap except precious metals such as gold and silver, most likely taken from captured Spanish and Portuguese ships. Going and returning, the sailors faced the ever-present dangers of typhoon, scurvy, attack by Spanish, Portuguese, and British ships, and (on land) malaria. A vase, acquired and surviving on such a journey, could command a good price from the well-to-do, ostentatious nobility in England.

3-16 The Royal College of Physicians

In the sixteenth century, London was one of the most prestigious and lucrative places in the world for doctors to set up their medical practices. Competition was fierce but protected by a guild-like organization for the healing arts. It was founded by King Henry VIII and called "The Royal College of Physicians," thus monopolizing medical practice for local doctors. Looked at another way, the College established standards for training doctors and defining their methods of practice. Needless to say, the standards of the time were largely based on textbook misconceptions perpetuated since the teachings of the physicians of ancient Greece.

Today, there is a Royal College of Physicians in three cities: London, Edinburgh, and Glasgow. Members must pass rigorous written and clinical examinations that are held in the United Kingdom and in several countries in Asia, Africa, and the Middle East. Membership in the College is required before entering the various medical and surgical specialties.

3-17 Deafness: Early Attitudes

The first edition of the *Encyclopedia Britannica* (published in 1771) explains deafness in two sentences: "DEAFNESS, the state of a person who either wants the sense of hearing or has it greatly impaired. See DUMB." Under DUMBNESS, there are two columns of small print. The text recognizes the privations caused by deafness. "... these unhappy people must forever be deprived of the use of language; and a language is the principle sense of knowledge; wherever [whoever] has the misfortune to want the sense of hearing, must remain in a state little superior to the text of the brute creature." The entry goes on to explain attempts of one expert in Edinburgh to teach children how to articulate words, an intensive live-in training requiring years. Their understanding of verbal conversation, however, was not clearly defined.

Even once realized, the child with profound deafness was virtually lost in society before the modern era. She was unable to communicate with the hearing world and—what may have been worse—unable to understand why. In reality, the fate of the born-deaf during the not-so-distant past was bleak. This "mistake of nature," on theological grounds, prejudiced the hearing world against the born-deaf by denying that they had the gift of reasoning. Theirs was an invisible handicap. This public sentiment was summed up in a statement in 1858; it said, in effect, there is no use trying to "cultivate the intellect and reason faculty" of deaf persons since they were on a par with "the savages of Patagonia or the North American Indians."

There is no question that language is essential for normal intellectual development. What long escaped educators was the practical belief that sign language is a language! The modern born-deaf person can master it at an early age, and it does not impair the ability to acquire spoken languages later. Electronic devices (hearing aids and/or cochlear implants) now enable the profoundly deaf to become bilingual, using both signing and speaking. Children, given appropriate opportunity, can readily navigate between the hearing and the silent worlds. Even so, deafness is the "invisible problem" that shapes in some way the interactions of people in everyday life.

While it is not easy to get into the mindset of previous ages, exploring what is available in the older literature on deafness leads to one conclusion: the problem was the inability to speak, that most human of all human characteristics. What seems to have been not fully appreciated through the ages was that a person deaf at an early age cannot speak because he cannot hear; these are not two separate entities. The inability of a child to learn to speak is what a family is likely to notice before (and perhaps years before) anyone realizes that the child does not hear.

"Hearing" by tactile sensations alone comes up in the remarkable story of Helen Keller, rendered both deaf and blind at the age of nineteen months, probably by the viral infection German measles (or rubella). Through the devoted and ingenious teaching of Ann Sullivan, Helen learned to understand spoken words and to speak. This accomplishment was achieved over many years by Helen holding her left hand so that the thumb rested on Ann's throat, the second finger over her lips and the third finger on her nose. The first full sentence spoken by Helen after extensive training over years was, "I am not dumb now."

Parents and physicians throughout the ages could do little to alleviate the burden of deafness in a child. Still, they tried mightily. The 1771 first edition of the *Encyclopedia Britannica* cites various treatment strategies when there is no obvious explanation, such as blockage of the ear canals.

This section begins by stating that deafness since birth meant that there was little hope of recovery.

3-18 Deafness: Traditional Treatment

One long-standing tradition for treating deafness was pouring warmed beeswax into the ear canal. In another, fumes from sulfa could be conveyed into the ear canal by a pipe or funnel. Alternatively, "If there is occasion to syringe the ear, a decoction of sage and rosemary-flowers will be proper, with equal parts of water and white wine; but great caution should be used." On the basis that deafness might be due to excessive humidity that causes the auditory nerves to become slack, one antidote was to instill a mixture of Hungary water containing strong perfumes in strong alcohol. Another treatment was wine containing the bitter fluid extracted from the gall bladder of an eel.

3-19 Deaf: Education

Early schools

Despite such an age-old, doom-monger's attitude about hearing-deficient children, there were scattered but serious attempts to address their education by the latter part of the nineteenth century. The effort evolved into an intense competition between two approaches: lip reading and signing by hand movement. In 1880, the Second International Congress on Education of the Deaf was held in Milan, Italy. The Congress embraced lip reading, decreeing that learning to sign would impair the student's ability to learn to read lips. A subtler rationale might be the illusion that a deaf person who learns to read lips is more "normal" than another who converses only in hand-dominated language. Thus, educators were restrained from using manual signing in the classroom. The concept, opposed by a few who favored sign language, dominated deaf-education methods for decades, well into the 20th century.

A. Lip-reading

Reading lips is an important skill for someone who is hard of hearing. A person who is profoundly deaf, however, misses much of a conversation when lip-reading alone. No matter how proficient one is in reading lips, it requires concentration and is quickly tiresome. Furthermore, the speaker must be directly in front of the reader. Even so, there are many chances for misjudging words even when clearly spoken. Experts at reading lips may pick up less than twenty percent of the words in ordinary conversation. A computerized program has proven much more proficient at recognizing lip-shaped words. (ref. "Watch, Attend and Spell," *The Limping Chicken,* March 18, 2017)

The meanings of words that look alike when spoken are conveyed by context and by accompanying facial expressions and hand gestures. The words "bee," "beet," and "bead" are thus distinguished, where the difference in sound is produced unseen at the end by the tongue. Those that sound alike and are shaped alike by the lips—wind, for example—can be easily understood with a simple gesture; in this instance by a hand-turning or a blowing gesture.

B. Signing

The modern born-deaf person can master sign language at an early age. Learning does not impair the ability to acquire spoken languages later. It has been fully demonstrated that signing at an early age is as effective in promoting intellectual development as learning a verbal language.

The pre-eminent center for developing a sign language was in Paris where, in 1760, the first free school of the deaf was founded. A French educator, L. Clerc, brought this discipline to America in 1817 with the founding of the American School for the Deaf in Hartford, Connecticut. The school was led by the famous deaf-educator, Thomas Hopkins Gallaudet. It was the first school in the western continents specifically dedicated to teaching children with handicaps. The ASD continues today in West Hartford; it provides full educational opportunities from an early age through the high school years.

Gallaudet founded the first college for the disabled in 1857 in Washington, DC. Gallaudet University graduated its first class in 1864. Ever since, the college has been a world-wide leader in promoting higher education of the deaf and of the hard of hearing. In 1965, the U.S. Congress established another milestone at the Rochester Institute of Technology in New York. Ten percent of its entering students are profoundly deaf. A professional signer attends each lecture; over the years, electronic innovations have facilitated the student's visual experience.

Sign language may have developed by finger spelling, which is making a certain hand shape to represent each letter. Of course, communication by this method is slow, even with the most skilled signers. Modern signing, however, has developed into a language that uses the hands in specific configurations, positions, and movements, all augmented by facial expressions.

The following description appeared in the UK deaf blog, *The Limping Chicken* on July 24, 2017: "...Eventually, sign language has evolved into a highly efficient means of communication, using the configuration of one or both hands in addition to motion and synchronization with facial expressions. A conversation does not depend upon stringing together individual words but rather is the art of conveying ideas in the form of meaningful bites that capture the intended information, separated by pauses and other forms of visible punctuation. Anyone not familiar with sign language can only watch signers with awe as they communicate with equal facility focused on the most complex or emotional subjects. At an address to the American Association for the Deaf in 1910, George Veditz put it in words, "[The deaf] are first, last and all time the people of the eye."

Is there an international sign language? Yes, but it is not as well developed nor as widely practiced as national and regional sign languages. As written In *The Limping Chicken* by Elisa Nuevo Vallin, who works with the deaf in London:

"Sign languages are independent of spoken languages and follow their own paths of development. For example, although the hearing people of

Spain and Argentina (or Chile, Costa Rica, México ...) share the same spoken language, the Spanish Sign language (LSE) and Argentine Sign Language (LSA) are quite different and mutually unintelligible.

Similarly, countries which use a single spoken language may have two or more sign languages (Great Britain is an example of this ...), or an area that contains more than one spoken language, like South Africa which has eleven official spoken languages, might use only one sign language.

Sign languages evolve wherever there are Deaf people, and they show all the variation (sic) you would expect from different spoken languages. There are regional dialects and 'accents' just like every language."

C. Augmented hearing

1.) Ear horn

Gadgets that funnel sounds toward the outer ear have been used for centuries to improve failing hearing. Amplifying sound in this way may be any conical or trumpet-shaped device. They have been made from animal horns, sea-shells, wood, and metal. Such gadgets have been depicted in caricature for centuries.

2.) Hearing aid

The electronic hearing aid boosts the volume of sound so that vibrations conveyed provide a stronger stimulus on the ear drum. Miniaturization and clarity of sound within the speaking range have been highly developed. The devices are effective when the fault of hearing is in the ear canal, tympanic membrane, or the auditory ossicles. They are not useful in persons whose deafness comes from lost function of the cochlear membrane or from damage to the auditory nerve.

Advanced hearing aids can filter out background noise while retaining voice reception and can dampen excessively loud sounds. The newest models provide a sense of direction and space, allowing the wearer to turn toward (or away from) the voice or noise activator.

3.) Cochlear implant

When the cause of a defect in hearing is in the inner ear, amplification alone is not useful. The cochlear implant provides direct stimulation of the auditory nerve within the cochlea, thus skipping the initial physical apparatus of hearing and going directly to the nerve receptors.

A cochlear implant consists of two elements. (1.) A microphone/transmitter, placed near the external ear, picks up ambient sound and converts it into a digital format. (2.) A receiver/stimulator, placed surgically beneath the skull, senses the digital signal. It then transmits the information as an electronic signal and passes it along a bundle of electrodes that extend into the cochlea. The electrodes end at varying positions along the length of the cochlea, stimulating the nerve receptors responsible for sensing different pitches. The external and the internal components are held together through magnetic attraction.

First tried in humans in 1985, the cochlear implant has become an extensively applied intervention to allow the profoundly deaf to navigate more easily in a hearing world. It is important to realize that "normal" hearing is not achieved. The artificial auditory signal is not analogous to correcting nearsightedness with a pair of prescribed glasses when perfect vision may be attained. Yet, the electronic stimulus provides a highly sensitive access to the sounds of conversation, even if very different from normal sound perception. What is required is a period of intensive training to learn to interpret the electronic stimuli as comprehensible speech and to articulate clearly. The process can begin in early childhood.

What modern hearing technology has given children is an opportunity to navigate more easily between the hearing and the silent worlds. The rivalry between the cochlear implant and alternate methods of teaching the deaf is slowly abating. An approach accepted by many parents of deaf children appears to be gaining hold: make use of every modality available that will enhance communications. Thus, the task of learning to communicate during the most formative years is greatly facilitated by a variety of techniques: hand figures, facial expression, lip reading and electronic devices.

D. Deaf gain

Many who are profoundly deaf opt to remain in the silent world. The reliance on signing and other means of non-verbal communication is preferred by those who choose to live free of ambient noise. Certainly, sparing the annoyance of noise can be appreciated in an age when screeching and droning machinery and advertising are ubiquitous and when some forms of popular music depend as much on high volume as on musicality. Even more, communicating solely by visual expression has an incomparable intimacy. Currently, there is a strong international movement to increase subtitles in movies and television and to provide plays and stage shows with deaf-friendly scripts.

The term "deaf gain" is not meant as an oxymoron. Rather, lost hearing emphasizes the increased ability that non-hearing people develop in their tactile, visual, and olfactory acuity. The marvels of auditory technology do not make communication by voice any more efficient than that by hand and facial expression. The downside for those choosing to stay in the silent world is, of course, a much more limited social interaction with the general population.

E. Deaf community

The internet has made possible the shared conversations of a global community of the deaf with those who are concerned about the rights and education of deaf people. The largest website is *The Limping Chicken* with its central location in London, England. Daily entries provide experiences and insight about the problems and accomplishments within the deaf culture. How the blog got its name is a story in itself.

One of the pet peeves of deaf people, when conversing with hearing people, is the tendency of the speakers not to look directly at them. Natural facial expressions and lip movement, therefore, cannot be interpreted. These actions can be a critical part of the communicating process. A hearing person, speaking much louder than in ordinary conversation, does not help the profoundly deaf. Rather, near-shouting usually changes the flow of conversation into a series of short sound bites. In this manner, hearing people may communicate verbally as though speaking to a child. This tendency is, of course, demeaning to the average deaf adult. Furthermore, hearing people—aware of talking to someone who is hearing deficient—may speak more slowly and articulate carefully at first, but, soon forget, lapsing eventually into their usual conversational

3-20 Prism

The magic of a rainbow is basically a matter of separating the different wavelengths that make up "white" light. A rainbow-making prism is a triangular shaped, solid figure that is transparent and usually of glass. Two of the opposing flat surfaces are at a critical angle to each other. White sunlight entering the prism is bent (or refracted) to a slight degree. It is bent again as it emerges from the opposite surface into the air. The shortest wavelengths of light are bent the most; these are at the violet end of the visual spectrum. The longer wavelengths, at the red end, bend the least. In between are included all the other colors that make up a rainbow.

In the sky, a layer of raindrops can also disperse sunlight into its spectral colors. The rainbow effect is caused by the light reflecting against the inside layer of a raindrop and emerging on the distant side to produce the spectrum. Red appears on the upper side of the arch and violet on the lower side. Rarely, a second rainbow appears above the primary one. Then the colors are reversed with violet now on top.

3-21 The River Thames

From its groundwater sources near Oxford, the Thames courses sixty miles in a southeasterly direction to Shepperton where it makes a sharp turn northward. From there, the river proceeds another eighteen miles easterly toward London. Flowing past London Center and beyond, it takes a snake-like winding course to the North Sea thirty-five miles away.

The Thames has provided the main transportation in England since Roman times. Medieval farmers and weavers from far inland had access to the rapidly expanding city of London for animals and their products: meat, vegetables, and cloth. The river also served to bring waste matter downstream, becoming ever more polluted on approaching the city.

Londoners with wealth tended to live in the western part of the city where the Thames was less foul smelling and where the prevalent direction of the wind and the flow of water were in an easterly direction.

Today, the town of Shepperton at the great bend of the river is most notable for an important lock and canal system that bypasses the fishhook curve in the natural river. The locks provide a closed chamber to raise or lower boats; this process enables the boats to re-enter the river at a different water level. The Thames has forty-five such locks. The locks and the weirs around them control the flow of water and allow safe navigation in times of floods or dangerous tides.

Near the locks of Shepperton is the picturesque Church Square where centuries ago an Anglican church was built. It was named for St. Nicholas, the Patron Saint of Sailors. The nearby Anchor Inn dates back four hundred years. The names attest to the dominance of mercantile traffic along the waterway.

The towns of Shepperton and Littleton, while adjoining physically, are separate parishes. In recent times, they have come together administratively.

3-22 Orangery

The "hot house" or "greenhouse" was a highly prized facility in well-to-do estates in Europe and England of the pre-electrical era. It provided a source of flowers and vegetables all year round. Indeed, much pride was taken by the aristocracy in their off-season "creativity"'of tulips and tubers.

The success of the orangery was based on its ability to trap the sun of winter. This was accomplished through roofs made of glass, or more likely in early modern history, through oiled cloth. A stove or series of stoves in the orangery kept a favorable temperature.

3-23 Horse: Domestication

The horse has a universal appeal for its immense size, gentleness, speed, and sheer beauty. In particular, the horse has innocently stolen the heart of many an adolescent girl who finds joy in the discipline of grooming, cleaning, riding, and loving this resplendent creature. After all, the horse is a great listener. It seems to absorb and then reflect the thoughts and touch of the one who offers them. With a nuzzle, a twitch of the ears, a shake of the head, or a flip of the tail, the horse responds in kind. The relationship between girl and horse is a safe place for expressing one's deepest feelings. During those turbulent years of adolescence, a horse can provide a stabilizing focus for her love. Overall, the experience is very zen.

It is, in fact, hard to realize that this gigantic and powerful animal is actually designed as prey. The quick reactions, natural wariness and amazing speed are its inborn defenses against predators.

Preparing a horse to not flinch when exposed to loud noises is, of course, essential for hunting and battle. The horse with rider has to learn to stay calm despite chaos and explosions all around. For training, sounds that are progressively louder and closer to the ear gradually accustom the horse to loud noises. Eventually, guns are shot close to the ear. One wonders if the close-up blasts actually conditioned the horse, or if they caused enough damage of the auditory system to cause deafness.

3-24 Blacksmith

The metalsmith expert who could creating various products necessary for maintaining an estate, and later even an entire village, was the blacksmith. Creating horseshoes with his forge and hammer and then nailing them to a horse's hoof was just one of his many tasks.

The art of heating metals to the point when they can be bent, pounded, and cut into useful instruments for the house, farm, and combat goes back a long time. The basic raw material of this ancient industry was iron. The necessary tools were a hammer, anvil, and a chisel. In addition, a really, really hot fire was essential.

Back in pharaonic Egypt, there were knives and other small tools made from iron. Iron, however, was not present in the Egyptian landscape but rather was found in meteorites. Indeed, one tool used in the embalming process (for "Opening the Mouth" of the recently deceased) was shaped like the constellation of the Big Dipper, thereby acknowledging its origin from the heavens.

Our image of a hardworking, strong-armed blacksmith, pounding away at a glob of yellow, glowing metal in a sweltering, dark workshop is one of steadfast industry. Longfellow portrayed him "Under a spreading chestnut-tree ...," as the model of a strong, diligent and caring individual who fulfilled life's obligations every day without complaint.

> *"...Week in, week out, from morn till night ...*
> *... Thus, at the flaming forge of life*
> *Our fortunes must be wrought;*
> *Thus on its sounding anvil shaped*
> *Each burning deed and thought."*

A key to smelting iron ore was getting the fire hot enough, much hotter than the ordinary open fire. The blacksmith used a brick oven shaped like a bee-hive and huge leather bellows to direct a blast of air into the burning fuel. From the hearth came an endless variety of objects ranging from huge (ploughs, weapons, chains, armor, and rims for wooden wagon wheels) to little (fish hooks, buttons, and nails). With an ever-growing population of horses, the flow of things made by the blacksmith (mostly horseshoes) rose exponentially.

3-25 Vibrations

The basis of sound is the vibration of air as it strikes a hearing-sensitive apparatus. There are pure tones produced by a tuning fork, and there are complex tones from blended vibrations. It is this blend that determines the quality of sound and, for example, allows us to identify the origin of the same tone played on a flute and a clarinet. This mixture has an infinite number of possibilities. To this point, every human voice has its distinctive quality, unique enough to form the basis of identification at future ATMs.

The human ear can detect an enormous range of pitches. Representing the low end in music is the double bass viol with its very long and thick strings. Even lower (and inaudible to humans) is the vocalized rumble of an elephant that can call together other elephants miles away. The violin and piccolo provide notes at the highest end of the audible scale.

Music for someone who is hearing-deficient is usually limited to the lowest register. A rock band concert may be enjoyed mostly by its throbbing beat.

3-26 Iron Horse

The weathervane has its place on many a steeple of a church or peak of a barn. It simply pivots according to wind pressure. The larger surface rotates downwind whereas the smaller surface points into the wind. The rooster is a prime example of an appropriate configuration with its small head and large tail. A horse, as in this story, makes a good weathervane when the size of the tail is exaggerated.

CHAPTER 4: OUTWARD BOUND

4-27 Foal

A newborn horse, male or female, is called a foal. (Until the age of three or four, a young male horse may be called a colt and a female horse, a filly.) At birth, its eyes are fully open as it takes its first look at life. Aside from its eyes, the creature seems to consist of all legs. In fact, the legs are already almost adult length. That this ungainly creature, after a few staggering attempts to rise, can stand within the hour is truly astonishing. Give it a couple more hours, and it is ready to trot or canter. A day-old horse is able to gallop alongside its mare. This precocious ability is some degree of reassurance that a newborn animal of prey, in the wild, is soon ready to move on with the herd.

The slender body fills out rapidly from its first day. Within two months food in addition to the mare's milk will be required. At one year, the horse will be about half its adult size, and its name will change to "yearling." It is another year or two before growth is complete. Some consider the horse not fully mature until its fourth or fifth year.

4-28 Horse

A. Care

Anyone who takes care of a horse soon learns that there are multiple needs that cannot be compromised. The horse will eat amazing amounts of food and, in fact, is a rather fussy eater. Also required is lots of drinking water. Then there is the grooming: the hands-on combing and the caressing of hide, mane, and tail. Regular inspection for problems of the skin, hooves, joints, teeth, mane, tail, and droppings are essential to maintain good health. There is the art of fitting a harness (saddle and bridle) so that it is secure and yet comfortable for the horse. Then there is, of course from the very beginning, the need to clean the stall frequently, a task that sentimental horse people call "mucking up."

B. Communication

The horse tends to speak with its whole body. Those who know a horse well learn to read its mood by listening to its vocal expressions as well as by observing its ears, head and neck position, tail, eyes, and legs. The equine language is remarkably similar in all breeds around the world, although the messages can be subtle and unique for an individual horse.

A horse may neigh (or whinny) to simply announce, "I am here," in the same way a dog barks when left alone, and an owl hoots through the night. The eyelids may flutter, and tail will lift a little to emphasize its presence.

When relaxed, the ears of the horse will appear relaxed and point forward or backward. The head is held level. Affection may be expressed by a soft, fluttering vocalization, often accompanied by nudging of its nose. The legs are planted solid. Flagging of the tail may indicate a playful mood. Rapid swishing, however, could be a sign of discomfort or simply an attempt to shoo away flies. Recent investigations on the movement of lips disclosed complex patterns of expression.

A horse is easily spooked by threatening sounds or sights. After all, the horse's only defense in the wild is its speed coupled with the ability to detect danger quickly and react immediately. An unfamiliar object or movement commands intense gaze. The head is outstretched. The ears become stiff and flicker. The eyes are opened wide. The horse may give out a brief but loud snort. These characteristics of alarm could also mean "It's time to feed me."

When anxiety turns to fear, several things may happen: the eyes may show white all around, the ears may prick up and move agitatedly, or flatten forward or rearward; additionally, the nostrils may flare, and the eyes may roll. The fearful horse will stand stiffly, the head held high, tight-lipped and breathing heavily, and its tail clamped down. A high-pitched squeal indicates fear. Pawing or stamping the ground usually follows. Be aware that a bite or kick from a heretofore placid horse could be next.

Horses sleep standing, seemingly always on the ready to run. The eyelids of the sleeping horse will be half closed and the lip drooping. To approach safely a horse in this state, make a familiar noise (calling its name is a good start) and from one side (not directly behind!) gently touch the flank.

C. Training

Humans have tamed wild animals throughout antiquity. Cats and dogs have long served as pets, for entertainment, and as an alarm system. The tamed and chained bear of the medieval town-to-town entertainer comes to mind. Teaching an animal to labor for humans, however, is something else. Making an animal several times larger and more powerful than a human perform work requires skilled training. The first lesson that must be instilled is the one that teaches who is in command and who obeys.

Traditionally, training a horse has been achieved with varying measures of reward and punishment. To demonstrate the dominance of man over beast, trainers are likely to apply the least pressure possible to get their subjects to obey basic commands. They begin with gentle persuasion and move on to apply as much force as is necessary.

The concept of training at the time of this story was to break the horse's spirit by instilling fear in order to achieve unquestioned obedience. In this way, it was believed, the horse would respect and perhaps even come to feel devoted to its human master. Once this relationship was accepted, the horse learned various simple commands by voice or switch: go forward, stop, turn right, and turn left. It was during this time that deciding on the horse's destiny might be made, depending on its size, speed, and response to command. The decision depended upon the essential question: would the horse be better at hauling heavy burdens or at carrying a rider?

If a horse resisted training, harsher measures were used. Sometimes a sharp blow between the ears made the point. Painful bits, whips, clubs, and spurs were all part of the trainer's tackle. Throughout history, trainers were not shy about inflicting inhuman punishment. The horse that would not respond submissively to these "enhanced" techniques was doomed.

The level of training for the draft horse meant little more than learning to push ahead against great resistance. (The term "pushing" is used here since the horse does not actually "pull" a plough or wagon but rather pushes against a collar or other device at the shoulders that is hitched behind to the tool or vehicle.) Following simple commands was enough.

A "saddle horse" however, demanded a higher degree of training. It needed to learn how to respond to various tactile and voice commands for speed and direction. "Breaking in" a horse included developing a proper gait at the walk, trot, canter, and gallop. Such training usually did not begin until the horse was two or three years old.

A trainer at a noble's manor house was only one of a small army of servants who cared for the horses. Included were husbandmen to feed and clean livestock, blacksmiths to make iron shoes, leather workers to make harnesses, and carpenters to build the stables. In addition, someone skilled in treating the various ailments and injuries of large animals needed to be close at hand. This person was the farrier.

Additional training was necessary to pursue the pastimes of the wealthy, such as hunting and hawking. Expected of the well-schooled saddle horse was running across rough ground, jumping streams and fences, and staying calm after an explosion from a nearby gun. All were meant to prepare the horse for battle, but perhaps served more as an excuse for a jolly good romp in the fields after a fox or wart hog. There was also the sense of pride in having a good mount. Many a noble in early modern England has had a lasting portrait of himself, resplendent in full armor, painted while posing on horseback.

The middle of the 17th century saw a more progressive and caring attitude to get horse and man to work in harmony, although the brutality intended to break a horse's spirit hardly disappeared. In today's world, the emphasis is on gentle training.

Much has been written about the early training of horses in a book by the American author, Dennis Manger. Called *The Classic Encyclopedia of the Horse,* the liberally illustrated book was originally published in 1887.

D. Untrainable Horse

Some horses resisted all attempts of man to control them. The character of insubordination seemed irreversibly fixed. The expert believed that he could detect such a characteristic because of the excited bearing, its fearful and wide-open eyes, the head stretched forward and ears straight up and stiff. A horse that does not submit to strong physical provocation was considered bad-tempered. Such a horse did not have a promising future within the realm of providing human services. Idle or wild-roaming horses were not part of the early modern landscape; leather and meat were.

E. Counting

What may seem beyond reality, actually, is not. There are instances in which horses have counted. Or, at least, they were trained to look as if they were!

In 1891, "Hans" was a horse that could count. Its owner, Wilhelm von Osten from Berlin, Germany, showed his prized horse throughout Europe for a fee. The horse tapped on one hoof to count any requested number below ten. Hans could also read the numbers on a chart. Endless skeptics could find no way that the learned horse was coached by its owner. Hans was coached, of course, but in an entirely unobtrusive way. Hans was taught to respond to blinks of its owner's eyes. As might have been expected, Herr von Osten made a small fortune with his "super-intelligent" horse.

F. Sidesaddle

Since the Middle Ages, it was generally considered unladylike for a woman to ride horseback with legs dangling on both sides. (There were some famous exceptions.) The custom may have arisen from a sense of modesty but the awkwardness of mounting a horse in a long skirt could have been a practical reason.

A side-facing saddle chair was eventually designed to allow women to ride, but it required someone on foot to lead the horse. For facing the front and controlling a horse, a saddle was eventually designed in which one leg was extended into a stirrup and upper leg curved around a pommel. The bent leg acted as a shock-absorber, while maintaining balance and control. Along with the suffragette movement and emerging concept of women's equality in the early 20th century, the modern era saw women riding horseback astride. Yet, some hold that riding sidesaddle had its own elegance, and so the custom has enjoyed a renaissance. The young Queen Elizabeth II, as an example, reviewed her troops riding sidesaddle. Today, it is commonly seen in parades and dressage as well as in competitive events of running and jumping.

4-29 Staines

Staines is a market town along the eastern Thames and located southwest of London. At the confluence of two other rivers, it has attracted settlers throughout its history: first by Stone Age inhabitants and later by the Romans who built a wooden bridge. Residents during the Middle Ages were occasionally attacked by the Vikings, whose weapons turn up from time to time. In the early modern period, the rivers at this site provided hydropower for industrial-age mills. Londoners wealthy enough to have property in the western resort towns overnighted in Staines, a good day's stagecoach ride from the capital city. The name of the city (officially, Staines-upon-Thames) comes from an ancient Saxon word meaning "stone," related linguistically to the modern German, *Stein.*

Entering Staines, you will pass by St. Mary's Church, under construction at the times of this story. The designer was the famous London architect, Inigo Jones.

Continuing past Staines for six miles heading northwest, you will come to Runnymede. It is the place where King John, in 1215, acceded to the demands of his nobles and signed the Magna Carta. The signing secured some rights of the nobles and heralded the dawn of parliamentary government. It was a small but crucial step in the long, erratic and—at the time—unimaginable staircase to democracy.

4-30 Windsor Castle

The castle in Windsor, just north of Staines, is virtually synonymous with royalty. The castle has served English kings and queens for a thousand years. It continues to do so today.

Windsor Castle was once the site of a Roman fort. It is said that King Arthur lived (or camped) here. The ensuing centuries saw the castle become ever more awesome by a succession of English rulers. William the Conqueror lodged here soon after the Norman Invasion in 1066. By the fourteenth century, it had become a massive fortress. It was substantial enough to survive several prolonged sieges. It offered a safe retreat during times when periodic uprisings against the Crown were occurring in London. Queen Elizabeth I stayed in the castle in 1563 to avoid the bubonic plague, forbidding anyone from London from entering the castle on pain of death. *The Merry Wives of Windsor*, a comedy by Shakespeare, was written at her invitation.

The seven-year Civil War ended badly for King Charles I who was imprisoned at Windsor Castle in 1649. During the ensuing Reformation years under the government of Parliament, the castle's upkeep deteriorated severely. It was Charles II, in the Restoration era, who had the castle restored and further developed.

Windsor Castle is certainly a major attraction for tourists who may see the Queen's Guardsmen, the parlor rooms, paintings and drawings by legendary masters, priceless antique furniture, and Queen Mary's doll house, the largest and most well-furnished doll house in the world. Its miniature portraits and books, in addition to electricity and running water, give some indication of the intricacy of the reproduction.

4-31 Puritans: Plymouth and the Massachusetts Bay Colony

In the 1600s, the English Crown insisted that all citizens follow the dictates of the Anglican Church with its emphasis on rituals, images, and the authority of bishops. Those who dissented were deprived of possessions and occupations. Most notable of the dissenters were those who wanted to return to a strict interpretation of the Bible and a simpler, "pure" way of worshiping God.

To escape the yoke of King Charles's grip on religious practices, some Puritans fled to the New World in 1620, settling in Plymouth on the New England coast. They were the English "Separatists" (later called the Pilgrims). Most had lived in Holland for years. They came to the New World without a charter, intending to sever completely their allegiance to the Crown. They arrived ill-prepared for the rigors of the winter and suffered immensely. Their endurance convinced Puritans back home that the New World could offer a place where they could reach out to God directly, not through a bishop.

Ten years later, another group of Puritans came to New England, this time under a charter granted by King Charles I. Although they were troublesome objectors to the official Anglican Church, these Puritans were few in number and seemingly not a threat to the Crown. Yet, one imagines that the King was not unhappy about getting rid of such pesky and persistent discontents.

In 1630, some four hundred Puritans came in eleven ships, determined to create a godly society that was of benefit to all (e.g., a commonwealth), what they envisioned as a shining "City Upon a Hill." On the way over, its leader, Reverend John Winthrop, wrote "we must knit together in this work, rejoice together, mourn together, labor and suffer together." The intention was to create and maintain an ideal society centered on a unified interpretation of the Bible. Steadfast religious zeal along with hard work would make such a Paradise on Earth possible. Unlike the Pilgrims, they came with a good supply of staples: food, animals, and tools for clearing land and tilling the soil.

Winthrop and his followers landed in a bay situated forty miles north of Plymouth. They arrived where a small settlement had been started two years before. The place name was *Naumkeag*, referring to the local Massachusett-Pawtucket tribe; it was soon changed to "Salem." The rocky soil soon proved poor as farmland. Furthermore, the population swelled ten-fold within a decade. The rapidly increased pressure for living space led to the formation of new villages farther south.

Most of those leaving Salem went to the mouth of the Charles River, a place they called Charleston. Here, they found fresh water lacking and so made another move across the river where an intrepid trader kept a small orchard on Beacon Hill. It was a place called *Shawmut* by the native population but renamed eventually to "Boston" after the English village, the origin of many of the settlers.

The settlers of the region formed the Massachusetts Bay Colony on "English property." Their charter gave them generally free reign over their destiny. The colony, all understood, would retain its loyalty to the Crown if not to the bishops. Those who disagreed with the mono-theocratic government imposed by the Company were invited to leave. A notable example of such dissenters was Roger Williams; he went on to found Providence in Rhode Island where total religious tolerance was fostered. Another was the outspoken, free-thinking Anne Hutchinson. Banished from Boston for heresy in 1638, she went to Narragansett Bay in Rhode Island where she was an activist for the female role in religious affairs. Fearing intervention by the fundamentalists, this mother of fifteen children moved in 1642 to the Dutch colony at Pelham Bay in The Bronx. A year later, Hutchinson along with all but one of her accompanying children was killed in an Indian raid.

4-32 Pudding Lane

London in the early seventeenth century was one of the largest cities in the world. It was renowned for other excesses as well: crowding, filth, noise, and crime. Narrow streets of high peaked buildings with overhanging second stories and lots of chimneys and steeples characterized the landscape. Wares, vegetables, fresh meat, candles, gloves, and countless other commodities were available in stalls set up along the busiest streets.

An amazing virtual tour of downtown Elizabethan London can be experienced in a video. It was produced in 2013 by students of game art design at De Montford University. The drone-like presentation, called "Fly through 17th century London," brings us onto narrow, cobblestone streets, laden with debris and sewage edged by leaning Tudor-style houses that stand shoulder-to-shoulder, all in an oppressive, dark atmosphere. Still, there is something exhilarating about the ability to be there in virtual reality. This amazing video was made before drones became readily available: https://www.youtube.com/watch?v=SPY-hr-8-M0 (Pudding Lane Productions, Crytek Off the Map).

An excellent book on the subject of Elizabethan England has been written by Ian Mortimer, *The Time Traveler's Guide to Elizabethan England.* For an audio or audio-visual review of London's history during this period, an authoritative and engaging source is Robert Bucholz's lecture series "The History of England from the Tudors to the Stuarts." It has been produced by The Great Courses, The Teaching Company.

4-33 Countrey Contentments or the English Huswife

A best-seller of English books in the seventeenth century was *Countrey Contentments.* It was written for women, yet, ironically, only a small percentage of women at that time in England could read. The book described in detail what was expected of them. Advice and instructions on a variety of topics were presented, such as: preparing meals, making sauces with fruit and wine, housekeeping, treating common illnesses and injuries, raising children, making cheese and butter from milk, and dying and weaving fabrics. A short biography of the author, Gervase Markham is provided in note # 36.

This book, published by R. Lackson in 1623, can be read online at https://books.google.com. The British Library has an original copy.

4-34 Quayside: London

In the seventeenth century, quays (pronounced "keys") were platforms built alongside the marshy riverbank between London Bridge and the Tower of London, a region known as the "Pool of London." Here, boats and ships would dock parallel to the shore. Barges from inland brought wool, linen, vegetables, and animals that were destined for distant markets. They docked alongside ships that came upriver from the North Sea. These vessels carried coal, fish, and foreign-made commodities. Other ships brought pepper, nutmeg, and other spices--precious seasonings for a country famous for its bland food. Then again, a few ships arrived with treasures pirated from Spanish and Portuguese ships.

A wharf included all that was necessary to load and unload cargo: storage areas or, in time, more docking space in platforms built perpendicular to the shoreline. Across the landscape of the quay would be seen a forest of slowly rocking masts, the bustle of laborers loading and unloading goods, and merchants licking their chops at the prospect of new opportunities. There were, too, some stone towers from which long arms projected. These were the cranes that made it possible to lift heavy loads and transfer them onto and off the ships. Men and beasts of burden provided the power to operate the crane with mechanical advantage by pulling on ropes or turning capstans. Frugal Queen Elizabeth I saw to it that all twenty quays at the "Pool of London" were under the watchful eyes of her customs officers who collected revenue with each shipment.

4-35 Animals: Ship Transport

Carrying large animals on a sailing ship was no easy matter. Not accustomed to movement underfoot, an animal had no experience with rocking at sea. If the rocking was severe, an untethered horse, cow, or ox could easily break a leg or, worse, act as a "loose cannon." During a storm, a cow or horse could be thrown about and become injured, or else cause damage to the cargo or other animals. To prevent such harm, these animals were restrained in slings (hammocks) with the hind feet touching the floor and bearing weight, and the forefeet bound and raised just above the floor to avoid thrashing. A trough of canvas was placed near the restrained head for feeding. This position, forced during a journey of several weeks, led to massive physical deconditioning; the animals required several weeks afterwards to regain fitness. Furthermore, horses were subject to developing colic, a painful and often fatal complication of seasickness. Even with the best of care, it is estimated that half of the horses transported across the Atlantic Ocean during this time died on the way.

Of course, large animals require large amounts of water. When a ship's progress was delayed for many days or weeks for lack of wind, water supplies became critically short. It was during such periods of the "doldrums" that large animals were sacrificed by being pushed overboard. It is this practice that gave name to the "horse latitude," that region between eastern and western directed winds on the Atlantic Ocean where ships could be becalmed for long periods.

4-36 Gervase Markham (1568-1637)

Certainly, this man well represented the "Renaissance Man." He had military experience as an officer, was conversant in several languages and wrote extensively on a diversity of subjects: horsemanship, hunting, agriculture, forestry, archery, bowling, and tennis. He also wrote poetry, comedies and tragedies, and evidently, had a great interest in cooking and wines.

4-37 Fishers Island

Nine miles long and very narrow with a highly irregular shoreline, Fishers Island lies at the eastern end of Long Island Sound. In 1614, explorer Adriaen Block dubbed it Visher's Island, to use the name of a crew member.

The island was ceded to the English in 1664 when New Netherland became New York. (Its anglicized name today is spelled without the apostrophe.) It still belongs to the State of New York, although its northern tip is only two miles from Connecticut. Both the utilities supplying the island and the ferry boat service come from Connecticut; otherwise taxes go to New York.

The Pequot tribe on Fishers Island called it *Munnawtawik*. There is archeological evidence of Indian settlements on the island, including char-preserved kernels of corn. The first European to take over the island was John Winthrop (Governor of Connecticut and son of the founder of the Massachusetts Bay Colony). He raised cattle here. The island changed hands through the ensuing centuries. Along came gentleman farming, raising sheep for wool, day trips for tourists, a Coast Guard facility, and a fortification in World War II. Today, there is mixed utilization in which the population of about two hundred swells ten-fold in the summer. Estate houses, cottages, yacht clubs, bicycle paths, golf links, and an airplane strip dot the island. The internet provides a decided advantage to the island's primary and middle schools. High school students take the ferry to New London. The protected environment harbors a highly varied population of ferns, flowering plants, and birds.

Swift tidal currents, changing in direction twice a day, occur off both ends of the island. The currents are especially strong in "The Race" at the southern end, where the island opposes Orient Point (the upper fork of Long Island). These powerful, shifting currents in addition to multiple small islands make the area hazardous for navigation, as attested to by the numerous lighthouses and warning buoys in the area. Old-time Atlantic-crossing navigators could determine their north-south location quite accurately by referring to the North Star and to the sun at high-noon. Distance east-west, however, could not be reliably determined until a sea-going clock became available in the mid-1800s. Nighttime or limited visibility from fog accounts for the many ships wrecked on Fishers Island and other islands at the mouth of Long Island Sound.

4-38 Connecticut River

Fed by trickles of water from the surrounding highlands, a beaver pond at the border of Quebec and New Hampshire spills over. The water begins a journey, collecting water from more than a hundred tributaries, and finally ends beyond Old Saybrook, four hundred ten miles due south where fresh water mixes with salt water in Long Island Sound. This long waterway is the Connecticut River. It is the major watershed for four of the New England States as well as the southwestern corner of Maine. The river defines the borders of Vermont and New Hampshire (by decree of King George III in 1764) and splits both Massachusetts and Connecticut into two almost equal parts.

At its mouth the river passes between two long breakwaters. At the end of one stands a lighthouse, operating there since 1886. Today, it flashes a green light every three seconds and in times of heavy fog, it sounds a horn every thirty seconds.

The State of Connecticut owes its name to the Indigenous people who called it *Quinnehtukqut*, a phonetic version of an Algonquian name meaning "beside the long, tidal river." The tidal flow may extend as far as Enfield, fifty-eight miles from the mouth, but seasonal rainfall and snowmelt are determining factors in its length. It was here at the Enfield shallow rapids, fifteen miles north of Hartford, where the Dutch explorer Adriaen Block came in 1615 but could navigate no farther. He called it the "Fresh River" (or *Versche Rivier*), perhaps calling attention to the difference between it and the saline Hudson River that is an estuary for about one hundred miles. (He and his crew had been in a makeshift boat built during the previous winter in Manhattan.) The English would later call it the "Great River."

The Connecticut River begins at an elevation one mile above sea level. By the time it enters the state of Connecticut, it is only one hundred ninety feet above sea level, having passed many waterfalls up to that point, the largest at South Hadley in Massachusetts. The river is remarkably determined in its rush to the south, but does make a sharp bend eastward in Middletown.

Heavy silt and periodic flooding account for the most fertile farmland in New England. The floods deposit mineral-rich silt along the banks of the river. Native Americans have planted corn here for more than a thousand years. Shifting shoals at the mouth, however, excludes navigation of large ships with deep draft. Smaller oil tankers do, however, ply the river as far north as Hartford.

4-39 Leadsman or Plumb Lead Line

The Connecticut River is notorious for its shallows, making navigation of large boats challenging. Hartford, located forty-three miles upriver, is unusual for a large city because its lack of sufficient depth does not favor water-borne trade with big ocean-going ships.

Before the days of sonar, the depth of a river was determined by a lead weight attached to a rope thrown repeatedly from the bow as the ship proceeded. In the boatman's tradition, the depth would be measured in fathoms, a fathom being equal to six feet. The author Samuel Clemens chose as his pen name "Mark Twain," meaning mark two fathoms (or a depth of 12 feet) and safe for his boat. His most famous book, *The Adventures of Huckleberry Finn,* was about a free-spirited ragamuffin rafting along the Mississippi River; it was actually written in 1884 at his home on the Connecticut River in Hartford.

4-40 Bodkin Rock

Bodkin Rock juts out into the Connecticut River on the eastern shore about a mile south of the bridge at Middletown. The river is shallow at this point, and heavily-laden ships must stay close to Bodkin Rock to find its greatest depth. Navigators on large sailing ships found this reach particularly challenging. In modern times the Coast Guard erected a frame-only tower at the point of the Rock. Bright red, triangular reflection plates on top, one facing upriver and the other facing downstream, give fair warning to a passing ship.

Getting to Bodkin Rock on foot takes a bit of ingenuity. Route 66 (Portland Cobalt Road) runs north-south on the eastern side of the Connecticut River. From there, check Google Earth for possible access points. In any case, it will be a hike to scoot around private property, greenhouses and industrial complexes.

Alternatively, one can get a look at Bodkin Rock from the west side of the Connecticut River by heading south on River Road from Middletown center.

CHAPTER 5: THE NEW WORLD

5-41 Fainting

Who has not experienced a little light-headedness from time to time from getting up too fast? The chances are much more likely if you have been sitting or lying in the sun for a long time, as at the beach. Prolonged exposure to heat causes a massive dilation of blood vessels in the skin to dissipate the heat more effectively. On standing, it takes a half minute or so for the cutaneous blood vessels in the lower body to constrict enough to support the vertical flow of blood; during the initial adjustment the result can be a momentary reduction of blood pressure and circulation to the brain; the symptom produced is described as light-headedness or feeling giddy. Usually, the earliest symptom is loss of color vision.

A similar sensation may be experienced from prolonged over-breathing, known as "hyperventilation." It commonly occurs during moments of high anxiety. Here there is a dilation of visceral blood vessels and a delayed response of a blood pressure regulating mechanism. A compensatory reaction occurs in the skin, causing the constriction of blood vessels and the blanching of the skin. Blowing off excessive carbon dioxide creates a disturbance in other body fluid components, such as calcium and magnesium. The result can be a destabilization of those essential physiological mechanisms that regulate blood pressure: vascular tone and heart rate. At some critical point, blood pressure falls and "benign syncope" occurs, that is the sudden loss (or near loss) of consciousness without any underlying disease. Recovery is rapid and full unless there had been injury sustained from falling. Such an episode is most likely to occur during periods of anxiety or heightened emotions that are associated with over-breathing. The latter may not bring an awareness of shortness of breath but is often described as an inability to take a deep breath. Sometimes hyperventilation occurs over a fairly long period and the person is not aware of air hunger.

5-42 Hartford: The Beginning

Settlers in the Massachusetts Bay Colony in Newtowne (later called Cambridge) earned their livelihood mostly by farming. Unfortunately, the ground was rocky, and the soil was soon exhausted by repeated plantings. Fertilization of soil was not a well-understood concept. Furthermore, land cleared of trees and boulders was at a premium. Farmers looking elsewhere were attracted by the fabled fertile lands along the Connecticut River (then, called the "Great River"). Unlimited land in the "Fruitfulness and commodiousness of Connecticut" seemed to be available.

A weary band of Puritans trekked from Newtowne with their animals to the Great River where a small tributary (the "Little River") joined it. There, along the riverside plains in the spring of 1636, they built primitive dwellings and began to clear the land and till the soil. It is said that some men had arrived some weeks or months before in order to construct a meeting house for the new arrivals. Such was the beginning of the City of Hartford.

Two small English settlements were already in the area. One was the palisaded village at Windsor, up the Little River about ten miles from its mouth. The other was Wethersfield to the southwest. The settlers there were a Separatist group that had left the Colony of Plymouth a few years earlier. Descendants from both places claim priority as the first permanent European settlement in the State of Connecticut.

The families of settlers came to a place where land rights, they claimed, had been rightfully purchased from the local Indians. This issue became seriously disputed with the neighboring Dutch at the nearby trading post; they claimed that they had purchased the same land from the Pequot Indians to the south. No one considered what "purchasing" meant to the Native peoples.

5-43 Nutmeg

Nutmeg has a sweet, musty flavor that matches well with many foods. It is said to also create a mild euphoria. In early modern European times, nutmeg had a reputation for curing everything from the common cold and stomach ailments to the plague. Today, its powdered form is used to flavor stews, soups, various meats, and potatoes. During the holidays of winter, nutmeg is just right for eggnogs and pumpkin pies. When roasted, nutmeg provides a pleasing aroma to the kitchen. The history of nutmeg, however, has not always been so pleasing.

Originally brought from Indonesia by sea-going Arabs to Europe, nutmeg was sold for exorbitant prices. In the 1500s, the Portuguese got wind of its unique origin in a small chain of volcanic islands in the Pacific and started their own trade, also for high profit. One can only begin to imagine the hardships and dangers of traveling to the other side of the globe to the "Spice Islands" and back, a journey of about two years, all to fill their ship's hold with the precious nutmeg and maybe with a supply of cloves.

After a struggle with the Portuguese, the Dutch in the 1620s became the dominant world-wide traders in nutmeg. On one island, the Dutch conquered and virtually wiped out the native population and started their own plantation. The English eventually got into the nutmeg trade and a ruthless, long-distant competition began. In 1667, a deal to reduce tension by territorial compromise was made by which the English ceded the island's spice trade as well as some Caribbean holdings, to the Dutch. In turn, the Dutch agreed to give up any claim they might still have in English-controlled Manhattan Island.

Why is Connecticut known as the "Nutmeg State"? Folklore says that the name came from a disreputable practice in the state where ordinary wood was carved into the shape of nutmeg and peddled on the street as such for a premium price. The idea somehow conjures up the idea of Yankee ingenuity, not bogus merchandise. However, an alternate name, and its official one, the "Constitution State," has more appeal.

5-44 Food

A modern person transposed into a Puritan home in colonial times would experience a numbing change at the dinner table. Modern life quells our appreciation of the seasonable variations of food. In fact, colonials had little choice about their food supplies from season to season aside from what meat and vegetables they could smoke, char, or salt through the winter. Puritans, observing God to the fullest, did not indulge in tasty foods. Food was meant for sustenance, not for any sensual gratification.

The table setting included wooden bowls. Each family member had his or her own knife. Forks were rare so that diners may have had to rely on their fingers to fetch meat and vegetables from stews. Clearly, eating with the hands was a common practice. Although the discovery of bacteria was more than two centuries ahead, there was enough already known about sanitation to prompt hand washing prior to eating.

Meat was boiled and then served only on certain days, never on the Sabbath. Certainly, large domestic animals were too valuable for supplying milk and hoof power to provide meat on a regular basis. Hunting required fine-tuned skills and a lot of time; it was especially challenging to use firearms that had little accuracy. Chickens were most important not for meat but for producing eggs. Sheep, of course, had a dual role: providing both wool and meat. Pigs, on the other hand, were raised solely to eat. The English of Hartford did not seem to take much to fishing, unlike their Indigenous neighbors.

Like rice and beans in other parts of the world, corn (maize) is almost the perfect food for complete nutrition. The Indians made full use of it, grinding the kernels into meal for porridges and journey cakes. They would also place charred corn into storage underground throughout the winter.

The English were not familiar with corn until they came to the colonies. There, they found that the crops with which they were familiar (wheat and rye) did not grow well. Corn flourished. The proud English were probably a little put off when they had to resort to eating corn to survive. It is noted that the Separatists, upon landing in Plymouth and expecting a plentiful supply of food just for the picking, were spared starving by finding corn that the Indigenous people had buried.

Puddings, pies, and stews made good use of whatever wild berries were available. Imported apple and cherry trees were planted soon after arrival of the settlers. Although fruit soon became an important crop, the settlers had to wait a few years before a newly planted tree bore fruit.

During the winter, food supplies always became critical. Much of the work of the autumn season went to preserve food by salting, smoking, and pickling.

5-45 Horses: North America

Even though the explorers and settlers in the New World took their horses with them, these mammals had already existed in the Western Hemisphere for a very long time. Archeologists have found ancestral bones of the horse in places that extend from Alaska to southernmost Chile. Called *eohippus* (Latin for "dawn horse"), this early horse was small, no larger than a medium-sized dog, and it had three or four toes. For reasons unknown, *eohippus* became extinct about eight centuries ago. It has been conjectured that the extinction of the native horse in the Americas might somehow be related to the rapid spread of humans across the continents ten or more centuries ago.

Horses were re-introduced into the Americas by the conquistadores of Spain in the 1500s. The animal was so strange to the Indigenous people that a man-on-horseback was perceived at first as a single creature. It did not take the Plains Indians long, however, to acquire horses, learn to breed and care for them, use them in hauling, and adapt horse and rider to hunting and warfare. They soon became expert in bare-back riding.

CHAPTER 6: THE PURITAN PLANTATION

6-46 Colonial Houses

A. Outside

At first, in 1636, a livable shelter was made in the most expedient way. It was often a dugout scooped out of the brow of a hill. A roof consisted of long planks covered by a thatch of wild grass. With earth on three sides, moveable wooden siding covered the exposed side. The planks were split from short logs. Fire pits and a good supply of fire wood were essential. During the construction of such early dwellings, the homesteaders were thankful for the peaceful breathing space that the nearby Dutch traders and local Indians allowed them.

Over time, the dugout houses were replaced with framed houses and the original living quarters became the basement. Each house had a thatched pitched roof, usually with a small second story. Trees had to be cut, trimmed of branches, dragged by oxen to the house lot, and sawn into boards and beams. Red clay mixed with wiry meadow grass served as insulating stuffing between the cracks of boards. A broad stone or brick chimney stood on one side of the house or was built into the center of the rear wall. The upper chimney was usually made of wood.

Many houses took on a "saltbox" shape. That is, the peaked roof on a two-story building projected out in back to become the roof of a one-story extension. Here was room for the kitchen and for a place to store necessities. The fireplace may have sat between the kitchen and the main house.

Humble as they were, the houses provided a place where the pious could raise their families with independence, honor, and decency—all granted by hard work and the belief that God approved.

B. Inside

Try to imagine stepping into a rudely built house along the Connecticut River in 1639. At first, the eyes would have to adjust to the semi-darkness in broad daylight. Windows were shuttered. Oiled cloth served as screens. The floor was pounded earth covered with straw. A dining table would be little more than some long narrow boards propped up on packing boxes or chests from England, all covered with a linen cloth.

The hearth dominated the interior view with its mantel above and andirons below. Usually a large, iron pot hung nearby. There would likely be a spinning wheel in view as well as a rocking cradle. A string of candle molds was likely draped along one wall into which fat from roasting could be poured. Some walls would be burdened with hanging coats and outerwear. Bedding was on a loft above and accessible by ladder.

C. Indoor lighting

Lighting in the colonial house was critically important. The low flame from a fireplace was not enough to allow reading and performing needlework. High flames depleted the wood supply much faster and were dangerous. (Remember the wooden upper chimney.) Lanterns lit by the oil of sperm whales were bright and burned with a pure white flame, but they were expensive. Readers and sewers had to make do with candles.

Some candles were contained in shipments from England. Mostly, however, each family had to make its own. Candle-making was most active in the autumn as days got progressively shorter and nights longer. Tallow from animal fat was the basic ingredient for making candles. Because meat was not plentiful during early colonial times, a supply of tallow was precious. In every kitchen, a great kettle hung from irons at the fireplace where equal amounts of melted tallow and water were kept at a near boil. One process required repeatedly dipping cotton strands or silky down from milkweed into the mix, gradually building up the elongated waxy mass around the central wick. Alternatively, the mix could be poured into candle molds and hung to solidify.

Candlewood was another source of nightlight. It was a traditional source for the Indians. A sticky tar-like substance can be found at the knots of pine trees where branches are attached to the trunk. These lighter knots burn readily, produce a clear "dancing light" and give a strong, pleasant smell. To prepare it for burning, the pine knot was shaved into two thin slices. Since hot pitch would drop from the lighter knot when alit, the knot had to be placed on a flat stone at one corner of the fireplace. Along with making candles, a colonial family in New England learned to lay in a good supply of candlewood that would last throughout the winter.

6-47 Diaspora

On May 31st, 1636, sixty men with women and children (about one hundred in all) set off from Newtowne and Dorchester in Massachusetts on a journey to the Connecticut River Valley. Along with horses, cattle, pigs, and chickens, they followed old Indian trails through the forest, over hills and through swamps, trusting Jehovah to show them the way but also using a compass and help from the Indians. They covered about ten miles a day. For food, they brought little. Acorns and berries picked up along the way were barely enough to sustain them. The overly stressed cows did not supply the milk for porridge in the quantity counted on. Cornmeal mush was the staple. It is said that Indians met along the way provided much needed food. For sleeping the travelers had little more than matted pine needles to lie on and leaves for cover. Accompanying the screeches and howls of the wild animals, cowbells provided journey music. The charismatic preacher, Thomas Hooker, led the group. He offered prayers all along the way. On the Sabbath, the entourage rested the entire day.

The company proceeded westerly toward Agawam, then turned south. The trail, known as the "Old Connecticut Path," was once an ancient Indian trail. After a fortnight of footslogging the weary travelers broke out of the forest somewhere along the east side of the Connecticut River. Whether this location was way upriver from Hartford (where the water is shallow enough to cross by wading) and whether rafts were improvised for poling across remain two unanswered questions. Ropes and a great deal of pushing and pulling were probably required to get livestock and pigs to cross. A sandbar at Hartford near the present-day I-84 bridge may have provided a natural bridge for wading. What we do know for sure is that the pioneers crossed onto the western shore.

The artist Frederick Church portrayed the trek in a stretched-arms-wide painting that hangs in the Wadsworth Atheneum Museum of Art in Hartford. Painted about two hundred years after the event, it shows only a few of the hundred people and at least as many livestock. Here in a clearing in the forest, we see two boys on horseback and a woman holding a baby, also on horseback, and a man guarding them, musket in hand. Some cows wade a stream. In the distance is a stretcher slung between two horses.

It is interesting that Church had a male ancestor in the company. He entitled his painting "Reverend Thomas Hooker and Company Journeying Through the Wilderness in 1636 from Plymouth to Hartford. 1846." Twenty-one years old at the time, Church sold the painting to the Wadsworth Atheneum for $130. His error referring to the origin of Hooker and company as Plymouth may be simply confusing the origin of the settlers with those of Windsor and Wethersfield.

6-48 Reverend Thomas Hooker

In Colonial times the general public looked up to the clergy (who were literate) for knowledge, guidance, and leadership. Rev. Thomas Hooker was a clergyman who had earned respect as a gifted speaker from the pulpit. He was also an idealist who had a radical viewpoint of community order.

Hooker had earned a Master of Arts degree at Emmanuel College, Cambridge University. Evidently, Hooker and the Archbishop in England did not see eye-to-eye. Hooker moved to Rotterdam, Holland for some years, then left to join the Massachusetts Bay Colony. He was appointed minister in Newtowne (later renamed Cambridge). There, Rev. Hooker found himself at odds about one issue with his senior, Pastor John Cotton. He argued that restricting the rights to vote to only freemen (i.e., land owners) was too limited. Indeed, his ideals were far more liberal than those by which Governor John Winthrop meant to keep the Bay Colony unified in principles and purpose.

It was Hooker's conviction and his charisma that convinced some of the settlers to start a new colony. Inspired by thoughts of forming a new concept of government, Hooker led his group on a difficult trek overland to the valley of the Great River (later, the Connecticut River).

We have, alas, no images showing what Thomas Hooker looked like. We do know that he was forty-six years old when he led the march from Boston to Hartford and that he died from an "epidemical sickness" in 1647 at the age of sixty-one.

6-49 Oxen and Horses

Oxen and horses were the tractors of the pre-mechanized Age. Pound-for-pound, oxen are stronger than horses. When straining against strong resistance, they pulled a plough with a steadier force, not with the sudden jerk of a horse. This characteristic is more advantageous for breaking through root-laden new soil. A yoke can be put on an ox much faster than a horse can be harnessed. Also, oxen do not require grooming. Nor are they fussy eaters: a horse would turn its nose up at moldy grass and hay that an ox would not hesitate to eat. Oxen digest corn with the kernels intact; it is necessary that each kernel be cracked for horses. Oxen are less susceptible to injury and when injured seem to heal faster. They do not become as easily fatigued or overheated as do horses. Eventually, at the end of a working life, oxen are valuable as meat.

Draft horses had advantages over oxen on the Colonial farm. They were faster and could turn at a sharper angle at the end of a furrow. They were much better on rough roads and going through the forest. Furthermore, a horse—including plough horses—could be ridden and could be driven to a fast pace. The general aversion to the consumption of horse meat limited the value of a "retired" horse to supplying leather.

6-50 First People

Several Eastern Algonquin tribes and clans lived along the Connecticut River. Their agricultural communities took full advantage of the rich riparian soil. For their farmlands, the Indians used the term *Suckiaug,* meaning "black earth."

The domed wigwams of these Indigenous farmers were scattered along elevated clearings. Their survival depended mainly on their ability to grow their own food. The main vegetables were corn, pumpkins, and beans (traditionally known as the "Three Sisters"). The Indians charred them to prevent rotting during storage. In addition to agriculture, they fished for shad and salmon using dugout canoes and hanging nets.

The Podunks resided east of the Connecticut River, while the Poquonocks had the territory north and west of what became Hartford. Other tribes in and around Hartford were the Massacoes, Tunxis, Wangunks, and Saukiog. These names are anglicized versions of the original.

A recently published book on the Podunks and other local tribes is entitled *Connecticut's Indigenous Peoples (What Archaeology, History, and Oral*

Traditions Teach Us About Their Communities and Cultures). The author is Licianne Lavin at the Institute for American Indian Studies in Washington, CT. (Yale University Press).

6-51 Migraine

A. Headache

Not every headache is a migraine. Typically, a migraine begins on one side of the head and sooner or later involves the entire head. In intensity, it ranges from annoying to incapacitating. What separates it from other kinds of headaches is the presence of at least one other symptom. Nausea (or a nausea-equivalent, such as an aversion to food or other gastrointestinal symptoms) is the most typical associated symptom. The spectrum ranges, however, from intolerance of light, to the tearing of bloodshot eyes and then to blurry or double vision. Smells and sounds can become distorted. Thirst along with retention of water with swelling in the face or eyelids sometimes occurs.

Emotional changes, including apathy, depression, lethargy, and malaise during these episodes are very common. Certainly, migraine headaches along with associated symptoms are an invisible infirmity that can take a powerful toll on the long-suffering person and family members.

The migraine experience may begin well before the headache. There is often a pattern of experiences that define an attack: excitability followed by a period of paralytic numbness. The onset of headache completes the cycle. All could happen in one day. Other times, the cycle plays out over many days. While the duration of an attack is unpredictable, the order of events for each person occurs with regularity akin to the motion of the planets.

During the pre-headache stage of migraine, there may be an enhanced sense of well-being, euphoria, arousal, and mania-like ideation. Hyperactivity and intentions of accomplishing great things may be part of the early illusions. Following this phase, the sufferer may collapse from sheer exhaustion and await the inevitable coming of a headache.

B. Aura

An identifying feature of a migraine headache is the aura, a hallucination that usually comes before the headache. Auras are strange distortions of vision such as dancing stars, flashes of colors, rotating or swirling images and changing geometric patterns of zigzagging angles. Most weirdly, parts of familiar objects, such as the nose or eye of some else's face, may seem missing.

Another form of aura is a sense of distortion of one's own body. Lewis Carroll, himself a sufferer of migraine headaches, described this strange symptom in *Alice in Wonderland*. Alice experiences her legs being too long and other sensations in which images of her own body are grotesquely unnatural. Some people with fever experience warped perceptions of their own body proportions; the symptom is especially common in children.

C. Treatment, Traditional

In 1672, the Oxford anatomist, Thomas Willis, wrote of the migraine headache, "no remedy or method of Curing ... [that] rebellious Disease refused to be tamed, being deaf to the charms of every Medicine." Still, history saw no paucity of remedies.

The age-honored tradition of ridding the body of "toxic substances" was applied to the treatment of the migraine headache. These attempts included various ways of removing blood and body fluid (diuretics, cupping, emetics, laxatives, purges). Herbs, barks, chemicals, and drugs were tried. Boring a hole in the skull to let out evil spirits dates back to pharaonic Egypt. Making an incision in the skull and packing it with garlic was widely performed throughout the Middle Ages. Practitioners of the art of medicine applied hot irons over the area of the headache or they bound the head tightly.

Clearly, rational treatment of a migraine headache and its attending symptoms could progress only by a clearer understanding of its cause. Although significant advances have been made, the cause of a migraine has not been precisely identified.

D. Treatment, Modern

Various medications have been used to relieve the dilation of blood vessels in the brain, long suspected as the cause of migraines. Certainly, the diversity of symptoms occurring with a migraine attack suggests that the autonomic nervous system is involved. Indeed, medications can control resulting autonomic symptoms to some extent. There is now evidence that a genetically determined hypersensitivity of brain cells may be the key to this malady. The findings have led to trials with a new generation of drugs. The clinician now has a wide assortment of medications that can lessen symptoms and help to reduce the frequency and duration of attacks.

E. Prevention

A wide assortment of triggers can precipitate an attack of the migraine headache. They include exposure to loud noises, bright or flashing lights, or certain smells. In addition, there may be migraine-producing stimuli in some foods (particularly those with additives for preservation), and in red wine and soft cheeses. Missing a meal, disturbed sleep, under-hydration, hormonal changes (especially in women), emotional stress, and certain stimuli (such as caffeine) may initiate symptoms. Identifying and avoiding suspected triggers is the key to effective prevention.

6-52 Colonial Women

Little is really known about the personal lives of the earliest Colonial women. Some may have been able to read the Bible, but curiously, they were typically not taught or expected to write. Consequently, we have precious few memoirs of women living during the early period of New England settlements. What was their relationship with their husbands? We know that they had many children. That they were hard-working is undeniable. Perhaps necessary and unending household chores left no time for writing.

The role of a woman of Colonial times was to provide the household with a demanding service. She was expected to master and conduct the many chores of cooking, sewing, perhaps weaving, laundering, and making candles. She was often left to dress poultry and other animals and prepare the meat and vegetables for meals and for storage. Of course, she became the in-house doctor: staunching bleeding and bandaging injuries, making remedies from various herbs, helping a neighbor during childbirth, and providing what psychological support a child or spouse may require during difficult times.

In addition, women of the time married young and had many children. Five to eight children were usual. Tending to children—from diapers to education—was challenging enough. Still, Colonial women were expected to be industrious, modest, resourceful, soft-spoken, and of pristine reputation.

While women in Colonial times were presumed to be obedient to their husbands, we have no reason to believe that there was abuse or lack of mutual respect and love. After all, cooperation in the household was essential for functioning in such hard-driven times of the early American settlements.

A custom of the time was that an early Colonial woman remained more or less anonymous. She may have been referred to only as the "goodwife." Names on family gravestones of the 1600s give the full name of the man but often recognize his spouse only as "AND HIS WIFE."

A Puritan woman of the time wore long hair that was tightly contained beneath a bonnet. She wore a shift, stay, petticoats, gown, apron, and sometimes a cloak. When working near the hearth, she may have worn an overskirt made of wool because of its resistance to fire. Of course, she wore no jewelry or adornments of any kind. Skin exposed above the wrists and ankles was considered shamefully immodest.

Then there were the real dangers of childbirth. It is estimated that one in twenty births proved fatal for the mother. Babies were mostly swaddled to keep them calm. Nursing and cleaning diapers were probably on-going in virtually every household.

A generation or two later, Colonial women wrote extensively, especially to family members. Presumably, their demands were a little less all-consuming so that there was a bit more time for writing. Servants or slaves may have taken up many of the household burdens. Moreover, their letters tend to be preserved. One of most prolific and revealing women of the Colonial Period was Abigail Adams (wife of President John Adams, and no relation to Master Jeremy Adams). From her letters, we read much of the way of life, habits, and attitudes of women of the time, all written more than a century after our story. Spelling and grammatical errors throughout her letters reveal that she did not have the refined education of her male peers. Nevertheless, she wrote in rather formal terms and in down-to-earth language. Many of her written concerns were related to the health of her family.

6-53 Historical Data

The children in the Adams household in 1639: Rebecca Greenhill (stepdaughter of Jeremy) was born in 1628. She died the same year as her mother. Thomas Greenhill (stepson of Jeremy) was younger than Rebecca. He died in 1653 at the age of 23 from an unknown cause. Jeremy's twin daughters were Sarah and Hannah, born in 1637, and his baby son was John.

As in most genealogical accounts, we have vital statistics of birth and death but precious little about personal characteristics, occupations, and situational issues. Some liberties have been taken with the stated ages of the older children for purposes of this story. Additional children, Samuel and Hester, were evidently born after the time of this story. (See Note 9-61: which refers to the map of 1640 and neighbors Easton and Ensign.)

6-54 Dutch Fort and Trading Post: House of Good Hope

Within a decade of Block's voyage of discovery up Versche Rivier, the Dutch in New Amsterdam extended their reach by constructing a trading post along the Connecticut River. They chose the high rise of a natural clearing of land that jutted out into the river near the confluence of a major tributary, the Little River. The Indigenous people of the land called it *Suckiage* (their word for "black earth"). The Dutch claimed land that was about as large as present-day Hartford. The arrangements for use of the land were made not with the local tribes but with a tribe to the south, the Pequots. One end of the exchange involved metal tools (such as axes, knives, and kettles) along with some duffel (woolen cloth manufactured in Duffel, Dutch Republic), some toys, and a musket. It was the Pequots who became the Dutch trader's major supplier of pelts.

The Dutch named their trading post *Huys de Goede Hoop* (House of Good Hope). There, they received fur from beaver, bear, mink, wildcat, and otter in exchange for goods made in Europe. The inclusion of guns as trading items, however, was soon forbidden. Two hundred years later, an interesting development occurred at the site of the trading post. It was the beginning of the Colt Firearms Company that morphed into a giant producer of guns.

What began as a small Dutch stockade was enlarged to a small fort with earthen walls except for some bricks from Holland, perhaps intended to strengthen the corners. Inside the palisade, the soldiers built a simple block house of two stories. Two small cannons pointed outward aimed from strategic places. The intent, clearly, was to protect against an attack by Indians, the very people with whom they actively traded.

In 1639, the Dutch had fourteen or fifteen soldiers and traders stationed at the fort. In addition, there may have been a few women and children. Although the land was famously fertile, the inhabitants maintained only small gardens (*bouwerie*) around the trading post. There was no serious interest in colonization and working the soil. The English, considered trespassers by the Dutch, pointed out the waste of letting such fertile soil go uncultivated.

A few geo-historical points are noteworthy. The land that protruded into the Connecticut River on which the Dutch built their trading post/fort was eventually washed away by periodic floods. The ruins of the fort and its burial grounds were discovered a hundred years later. Decayed timbers, cannon mounts without cannons and some bricks were all that was left. Some of the bricks are now under protection of the Connecticut

Historical Society. An adjacent commercial-residential area known as "Dutch Point" has preserved no traces of Dutch heritage except for names of a few streets: Huyshope Avenue, Wyllys Street, Van Dyke Avenue, and Van Block Avenue. It is good to know, incidentally, that there are streets in the City of Hartford that bear Indian names: Nepaquash, Pequot, and Sequassen.

6-55 Neighbors: The Dutch and the English

A festering tension between the Dutch at the Fort and the English settlers who surrounded them was inevitable. English ploughs turned up soil in Dutch-claimed meadows. A cow wandering into a foreign territory was reason for dispute. Every territorial incident provoked further strain. There were some skirmishes, but in general the two rival groups had the good sense to restrain from open warfare. It is ironic that Holland, a province in the Dutch Republic, was long a refuge where Puritans from England could live without fear of persecution from their king. Even Hartford's Founding Father, Reverend Thomas Hooker, and many of his followers came to the colonies directly from their homes in Rotterdam.

The Dutch considered the newcomers trespassers, pointing to their purchase of land rights from the Pequots in the south, not from the local tribes. They could not, however, provide a written deed to this effect. The English, by contrast, had a formalized agreement with the neighboring "River Indians," the Sequassen. Land rights were formerly deeded by Samuel Stone (from Hertford, England) and William Gardner. Furthermore, they stated that the Dutch had done scarcely anything with their rich land for farming over many years. It was "a sin to let such rich land which produced such fine corn lie uncultivated."

After years of rivalry, the Dutch up and left the House of Good Hope, having been overwhelmed by the sheer numbers of English settling in and by an ever-dwindling supply of animals providing fur. Their departure was in 1654, just three years before the full-scale war between England

and Holland. Parliament then authorized seizure of the Dutch property in Hartford by "virtue of the commission granted by the Providence Plantation."

6-56 Meetinghouse

Anticipating the arrival of Hooker, some workers came to the area much earlier to build a meeting/prayer house. Most likely, it was like other New England meeting houses: logs squared at the corners with spaces between filled with chunks of moss or clay mixed with hay. The door was made of planks and roof was covered with thatch. Openings for windows had boarded shutters.

Inside, the floor was just tamped-down earth. Narrow benches stood on two sides, one for men, the other for women. An elevated pulpit faced them. The setting offered all the opportunity to share the Word of God. It was a simple, primitive structure in contrast to its more elegant counterpart in Windsor, which may have served the Hartford community at first for hearing "fire and brimstone" sermons.

6-57 Connecticut Constitution

The first colonies established along the Connecticut River were at Windsor and Wethersfield, each a dozen or so miles from Hartford. Today, there is still some rivalry about which colony got there first.

Now independent, these settlements along with the one in Hartford, were outside the authority of the Massachusetts Bay Colony in Boston. In 1639, the three neighboring English plantations—Windsor, Hartford, Wethersfield—agreed to consolidate their governing bodies. The charter was known as the Warwick Patent. Advanced by Reverend Hooker, it held that "The foundation of authority is laid, firstly, in the free consent of the people." This agreement became the forerunner for the Constitution of the United States that was to come one hundred forty years later. It is this document that led to our calling Connecticut "The Constitution State."

Hooker's sermon on "Fundamental Orders of Connecticut" led to ratification of the charter by all three colonies on January 14, 1639. The bottom line was "self-rule."

6-58 Dutch Sloop

The practical and frugal Dutch came up with a small sailboat called the sloop (Dutch spelling: *sloep*) that could carry a lot of cargo, and was navigable in relatively shallow water and easy to handle by a few crew members. Their boat, from the seventeenth century on, had a single mast carrying a huge mainsail that was "gaff rigged." That is, the sail hung from a boom on top and stretched to a boom on the bottom that extended out well beyond the stern. A smaller headsail, the jib, billowed out in front. The crew raised, lowered, and positioned the sails from lines on the deck; there was no need to climb the rigging. Capacity for cargo was large, owing to the hull's wide breadth. While sailboats need a keel to limit being pushed sideways by a cross wind, the Dutch sloop had two retractable keels ("larboards"), one on each side of the hull.

A replica of the Dutch sloop has sailed the Hudson River and beyond since 1969. Called the "Clearwater," its construction was championed by legendary folk singer and environmentalist Pete Seeger. Its cargo today is mainly schoolchildren who get hands-on experience at sailing and exposure to ecological issues, all in a stream of folk music.

CHAPTER 9: SPRING

9-59 Spring Peepers

The high-pitched, incessant Song of Spring heard at the edge of woodlands comes from the accumulated voices of hundreds of small tree frogs called spring peepers. Each one is about the size of a paper clip. The vocalizations are from males with mating much in mind. The giveaway sound is made by sudden deflation of a ballooned-out sac in the throat, repeated about every three seconds from dusk to dawn.

These tiny critters have another astonishing characteristic. They hibernate hidden beneath a leaf, not deep in a cavern. There, the bodies freeze solid throughout the winter. This ice cube suspension of life is possible because they produce an antifreeze substance that protects all the organs from injury. It is small wonder that tree frogs celebrate their revival with the coming of warmer days.

The celebration also stirs the farmer to get ready for the next winter. The reawakening of Mother Earth means it is time to restart the cycle of turning the soil, planting, weeding, protecting from varmints (both big and small), harvesting, cooking or charring, and storing. Precious foals, calves, piglets, and lambs are usually born in the spring and, of course, require much attention. Trees must be cut, and from them, lumber made for houses and stables. Perhaps the peepers are offering gentle praise for the renewal of activity around a plantation.

9-60 Bathing

Bathing among the English in the seventeenth century was not an obsession. People could go through the winter, or longer, without a bath. Indeed, excessive bathing was generally considered bad for health; presumably it takes away the natural resistance to disease by destroying natural oils in the skin and opening the scrubbed pores to "contagion." For the Puritans, a bath was simply too sensuous for frequent indulgence.

Enough was known about basic sanitation that it was common to wash the hands and face before a meal, evidently regardless of social status. People were careful to avoid scrubbing the nose and eyes in order to prevent getting catarrhal disease (nose colds) and blurring of vision. Soap may have consisted of a mixture of mutton fat, wood ash and, if available, natural soda. The problem of body odor must have been so common that it was largely overlooked or thought to be natural—which, in fact, it is.

Rather than bathing to control body odor, there was sometimes an effort to cover it up with various oils from flowers, herbs, and spices.

"Necessary houses" (small outhouses) were sparsely furnished. There may have been one for men, whimsically marked with a star over the door. One for women was marked with a half moon.

9-61 Hartford: The City

A. Origin

One of the Founding Fathers of Hartford was Jeremy Adams. We know a good bit about him but little about his family other than their dates of births and deaths. The imbalance of personal history is quite typical for the period. This story is based upon fictionalized accounts of the family member's personalities and characteristics.

At the time of the story, Jeremy was thirty-five years old. A deeply religious man, as only expected, he was affable and generous with wit and wisdom. There is evidence, nevertheless, that he was a bit outspoken. Indeed, he was censored in 1644 for his "passionate, distempered speechess (sic), loud language, and womanly carriage before the court"—that is, unmannerly conduct.

Jeremy was born in Somerset, England in 1604. He became a Unitarian Pastor in Chelmsford, a city in the county of Essex, England and, in 1632, emigrated to the Colonies with Reverend Thomas Hooker. In Hartford, he eventually became a public constable, a tax assessor, a juror, and a collector of customs. He was also the innkeeper of a tavern that once stood at the site of the present Universalist Church. He died in 1683 at the age of seventy-nine, certainly a ripe old age for the times.

Jeremy's wife was Rebecca Baseden Greenhill, a widow and mother of two. She and Jeremy were married in 1637. She had been married previously to Samuel Greenhill. Rebecca lived until 1678.

By 1639, the Hartford plantation had increased to about thirty acres. A reconstructed map of 1640 depicts outlines of 137 plots but at this time there were only about thirty framed houses. The map shows early Hartford stretched out on both sides of Little River with access to meadows, pastures and woodland. The Jeremy Adams house on the southern shore is shown flanked by that of Joseph Easton to the west and James Ensign on the east. They were located but a long stone's throw to the confluence with the Great River (to be renamed the Connecticut River) and just beyond the Dutch fort.

Native people referred to the area as the "Black Fertile River-Enhanced Earth," summarized in the word *Suckiaug*. The new settlers did not choose this name for their plantation but rather picked Newtown. It was soon changed to Hartford. This name acknowledged the birthplace of one of the founding fathers, Rev. Samuel Stone who came from Hertford (spelled with an "e"), England. The name refers to a shallow place in a river easily forded or crossed by a stag deer or "hart."

The Indians grew corn, pumpkin, and beans with the seeds of each mixed together in small hills. The combination provided a tall growth for maximum sunlight and a thick ground cover to maintain moisture and discourage weeds. A fish buried beneath the seeds became fertilizer. The mineral-rich soil and favorable summer climate along the Connecticut River did the rest. These native farmers must have looked at the settler's gardens with curiosity, and perhaps a sense of self-righteousness, wondering why tending crops in the English way was so much more work. Paradoxically, the English attitude, naively, appears to be that they, as good neighbors, should teach the natives a thing or two about agriculture but found them reluctant to change.

The Charter Oak is a preeminent symbol of early Hartford. The tree is said to have had a cavity in which the Connecticut Charter of Independence was hidden from British soldiers in 1685. The King of England, James II, wanted to take away the colonists' right of self-governing that his father, King Charles II, had granted them in 1662. The colonists steadfastly refused to surrender their charter.

In 1856, a storm blew down the famous and long-battered Charter Oak. A craftsman carved some of the wood into an elaborate cradle for the son of industrialist and gunsmith Samuel Colt. The astonishing cradle consisted of a large decorative, boat-shaped basin that is suspended between two elaborately carved posts. Topping each post is a prancing colt or young horse, an artistic play on the gunsmith's name. The cradle can be seen at the Wadsworth Atheneum Museum of Art in Hartford.

B. Industry

By the 1880s, Hartford had evolved from an agricultural community to the capital city of Connecticut and into a huge industrial complex. Could the original settlers in their dugout huts and rude cabins have imagined what the village would look like within a few generations? On the banks of the Connecticut River, the face of Yankee ingenuity shows up in bold relief. Whereas most large old cities became established where the geography was favorable to shipping, industrial Hartford by contrast, evolved fifty miles up-river where the river is fairly shallow, and has a strong outgoing flow.

Most notable in this transformation was the manufacturing of fire arms. In this development, the name Samuel Colt is preeminent. Colt, in 1830 as a sixteen-year old seaman on the way to India, whittled an innovative pistol, constructed in a way that showed how it might discharge several times without reloading. The mechanism consisted of several gunpowder-containing cavities that rotated in the firing position with each pull of a trigger. The invention made it possible to fire multiple times with a single loading. At first, the barrels rotated, but Colt found that a rotating cylinder improved the design. Colt eventually gave his model to a gunsmith. Shooting a pistol made of wood was not a good idea, and the model was destroyed in the initial trial. When adapted to metal, however, the device became the Colt Revolver, a "six-shooter" soon known throughout the world.

The inventor purchased a large track of land near the former Dutch House of Good Hope. Here he started his business named the "Colt's Patent Fire Arms Manufacturing Company." The patent-conscious Colt designed gun parts that were interchangeable, and these were manufactured in an assembly line production. Concerned about the welfare of his workers, many of them immigrants, he built a sheltered community for them called Coltsville. Although Colt died in the early part of the Civil War, his huge factory provided great numbers of weapons to Union troops. In modern times, Colt's legacy, through the generosity of his widow, made possible the creation of extensive parklands in the city.

A second gun manufacturing competitor, the Sharps Rifle Manufacturing Company, came to Hartford in 1852. It took up a marshland known as Frog Hollow, now the home of Trinity College. Industrial Hartford also boasted precision manufacturing where bicycles, automobiles, typewriters, and sewing machines were made. Pratt & Whitney began in Hartford as a tool-making shop and evolved into the aerospace manufacturing giant, producing aircraft engines, gas turbines, and power generators.

In 1850, the Aetna (Fire) Insurance Company opened its offices in Hartford, at first to service the maritime trade. Other insurance businesses followed, offering coverage against fire, injury and death, loss of possessions, automotive mishaps, and anything else that clients wished to protect against risk. So gigantic was the growth of these insurance carriers that Hartford eventually became known as the "Insurance City of the World." One of the city's benefits from this concentration of risk-conscious industries was to promote excellent fire departments and companies of local fire brigades. Aetna's name, incidentally, refers to an active volcano in Sicily, suggesting that having insurance provided a safeguard against an impending disaster.

Much earlier in the century, in 1817, a primary school for the deaf began in the city. It was first called the "American Asylum for the Education of Deaf and Dumb Persons." For teaching visible communication, the school turned to the French Institute for the Deaf in Paris where teaching sign language was already well advanced. The school in Hartford is still there but is now located in West Hartford; it is known as "The American School for the Deaf." One of the founders was Thomas Gallaudet. His son, Edward, became the principal of America's first college for deaf students, Gallaudet University in Washington, D.C. In September 2013, the University celebrated its 150th birthday.

Hartford also had a strong social-minded side. In the early nineteenth century, the city became a center for abolitionist activities. In this movement, the surname Beecher reverberates. Rev. Lyman Beecher and his son, Henry Ward, were both known for their stirring anti-slavery sermons. His daughter, Harriet Beecher Stowe, wrote *Uncle Tom's Cabin.* When Abraham Lincoln spoke in Hartford in March of 1860, he said, "Whether we know it so or not, the slave question is the prevailing question before the nation." An editorial in *The Daily Courant* the following day commented on the speech, "There could not have been even a ten-year old boy in the crowd at the City Hall who did not leave the room satisfied that Mr. Lincoln was right, and he argued his points man-fashion." The newspaper, incidentally, was renamed the *Hartford Courant*; it happens to be the oldest continually printed newspaper in the country.

C. Modern

Industrial and financial Hartford has seen better days. The vicissitudes of economics have led what was for decades the richest city in the country into an economic downturn. A flight to the suburbs and beyond marks a trend of the past few decades. The gun manufacturers and most of the insurance companies have sought other locations. But they have left a precious legacy. These include Bushnell Park, a lawn with sculptures and fountains. On land purchased from Colt's estate, it is the first publicly funded park in the United States. At Nook Farmland, visitors are invited to the historic home of Harriet Beecher Stowe and, next door, to the home of Mark Twain.

The flight of the large insurance companies had a powerfully adverse effect on Hartford's financial health. In January of 2018, however, Aetna announced that it would stay put, along with its 6,000 employees.

The oldest public art museum in the country is Wadsworth Athenaeum, housing treasures by old and modern masters. A vigorous sign of renewed life in the old city is a new campus of the University of Connecticut centered in the old *Hartford Times* building.

D. The Little River

The Little River in Hartford has seen some transformations. Waterpower used for running machinery led to its being renamed the "Mill River." In time, it acquired the reputation of "hell without the fire" as it served as a convenient disposal site for human, livestock, and factory waste. Consequently, its name for a while was changed to "Hog River." Furthermore, seasonal flooding of the river created a massive problem for the city. After an urban renewal program that included development of Bushnell Park, it became "Park River," a name that sticks today. Massive open conduits were then constructed for flood control within the watershed area. The great floods of 1936 and 1938, however, proved that even these conduits were wholly inadequate to prevent the inundation of the City of Hartford.

In the 1940s, the Army Corps of Engineers buried the original Little River thirty feet or more beneath center city in subway-sized concrete tunnels. Extended tunneling into the North Branch and the South Branch occurred well into the 1980s. During flood stage, a series of pumps along the way can transfer accumulating street water over an extensive area into the underground river. In conduits that now extend nine miles, the original Little River flows unceremoniously into the Connecticut River where the Whitehead Highway and Route I-91 merge.

The long-enduring, much-abused, and now entombed Little River still has some bragging rights. A brownstone bridge once crossed the open culvert where the Little River entered the Connecticut River. When built, it was the largest bridge of its kind in the United States. In addition, the burial of the river was, at the time, the biggest and most expensive project undertaken by the Army Corps of Engineering. It is also the only river in America that runs underneath a State Capitol.

9-62 Flood

Native people and the settlers along the Connecticut River were certainly familiar with spring flooding. Snowmelt coupled with copious rain periodically causes the Connecticut River and its tributaries to overflow onto the low-lying plains.

The two features of the river banks, namely, the remarkably fertile soil and the periodic flooding, were long considered separate phenomena. It was the intrepid, German explorer and naturalist, Alexander Humboldt, who connected these conditions in the early 1800s by pointing out that periodic flooding was good for the soil. It was then a matter for riparian scientists to document that fresh water overflowing onto farmland left behind minerals when it receded. The deposits were from erosions upstream that would replenish the minerals taken up by growing vegetables in preceding seasons. The same phenomenon has created the fertile banks of the Nile River where vital agriculture is possible in an otherwise desert landscape.

While the grains best known by English farmers (wheat, oats, barley) did not flourish as crops along the Connecticut Valley, corn grew remarkably well. Indeed, corn provided the principle food of indigenous people and eventually that of the settlers.

In more modern times, another crop, tobacco, proved especially suited to the Valley. The leaves were prized for providing the outer wrapping of cigars made from tobacco grown farther south. To prevent damage from hail, the tobacco fields were covered with tents of gauze. The author of this book, as a teenager, picked tobacco along with migrant laborers from Jamaica in the shade-covered fields of the Connecticut River. The going pay rate was thirty-five cents an hour.

9-63 Quinsy

The term "quinsy" in folk medicine refers to a severe sore throat associated with fever. Tonsillitis (viral or streptococcal, the most common causes) and tonsillar abscesses occur frequently where people are in crowded living spaces. Usually, the condition clears, although complications such as rheumatic heart disease and arthritis can occur. The infection at its most advanced stage may cause enough swelling of the pharynx to restrict the airway. It is this complication of quinsy that finally did in George Washington at the age of sixty-seven.

CHAPTER 10: SUMMER

10-64 Almandine

That a hunk of dried mud could contain radiant jewels is not a figment of the imagination. Given the right elements in the soil and the unimaginably high pressures and high temperatures of geological creation, some combination of elements is rearranged in highly specialized ways to form crystals. Such is the case of almandine in which iron, aluminum, and silicone are fused into a precise, unique structure. White light entering the stone emerges in an intense purplish-red color. When cut and its many facets polished, the gemstone becomes an attractive jewel in a ring or necklace.

Long ago, its deep redness earned the gemstone the reputation of having something to do with blood. Consequently, crude almandine was incorporated in traditional remedies and rituals intended to counteract various forms of hemorrhage and inflammation. William Rowland, Doctor of Physics in the 1600s, advocated the use of almandine to stimulate the heart, decrease palpitations, increase blood flow, remove toxins, and treat melancholy.

Almandine is a species within the family of stone, the garnets. Garnet is the official mineral of the State of Connecticut. Today, alas, there is no source of garnet in the state. Rather, the only known origin is the Red Ember Mine in Erving, a small town in upstate Massachusetts. Who is to say that, four or five hundred years ago, a huge, hardened piece of almandine-laden mud did not break off in the flood waters of Mills River that runs through Erving? It would be carried by the rapids and enter the Connecticut River near Turner Falls, breaking into jagged fragments along the way. Tossed and spun wildly, fragments could reach Hartford where the receding waters left them high and dry on the flood plains. There, a curious river-comber might have picked up a piece and discovered by chance its unique quality: when illuminated from behind the dried mud reveals a magical property: a bright red glow.

10-65 Witch

To say that the Puritans were serious about their faith is a colossal understatement. Fundamental was their view that Good and Evil existed as a continuous struggle. God, it seemed, tolerated the Devil's misdeeds as a test of the strength of Man; it was faith in God that enabled them to resist. In their insecure world of primitive settlements at the edge of the forested wilderness overrun by (in their minds) "savages," imaginations were not always harnessed by reality. The settlers, huddled up in their dark, drafty houses, felt vulnerable to any random force that might act against them in strange ways.

Fearsome and unfavorable events were often explained as the deliberate work of the devil. Of course, carrying out such terrible deeds required agents. Those were persons identified by strange behaviors or physical liabilities, or more "normal" people in disguise. Often the capacity for performing misdeeds was exposed by strange grimaces, trances, or shaking. Especially suspect were those individuals with birth defects, including children who were deaf and who could not speak, and the blind. These agents were the witches of Colonial New England, mostly elderly women and girls.

According to the Puritan viewpoint, a sudden, devastating illness, even an epidemic (which was common) may have been the work of the devil put into action by an agent within the community. A sudden-onset gale might blow off the roof of a house, a dog or wolf could spring at one's throat during the night, and black and blue spots ("witch marks")could appear on the body without explanation. Terrifying howling of the wolves at night added to the anxiety.

There were plenty of reasons to be wary in the colonies, but the pervasive insecurity nurtured explanations for bad luck that spun well beyond reason. By the 1690s, blaming adversities on the machinations of the devil and his agents developed into epidemic hysteria, leading in 1692 to the infamous "witch trials" of Salem, Massachusetts. The trials implicated local residents who had some quirks, and their quirks were interpreted as clues to an evil force.

The reasoning for witchcraft—if one chooses to call it that—was that bad times came because God's adversary, the Devil, found it easier to enter a woman's body than a man's body. Once inside, Satan could use her as an operative agent to counter the good works of God. God allowed this as punishment for misdeeds or lagging spiritual beliefs, and the penalty for such transgressions was expressed by poor harvests, fires, epidemics, and birth defects. Some claimed that being mute or blind were forms of the Devil's interventions. Witches were the designated scapegoats for such misfortunes. Indeed, their ability to inflect harm to ordinary people was a way to test the faith of believers. How to determine who was a witch and who was not was the stuff of pure superstition and prejudice.

10-66 John Donne

The most famous poet in seventeenth century England was John Donne who lived from 1572 to 1631. Raised as a Catholic, he left his Oxford home at the age of sixteen to avoid taking the required oath of allegiance to the queen's supremacy as sovereign of the Church of England. He then studied at Cambridge and eventually went to Europe to study law. Donne, astute observer of human nature, wrote satires, elegies, and lyrics. He wrote with a powerful new style, especially in his love poems. Few of these works were published during his lifetime, and he remained generally forgotten until early in the twentieth century.

Of Donne's extensive writing, his most enduring is the passage, "No man is an Island, entirely of itself ...And therefore never send to know for whom the bell tolls; it tolls for thee." The quotation is the seventeenth "meditation" in *Devotions upon Emergent Occasions,* written in 1624.

10-67 Cavern versus Cave

A cavern is an underground space where soft rock, such as sandstone, is eroded by below-surface streams of "ground water." Visitor-friendly Howe's Caverns in New York and Shenandoah Caverns in Virginia are examples in gigantic scale. None, alas, have been identified in Connecticut but that does not mean that there were none or that there are yet undiscovered caverns.

Connecticut does have its share of caves. These are hollows between large hunks of rocks that lean helter-skelter against one another. Notable is a complex of caves at Bolton Notch State Park. It is said that around 1640 one of these caves (subsequently called "the Squaw's Cave") became the refuge of a European and his Podunk wife. Their mixed racial marriage had scandalized their respective cultures.

Connecticut's most famous cave is in Hamden. Named Judges Cave, it is not a cave but a giant glacial erratic boulder which over time has split into several cleavages. The rock, sitting on top of West Rock State Park, has a commanding view of New Haven and its harbor. The name recognizes members of the English Parliament who, with fifty-six others, signed the death certificate of King Charles I back in 1649. His son Charles II, returning to England to restore the throne in 1660, sought to arrest all signatories and to exact hideous revenge. Some signers escaped to the Colonies only to be hunted down here by British soldiers.

Two of the fugitives, Edward Whalley and his son-in-law, William Goffe, spent about a month in 1661 hiding in crevices of the rock before further flight to Massachusetts. The third fugitive, John Dixwell, lived undercover with an assumed name, but may have joined the others in the cave at some point. Although the plaque on the rock identifies the signers of the death warrant as judges, not one of these men was a judge by occupation; all had been military officers before becoming members of Parliament. Their names are perpetuated in New Haven as Whalley Avenue and Goffe Street and in Hamden as Dixwell Avenue.

10-68 Sonnet

The poem cited, "Sonnet #18," is one of 154 sonnets written by William Shakespeare. It is the most beloved and the most analyzed of all. The sonnet compares the perfect beauty of a loved one to that of summer day. The day loses out due to the imperfections of the season. The beloved's beauty will be appreciated forever through the immortality of the written word.

The sonnet is a verse of fourteen lines in which the second of each foot (a two-syllable group) is emphasized in the reading. The "lub-DUB" of each heartbeat is a physiological analogy. The form is known as "iambic pentameter." A well-known example is William Wordsworth's "I wandered lonely as a cloud."

That floats on high o'er vales and hills,
When all at once I saw a crowd,
A host, of golden daffodils;
Beside the lake, beneath the trees,
Fluttering and dancing in the breeze.

In contrast is an ancient poetic form that originated in Kalevala, northern Finland. Its rhythm calls for accenting the first syllable of each foot (not the second syllable). The form is denoted "trochaic tetrameter."

Although rarely used, the meter has its own hypnotic ring, as in this example by Henry Wadsworth Longfellow's "Song of Hiawatha."

By the shore of Gitche Gumee,
By the shining Big-Sea-Water,
At the doorway of his wigwam,
In the pleasant Summer morning,
Hiawatha stood and waited.

CHAPTER 11: AUTUMN, AGAIN

11-69 Horse: Leg Injury

Horses incur injuries of the legs fairly often. A simple misstep into a gopher hole, a trip on an unseen rock, and sometimes just running at a gallop will strain or tear the complex ligaments and tendons within the leg. The principal means of treating such a limp-producing injury is to reduce weight bearing, and then only gradually return to normal activity.

A fracture of the leg, however, is a different matter. Because the bones have developed for speed, they are very strong but thin. When they break, they tend to shatter. Healing by fusing all the separated pieces generally results in a deformed leg. In the simple act of walking, the horse, weighing 1,000 pounds or more, shifts its weight alternatively onto each leg, an excessive load for a recently broken bone. Over the centuries, splints, casts, and methods of avoiding weight bearing for many weeks have usually proven futile. A horse with a broken leg has little prospect of returning to its former productivity, and its fate is usually a forgone conclusion: euthanasia. The advances of the modern technological sciences in promoting limb and joint healing and replacement add a glimmer of hope.

11-70 Aspererger's Syndrome

One quirk of personality is a tendency to be highly focused on narrow subjects at the expense of social grace. Such individuals can be smart, sometimes surprisingly so. A young person, even a child, with this trait may be extremely knowledgeable about a favorite subject, and may even be called "The Little Professor;" focus may be about old car models, flags of nations, sports personalities, or details on maps of remote places. In modern lingo, the term Asperger's syndrome might be applied.

People with Asperger's syndrome find difficulty in common social interactions and in forming close friendships. They often miss the subtleties of humor and friendly chatty exchanges. Instead, they are detail-driven about their collections and expertise. Their one-sided perspective tends to dominate conversations. Inflexible and fiercely independent, they may be insensitive to social customs but can be super-sensitive to noises, textures, tastes, smells, or temperatures. Additional characteristics are an obsession with the order of things, clumsy social skills (such as being bluntly honest), and literal interpretation of everyday affairs.

A wide variation of expression in what might be termed Asperger's syndrome includes those on one side of the scale who function quite normally and those who are quite disabled in dealing with the social world. One can only wonder who might have fit within the modern concept of an Asperger profile among the famous, historical geniuses who composed music, wrote long novels, painted huge landscapes, made breakthroughs in science, and led nations. How is it possible to write a full orchestral symphony in one week? It was done by Mozart and at a very young age. After all, the ability to carry on a sustained focus requiring a high intellectual capacity can be considered a gift for creative people.

First recognized as a psychiatric condition in the 1940s, Asperger's syndrome was not generally accepted as a genuine medical diagnosis until the 1990s. Today, the condition is considered a subheading under autism where there is a very fuzzy line of separation. Yet about 1% of the population fits such behavioral criteria. Perhaps we all have a touch of Asperger's syndrome. It could help at times that call for intense concentration.

11-71 Delftware Potter

"Porcelain mania" in the early 1600s was a period in Europe when white, decorated pottery from China was worth a fortune. Clay was the building material of pottery. The kind available in Europe was, alas, not the natural white clay that gave Chinese porcelain an edge on marketing. Technology developed in Italy, however, eventually turned plates, vessels, and tiles made from dull-colored clay to white. The art of making fine earthenware spread rapidly through Europe, most especially in The Netherlands. Of course, the prices dropped sharply as the products became more available. Nowhere was the manufacture of decorative pottery more active than in the town of Delft in Holland.

The production of Delftware required three firings: that is, subjecting an object of clay to high heat in a kiln.

Firing #1: the sculptured, soft-bodied, and porous clay was covered with a coat of lead oxide. Impurities in the veneer often gave a green or brown hue. Baking fused a glaze that was transparent and rendered the ceramic product watertight and glassy.

Firing #2: an opaque tin oxide then coated the object that, after baking, turned it white. Before the next kiln exposure, designs with a blue pigment made from cobalt were then brushed on.

Firing #3: a clear lead glaze was added to the object for a smooth and glistening surface.

This method of producing earthenware products was soon adapted in England and other countries. The numerous manufacturers once thriving in Delft were reduced to one: The Royal Delft Pottery Factory. The company ships its products worldwide and conducts popular tours of its factory.

Lead coating the inside of a cup or bowl presents a hazard to health. Absorbed into the body, it causes damage to the skin and loss of hair. Lead overload is detrimental to the mental development of children. Toxicity from lead ingestion can also produce one form of anemia. Looking back, one wonders if the pale complexion so admired in earlier times was in fact a low red blood cell mass from the absorption of lead. After all, pallor was a sign of high-fashion and certainly more likely to occur among those who could afford pottery.

The initial glaze in pottery no longer contains lead but potters have avidly searched for elements that can produce such brilliant colors. Now, the initial recipe for glazing calls for mixtures containing zinc, boron, silicates, cobalt, and others.

11-72 Grass

What is more common than a strand of grass? There are several thousand species of grasses known in various niches of the globe. They grow in deserts, swamps, sand dunes, heavily shaded woodlands, windswept plains, and in arctic and tropical climates. Some grow in a tight cluster, while others tend to spread out. Complex in basic structure, each variety has its own adaptive characteristics.

Pull up a stalk of mature grass, a stalk with a feathery top. Chances are that the plant will break off at the crown (where the roots and stem are joined). The deepest, thread-like roots of fiber maintain a strong anchor for the plant. Roots that run more horizontally and are shallow may bear a new growth that pops above the ground and forms its own roots and stem. The system of reproduction is an asexual process, meaning that male and female parts were not combined; the new plant is a clone.

The stem (or "culm") is made of tough fibrous cellulose that is very flexible and highly resistant against tearing, bending, or trampling. Cut across the culm and notice that it is hollow except at a thickened area (collar) where the blades branch out. The blades have nearly parallel edges that come to a tapered point. There is a central stem in each blade with parallel veins alongside. Note that the blades emerge on alternating sides of the culm, reducing the chances of a blade being left in the shadow of another blade.

The blades absorb radiant energy from the sun and convert it into metabolic energy. The process, called "photosynthesis," involves combining carbon dioxide from soil with water from air. The combination is the fundamental energy-containing unit of biology, the carbohydrate. Glucose is the prototypical molecule. Chlorophyll, a greenish enzyme in the blade, facilitates the transfer of solar energy to biological energy.

Photosynthesis is the essential process that makes life possible. There are no exceptions in either the plant or animal kingdoms. Only plants, however, have this capability (with the single exception of the chlorophyll-bearing, mobile, single-cell euglena). Animals that do not eat plants eat animals that eat plants.

When "gone to seed" (meaning fully mature), the tip of the stem will appear feather-like. Here is a cluster of many small flowers, called florets. A male component (stamen) at maturity produces several thousand microscopic spores. A spore (pollen) is borne by wind or by insects to a neighboring plant where it may enter a leafy chamber (pistil) containing the female reproductive organ (ovary). Once the egg is fertilized, the embryo will grow, surrounded by a nutritious and protective coat of starch. The complex becomes a seed that, when mature, will fall to the ground, root into the soil, and become a new grass plant. In a well-manicured lawn, we see the cut-off blades of grass, not the clusters of florets.

Fast growing bamboo has stiff, woody stems that are light and strong and may grow as tall as trees. It is hard to think of a more versatile substance, useful from cradle to coffin and serving for everything from beautiful laminated wood panels to the framework of scaffolds and bridges. It makes baskets and fine, textured paper and textiles. Bamboo is the only grass that can be made into a flute or drum. From an ecological perspective, bamboo once cut regrows, and rapidly, too. There is no need for replanting.

Corn is another radical variant of grass. Farmers have bred many useful varieties over thousands of years. Long before the Europeans came, corn was a staple in the American Indian diet. Then, cobs of corn were multicolored and very small.

Corn is an exception to the rule that grasses fertilize neighboring plants. Corn fertilizes itself in a process called monoecious reproduction. The tassels growing at the top of the stalk are the male component of the system. They contain the pollen that eventually falls on the tufts (or silk) at the tip of the ear. Each thread in the silk serves as a pathway for the male genetic material to reach an individual kernel that contains the ovule, the female component. It is the kernel that is the edible part.

It is impossible to overestimate the importance of corn during the past centuries in the sustenance of people in the Americas. It was probably developed in central Mexico from a grass containing edible seeds along its length. With continuous agricultural manipulations throughout past centuries, corn has gone from a scrawny ear to one chock-full of robust kernels.

In the northeastern woodlands perhaps a thousand years ago, a rapid-growing variety was cultured to best address a relatively short growing season. For winter consumption dried kernels were kept in pits underground. Strips from the husks were made into mats, twine and moccasins. Husks also served to fill bedding. Cobs made good scrubbers, and silk was used as hair on a cornhusk doll.

Corn has a central role in the Iroquois Legend of Creation. Along with squash and beans, it grew on Turtle Island from the grave of the Daughter of the Sky Woman. The daughter died in the childbirth of twin boys—one right-handed, the other left-handed. But that is another story!

Milton Keynes UK
Ingram Content Group UK Ltd.
UKHW011100230424
441551UK00023B/616

9 798989 906284